ELDRITCH

&

ANTIQUARY

TALES OF

HORROR

BY

H. P. LOVECRAFT

AND

M. R. JAMES

ILLUSTRATED

BY

ZACK TRAUM

EDITED

BY

ZACHARY VON HOUSER

OFF SOUTH PRESS
PHILA. PA

OFF SOUTH PRESS
PHILA. PA

Printed in the United States of America

First Printing, 2022

ISBN 979-8-9851855-3-9

Off South Press
Philadelphia, PA
USA

https://OffSouthPress.square.site/

ACKNOWLEDGEMENTS

Two years is a long time for me to dedicate to any project, and I was only able to get through it with the help of many people. No one wants to read a long list of every person that a stranger has ever met, so, in the interest of brevity, I'll cut it down a bit.

First and foremost, I need to thank Ronnie Osbeck; without him introducing me to Lovecraft, I never would have had a subject to obsess over for the past couple of decades. I need to thank my ma, Aunt Cass, and Aunt Meg for instilling a, some would say obsessive, passion for literature in me. Finally, and far from least, I need to thank Cacey for not murdering me in my sleep many times over for how difficult I surely was during the process of working on this.

I love you all,

Zachary Von Houser

CONTENTS

Introduction By The Editor

Zachary Von Houser

'The oldest and strongest emotion of mankind is fear, and the oldest and strongest kind of fear is fear of the unknown', Lovecraft said it and every hackneyed editor, soon-to-be-scholar, English teacher, and edgy teenager has used it for the introduction to every Lovecraft collection/essay/assignment/hitting-on-someone-that-you-found-attractive since Lovecraft came back into vogue. It's old, it's tired, and to Lovecraft at the time, it was a fundamental truth. It's hard to come to terms with M. R. James and H. P. Lovecraft both being so fundamental to horror, when their perceived notions of where horror should be built from couldn't be more different in some ways.

That Lovecraftian ideal of horror, to glimpse upon something so grand, so unbelievable, so indifferent as to destroy the subject's whole conception of the universe (where mankind is the perpetual infant in the grand battle of minds across the universe) is completely at odds with James. James' protagonists are rarely blind to the concept that becomes their doorway into darkness. It is in their knowledge that the key to horror is found. More often than not they seek, they search, they find; and with that discovery the horror is only the greater because each incremental piece of knowledge that they uncover along the way does nothing to subdue their fears, but brings the monstrosity more to light. They are not ignorant, they are not a canvas rube for the horror to paint its strokes across.

Still, known or unknown, I believe that they both understood that the singular component to fear is a scale (whether of mind or space) that is so far beyond what man thought possible as to become life altering.

We were in that ceaseless state of boredom that cloaks its great black wings over the lives of teenagers, drinking poor quality, warm beer in a room that I had never been in before when the idea was presented.

"Why don't we go to Lakeland?" someone whose name I've forgotten suggested.

"Fuck yeah," Ron said, and, Ron being my best friend, that meant that I would go along as well.

Stories of Lakeland had been dancing around from a few of the smaller, tight-knit clusters of kids that made up our base friend group. There were Satanic cults in there; there were secret tunnels underneath that took you into a secret other building for secret psychotics; if you stepped on a certain tile inside any of the patients' rooms, the door would slam shut and lock forever; there were lizard and birds nailed to the walls in the basement (I always believed that one. I mean, most people are assholes). The whole contingent of myths that have probably been attached to every abandoned asylum in America. I would imagine the rest of the world probably has better ideas for giant, expensive closed structures than to just let them rot until nature and time tumble their walls; I've never bothered to ask around though, so maybe every culture had teenagers with dark, forgotten corridors to wander in the middle of the night. It would be a shame if they didn't.

So, we packed into cars just after midnight. One of Jello Biafra's many, horrible side-projects were playing on the radio (some Polynesian/folk-punk ballads, or some sort of equally terrible nonsense), but since I didn't have a driver's license I didn't have much say in what blared into my ears and dug pits from my mind. Luckily it was a nice summer night, without the polyester-stuffing-thick humidity that usually plagued our summer nights, and the beer that I had grabbed on the way out was a little cooler than the previous seven had been that night.

It was said that if you parked in front of the hospital, Johnny Law would be on you before you could even get out of the car, so we parked two blocks away, at the end of a dark cul-de-sac. The asylum had been closed for nearly twenty years but, instead of tearing it down and building on the site of the original hospital, the state had figured it would save some money by building on the grounds, but right next to the mouldering tomb that they have vacated. I suppose they thought it would be a nice view, the bleak, damp degradation, for their current patients. At least they did have the courtesy to keep a single line of decrepit trees between the two, so only those in the penthouse would have a clear view. You have to keep a separation of classes after all.

A fence blocked entry or egress from the street and a deep and unknown wood capped in the back, so the best means of trespassing was to cut through the parking lot of the active asylum. In my current, less than cautious state, being both youthful and slightly tipsy, I opted for a spot toward the front of our group of eight, though I had never been there and in turn had no idea where the hell I was going. Ah, the joys of youth.

The parking lot held five or six rows of cars, which gave a decent amount of distance and cover as we hunched down and scrambled across the blacktop. It was going well, it was going smoothly, and I couldn't see a way that this could possibly go awry. Unfortunately the mixture of beer, excitement, and my hunched over state proved me wrong. The bubbly bile hit the back of my throat with no warning, panic sunk in as it is wont to do with such surprises, and I stopped dead to prevent the ruin of my shoes.

James crashed into the back of me, uttering a quick but loud, "Fuck," as we both tumbled to the ground. Which gave way to an even louder, "Shut the fuck up," from the person whose name I forget. As I got up, brushing away the little rocks that had embedded themselves into my palms, the inevitable happened. A flashlight scanned across the cars toward us from some hitherto unseen security guard. And what do you do when someone is trying to find you via flashlight? Sit still? Get as low to the ground as possible? No, of course not. We bolted for the tree line, hoping that the studs on jackets or clomp of Doc Martens would be as dull and soundless as possible.

Catching our breath, crouched down amongst the low-lying plants between trees, a long series of minutes passed, considering plausible excuses for our late-night excursion to their hallowed facility (all of which were utter bullshit). It seemed as though we might have been graced with possibly the least observant security guard in the history of security or guards, when I felt a tap on my shoulder. It was James, with a strange mix of excitement and concern splattered across his face, and he pointed over his shoulder.

It was a behemoth. Seven stories of harsh, brick angles towered less than a hundred feet away, with a growing half moon casting coldness upon it. The third floor window, the only one not boarded up and known to be the only way in, with an iron downspout to climb nearby was there as advertised. The next bit of detail (and the part that sounds like a lie to any advanced trespasser of creepy places, due to them never having the good luck to observe it) was a thick mist that crept across the ground at hip to knee height.

I could feel it, and I imagine everyone else could, that crackling charge of a place where something was happening. I looked over at Ron, who was crouched beside me, and he looked over at me, and we gave that brief, eyes-only discussion that you can have if you've been friends with someone since the first few months of your life. This was fun, this was novel, this was a fuck-ton better than sitting in a bedroom that smelled like old beer, feet, and stale weed and cigarettes. Ron turned back to the hospital before I did, and I saw his brow furrow, and even in the pale moonlight I could see some of the color seep from his face. He turned back to me and nodded in the direction that he had been looking. At first I couldn't clock what it was that he had been looking at. Was there a cop? Some easier way to enter? A sniper in the trees? Then it came into view, and I imagine my face went about the same as Ron's had.

From a darkened corner of the building, out of a higher crest of mist, someone was walking.

"The fuck?" I mumbled, or maybe just thought.

Ron hefted his Maglite, and I brought up the section of metal pipe that I had brought (both essential tools for breaking into old asylums) and, to our amazement, almost as if on cue, he turned toward us and started walking. Maybe he was a cop, or security guard. But, why was he wearing white? And why didn't he say 'freeze' or ask what we were doing there. Maybe he was just some normal guy, or one of the patients from the new asylum that was allowed to go out? Even a patient would know better than to wander over to a bunch of kids with pipes and heavy, metal flashlights. All of these questions and responses were crashing through my mind as he got ever closer. Ron's leg was jumping and I heard twigs snapping and someone in the group talking farther down the line and as close as this guy had gotten I couldn't make up his face.

"Fuck this, I'm out," I heard James say from the other side of the group, and in unison we all silently agreed.

I was the last to get up, and in the back of the line as we ran, and in the last moment just as I had stood and started, I turned back to look one more time. He was still coming, the same slow stroll that he had been doing, and a wave of mist cascaded over him. When it passed, he was gone. Sure he could have decided to sit down or lay down at that very moment in the damp grass and weeds, but it seems an odd time for a nap.

Whatever the case neither I nor anyone else in the group decided to stop and check; nor did we have the time to consider it because, as he neared the halfway point of the parking lot, Kat (who was dating James, or maybe they were broken up at the moment) tripped over something and crashed fast into the hard asphalt. I heard her knee hit the pavement, that heavy dull thud of something bad happening to bone, and then her muffled shout. I'll give her that, she had the mind to cover her cry, but she wasn't going anywhere and we needed to be anywhere.

James grabbed her under her armpits, Ron lifted one leg and I did the other. Luckily Ron got the injured leg, because I never have been known for grace, and we hurried off as quickly as we could. Kat was always small, so we had that on our side, but it was still awkward and slowing, and if the guard hadn't seen us on our first pass he was sure to have now and that meant cops. We never did well around cops. It would have taken more time than we had to finish cutting across the parking lot, carry Kat down the driveway, down streets with no sidewalk and finally get to the car. That's how you get caught. We weren't going to just dump Kat like an old couch though, so we did the only thing we could think and made for the woods.

A streetlight shined distantly through the trees, and James was sure that this was the very streetlight beside which sat the car, so we made as much of a quick and careful path as we could hefting the shared weight of a human. 'Don't get fucking caught, don't get fucking caught, you're too poor for a lawyer or bail, don't get fucking caught,' the mantra rolled in my mind. The light, sure enough was getting closer. Maybe we would make it. That's when someone up ahead stopped, and I had to struggle not to drop Kat as I stumbled to a halt.

Kat propped herself against a tree as we pushed forward to see what the holdup was. Why couldn't we have taken the street? Why couldn't we have just waited in the line of trees until morning? Why couldn't we have chosen any path besides this? I was a maelstrom of such questions as I pushed up beside Ron and saw what had stopped us. In a small clearing was sat a child's plastic table, all bleached, ugly purple, with bleached, plastic chairs around it and on the table a group of disfigured dolls around a pile of moldy, rotting food.

"Let's... fucking... go." James said with Kat clinging to his back.

We ran through the woods, branches scraping through our faces and scalps, preferring that to seeing who or what had set that horrid table. My lungs felt heavy with air turned thick, my clothes damp with sweat and brushed off dew. I wouldn't stop, I wouldn't slow, and most of all I wouldn't look back. I was thinking of the irony that the night had become so fucked because I was scared when the whole plan for the night had been to be scared, when we suddenly broke from the trees and were in a happy, suburban backyard.

We snuck through the yard, trotted past two houses, and were in the cars within a minute.

No one really spoke on the ride back, at least not in our car. Quiet houses swept past and the windows were down to clear the car of the acrid stink of fear. There I was, not so much with thoughts because my mind was too busy trying to make sense of everything, until we were back at that kid's house.

We slept on the floor, sleeping refusing to come to me until morning, and I know Ron was having just as much trouble because he kept trying to make bad jokes and tell creepy stories that I periodically ignored. When we woke up Ron offered to give me a ride home. On the way, we stopped at his house and he ran in on his own, giving me a reprieve from one of the long, but pleasant, sets of questioning that his mom would always give me. When he got back into the car, he threw a box of books into my lap. There were some sci-fi and cyber-punk books in there, which weren't (and still aren't) really my thing as well as some Bradbury and Matheson (which most definitely are), but mixed in with it all was a collection of James' ghost stories and one of the 'Best of Lovecraft' collections.

At that moment, I had no idea who James or Lovecraft (or a few of the authors of books that weren't suited to me) were, but after reading it I wonder how I would have felt running through those woods in the dark, desolate night if I had.

INTRODUCTION

Zachary Von Houser

ELDRITCH

&

ANTIQUARY

TALES OF

HORROR

BY

H. P. LOVECRAFT

AND

M. R. JAMES

ILLUSTRATED

BY

ZACK TRAUM

EDITED

BY

ZACHARY VON HOUSER

Zachary Von Houser

Zachary Von Houser

At the Mountains of Madness

by H. P. Lovecraft

I.

I am forced into speech because men of science have refused to follow my advice without knowing why. It is altogether against my will that I tell my reasons for opposing this contemplated invasion of the antarctic—with its vast fossil-hunt and its wholesale boring and melting of the ancient ice-cap—and I am the more reluctant because my warning may be in vain. Doubt of the real facts, as I must reveal them, is inevitable; yet if I suppressed what will seem extravagant and incredible there would be nothing left. The hitherto withheld photographs, both ordinary and aërial, will count in my favour; for they are damnably vivid and graphic. Still, they will be doubted because of the great lengths to which clever fakery can be carried. The ink drawings, of course, will be jeered at as obvious impostures; notwithstanding a strangeness of technique which art experts ought to remark and puzzle over.

In the end I must rely on the judgment and standing of the few scientific leaders who have, on the one hand, sufficient independence of thought to weigh my data on its own hideously convincing merits or in the light of certain primordial and highly baffling myth-cycles; and on the other hand, sufficient influence to deter the exploring world in general from any rash and overambitious programme in the region of those mountains of madness. It is an unfortunate fact that relatively obscure men like myself and my associates, connected only with a small university, have little chance of making an impression where matters of a wildly bizarre or highly controversial nature are concerned.

It is further against us that we are not, in the strictest sense, specialists in the fields which came primarily to be concerned. As a geologist my object in leading the Miskatonic University Expedition was wholly that of securing deep-level specimens of rock and soil from various parts of the antarctic continent, aided by the remarkable drill devised by Prof. Frank H. Pabodie of our engineering department. I had no wish to be a pioneer in any other field than this; but I did hope that the use of this new mechanical appliance at different points along previously explored paths would bring to light materials of a sort hitherto unreached by the ordinary methods of collection. Pabodie's drilling apparatus, as the public already knows from our reports, was unique and radical in its lightness, portability, and capacity to combine the ordinary artesian drill principle with the principle of the small circular rock drill in such a way as to cope quickly with strata of varying hardness. Steel head, jointed rods, gasoline motor, collapsible wooden derrick, dynamiting paraphernalia, cording, rubbish-removal auger, and sectional piping for bores five inches wide and up to 1000 feet deep all formed, with needed accessories, no greater load than three seven-dog sledges could carry; this being made possible by the clever aluminum alloy of which most of the metal objects were fashioned. Four large Dornier aëroplanes, designed especially for the tremendous altitude flying necessary on the antarctic plateau and with added fuel-warming and quick-starting devices worked out by Pabodie, could transport our entire expedition from a base at the edge of the great ice barrier to various suitable inland points, and from these points a sufficient quota of dogs would serve us.

We planned to cover as great an area as one antarctic season—or longer, if absolutely necessary—would permit, operating mostly in the mountain-ranges and on the plateau south of Ross Sea; regions explored in varying degree by Shackleton, Amundsen, Scott, and Byrd. With frequent changes of camp, made by aëroplane and involving distances great enough to be of geological significance, we expected to unearth a quite unprecedented amount of material; especially in the pre-Cambrian strata of which so narrow a range of antarctic specimens had previously been secured. We wished also to obtain as great as possible a variety of the upper fossiliferous rocks, since the primal life-history of this bleak realm of ice and death is of the highest importance to our knowledge of the earth's past. That the antarctic continent was once temperate and even tropical, with a teeming vegetable and animal life of which the lichens, marine fauna, arachnida, and penguins of the northern edge are the only survivals, is a matter of common information; and we hoped to expand that information in variety, accuracy, and detail. When a simple boring revealed fossiliferous signs, we would enlarge the aperture by blasting in order to get specimens of suitable size and condition.

Our borings, of varying depth according to the promise held out by the upper soil or rock, were to be confined to exposed or nearly exposed land surfaces—

these inevitably being slopes and ridges because of the mile or two-mile thickness of solid ice overlying the lower levels. We could not afford to waste drilling depth on any considerable amount of mere glaciation, though Pabodie had worked out a plan for sinking copper electrodes in thick clusters of borings and melting off limited areas of ice with current from a gasoline-driven dynamo. It is this plan—which we could not put into effect except experimentally on an expedition such as ours—that the coming Starkweather-Moore Expedition proposes to follow despite the warnings I have issued since our return from the antarctic.

The public knows of the Miskatonic Expedition through our frequent wireless reports to the Arkham Advertiser and Associated Press, and through the later articles of Pabodie and myself. We consisted of four men from the University—Pabodie, Lake of the biology department, Atwood of the physics department (also a meteorologist), and I representing geology and having nominal command—besides sixteen assistants; seven graduate students from Miskatonic and nine skilled mechanics. Of these sixteen, twelve were qualified aëroplane pilots, all but two of whom were competent wireless operators. Eight of them understood navigation with compass and sextant, as did Pabodie, Atwood, and I. In addition, of course, our two ships—wooden ex-whalers, reinforced for ice conditions and having auxiliary steam—were fully manned. The Nathaniel Derby Pickman Foundation, aided by a few special contributions, financed the expedition; hence our preparations were extremely thorough despite the absence of great publicity. The dogs, sledges, machines, camp materials, and unassembled parts of our five planes were delivered in Boston, and there our ships were loaded.

We were marvellously well-equipped for our specific purposes, and in all matters pertaining to supplies, regimen, transportation, and camp construction we profited by the excellent example of our many recent and exceptionally brilliant predecessors. It was the unusual number and fame of these predecessors which made our own expedition—ample though it was—so little noticed by the world at large.

As the newspapers told, we sailed from Boston Harbour on September 2, 1930; taking a leisurely course down the coast and through the Panama Canal, and stopping at Samoa and Hobart, Tasmania, at which latter place we took on final supplies. None of our exploring party had ever been in the polar regions before, hence we all relied greatly on our ship captains—J. B. Douglas, commanding the brig Arkham, and serving as commander of the sea party, and Georg Thorfinnssen, commanding the barque Miskatonic—both veteran whalers in antarctic waters. As we left the inhabited world behind the sun sank lower and lower in the north, and stayed longer and longer above the horizon each day. At about 62° South Latitude we sighted our first icebergs—table-like objects with vertical sides— and just before reaching the Antarctic Circle, which we crossed on October 20 with appropriately quaint ceremonies, we were considerably troubled with field ice. The falling temperature bothered me considerably after our long voyage through the tropics, but I tried to brace up for the worse rigours to come. On many occasions the curious atmospheric effects enchanted me vastly; these including a strikingly vivid mirage—the first I had ever seen—in which distant bergs became the battlements of unimaginable cosmic castles.

Pushing through the ice, which was fortunately

neither extensive nor thickly packed, we regained open water at South Latitude 67°, East Longitude 175°. On the morning of October 26 a strong "land blink" appeared on the south, and before noon we all felt a thrill of excitement at beholding a vast, lofty, and snow-clad mountain chain which opened out and covered the whole vista ahead. At last we had encountered an outpost of the great unknown continent and its cryptic world of frozen death. These peaks were obviously the Admiralty Range discovered by Ross, and it would now be our task to round Cape Adare and sail down the east coast of Victoria Land to our contemplated base on the shore of McMurdo Sound at the foot of the volcano Erebus in South Latitude 77° 9'.

The last lap of the voyage was vivid and fancy-stirring, great barren peaks of mystery looming up constantly against the west as the low northern sun of noon or the still lower horizon-grazing southern sun of midnight poured its hazy reddish rays over the white snow, bluish ice and water lanes, and black bits of exposed granite slope. Through the desolate summits swept raging intermittent gusts of the terrible antarctic wind; whose cadences sometimes held vague suggestions of a wild and half-sentient musical piping, with notes extending over a wide range, and which for some subconscious mnemonic reason seemed to me disquieting and even dimly terrible. Something about the scene reminded me of the strange and disturbing Asian paintings of Nicholas Roerich, and of the still stranger and more disturbing descriptions of the evilly fabled plateau of Leng which occur in the dreaded Necronomicon of the mad Arab Abdul Alhazred. I was rather sorry, later on, that I had ever looked into that monstrous book at the college library.

On the seventh of November, sight of the westward

range having been temporarily lost, we passed Franklin Island; and the next day descried the cones of Mts. Erebus and Terror on Ross Island ahead, with the long line of the Parry Mountains beyond. There now stretched off to the east the low, white line of the great ice barrier; rising perpendicularly to a height of 200 feet like the rocky cliffs of Quebec, and marking the end of southward navigation. In the afternoon we entered McMurdo Sound and stood off the coast in the lee of smoking Mt. Erebus. The scoriac peak towered up some 12,700 feet against the eastern sky, like a Japanese print of the sacred Fujiyama; while beyond it rose the white, ghost-like height of Mt. Terror, 10,900 feet in altitude, and now extinct as a volcano. Puffs of smoke from Erebus came intermittently, and one of the graduate assistants—a brilliant young fellow named Danforth—pointed out what looked like lava on the snowy slope; remarking that this mountain, discovered in 1840, had undoubtedly been the source of Poe's image when he wrote seven years later of

"—the lavas that restlessly roll
Their sulphurous currents down Yaanek
   In the ultimate climes of the pole—
That groan as they roll down Mount Yaanek
   In the realms of the boreal pole."

Danforth was a great reader of bizarre material, and had talked a good deal of Poe. I was interested myself because of the antarctic scene of Poe's only long story—the disturbing and enigmatical Arthur Gordon Pym. On the barren shore, and on the lofty ice barrier in the background, myriads of grotesque penguins squawked and flapped their fins; while many fat seals were visible on the water, swimming or sprawling across large cakes of slowly drifting ice.

Using small boats, we effected a difficult landing on Ross Island shortly after midnight on the morning of the 9th, carrying a line of cable from each of the ships and preparing to unload supplies by means of a breeches-buoy arrangement. Our sensations on first treading antarctic soil were poignant and complex, even though at this particular point the Scott and Shackleton expeditions had preceded us. Our camp on the frozen shore below the volcano's slope was only a provisional one; headquarters being kept aboard the Arkham. We landed all our drilling apparatus, dogs, sledges, tents, provisions, gasoline tanks, experimental ice-melting outfit, cameras both ordinary and aërial, aëroplane parts, and other accessories, including three small portable wireless outfits (besides those in the planes) capable of communicating with the Arkham's large outfit from any part of the antarctic continent that we would be likely to visit. The ship's outfit, communicating with the outside world, was to convey press reports to the Arkham Advertiser's powerful wireless station on Kingsport Head, Mass. We hoped to complete our work during a single antarctic summer; but if this proved impossible we would winter on the Arkham, sending the Miskatonic north before the freezing of the ice for another summer's supplies.

I need not repeat what the newspapers have already published about our early work: of our ascent of Mt. Erebus; our successful mineral borings at several points on Ross Island and the singular speed with which Pabodie's apparatus accomplished them, even through solid rock layers; our provisional test of the small ice-melting equipment; our perilous ascent of the great barrier with sledges and supplies; and our final assembling of five huge aëroplanes at the camp atop the barrier. The health of our land party—twenty men and 55 Alaskan sledge dogs—was remarkable, though of course we had so far encountered no really destructive temperatures or windstorms. For the most part, the thermometer varied between zero and 20° or 25° above, and our experience with New England winters had accustomed us to rigours of this sort. The barrier camp was semi-permanent, and destined to be a storage cache for gasoline, provisions, dynamite, and other supplies. Only four of our planes were needed to carry the actual exploring material, the fifth being left with a pilot and two men from the ships at the storage cache to form a means of reaching us from the Arkham in case all our exploring planes were lost. Later, when not using all the other planes for moving apparatus, we would employ one or two in a shuttle transportation service between this cache and another permanent base on the great plateau from 600 to 700 miles southward, beyond Beardmore Glacier. Despite the almost unanimous accounts of appalling winds and tempests that pour down from the plateau, we determined to dispense with intermediate bases; taking our chances in the interest of economy and probable efficiency.

Wireless reports have spoken of the breath-taking four-hour non-stop flight of our squadron on November 21 over the lofty shelf ice, with vast peaks rising on the west, and the unfathomed silences echoing to the sound of our engines. Wind troubled us only moderately, and our radio compasses helped us through the one opaque fog we encountered. When the vast rise loomed ahead, between Latitudes 83° and 84°, we knew we had reached Beardmore Glacier, the largest valley glacier in the world, and that the frozen sea was now giving place to a frowning and mountainous coastline. At last we were

truly entering the white, aeon-dead world of the ultimate south, and even as we realised it we saw the peak of Mt. Nansen in the eastern distance, towering up to its height of almost 15,000 feet.

The successful establishment of the southern base above the glacier in Latitude 86° 7', East Longitude 174° 23', and the phenomenally rapid and effective borings and blastings made at various points reached by our sledge trips and short aëroplane flights, are matters of history; as is the arduous and triumphant ascent of Mt. Nansen by Pabodie and two of the graduate students—Gedney and Carroll—on December 13–15. We were some 8500 feet above sea-level, and when experimental drillings revealed solid ground only twelve feet down through the snow and ice at certain points, we made considerable use of the small melting apparatus and sunk bores and performed dynamiting at many places where no previous explorer had ever thought of securing mineral specimens. The pre-Cambrian granites and beacon sandstones thus obtained confirmed our belief that this plateau was homogeneous with the great bulk of the continent to the west, but somewhat different from the parts lying eastward below South America—which we then thought to form a separate and smaller continent divided from the larger one by a frozen junction of Ross and Weddell Seas, though Byrd has since disproved the hypothesis.

In certain of the sandstones, dynamited and chiselled after boring revealed their nature, we found some highly interesting fossil markings and fragments—notably ferns, seaweeds, trilobites, crinoids, and such molluscs as lingulae and gasteropods—all of which seemed of real significance in connexion with the region's primordial history. There was also a queer triangular, striated marking about a foot in greatest diameter which Lake pieced together from three fragments of slate brought up from a deep-blasted aperture. These fragments came from a point to the westward, near the Queen Alexandra Range; and Lake, as a biologist, seemed to find their curious marking unusually puzzling and provocative, though to my geological eye it looked not unlike some of the ripple effects reasonably common in the sedimentary rocks. Since slate is no more than a metamorphic formation into which a sedimentary stratum is pressed, and since the pressure itself produces odd distorting effects on any markings which may exist, I saw no reason for extreme wonder over the striated depression.

On January 6, 1931, Lake, Pabodie, Danforth, all six of the students, four mechanics, and I flew directly over the south pole in two of the great planes, being forced down once by a sudden high wind which fortunately did not develop into a typical storm. This was, as the papers have stated, one of several observation flights; during others of which we tried to discern new topographical features in areas unreached by previous explorers. Our early flights were disappointing in this latter respect; though they afforded us some magnificent examples of the richly fantastic and deceptive mirages of the polar regions, of which our sea voyage had given us some brief foretastes. Distant mountains floated in the sky as enchanted cities, and often the whole white world would dissolve into a gold, silver, and scarlet land of Dunsanian dreams and adventurous expectancy under the magic of the low midnight sun. On cloudy days we had considerable trouble in flying, owing to the tendency of snowy earth and sky to merge into one mystical opalescent void with no visible horizon to mark the junction of the two.

At length we resolved to carry out our original plan of flying 500 miles eastward with all four exploring planes and establishing a fresh sub-base at a point which would probably be on the smaller continental division, as we mistakenly conceived it. Geological specimens obtained there would be desirable for purposes of comparison. Our health so far had remained excellent; lime-juice well offsetting the steady diet of tinned and salted food, and temperatures generally above zero enabling us to do without our thickest furs. It was now midsummer, and with haste and care we might be able to conclude work by March and avoid a tedious wintering through the long antarctic night. Several savage windstorms had burst upon us from the west, but we had escaped damage through the skill of Atwood in devising rudimentary aëroplane shelters and windbreaks of heavy snow blocks, and reinforcing the principal camp buildings with snow. Our good luck and efficiency had indeed been almost uncanny.

The outside world knew, of course, of our programme, and was told also of Lake's strange and dogged insistence on a westward—or rather, northwestward—prospecting trip before our radical shift to the new base. It seems he had pondered a great deal, and with alarmingly radical daring, over that triangular striated marking in the slate; reading into it certain contradictions in Nature and geological period which whetted his curiosity to the utmost, and made him avid to sink more borings and blastings in the west-stretching formation to which the exhumed fragments evidently belonged. He was strangely convinced that the marking was the print of some bulky, unknown, and radically unclassifiable organism of considerably advanced evolution, notwithstanding that the rock which bore it was of so vastly ancient a date—

Cambrian if not actually pre-Cambrian—as to preclude the probable existence not only of all highly evolved life, but of any life at all above the unicellular or at most the trilobite stage. These fragments, with their odd marking, must have been 500 million to a thousand million years old.

II.

Popular imagination, I judge, responded actively to our wireless bulletins of Lake's start northwestward into regions never trodden by human foot or penetrated by human imagination; though we did not mention his wild hopes of revolutionising the entire sciences of biology and geology. His preliminary sledging and boring journey of January 11–18 with Pabodie and five others—marred by the loss of two dogs in an upset when crossing one of the great pressure-ridges in the ice—had brought up more and more of the Archaean slate; and even I was interested by the singular profusion of evident fossil markings in that unbelievably ancient stratum. These markings, however, were of very primitive life-forms involving no great paradox except that any life-forms should occur in rock as definitely pre-Cambrian as this seemed to be; hence I still failed to see the good sense of Lake's demand for an interlude in our time-saving programme—an interlude requiring the use of all four planes, many men, and the whole of the expedition's mechanical apparatus. I did not, in the end, veto the plan; though I decided not to accompany the northwestward party despite Lake's plea for my geological advice. While they were gone, I would remain at the base with Pabodie and five men and work out final plans for the eastward shift. In preparation for

this transfer one of the planes had begun to move up a good gasoline supply from McMurdo Sound; but this could wait temporarily. I kept with me one sledge and nine dogs, since it is unwise to be at any time without possible transportation in an utterly tenantless world of aeon-long death.

Lake's sub-expedition into the unknown, as everyone will recall, sent out its own reports from the short-wave transmitters on the planes; these being simultaneously picked up by our apparatus at the southern base and by the *Arkham* at McMurdo Sound, whence they were relayed to the outside world on wave-lengths up to fifty metres. The start was made January 22 at 4 A.M.; and the first wireless message we received came only two hours later, when Lake spoke of descending and starting a small-scale ice-melting and bore at a point some 300 miles away from us. Six hours after that a second and very excited message told of the frantic, beaver-like work whereby a shallow shaft had been sunk and blasted; culminating in the discovery of slate fragments with several markings approximately like the one which had caused the original puzzlement.

Three hours later a brief bulletin announced the resumption of the flight in the teeth of a raw and piercing gale; and when I despatched a message of protest against further hazards, Lake replied curtly that his new specimens made any hazard worth taking. I saw that his excitement had reached the point of mutiny, and that I could do nothing to check this headlong risk of the whole expedition's success; but it was appalling to think of his plunging deeper and deeper into that treacherous and sinister white immensity of tempests and unfathomed mysteries which stretched off for some 1500 miles to the half-known, half-suspected coast-line of Queen Mary and Knox Lands.

Then, in about an hour and a half more, came that doubly excited message from Lake's moving plane which almost reversed my sentiments and made me wish I had accompanied the party.

"10:05 P.M. On the wing. After snowstorm, have spied mountain-range ahead higher than any hitherto seen. May equal Himalayas allowing for height of plateau. Probable Latitude 76° 15', Longitude 113° 10' E. Reaches far as can see to right and left. Suspicion of two smoking cones. All peaks black and bare of snow. Gale blowing off them impedes navigation."

After that Pabodie, the men, and I hung breathlessly over the receiver. Thought of this titanic mountain rampart 700 miles away inflamed our deepest sense of adventure; and we rejoiced that our expedition, if not ourselves personally, had been its discoverers. In half an hour Lake called us again.

"Moulton's plane forced down on plateau in foothills, but nobody hurt and perhaps can repair. Shall transfer essentials to other three for return or further moves if necessary, but no more heavy plane travel needed just now. Mountains surpass anything in imagination. Am going up scouting in Carroll's plane, with all weight out. You can't imagine anything like this. Highest peaks must go over 35,000 feet. Everest out of the running. Atwood to work out height with theodolite while Carroll and I go up. Probably wrong about cones, for formations look stratified. Possibly pre-Cambrian slate with other strata mixed in. Queer skyline effects—regular sections of

cubes clinging to highest peaks. Whole thing marvellous in red-gold light of low sun. Like land of mystery in a dream or gateway to forbidden world of untrodden wonder. Wish you were here to study."

Though it was technically sleeping-time, not one of us listeners thought for a moment of retiring. It must have been a good deal the same at McMurdo Sound, where the supply cache and the Arkham were also getting the messages; for Capt. Douglas gave out a call congratulating everybody on the important find, and Sherman, the cache operator, seconded his sentiments. We were sorry, of course, about the damaged aëroplane; but hoped it could be easily mended. Then, at 11 P.M., came another call from Lake.

"Up with Carroll over highest foothills. Don't dare try really tall peaks in present weather, but shall later. Frightful work climbing, and hard going at this altitude, but worth it. Great range fairly solid, hence can't get any glimpses beyond. Main summits exceed Himalayas, and very queer. Range looks like pre-Cambrian slate, with plain signs of many other upheaved strata. Was wrong about volcanism. Goes farther in either direction than we can see. Swept clear of snow above about 21,000 feet. Odd formations on slopes of highest mountains. Great low square blocks with exactly vertical sides, and rectangular lines of low vertical ramparts, like the old Asian castles clinging to steep mountains in Roerich's paintings. Impressive from distance. Flew close to some, and Carroll thought they were formed of smaller separate pieces, but that is probably weathering. Most edges crumbled and rounded off as if exposed to storms and climate changes for millions of years. Parts, especially upper parts, seem to be of lighter-coloured rock than any visible strata on slopes proper, hence an evidently crystalline origin. Close flying shews many cave-mouths, some unusually regular in outline, square or semicircular. You must come and investigate. Think I saw rampart squarely on top of one peak. Height seems about 30,000 to 35,000 feet. Am up 21,500 myself, in devilish gnawing cold. Wind whistles and pipes through passes and in and out of caves, but no flying danger so far."

From then on for another half-hour Lake kept up a running fire of comment, and expressed his intention of climbing some of the peaks on foot. I replied that I would join him as soon as he could send a plane, and that Pabodie and I would work out the best gasoline plan—just where and how to concentrate our supply in view of the expedition's altered character. Obviously, Lake's boring operations, as well as his aëroplane activities, would need a great deal delivered for the new base which he was to establish at the foot of the mountains; and it was possible that the eastward flight might not be made after all this season. In connexion with this business I called Capt. Douglas and asked him to get as much as possible out of the ships and up the barrier with the single dog-team we had left there. A direct route across the unknown region between Lake and McMurdo Sound was what we really ought to establish.

Lake called me later to say that he had decided to let the camp stay where Moulton's plane had been forced down, and where repairs had already progressed somewhat. The ice-sheet was very thin, with dark ground here and there visible, and he would sink some borings and blasts at that very point before making any sledge trips or climbing expeditions. He spoke of the ineffable majesty of the whole scene, and the queer state of his sensations

at being in the lee of vast silent pinnacles whose ranks shot up like a wall reaching the sky at the world's rim. Atwood's theodolite observations had placed the height of the five tallest peaks at from 30,000 to 34,000 feet. The windswept nature of the terrain clearly disturbed Lake, for it argued the occasional existence of prodigious gales violent beyond anything we had so far encountered. His camp lay a little more than five miles from where the higher foothills abruptly rose. I could almost trace a note of subconscious alarm in his words—flashed across a glacial void of 700 miles—as he urged that we all hasten with the matter and get the strange new region disposed of as soon as possible. He was about to rest now, after a continuous day's work of almost unparalleled speed, strenuousness, and results.

In the morning I had a three-cornered wireless talk with Lake and Capt. Douglas at their widely separated bases; and it was agreed that one of Lake's planes would come to my base for Pabodie, the five men, and myself, as well as for all the fuel it could carry. The rest of the fuel question, depending on our decision about an easterly trip, could wait for a few days; since Lake had enough for immediate camp heat and borings. Eventually the old southern base ought to be restocked; but if we postponed the easterly trip we would not use it till the next summer, and meanwhile Lake must send a plane to explore a direct route between his new mountains and McMurdo Sound.

Pabodie and I prepared to close our base for a short or long period, as the case might be. If we wintered in the antarctic we would probably fly straight from Lake's base to the Arkham without returning to this spot. Some of our conical tents had already been reinforced by blocks of hard snow, and now we decided to complete the job of making a permanent Esquimau village. Owing to a very liberal tent supply, Lake had with him all that his base would need even after our arrival. I wirelessed that Pabodie and I would be ready for the northwestward move after one day's work and one night's rest.

Our labours, however, were not very steady after 4 P.M.; for about that time Lake began sending in the most extraordinary and excited messages. His working day had started unpropitiously; since an aëroplane survey of the nearly exposed rock surfaces shewed an entire absence of those Archaean and primordial strata for which he was looking, and which formed so great a part of the colossal peaks that loomed up at a tantalising distance from the camp. Most of the rocks glimpsed were apparently Jurassic and Comanchian sandstones and Permian and Triassic schists, with now and then a glossy black outcropping suggesting a hard and slaty coal. This rather discouraged Lake, whose plans all hinged on unearthing specimens more than 500 million years older. It was clear to him that in order to recover the Archaean slate vein in which he had found the odd markings, he would have to make a long sledge trip from these foothills to the steep slopes of the gigantic mountains themselves.

He had resolved, nevertheless, to do some local boring as part of the expedition's general programme; hence set up the drill and put five men to work with it while the rest finished settling the camp and repairing the damaged aëroplane. The softest visible rock—a sandstone about a quarter of a mile from the camp—had been chosen for the first sampling; and the drill made excellent progress without much supplementary blasting. It was about three hours afterward, following the first really heavy blast of the operation, that the shouting of the drill crew was

heard; and that young Gedney—the acting foreman—rushed into the camp with the startling news.

They had struck a cave. Early in the boring the sandstone had given place to a vein of Comanchian limestone full of minute fossil cephalopods, corals, echini, and spirifera, and with occasional suggestions of siliceous sponges and marine vertebrate bones—the latter probably of teliosts, sharks, and ganoids. This in itself was important enough, as affording the first vertebrate fossils the expedition had yet secured; but when shortly afterward the drill-head dropped through the stratum into apparent vacancy, a wholly new and doubly intense wave of excitement spread among the excavators. A good-sized blast had laid open the subterrene secret; and now, through a jagged aperture perhaps five feet across and three feet thick, there yawned before the avid searchers a section of shallow limestone hollowing worn more than fifty million years ago by the trickling ground waters of a bygone tropic world.

The hollowed layer was not more than seven or eight feet deep, but extended off indefinitely in all directions and had a fresh, slightly moving air which suggested its membership in an extensive subterranean system. Its roof and floor were abundantly equipped with large stalactites and stalagmites, some of which met in columnar form; but important above all else was the vast deposit of shells and bones which in places nearly choked the passage. Washed down from unknown jungles of Mesozoic tree-ferns and fungi, and forests of Tertiary cycads, fan-palms, and primitive angiosperms, this osseous medley contained representatives of more Cretaceous, Eocene, and other animal species than the greatest palaeontologist could have counted or classified in a year. Molluscs, crustacean armour, fishes, amphibians, reptiles, birds, and early mammals—great and small, known and unknown. No wonder Gedney ran back to the camp shouting, and no wonder everyone else dropped work and rushed headlong through the biting cold to where the tall derrick marked a new-found gateway to secrets of inner earth and vanished aeons.

When Lake had satisfied the first keen edge of his curiosity he scribbled a message in his notebook and had young Moulton run back to the camp to despatch it by wireless. This was my first word of the discovery, and it told of the identification of early shells, bones of ganoids and placoderms, remnants of labyrinthodonts and thecodonts, great mososaur skull fragments, dinosaur vertebrae and armour-plates, pterodactyl teeth and wing-bones, archaeopteryx debris, Miocene sharks' teeth, primitive bird-skulls, and skulls, vertebrae, and other bones of archaic mammals such as palaeotheres, xiphodons, dinocerases, eohippi, oreodons, and titanotheres. There was nothing as recent as a mastodon, elephant, true camel, deer, or bovine animal; hence Lake concluded that the last deposits had occurred during the Oligocene age, and that the hollowed stratum had lain in its present dried, dead, and inaccessible state for at least thirty million years.

On the other hand, the prevalence of very early life-forms was singular in the highest degree. Though the limestone formation was, on the evidence of such typical imbedded fossils as ventriculites, positively and unmistakably Comanchian and not a particle earlier; the free fragments in the hollow space included a surprising proportion from organisms hitherto considered as peculiar to far older periods—even rudimentary

fishes, molluscs, and corals as remote as the Silurian or Ordovician. The inevitable inference was that in this part of the world there had been a remarkable and unique degree of continuity between the life of over 300 million years ago and that of only thirty million years ago. How far this continuity had extended beyond the Oligocene age when the cavern was closed, was of course past all speculation. In any event, the coming of the frightful ice in the Pleistocene some 500,000 years ago—a mere yesterday as compared with the age of this cavity—must have put an end to any of the primal forms which had locally managed to outlive their common terms.

Lake was not content to let his first message stand, but had another bulletin written and despatched across the snow to the camp before Moulton could get back. After that Moulton stayed at the wireless in one of the planes; transmitting to me—and to the Arkham for relaying to the outside world—the frequent postscripts which Lake sent him by a succession of messengers. Those who followed the newspapers will remember the excitement created among men of science by that afternoon's reports—reports which have finally led, after all these years, to the organisation of that very Starkweather-Moore Expedition which I am so anxious to dissuade from its purposes. I had better give the messages literally as Lake sent them, and as our base operator McTighe translated them from his pencil shorthand.

"Fowler makes discovery of highest importance in sandstone and limestone fragments from blasts. Several distinct triangular striated prints like those in Archaean slate, proving that source survived from over 600 million years ago to Comanchian times without more than moderate morphological changes and decrease in average size. Comanchian prints apparently more primitive or decadent, if anything, than older ones. Emphasise importance of discovery in press. Will mean to biology what Einstein has meant to mathematics and physics. Joins up with my previous work and amplifies conclusions. Appears to indicate, as I suspected, that earth has seen whole cycle or cycles of organic life before known one that begins with Archaeozoic cells. Was evolved and specialised not later than thousand million years ago, when planet was young and recently uninhabitable for any life-forms or normal protoplasmic structure. Question arises when, where, and how development took place."

———————————

"Later. Examining certain skeletal fragments of large land and marine saurians and primitive mammals, find singular local wounds or injuries to bony structure not attributable to any known predatory or carnivorous animal of any period. Of two sorts—straight, penetrant bores, and apparently hacking incisions. One or two cases of cleanly severed bone. Not many specimens affected. Am sending to camp for electric torches. Will extend search area underground by hacking away stalactites."

———————————

"Still later. Have found peculiar soapstone fragment about six inches across and an inch and a half thick, wholly unlike any visible local formation. Greenish, but no evidences to place its period. Has curious smoothness and regularity. Shaped like five-pointed star with tips broken off, and signs of other cleavage at inward angles and in centre of surface. Small, smooth depression in

centre of unbroken surface. Arouses much curiosity as to source and weathering. Probably some freak of water action. Carroll, with magnifier, thinks he can make out additional markings of geologic significance. Groups of tiny dots in regular patterns. Dogs growing uneasy as we work, and seem to hate this soapstone. Must see if it has any peculiar odour. Will report again when Mills gets back with light and we start on underground area."

————————

"10:15 P.M. Important discovery. Orrendorf and Watkins, working underground at 9:45 with light, found monstrous barrel-shaped fossil of wholly unknown nature; probably vegetable unless overgrown specimen of unknown marine radiata. Tissue evidently preserved by mineral salts. Tough as leather, but astonishing flexibility retained in places. Marks of broken-off parts at ends and around sides. Six feet end to end, 3.5 feet central diameter, tapering to 1 foot at each end. Like a barrel with five bulging ridges in place of staves. Lateral breakages, as of thinnish stalks, are at equator in middle of these ridges. In furrows between ridges are curious growths. Combs or wings that fold up and spread out like fans. All greatly damaged but one, which gives almost seven-foot wing spread. Arrangement reminds one of certain monsters of primal myth, especially fabled Elder Things in Necronomicon. These wings seem to be membraneous, stretched on framework of glandular tubing. Apparent minute orifices in frame tubing at wing tips. Ends of body shrivelled, giving no clue to interior or to what has been broken off there. Must dissect when we get back to camp. Can't decide whether vegetable or animal. Many features obviously of almost incredible primitiveness. Have set all hands cutting stalactites and looking for further specimens. Additional scarred bones found, but these must wait. Having trouble with dogs. They can't endure the new specimen, and would probably tear it to pieces if we didn't keep it at a distance from them."

————————

"11:30 P.M. Attention, Dyer, Pabodie, Douglas. Matter of highest—I might say transcendent—importance. Arkham must relay to Kingsport Head Station at once. Strange barrel growth is the Archaean thing that left prints in rocks. Mills, Boudreau, and Fowler discover cluster of thirteen more at underground point forty feet from aperture. Mixed with curiously rounded and configured soapstone fragments smaller than one previously found—star-shaped but no marks of breakage except at some of the points. Of organic specimens, eight apparently perfect, with all appendages. Have brought all to surface, leading off dogs to distance. They cannot stand the things. Give close attention to description and repeat back for accuracy. Papers must get this right.

"Objects are eight feet long all over. Six-foot five-ridged barrel torso 3.5 feet central diameter, 1 foot end diameters. Dark grey, flexible, and infinitely tough. Seven-foot membraneous wings of same colour, found folded, spread out of furrows between ridges. Wing framework tubular or glandular, of lighter grey, with orifices at wing tips. Spread wings have serrated edge. Around equator, one at central apex of each of the five vertical, stave-like ridges, are five systems of light grey flexible arms or tentacles found tightly folded to torso but expansible to maximum length of over 3 feet. Like arms of primitive crinoid. Single stalks 3 inches diameter branch after 6 inches into five sub-stalks, each of which

branches after 8 inches into five small, tapering tentacles or tendrils, giving each stalk a total of 25 tentacles.

"At top of torso blunt bulbous neck of lighter grey with gill-like suggestions holds yellowish five-pointed starfish-shaped apparent head covered with three-inch wiry cilia of various prismatic colours. Head thick and puffy, about 2 feet point to point, with three-inch flexible yellowish tubes projecting from each point. Slit in exact centre of top probably breathing aperture. At end of each tube is spherical expansion where yellowish membrane rolls back on handling to reveal glassy, red-irised globe, evidently an eye. Five slightly longer reddish tubes start from inner angles of starfish-shaped head and end in sac-like swellings of same colour which upon pressure open to bell-shaped orifices 2 inches maximum diameter and lined with sharp white tooth-like projections. Probable mouths. All these tubes, cilia, and points of starfish-head found folded tightly down; tubes and points clinging to bulbous neck and torso. Flexibility surprising despite vast toughness.

"At bottom of torso rough but dissimilarly functioning counterparts of head arrangements exist. Bulbous light-grey pseudo-neck, without gill suggestions, holds greenish five-pointed starfish-arrangement. Tough, muscular arms 4 feet long and tapering from 7 inches diameter at base to about 2.5 at point. To each point is attached small end of a greenish five-veined membraneous triangle 8 inches long and 6 wide at farther end. This is the paddle, fin, or pseudo-foot which has made prints in rocks from a thousand million to fifty or sixty million years old. From inner angles of starfish-arrangement project two-foot reddish tubes tapering from 3 inches diameter at base to 1 at tip. Orifices at tips. All these parts infinitely tough and leathery, but extremely flexible. Four-foot arms with paddles undoubtedly used for locomotion of some sort, marine or otherwise. When moved, display suggestions of exaggerated muscularity. As found, all these projections tightly folded over pseudo-neck and end of torso, corresponding to projections at other end.

"Cannot yet assign positively to animal or vegetable kingdom, but odds now favour animal. Probably represents incredibly advanced evolution of radiata without loss of certain primitive features. Echinoderm resemblances unmistakable despite local contradictory evidences. Wing structure puzzles in view of probable marine habitat, but may have use in water navigation. Symmetry is curiously vegetable-like, suggesting vegetable's essentially up-and-down structure rather than animal's fore-and-aft structure. Fabulously early date of evolution, preceding even simplest Archaean protozoa hitherto known, baffles all conjecture as to origin.

"Complete specimens have such uncanny resemblance to certain creatures of primal myth that suggestion of ancient existence outside antarctic becomes inevitable. Dyer and Pabodie have read Necronomicon and seen Clark Ashton Smith's nightmare paintings based on text, and will understand when I speak of Elder Things supposed to have created all earth-life as jest or mistake. Students have always thought conception formed from morbid imaginative treatment of very ancient tropical radiata. Also like prehistoric folklore things Wilmarth has spoken of—Cthulhu cult appendages, etc.

"Vast field of study opened. Deposits probably of late Cretaceous or early Eocene period, judging from associated specimens. Massive stalagmites deposited

above them. Hard work hewing out, but toughness prevented damage. State of preservation miraculous, evidently owing to limestone action. No more found so far, but will resume search later. Job now to get fourteen huge specimens to camp without dogs, which bark furiously and can't be trusted near them. With nine men—three left to guard the dogs—we ought to manage the three sledges fairly well, though wind is bad. Must establish plane communication with McMurdo Sound and begin shipping material. But I've got to dissect one of these things before we take any rest. Wish I had a real laboratory here. Dyer better kick himself for having tried to stop my westward trip. First the world's greatest mountains, and then this. If this last isn't the high spot of the expedition, I don't know what is. We're made scientifically. Congrats, Pabodie, on the drill that opened up the cave. Now will Arkham please repeat description?"

The sensations of Pabodie and myself at receipt of this report were almost beyond description, nor were our companions much behind us in enthusiasm. McTighe, who had hastily translated a few high spots as they came from the droning receiving set, wrote out the entire message from his shorthand version as soon as Lake's operator signed off. All appreciated the epoch-making significance of the discovery, and I sent Lake congratulations as soon as the Arkham's operator had repeated back the descriptive parts as requested; and my example was followed by Sherman from his station at the McMurdo Sound supply cache, as well as by Capt. Douglas of the Arkham. Later, as head of the expedition, I added some remarks to be relayed through the Arkham to the outside world. Of course, rest was an absurd thought amidst this excitement; and my only wish was to get to Lake's camp as quickly as I could. It disappointed me when he sent word that a rising mountain gale made early aërial travel impossible.

But within an hour and a half interest again rose to banish disappointment. Lake was sending more messages, and told of the completely successful transportation of the fourteen great specimens to the camp. It had been a hard pull, for the things were surprisingly heavy; but nine men had accomplished it very neatly. Now some of the party were hurriedly building a snow corral at a safe distance from the camp, to which the dogs could be brought for greater convenience in feeding. The specimens were laid out on the hard snow near the camp, save for one on which Lake was making crude attempts at dissection.

This dissection seemed to be a greater task than had been expected; for despite the heat of a gasoline stove in the newly raised laboratory tent, the deceptively flexible tissues of the chosen specimen—a powerful and intact one—lost nothing of their more than leathery toughness. Lake was puzzled as to how he might make the requisite incisions without violence destructive enough to upset all the structural niceties he was looking for. He had, it is true, seven more perfect specimens; but these were too few to use up recklessly unless the cave might later yield an unlimited supply. Accordingly he removed the specimen and dragged in one which, though having remnants of the starfish-arrangements at both ends, was badly crushed and partly disrupted along one of the great torso furrows.

Results, quickly reported over the wireless, were baffling and provocative indeed. Nothing like delicacy or accuracy was possible with instruments hardly able to cut the anomalous tissue, but the little that was achieved left

us all awed and bewildered. Existing biology would have to be wholly revised, for this thing was no product of any cell-growth science knows about. There had been scarcely any mineral replacement, and despite an age of perhaps forty million years the internal organs were wholly intact. The leathery, undeteriorative, and almost indestructible quality was an inherent attribute of the thing's form of organisation; and pertained to some palaeogean cycle of invertebrate evolution utterly beyond our powers of speculation. At first all that Lake found was dry, but as the heated tent produced its thawing effect, organic moisture of pungent and offensive odour was encountered toward the thing's uninjured side. It was not blood, but a thick, dark-green fluid apparently answering the same purpose. By the time Lake reached this stage all 37 dogs had been brought to the still uncompleted corral near the camp; and even at that distance set up a savage barking and show of restlessness at the acrid, diffusive smell.

Far from helping to place the strange entity, this provisional dissection merely deepened its mystery. All guesses about its external members had been correct, and on the evidence of these one could hardly hesitate to call the thing animal; but internal inspection brought up so many vegetable evidences that Lake was left hopelessly at sea. It had digestion and circulation, and eliminated waste matter through the reddish tubes of its starfish-shaped base. Cursorily, one would say that its respiratory apparatus handled oxygen rather than carbon dioxide; and there were odd evidences of air-storage chambers and methods of shifting respiration from the external orifice to at least two other fully developed breathing-systems—gills and pores. Clearly, it was amphibian and probably adapted to long airless hibernation-periods as well. Vocal organs seemed present in connexion with the main respiratory system, but they presented anomalies beyond immediate solution. Articulate speech, in the sense of syllable-utterance, seemed barely conceivable; but musical piping notes covering a wide range were highly probable. The muscular system was almost preternaturally developed.

The nervous system was so complex and highly developed as to leave Lake aghast. Though excessively primitive and archaic in some respects, the thing had a set of ganglial centres and connectives arguing the very extremes of specialised development. Its five-lobed brain was surprisingly advanced; and there were signs of a sensory equipment, served in part through the wiry cilia of the head, involving factors alien to any other terrestrial organism. Probably it had more than five senses, so that its habits could not be predicted from any existing analogy. It must, Lake thought, have been a creature of keen sensitiveness and delicately differentiated functions in its primal world; much like the ants and bees of today. It reproduced like the vegetable cryptogams, especially the pteridophytes; having spore-cases at the tips of the wings and evidently developing from a thallus or prothallus.

But to give it a name at this stage was mere folly. It looked like a radiate, but was clearly something more. It was partly vegetable, but had three-fourths of the essentials of animal structure. That it was marine in origin, its symmetrical contour and certain other attributes clearly indicated; yet one could not be exact as to the limit of its later adaptations. The wings, after all, held a persistent suggestion of the aërial. How it could have undergone its tremendously complex evolution on a new-born earth in time to leave prints in Archaean rocks was so far beyond conception as to make Lake whimsically recall the primal

myths about Great Old Ones who filtered down from the stars and concocted earth-life as a joke or mistake; and the wild tales of cosmic hill things from Outside told by a folklorist colleague in Miskatonic's English department.

Naturally, he considered the possibility of the pre-Cambrian prints' having been made by a less evolved ancestor of the present specimens; but quickly rejected this too facile theory upon considering the advanced structural qualities of the older fossils. If anything, the later contours shewed decadence rather than higher evolution. The size of the pseudo-feet had decreased, and the whole morphology seemed coarsened and simplified. Moreover, the nerves and organs just examined held singular suggestions of retrogression from forms still more complex. Atrophied and vestigial parts were surprisingly prevalent. Altogether, little could be said to have been solved; and Lake fell back on mythology for a provisional name—jocosely dubbing his finds "The Elder Ones".

At about 2:30 A.M., having decided to postpone further work and get a little rest, he covered the dissected organism with a tarpaulin, emerged from the laboratory tent, and studied the intact specimens with renewed interest. The ceaseless antarctic sun had begun to limber up their tissues a trifle, so that the head-points and tubes of two or three shewed signs of unfolding; but Lake did not believe there was any danger of immediate decomposition in the almost sub-zero air. He did, however, move all the undissected specimens closer together and throw a spare tent over them in order to keep off the direct solar rays. That would also help to keep their possible scent away from the dogs, whose hostile unrest was really becoming a problem even at their substantial distance and behind the higher and higher snow walls which an increased quota of the men were hastening to raise around their quarters. He had to weight down the corners of the tent-cloth with heavy blocks of snow to hold it in place amidst the rising gale, for the titan mountains seemed about to deliver some gravely severe blasts. Early apprehensions about sudden antarctic winds were revived, and under Atwood's supervision precautions were taken to bank the tents, new dog-corral, and crude aëroplane shelters with snow on the mountainward side. These latter shelters, begun with hard snow blocks during odd moments, were by no means as high as they should have been; and Lake finally detached all hands from other tasks to work on them.

It was after four when Lake at last prepared to sign off and advised us all to share the rest period his outfit would take when the shelter walls were a little higher. He held some friendly chat with Pabodie over the ether, and repeated his praise of the really marvellous drills that had helped him make his discovery. Atwood also sent greetings and praises. I gave Lake a warm word of congratulation, owning up that he was right about the western trip; and we all agreed to get in touch by wireless at ten in the morning. If the gale was then over, Lake would send a plane for the party at my base. Just before retiring I despatched a final message to the Arkham with instructions about toning down the day's news for the outside world, since the full details seemed radical enough to rouse a wave of incredulity until further substantiated.

III.

None of us, I imagine, slept very heavily or continuously that morning; for both the excitement of Lake's discovery and the mounting fury of the wind were against such a thing. So savage was the blast, even where we were, that we could not help wondering how much worse it was at Lake's camp, directly under the vast unknown peaks that bred and delivered it. McTighe was awake at ten o'clock and tried to get Lake on the wireless, as agreed, but some electrical condition in the disturbed air to the westward seemed to prevent communication. We did, however, get the Arkham, and Douglas told me that he had likewise been vainly trying to reach Lake. He had not known about the wind, for very little was blowing at McMurdo Sound despite its persistent rage where we were.

Throughout the day we all listened anxiously and tried to get Lake at intervals, but invariably without results. About noon a positive frenzy of wind stampeded out of the west, causing us to fear for the safety of our camp; but it eventually died down, with only a moderate relapse at 2 P.M. After three o'clock it was very quiet, and we redoubled our efforts to get Lake. Reflecting that he had four planes, each provided with an excellent short-wave outfit, we could not imagine any ordinary accident capable of crippling all his wireless equipment at once. Nevertheless the stony silence continued; and when we thought of the delirious force the wind must have had in his locality we could not help making the most direful conjectures.

By six o'clock our fears had become intense and definite, and after a wireless consultation with Douglas and Thorfinnssen I resolved to take steps toward investigation. The fifth aëroplane, which we had left at the McMurdo Sound supply cache with Sherman and two sailors, was in good shape and ready for instant use; and it seemed that the very emergency for which it had been saved was now upon us. I got Sherman by wireless and ordered him to join me with the plane and the two sailors at the southern base as quickly as possible; the air conditions being apparently highly favourable. We then talked over the personnel of the coming investigation party; and decided that we would include all hands, together with the sledge and dogs which I had kept with me. Even so great a load would not be too much for one of the huge planes built to our especial orders for heavy machinery transportation. At intervals I still tried to reach Lake with the wireless, but all to no purpose.

Sherman, with the sailors Gunnarsson and Larsen, took off at 7:30; and reported a quiet flight from several points on the wing. They arrived at our base at midnight, and all hands at once discussed the next move. It was risky business sailing over the antarctic in a single aëroplane without any line of bases, but no one drew back from what seemed like the plainest necessity. We turned in at two o'clock for a brief rest after some preliminary loading of the plane, but were up again in four hours to finish the loading and packing.

At 7:15 A.M., January 25th, we started flying northwestward under McTighe's pilotage with ten men, seven dogs, a sledge, a fuel and food supply, and other items including the plane's wireless outfit. The atmosphere was clear, fairly quiet, and relatively mild in temperature; and we anticipated very little trouble in reaching the latitude and longitude designated by Lake as the site of his camp. Our apprehensions were over what we might find, or fail to find, at the end of our journey; for silence

continued to answer all calls despatched to the camp.

Every incident of that four-and-a-half-hour flight is burned into my recollection because of its crucial position in my life. It marked my loss, at the age of fifty-four, of all that peace and balance which the normal mind possesses through its accustomed conception of external Nature and Nature's laws. Thenceforward the ten of us—but the student Danforth and myself above all others—were to face a hideously amplified world of lurking horrors which nothing can erase from our emotions, and which we would refrain from sharing with mankind in general if we could. The newspapers have printed the bulletins we sent from the moving plane; telling of our non-stop course, our two battles with treacherous upper-air gales, our glimpse of the broken surface where Lake had sunk his mid-journey shaft three days before, and our sight of a group of those strange fluffy snow-cylinders noted by Amundsen and Byrd as rolling in the wind across the endless leagues of frozen plateau. There came a point, though, when our sensations could not be conveyed in any words the press would understand; and a later point when we had to adopt an actual rule of strict censorship.

The sailor Larsen was first to spy the jagged line of witch-like cones and pinnacles ahead, and his shouts sent everyone to the windows of the great cabined plane. Despite our speed, they were very slow in gaining prominence; hence we knew that they must be infinitely far off, and visible only because of their abnormal height. Little by little, however, they rose grimly into the western sky; allowing us to distinguish various bare, bleak, blackish summits, and to catch the curious sense of phantasy which they inspired as seen in the reddish antarctic light against the provocative background of iridescent ice-dust clouds. In the whole spectacle there was a persistent, pervasive hint of stupendous secrecy and potential revelation; as if these stark, nightmare spires marked the pylons of a frightful gateway into forbidden spheres of dream, and complex gulfs of remote time, space, and ultra-dimensionality. I could not help feeling that they were evil things—mountains of madness whose farther slopes looked out over some accursed ultimate abyss. That seething, half-luminous cloud-background held ineffable suggestions of a vague, ethereal beyondness far more than terrestrially spatial; and gave appalling reminders of the utter remoteness, separateness, desolation, and aeon-long death of this untrodden and unfathomed austral world.

It was young Danforth who drew our notice to the curious regularities of the higher mountain skyline—regularities like clinging fragments of perfect cubes, which Lake had mentioned in his messages, and which indeed justified his comparison with the dream-like suggestions of primordial temple-ruins on cloudy Asian mountain-tops so subtly and strangely painted by Roerich. There was indeed something hauntingly Roerich-like about this whole unearthly continent of mountainous mystery. I had felt it in October when we first caught sight of Victoria Land, and I felt it afresh now. I felt, too, another wave of uneasy consciousness of Archaean mythical resemblances; of how disturbingly this lethal realm corresponded to the evilly famed plateau of Leng in the primal writings. Mythologists have placed Leng in Central Asia; but the racial memory of man—or of his predecessors—is long, and it may well be that certain tales have come down from lands and mountains and temples of horror earlier than Asia and earlier than any human world we know. A few daring

mystics have hinted at a pre-Pleistocene origin for the fragmentary Pnakotic Manuscripts, and have suggested that the devotees of Tsathoggua were as alien to mankind as Tsathoggua itself. Leng, wherever in space or time it might brood, was not a region I would care to be in or near; nor did I relish the proximity of a world that had ever bred such ambiguous and Archaean monstrosities as those Lake had just mentioned. At the moment I felt sorry that I had ever read the abhorred Necronomicon, or talked so much with that unpleasantly erudite folklorist Wilmarth at the university.

This mood undoubtedly served to aggravate my reaction to the bizarre mirage which burst upon us from the increasingly opalescent zenith as we drew near the mountains and began to make out the cumulative undulations of the foothills. I had seen dozens of polar mirages during the preceding weeks, some of them quite as uncanny and fantastically vivid as the present sample; but this one had a wholly novel and obscure quality of menacing symbolism, and I shuddered as the seething labyrinth of fabulous walls and towers and minarets loomed out of the troubled ice-vapours above our heads.

The effect was that of a Cyclopean city of no architecture known to man or to human imagination, with vast aggregations of night-black masonry embodying monstrous perversions of geometrical laws and attaining the most grotesque extremes of sinister bizarrerie. There were truncated cones, sometimes terraced or fluted, surmounted by tall cylindrical shafts here and there bulbously enlarged and often capped with tiers of thinnish scalloped discs; and strange, beetling, table-like constructions suggesting piles of multitudinous rectangular slabs or circular plates or five-pointed stars with each one overlapping the one beneath. There were composite cones and pyramids either alone or surmounting cylinders or cubes or flatter truncated cones and pyramids, and occasional needle-like spires in curious clusters of five. All of these febrile structures seemed knit together by tubular bridges crossing from one to the other at various dizzy heights, and the implied scale of the whole was terrifying and oppressive in its sheer giganticism. The general type of mirage was not unlike some of the wilder forms observed and drawn by the Arctic whaler Scoresby in 1820; but at this time and place, with those dark, unknown mountain peaks soaring stupendously ahead, that anomalous elder-world discovery in our minds, and the pall of probable disaster enveloping the greater part of our expedition, we all seemed to find in it a taint of latent malignity and infinitely evil portent.

I was glad when the mirage began to break up, though in the process the various nightmare turrets and cones assumed distorted temporary forms of even vaster hideousness. As the whole illusion dissolved to churning opalescence we began to look earthward again, and saw that our journey's end was not far off. The unknown mountains ahead rose dizzyingly up like a fearsome rampart of giants, their curious regularities shewing with startling clearness even without a field-glass. We were over the lowest foothills now, and could see amidst the snow, ice, and bare patches of their main plateau a couple of darkish spots which we took to be Lake's camp and boring. The higher foothills shot up between five and six miles away, forming a range almost distinct from the terrifying line of more than Himalayan peaks beyond them. At length Ropes—the student who had relieved McTighe at the controls—began to head

downward toward the left-hand dark spot whose size marked it as the camp. As he did so, McTighe sent out the last uncensored wireless message the world was to receive from our expedition.

Everyone, of course, has read the brief and unsatisfying bulletins of the rest of our antarctic sojourn. Some hours after our landing we sent a guarded report of the tragedy we found, and reluctantly announced the wiping out of the whole Lake party by the frightful wind of the preceding day, or of the night before that. Eleven known dead, young Gedney missing. People pardoned our hazy lack of details through realisation of the shock the sad event must have caused us, and believed us when we explained that the mangling action of the wind had rendered all eleven bodies unsuitable for transportation outside. Indeed, I flatter myself that even in the midst of our distress, utter bewilderment, and soul-clutching horror, we scarcely went beyond the truth in any specific instance. The tremendous significance lies in what we dared not tell—what I would not tell now but for the need of warning others off from nameless terrors.

It is a fact that the wind had wrought dreadful havoc. Whether all could have lived through it, even without the other thing, is gravely open to doubt. The storm, with its fury of madly driven ice-particles, must have been beyond anything our expedition had encountered before. One aëroplane shelter—all, it seems, had been left in a far too flimsy and inadequate state—was nearly pulverised; and the derrick at the distant boring was entirely shaken to pieces. The exposed metal of the grounded planes and drilling machinery was bruised into a high polish, and two of the small tents were flattened despite their snow banking. Wooden surfaces left out in the blast were pitted and denuded of paint, and all signs of tracks in the snow were completely obliterated. It is also true that we found none of the Archaean biological objects in a condition to take outside as a whole. We did gather some minerals from a vast tumbled pile, including several of the greenish soapstone fragments whose odd five-pointed rounding and faint patterns of grouped dots caused so many doubtful comparisons; and some fossil bones, among which were the most typical of the curiously injured specimens.

None of the dogs survived, their hurriedly built snow enclosure near the camp being almost wholly destroyed. The wind may have done that, though the greater breakage on the side next the camp, which was not the windward one, suggests an outward leap or break of the frantic beasts themselves. All three sledges were gone, and we have tried to explain that the wind may have blown them off into the unknown. The drill and ice-melting machinery at the boring were too badly damaged to warrant salvage, so we used them to choke up that subtly disturbing gateway to the past which Lake had blasted. We likewise left at the camp the two most shaken-up of the planes; since our surviving party had only four real pilots—Sherman, Danforth, McTighe, and Ropes—in all, with Danforth in a poor nervous shape to navigate. We brought back all the books, scientific equipment, and other incidentals we could find, though much was rather unaccountably blown away. Spare tents and furs were either missing or badly out of condition.

It was approximately 4 P.M., after wide plane cruising had forced us to give Gedney up for lost, that we sent our guarded message to the Arkham for relaying; and I think we did well to keep it as calm and non-committal

as we succeeded in doing. The most we said about agitation concerned our dogs, whose frantic uneasiness near the biological specimens was to be expected from poor Lake's accounts. We did not mention, I think, their display of the same uneasiness when sniffing around the queer greenish soapstones and certain other objects in the disordered region; objects including scientific instruments, aëroplanes, and machinery both at the camp and at the boring, whose parts had been loosened, moved, or otherwise tampered with by winds that must have harboured singular curiosity and investigativeness.

About the fourteen biological specimens we were pardonably indefinite. We said that the only ones we discovered were damaged, but that enough was left of them to prove Lake's description wholly and impressively accurate. It was hard work keeping our personal emotions out of this matter—and we did not mention numbers or say exactly how we had found those which we did find. We had by that time agreed not to transmit anything suggesting madness on the part of Lake's men, and it surely looked like madness to find six imperfect monstrosities carefully buried upright in nine-foot snow graves under five-pointed mounds punched over with groups of dots in patterns exactly like those on the queer greenish soapstones dug up from Mesozoic or Tertiary times. The eight perfect specimens mentioned by Lake seemed to have been completely blown away.

We were careful, too, about the public's general peace of mind; hence Danforth and I said little about that frightful trip over the mountains the next day. It was the fact that only a radically lightened plane could possibly cross a range of such height which mercifully limited that scouting tour to the two of us. On our return at 1 A.M.

Danforth was close to hysterics, but kept an admirably stiff upper lip. It took no persuasion to make him promise not to shew our sketches and the other things we brought away in our pockets, not to say anything more to the others than what we had agreed to relay outside, and to hide our camera films for private development later on; so that part of my present story will be as new to Pabodie, McTighe, Ropes, Sherman, and the rest as it will be to the world in general. Indeed—Danforth is closer mouthed than I; for he saw—or thinks he saw—one thing he will not tell even me.

As all know, our report included a tale of a hard ascent; a confirmation of Lake's opinion that the great peaks are of Archaean slate and other very primal crumpled strata unchanged since at least middle Comanchian times; a conventional comment on the regularity of the clinging cube and rampart formations; a decision that the cave-mouths indicate dissolved calcareous veins; a conjecture that certain slopes and passes would permit of the scaling and crossing of the entire range by seasoned mountaineers; and a remark that the mysterious other side holds a lofty and immense super-plateau as ancient and unchanging as the mountains themselves—20,000 feet in elevation, with grotesque rock formations protruding through a thin glacial layer and with low gradual foothills between the general plateau surface and the sheer precipices of the highest peaks.

This body of data is in every respect true so far as it goes, and it completely satisfied the men at the camp. We laid our absence of sixteen hours—a longer time than our announced flying, landing, reconnoitring, and rock-collecting programme called for—to a long mythical spell of adverse wind conditions; and told truly of our landing

on the farther foothills. Fortunately our tale sounded realistic and prosaic enough not to tempt any of the others into emulating our flight. Had any tried to do that, I would have used every ounce of my persuasion to stop them—and I do not know what Danforth would have done. While we were gone, Pabodie, Sherman, Ropes, McTighe, and Williamson had worked like beavers over Lake's two best planes; fitting them again for use despite the altogether unaccountable juggling of their operative mechanism.

We decided to load all the planes the next morning and start back for our old base as soon as possible. Even though indirect, that was the safest way to work toward McMurdo Sound; for a straight-line flight across the most utterly unknown stretches of the aeon-dead continent would involve many additional hazards. Further exploration was hardly feasible in view of our tragic decimation and the ruin of our drilling machinery; and the doubts and horrors around us—which we did not reveal—made us wish only to escape from this austral world of desolation and brooding madness as swiftly as we could.

As the public knows, our return to the world was accomplished without further disasters. All planes reached the old base on the evening of the next day—January 27th—after a swift non-stop flight; and on the 28th we made McMurdo Sound in two laps, the one pause being very brief, and occasioned by a faulty rudder in the furious wind over the ice-shelf after we had cleared the great plateau. In five days more the Arkham and Miskatonic, with all hands and equipment on board, were shaking clear of the thickening field ice and working up Ross Sea with the mocking mountains of Victoria

Land looming westward against a troubled antarctic sky and twisting the wind's wails into a wide-ranged musical piping which chilled my soul to the quick. Less than a fortnight later we left the last hint of polar land behind us, and thanked heaven that we were clear of a haunted, accursed realm where life and death, space and time, have made black and blasphemous alliances in the unknown epochs since matter first writhed and swam on the planet's scarce-cooled crust.

Since our return we have all constantly worked to discourage antarctic exploration, and have kept certain doubts and guesses to ourselves with splendid unity and faithfulness. Even young Danforth, with his nervous breakdown, has not flinched or babbled to his doctors—indeed, as I have said, there is one thing he thinks he alone saw which he will not tell even me, though I think it would help his psychological state if he would consent to do so. It might explain and relieve much, though perhaps the thing was no more than the delusive aftermath of an earlier shock. That is the impression I gather after those rare irresponsible moments when he whispers disjointed things to me—things which he repudiates vehemently as soon as he gets a grip on himself again.

It will be hard work deterring others from the great white south, and some of our efforts may directly harm our cause by drawing inquiring notice. We might have known from the first that human curiosity is undying, and that the results we announced would be enough to spur others ahead on the same age-long pursuit of the unknown. Lake's reports of those biological monstrosities had aroused naturalists and palaeontologists to the highest pitch; though we were sensible enough not to shew the detached parts we had taken from the actual

buried specimens, or our photographs of those specimens as they were found. We also refrained from shewing the more puzzling of the scarred bones and greenish soapstones; while Danforth and I have closely guarded the pictures we took or drew on the super-plateau across the range, and the crumpled things we smoothed, studied in terror, and brought away in our pockets. But now that Starkweather-Moore party is organising, and with a thoroughness far beyond anything our outfit attempted. If not dissuaded, they will get to the innermost nucleus of the antarctic and melt and bore till they bring up that which may end the world we know. So I must break through all reticences at last—even about that ultimate nameless thing beyond the mountains of madness.

IV.

It is only with vast hesitancy and repugnance that I let my mind go back to Lake's camp and what we really found there—and to that other thing beyond the frightful mountain wall. I am constantly tempted to shirk the details, and to let hints stand for actual facts and ineluctable deductions. I hope I have said enough already to let me glide briefly over the rest; the rest, that is, of the horror at the camp. I have told of the wind-ravaged terrain, the damaged shelters, the disarranged machinery, the varied uneasinesses of our dogs, the missing sledges and other items, the deaths of men and dogs, the absence of Gedney, and the six insanely buried biological specimens, strangely sound in texture for all their structural injuries, from a world forty million years dead. I do not recall whether I mentioned that upon checking up the canine bodies we found one dog missing. We did not think much about that till later—indeed, only Danforth and I have thought of it at all.

The principal things I have been keeping back relate to the bodies, and to certain subtle points which may or may not lend a hideous and incredible kind of rationale to the apparent chaos. At the time I tried to keep the men's minds off those points; for it was so much simpler—so much more normal—to lay everything to an outbreak of madness on the part of some of Lake's party. From the look of things, that daemon mountain wind must have been enough to drive any man mad in the midst of this centre of all earthly mystery and desolation.

The crowning abnormality, of course, was the condition of the bodies—men and dogs alike. They had all been in some terrible kind of conflict, and were torn and mangled in fiendish and altogether inexplicable ways. Death, so far as we could judge, had in each case come from strangulation or laceration. The dogs had evidently started the trouble, for the state of their ill-built corral bore witness to its forcible breakage from within. It had been set some distance from the camp because of the hatred of the animals for those hellish Archaean organisms, but the precaution seemed to have been taken in vain. When left alone in that monstrous wind behind flimsy walls of insufficient height they must have stampeded—whether from the wind itself, or from some subtle, increasing odour emitted by the nightmare specimens, one could not say. Those specimens, of course, had been covered with a tent-cloth; yet the low antarctic sun had beat steadily upon that cloth, and Lake had mentioned that solar heat tended to make the

strangely sound and tough tissues of the things relax and expand. Perhaps the wind had whipped the cloth from over them, and jostled them about in such a way that their more pungent olfactory qualities became manifest despite their unbelievable antiquity.

But whatever had happened, it was hideous and revolting enough. Perhaps I had better put squeamishness aside and tell the worst at last—though with a categorical statement of opinion, based on the first-hand observations and most rigid deductions of both Danforth and myself, that the then missing Gedney was in no way responsible for the loathsome horrors we found. I have said that the bodies were frightfully mangled. Now I must add that some were incised and subtracted from in the most curious, cold-blooded, and inhuman fashion. It was the same with dogs and men. All the healthier, fatter bodies, quadrupedal or bipedal, had had their most solid masses of tissue cut out and removed, as by a careful butcher; and around them was a strange sprinkling of salt—taken from the ravaged provision-chests on the planes—which conjured up the most horrible associations. The thing had occurred in one of the crude aëroplane shelters from which the plane had been dragged out, and subsequent winds had effaced all tracks which could have supplied any plausible theory. Scattered bits of clothing, roughly slashed from the human incision-subjects, hinted no clues. It is useless to bring up the half-impression of certain faint snow-prints in one shielded corner of the ruined enclosure—because that impression did not concern human prints at all, but was clearly mixed up with all the talk of fossil prints which poor Lake had been giving throughout the preceding weeks. One had to be careful of one's imagination in the lee of those overshadowing mountains of madness.

As I have indicated, Gedney and one dog turned out to be missing in the end. When we came on that terrible shelter we had missed two dogs and two men; but the fairly unharmed dissecting tent, which we entered after investigating the monstrous graves, had something to reveal. It was not as Lake had left it, for the covered parts of the primal monstrosity had been removed from the improvised table. Indeed, we had already realised that one of the six imperfect and insanely buried things we had found—the one with the trace of a peculiarly hateful odour—must represent the collected sections of the entity which Lake had tried to analyse. On and around that laboratory table were strown other things, and it did not take long for us to guess that those things were the carefully though oddly and inexpertly dissected parts of one man and one dog. I shall spare the feelings of survivors by omitting mention of the man's identity. Lake's anatomical instruments were missing, but there were evidences of their careful cleansing. The gasoline stove was also gone, though around it we found a curious litter of matches. We buried the human parts beside the other ten men, and the canine parts with the other 35 dogs. Concerning the bizarre smudges on the laboratory table, and on the jumble of roughly handled illustrated books scattered near it, we were much too bewildered to speculate.

This formed the worst of the camp horror, but other things were equally perplexing. The disappearance of Gedney, the one dog, the eight uninjured biological specimens, the three sledges, and certain instruments, illustrated technical and scientific books, writing materials, electric torches and batteries, food and fuel, heating apparatus, spare tents, fur suits, and the like,

was utterly beyond sane conjecture; as were likewise the spatter-fringed ink-blots on certain pieces of paper, and the evidences of curious alien fumbling and experimentation around the planes and all other mechanical devices both at the camp and at the boring. The dogs seemed to abhor this oddly disordered machinery. Then, too, there was the upsetting of the larder, the disappearance of certain staples, and the jarringly comical heap of tin cans pried open in the most unlikely ways and at the most unlikely places. The profusion of scattered matches, intact, broken, or spent, formed another minor enigma; as did the two or three tent-cloths and fur suits which we found lying about with peculiar and unorthodox slashings conceivably due to clumsy efforts at unimaginable adaptations. The maltreatment of the human and canine bodies, and the crazy burial of the damaged Archaean specimens, were all of a piece with this apparent disintegrative madness. In view of just such an eventuality as the present one, we carefully photographed all the main evidences of insane disorder at the camp; and shall use the prints to buttress our pleas against the departure of the proposed Starkweather-Moore Expedition.

Our first act after finding the bodies in the shelter was to photograph and open the row of insane graves with the five-pointed snow mounds. We could not help noticing the resemblance of these monstrous mounds, with their clusters of grouped dots, to poor Lake's descriptions of the strange greenish soapstones; and when we came on some of the soapstones themselves in the great mineral pile we found the likeness very close indeed. The whole general formation, it must be made clear, seemed abominably suggestive of the starfish-head of the Archaean entities; and we agreed that the suggestion must have worked potently upon the sensitised minds of Lake's overwrought party. Our own first sight of the actual buried entities formed a horrible moment, and sent the imaginations of Pabodie and myself back to some of the shocking primal myths we had read and heard. We all agreed that the mere sight and continued presence of the things must have coöperated with the oppressive polar solitude and daemon mountain wind in driving Lake's party mad.

For madness—centring in Gedney as the only possible surviving agent—was the explanation spontaneously adopted by everybody so far as spoken utterance was concerned; though I will not be so naive as to deny that each of us may have harboured wild guesses which sanity forbade him to formulate completely. Sherman, Pabodie, and McTighe made an exhaustive aëroplane cruise over all the surrounding territory in the afternoon, sweeping the horizon with field-glasses in quest of Gedney and of the various missing things; but nothing came to light. The party reported that the titan barrier range extended endlessly to right and left alike, without any diminution in height or essential structure. On some of the peaks, though, the regular cube and rampart formations were bolder and plainer; having doubly fantastic similitudes to Roerich-painted Asian hill ruins. The distribution of cryptical cave-mouths on the black snow-denuded summits seemed roughly even as far as the range could be traced.

In spite of all the prevailing horrors we were left with enough sheer scientific zeal and adventurousness to wonder about the unknown realm beyond those mysterious mountains. As our guarded messages stated, we rested at midnight after our day of terror and bafflement; but not without a tentative plan for one or more range-crossing altitude flights in a lightened plane

53

with aërial camera and geologist's outfit, beginning the following morning. It was decided that Danforth and I try it first, and we awaked at 7 A.M. intending an early trip; though heavy winds—mentioned in our brief bulletin to the outside world—delayed our start till nearly nine o'clock.

I have already repeated the non-committal story we told the men at camp—and relayed outside—after our return sixteen hours later. It is now my terrible duty to amplify this account by filling in the merciful blanks with hints of what we really saw in the hidden trans-montane world—hints of the revelations which have finally driven Danforth to a nervous collapse. I wish he would add a really frank word about the thing which he thinks he alone saw—even though it was probably a nervous delusion—and which was perhaps the last straw that put him where he is; but he is firm against that. All I can do is to repeat his later disjointed whispers about what set him shrieking as the plane soared back through the wind-tortured mountain pass after that real and tangible shock which I shared. This will form my last word. If the plain signs of surviving elder horrors in what I disclose be not enough to keep others from meddling with the inner antarctic—or at least from prying too deeply beneath the surface of that ultimate waste of forbidden secrets and unhuman, aeon-cursed desolation—the responsibility for unnamable and perhaps immensurable evils will not be mine.

Danforth and I, studying the notes made by Pabodie in his afternoon flight and checking up with a sextant, had calculated that the lowest available pass in the range lay somewhat to the right of us, within sight of camp, and about 23,000 or 24,000 feet above sea-level. For this point, then, we first headed in the lightened plane as we embarked on our flight of discovery. The camp itself, on foothills which sprang from a high continental plateau, was some 12,000 feet in altitude; hence the actual height increase necessary was not so vast as it might seem. Nevertheless we were acutely conscious of the rarefied air and intense cold as we rose; for on account of visibility conditions we had to leave the cabin windows open. We were dressed, of course, in our heaviest furs.

As we drew near the forbidding peaks, dark and sinister above the line of crevasse-riven snow and interstitial glaciers, we noticed more and more the curiously regular formations clinging to the slopes; and thought again of the strange Asian paintings of Nicholas Roerich. The ancient and wind-weathered rock strata fully verified all of Lake's bulletins, and proved that these hoary pinnacles had been towering up in exactly the same way since a surprisingly early time in earth's history— perhaps over fifty million years. How much higher they had once been, it was futile to guess; but everything about this strange region pointed to obscure atmospheric influences unfavourable to change, and calculated to retard the usual climatic processes of rock disintegration.

But it was the mountainside tangle of regular cubes, ramparts, and cave-mouths which fascinated and disturbed us most. I studied them with a field-glass and took aërial photographs whilst Danforth drove; and at times relieved him at the controls—though my aviation knowledge was purely an amateur's—in order to let him use the binoculars. We could easily see that much of the material of the things was a lightish Archaean quartzite, unlike any formation visible over broad areas of the general surface; and that their regularity was extreme

55

and uncanny to an extent which poor Lake had scarcely hinted.

As he had said, their edges were crumbled and rounded from untold aeons of savage weathering; but their preternatural solidity and tough material had saved them from obliteration. Many parts, especially those closest to the slopes, seemed identical in substance with the surrounding rock surface. The whole arrangement looked like the ruins of Machu Picchu in the Andes, or the primal foundation-walls of Kish as dug up by the Oxford–Field Museum Expedition in 1929; and both Danforth and I obtained that occasional impression of separate Cyclopean blocks which Lake had attributed to his flight-companion Carroll. How to account for such things in this place was frankly beyond me, and I felt queerly humbled as a geologist. Igneous formations often have strange regularities—like the famous Giants' Causeway in Ireland—but this stupendous range, despite Lake's original suspicion of smoking cones, was above all else non-volcanic in evident structure.

The curious cave-mouths, near which the odd formations seemed most abundant, presented another albeit a lesser puzzle because of their regularity of outline. They were, as Lake's bulletin had said, often approximately square or semicircular; as if the natural orifices had been shaped to greater symmetry by some magic hand. Their numerousness and wide distribution were remarkable, and suggested that the whole region was honeycombed with tunnels dissolved out of limestone strata. Such glimpses as we secured did not extend far within the caverns, but we saw that they were apparently clear of stalactites and stalagmites. Outside, those parts of the mountain slopes adjoining the apertures seemed invariably smooth and regular; and Danforth thought that the slight cracks and pittings of the weathering tended toward unusual patterns. Filled as he was with the horrors and strangenesses discovered at the camp, he hinted that the pittings vaguely resembled those baffling groups of dots sprinkled over the primeval greenish soapstones, so hideously duplicated on the madly conceived snow mounds above those six buried monstrosities.

We had risen gradually in flying over the higher foothills and along toward the relatively low pass we had selected. As we advanced we occasionally looked down at the snow and ice of the land route, wondering whether we could have attempted the trip with the simpler equipment of earlier days. Somewhat to our surprise we saw that the terrain was far from difficult as such things go; and that despite the crevasses and other bad spots it would not have been likely to deter the sledges of a Scott, a Shackleton, or an Amundsen. Some of the glaciers appeared to lead up to wind-bared passes with unusual continuity, and upon reaching our chosen pass we found that its case formed no exception.

Our sensations of tense expectancy as we prepared to round the crest and peer out over an untrodden world can hardly be described on paper; even though we had no cause to think the regions beyond the range essentially different from those already seen and traversed. The touch of evil mystery in these barrier mountains, and in the beckoning sea of opalescent sky glimpsed betwixt their summits, was a highly subtle and attenuated matter not to be explained in literal words. Rather was it an affair of vague psychological symbolism and aesthetic association—a thing mixed up with exotic poetry and paintings, and with archaic myths lurking in shunned

and forbidden volumes. Even the wind's burden held a peculiar strain of conscious malignity; and for a second it seemed that the composite sound included a bizarre musical whistling or piping over a wide range as the blast swept in and out of the omnipresent and resonant cave-mouths. There was a cloudy note of reminiscent repulsion in this sound, as complex and unplaceable as any of the other dark impressions.

We were now, after a slow ascent, at a height of 23,570 feet according to the aneroid; and had left the region of clinging snow definitely below us. Up here were only dark, bare rock slopes and the start of rough-ribbed glaciers—but with those provocative cubes, ramparts, and echoing cave-mouths to add a portent of the unnatural, the fantastic, and the dream-like. Looking along the line of high peaks, I thought I could see the one mentioned by poor Lake, with a rampart exactly on top. It seemed to be half-lost in a queer antarctic haze; such a haze, perhaps, as had been responsible for Lake's early notion of volcanism. The pass loomed directly before us, smooth and windswept between its jagged and malignly frowning pylons. Beyond it was a sky fretted with swirling vapours and lighted by the low polar sun—the sky of that mysterious farther realm upon which we felt no human eye had ever gazed.

A few more feet of altitude and we would behold that realm. Danforth and I, unable to speak except in shouts amidst the howling, piping wind that raced through the pass and added to the noise of the unmuffled engines, exchanged eloquent glances. And then, having gained those last few feet, we did indeed stare across the momentous divide and over the unsampled secrets of an elder and utterly alien earth.

V.

I think that both of us simultaneously cried out in mixed awe, wonder, terror, and disbelief in our own senses as we finally cleared the pass and saw what lay beyond. Of course we must have had some natural theory in the back of our heads to steady our faculties for the moment. Probably we thought of such things as the grotesquely weathered stones of the Garden of the Gods in Colorado, or the fantastically symmetrical wind-carved rocks of the Arizona desert. Perhaps we even half thought the sight a mirage like that we had seen the morning before on first approaching those mountains of madness. We must have had some such normal notions to fall back upon as our eyes swept that limitless, tempest-scarred plateau and grasped the almost endless labyrinth of colossal, regular, and geometrically eurhythmic stone masses which reared their crumbled and pitted crests above a glacial sheet not more than forty or fifty feet deep at its thickest, and in places obviously thinner.

The effect of the monstrous sight was indescribable, for some fiendish violation of known natural law seemed certain at the outset. Here, on a hellishly ancient table-land fully 20,000 feet high, and in a climate deadly to habitation since a pre-human age not less than 500,000 years ago, there stretched nearly to the vision's limit a tangle of orderly stone which only the desperation of mental self-defence could possibly attribute to any but a conscious and artificial cause. We had previously dismissed, so far as serious thought was concerned, any theory that the cubes and ramparts of the mountainsides

were other than natural in origin. How could they be otherwise, when man himself could scarcely have been differentiated from the great apes at the time when this region succumbed to the present unbroken reign of glacial death?

Yet now the sway of reason seemed irrefutably shaken, for this Cyclopean maze of squared, curved, and angled blocks had features which cut off all comfortable refuge. It was, very clearly, the blasphemous city of the mirage in stark, objective, and ineluctable reality. That damnable portent had had a material basis after all—there had been some horizontal stratum of ice-dust in the upper air, and this shocking stone survival had projected its image across the mountains according to the simple laws of reflection. Of course the phantom had been twisted and exaggerated, and had contained things which the real source did not contain; yet now, as we saw that real source, we thought it even more hideous and menacing than its distant image.

Only the incredible, unhuman massiveness of these vast stone towers and ramparts had saved the frightful thing from utter annihilation in the hundreds of thousands—perhaps millions—of years it had brooded there amidst the blasts of a bleak upland. "Corona Mundi . . . Roof of the World . . ." All sorts of fantastic phrases sprang to our lips as we looked dizzily down at the unbelievable spectacle. I thought again of the eldritch primal myths that had so persistently haunted me since my first sight of this dead antarctic world—of the daemoniac plateau of Leng, of the Mi-Go, or Abominable Snow-Men of the Himalayas, of the Pnakotic Manuscripts with their pre-human implications, of the Cthulhu cult, of the Necronomicon, and of the Hyperborean legends of formless Tsathoggua and the worse than formless star-spawn associated with that semi-entity.

For boundless miles in every direction the thing stretched off with very little thinning; indeed, as our eyes followed it to the right and left along the base of the low, gradual foothills which separated it from the actual mountain rim, we decided that we could see no thinning at all except for an interruption at the left of the pass through which we had come. We had merely struck, at random, a limited part of something of incalculable extent. The foothills were more sparsely sprinkled with grotesque stone structures, linking the terrible city to the already familiar cubes and ramparts which evidently formed its mountain outposts. These latter, as well as the queer cave-mouths, were as thick on the inner as on the outer sides of the mountains.

The nameless stone labyrinth consisted, for the most part, of walls from 10 to 150 feet in ice-clear height, and of a thickness varying from five to ten feet. It was composed mostly of prodigious blocks of dark primordial slate, schist, and sandstone—blocks in many cases as large as $4 \times 6 \times 8$ feet—though in several places it seemed to be carved out of a solid, uneven bed-rock of pre-Cambrian slate. The buildings were far from equal in size; there being innumerable honeycomb-arrangements of enormous extent as well as smaller separate structures. The general shape of these things tended to be conical, pyramidal, or terraced; though there were many perfect cylinders, perfect cubes, clusters of cubes, and other rectangular forms, and a peculiar sprinkling of angled edifices whose five-pointed ground plan roughly suggested modern fortifications. The builders had made constant and expert use of the principle of the arch, and domes had probably

existed in the city's heyday.

The whole tangle was monstrously weathered, and the glacial surface from which the towers projected was strewn with fallen blocks and immemorial debris. Where the glaciation was transparent we could see the lower parts of the gigantic piles, and noticed the ice-preserved stone bridges which connected the different towers at varying distances above the ground. On the exposed walls we could detect the scarred places where other and higher bridges of the same sort had existed. Closer inspection revealed countless largish windows; some of which were closed with shutters of a petrified material originally wood, though most gaped open in a sinister and menacing fashion. Many of the ruins, of course, were roofless, and with uneven though wind-rounded upper edges; whilst others, of a more sharply conical or pyramidal model or else protected by higher surrounding structures, preserved intact outlines despite the omnipresent crumbling and pitting. With the field-glass we could barely make out what seemed to be sculptural decorations in horizontal bands—decorations including those curious groups of dots whose presence on the ancient soapstones now assumed a vastly larger significance.

In many places the buildings were totally ruined and the ice-sheet deeply riven from various geologic causes. In other places the stonework was worn down to the very level of the glaciation. One broad swath, extending from the plateau's interior to a cleft in the foothills about a mile to the left of the pass we had traversed, was wholly free from buildings; and probably represented, we concluded, the course of some great river which in Tertiary times— millions of years ago—had poured through the city and into some prodigious subterranean abyss of the great barrier range. Certainly, this was above all a region of caves, gulfs, and underground secrets beyond human penetration.

Looking back to our sensations, and recalling our dazedness at viewing this monstrous survival from aeons we had thought pre-human, I can only wonder that we preserved the semblance of equilibrium which we did. Of course we knew that something—chronology, scientific theory, or our own consciousness—was woefully awry; yet we kept enough poise to guide the plane, observe many things quite minutely, and take a careful series of photographs which may yet serve both us and the world in good stead. In my case, ingrained scientific habit may have helped; for above all my bewilderment and sense of menace there burned a dominant curiosity to fathom more of this age-old secret—to know what sort of beings had built and lived in this incalculably gigantic place, and what relation to the general world of its time or of other times so unique a concentration of life could have had.

For this place could be no ordinary city. It must have formed the primary nucleus and centre of some archaic and unbelievable chapter of earth's history whose outward ramifications, recalled only dimly in the most obscure and distorted myths, had vanished utterly amidst the chaos of terrene convulsions long before any human race we know had shambled out of apedom. Here sprawled a palaeogean megalopolis compared with which the fabled Atlantis and Lemuria, Commoriom and Uzuldaroum, and Olathoë in the land of Lomar are recent things of today—not even of yesterday; a megalopolis ranking with such whispered pre-human blasphemies as Valusia, R'lyeh, Ib in the land of Mnar, and the Nameless City of

Arabia Deserta. As we flew above that tangle of stark titan towers my imagination sometimes escaped all bounds and roved aimlessly in realms of fantastic associations—even weaving links betwixt this lost world and some of my own wildest dreams concerning the mad horror at the camp.

The plane's fuel-tank, in the interest of greater lightness, had been only partly filled; hence we now had to exert caution in our explorations. Even so, however, we covered an enormous extent of ground—or rather, air—after swooping down to a level where the wind became virtually negligible. There seemed to be no limit to the mountain-range, or to the length of the frightful stone city which bordered its inner foothills. Fifty miles of flight in each direction shewed no major change in the labyrinth of rock and masonry that clawed up corpse-like through the eternal ice. There were, though, some highly absorbing diversifications; such as the carvings on the canyon where that broad river had once pierced the foothills and approached its sinking-place in the great range. The headlands at the stream's entrance had been boldly carved into Cyclopean pylons; and something about the ridgy, barrel-shaped designs stirred up oddly vague, hateful, and confusing semi-remembrances in both Danforth and me.

We also came upon several star-shaped open spaces, evidently public squares; and noted various undulations in the terrain. Where a sharp hill rose, it was generally hollowed out into some sort of rambling stone edifice; but there were at least two exceptions. Of these latter, one was too badly weathered to disclose what had been on the jutting eminence, while the other still bore a fantastic conical monument carved out of the solid rock and roughly resembling such things as the well-known Snake Tomb in the ancient valley of Petra.

Flying inland from the mountains, we discovered that the city was not of infinite width, even though its length along the foothills seemed endless. After about thirty miles the grotesque stone buildings began to thin out, and in ten more miles we came to an unbroken waste virtually without signs of sentient artifice. The course of the river beyond the city seemed marked by a broad depressed line; while the land assumed a somewhat greater ruggedness, seeming to slope slightly upward as it receded in the mist-hazed west.

So far we had made no landing, yet to leave the plateau without an attempt at entering some of the monstrous structures would have been inconceivable. Accordingly we decided to find a smooth place on the foothills near our navigable pass, there grounding the plane and preparing to do some exploration on foot. Though these gradual slopes were partly covered with a scattering of ruins, low flying soon disclosed an ample number of possible landing-places. Selecting that nearest to the pass, since our next flight would be across the great range and back to camp, we succeeded about 12:30 P.M. in coming down on a smooth, hard snowfield wholly devoid of obstacles and well adapted to a swift and favourable takeoff later on.

It did not seem necessary to protect the plane with a snow banking for so brief a time and in so comfortable an absence of high winds at this level; hence we merely saw that the landing skis were safely lodged, and that the vital parts of the mechanism were guarded against the cold. For our foot journey we discarded the heaviest of our flying

furs, and took with us a small outfit consisting of pocket compass, hand camera, light provisions, voluminous notebooks and paper, geologist's hammer and chisel, specimen-bags, coil of climbing rope, and powerful electric torches with extra batteries; this equipment having been carried in the plane on the chance that we might be able to effect a landing, take ground pictures, make drawings and topographical sketches, and obtain rock specimens from some bare slope, outcropping, or mountain cave. Fortunately we had a supply of extra paper to tear up, place in a spare specimen-bag, and use on the ancient principle of hare-and-hounds for marking our course in any interior mazes we might be able to penetrate. This had been brought in case we found some cave system with air quiet enough to allow such a rapid and easy method in place of the usual rock-chipping method of trail-blazing.

Walking cautiously downhill over the crusted snow toward the stupendous stone labyrinth that loomed against the opalescent west, we felt almost as keen a sense of imminent marvels as we had felt on approaching the unfathomed mountain pass four hours previously. True, we had become visually familiar with the incredible secret concealed by the barrier peaks; yet the prospect of actually entering primordial walls reared by conscious beings perhaps millions of years ago—before any known race of men could have existed—was none the less awesome and potentially terrible in its implications of cosmic abnormality. Though the thinness of the air at this prodigious altitude made exertion somewhat more difficult than usual; both Danforth and I found ourselves bearing up very well, and felt equal to almost any task which might fall to our lot. It took only a few steps to bring us to a shapeless ruin worn level with the snow, while ten or fifteen rods farther on there was a huge roofless rampart still complete in its gigantic five-pointed outline and rising to an irregular height of ten or eleven feet. For this latter we headed; and when at last we were able actually to touch its weathered Cyclopean blocks, we felt that we had established an unprecedented and almost blasphemous link with forgotten aeons normally closed to our species.

This rampart, shaped like a star and perhaps 300 feet from point to point, was built of Jurassic sandstone blocks of irregular size, averaging 6 × 8 feet in surface. There was a row of arched loopholes or windows about four feet wide and five feet high; spaced quite symmetrically along the points of the star and at its inner angles, and with the bottoms about four feet from the glaciated surface. Looking through these, we could see that the masonry was fully five feet thick, that there were no partitions remaining within, and that there were traces of banded carvings or bas-reliefs on the interior walls; facts we had indeed guessed before, when flying low over this rampart and others like it. Though lower parts must have originally existed, all traces of such things were now wholly obscured by the deep layer of ice and snow at this point.

We crawled through one of the windows and vainly tried to decipher the nearly effaced mural designs, but did not attempt to disturb the glaciated floor. Our orientation flights had indicated that many buildings in the city proper were less ice-choked, and that we might perhaps find wholly clear interiors leading down to the true ground level if we entered those structures still roofed at the top. Before we left the rampart we photographed it carefully, and studied its mortarless Cyclopean masonry

with complete bewilderment. We wished that Pabodie were present, for his engineering knowledge might have helped us guess how such titanic blocks could have been handled in that unbelievably remote age when the city and its outskirts were built up.

The half-mile walk downhill to the actual city, with the upper wind shrieking vainly and savagely through the skyward peaks in the background, was something whose smallest details will always remain engraved on my mind. Only in fantastic nightmares could any human beings but Danforth and me conceive such optical effects. Between us and the churning vapours of the west lay that monstrous tangle of dark stone towers; its outré and incredible forms impressing us afresh at every new angle of vision. It was a mirage in solid stone, and were it not for the photographs I would still doubt that such a thing could be. The general type of masonry was identical with that of the rampart we had examined; but the extravagant shapes which this masonry took in its urban manifestations were past all description.

Even the pictures illustrate only one or two phases of its infinite bizarrerie, endless variety, preternatural massiveness, and utterly alien exoticism. There were geometrical forms for which an Euclid could scarcely find a name—cones of all degrees of irregularity and truncation; terraces of every sort of provocative disproportion; shafts with odd bulbous enlargements; broken columns in curious groups; and five-pointed or five-ridged arrangements of mad grotesqueness. As we drew nearer we could see beneath certain transparent parts of the ice-sheet, and detect some of the tubular stone bridges that connected the crazily sprinkled structures at various heights. Of orderly streets there seemed to be none, the only broad open swath being a mile to the left, where the ancient river had doubtless flowed through the town into the mountains.

Our field-glasses shewed the external horizontal bands of nearly effaced sculptures and dot-groups to be very prevalent, and we could half imagine what the city must once have looked like—even though most of the roofs and tower-tops had necessarily perished. As a whole, it had been a complex tangle of twisted lanes and alleys; all of them deep canyons, and some little better than tunnels because of the overhanging masonry or overarching bridges. Now, outspread below us, it loomed like a dream-phantasy against a westward mist through whose northern end the low, reddish antarctic sun of early afternoon was struggling to shine; and when for a moment that sun encountered a denser obstruction and plunged the scene into temporary shadow, the effect was subtly menacing in a way I can never hope to depict. Even the faint howling and piping of the unfelt wind in the great mountain passes behind us took on a wilder note of purposeful malignity. The last stage of our descent to the town was unusually steep and abrupt, and a rock outcropping at the edge where the grade changed led us to think that an artificial terrace had once existed there. Under the glaciation, we believed, there must be a flight of steps or its equivalent.

When at last we plunged into the labyrinthine town itself, clambering over fallen masonry and shrinking from the oppressive nearness and dwarfing height of omnipresent crumbling and pitted walls, our sensations again became such that I marvel at the amount of self-control we retained. Danforth was frankly jumpy, and began making some offensively irrelevant speculations

about the horror at the camp—which I resented all the more because I could not help sharing certain conclusions forced upon us by many features of this morbid survival from nightmare antiquity. The speculations worked on his imagination, too; for in one place—where a debris-littered alley turned a sharp corner—he insisted that he saw faint traces of ground markings which he did not like; whilst elsewhere he stopped to listen to a subtle imaginary sound from some undefined point—a muffled musical piping, he said, not unlike that of the wind in the mountain caves yet somehow disturbingly different. The ceaseless five-pointedness of the surrounding architecture and of the few distinguishable mural arabesques had a dimly sinister suggestiveness we could not escape; and gave us a touch of terrible subconscious certainty concerning the primal entities which had reared and dwelt in this unhallowed place.

Nevertheless our scientific and adventurous souls were not wholly dead; and we mechanically carried out our programme of chipping specimens from all the different rock types represented in the masonry. We wished a rather full set in order to draw better conclusions regarding the age of the place. Nothing in the great outer walls seemed to date from later than the Jurassic and Comanchian periods, nor was any piece of stone in the entire place of a greater recency than the Pliocene age. In stark certainty, we were wandering amidst a death which had reigned at least 500,000 years, and in all probability even longer.

As we proceeded through this maze of stone-shadowed twilight we stopped at all available apertures to study interiors and investigate entrance possibilities. Some were above our reach, whilst others led only into ice-choked ruins as unroofed and barren as the rampart on the hill. One, though spacious and inviting, opened on a seemingly bottomless abyss without visible means of descent. Now and then we had a chance to study the petrified wood of a surviving shutter, and were impressed by the fabulous antiquity implied in the still discernible grain. These things had come from Mesozoic gymnosperms and conifers—especially Cretaceous cycads—and from fan-palms and early angiosperms of plainly Tertiary date. Nothing definitely later than the Pliocene could be discovered. In the placing of these shutters—whose edges shewed the former presence of queer and long-vanished hinges—usage seemed to be varied; some being on the outer and some on the inner side of the deep embrasures. They seemed to have become wedged in place, thus surviving the rusting of their former and probably metallic fixtures and fastenings.

After a time we came across a row of windows—in the bulges of a colossal five-ridged cone of undamaged apex—which led into a vast, well-preserved room with stone flooring; but these were too high in the room to permit of descent without a rope. We had a rope with us, but did not wish to bother with this twenty-foot drop unless obliged to—especially in this thin plateau air where great demands were made upon the heart action. This enormous room was probably a hall or concourse of some sort, and our electric torches shewed bold, distinct, and potentially startling sculptures arranged round the walls in broad, horizontal bands separated by equally broad strips of conventional arabesques. We took careful note of this spot, planning to enter here unless a more easily gained interior were encountered.

Finally, though, we did encounter exactly the opening we wished; an archway about six feet wide and ten feet

high, marking the former end of an aërial bridge which had spanned an alley about five feet above the present level of glaciation. These archways, of course, were flush with upper-story floors; and in this case one of the floors still existed. The building thus accessible was a series of rectangular terraces on our left facing westward. That across the alley, where the other archway yawned, was a decrepit cylinder with no windows and with a curious bulge about ten feet above the aperture. It was totally dark inside, and the archway seemed to open on a well of illimitable emptiness.

Heaped debris made the entrance to the vast left-hand building doubly easy, yet for a moment we hesitated before taking advantage of the long-wished chance. For though we had penetrated into this tangle of archaic mystery, it required fresh resolution to carry us actually inside a complete and surviving building of a fabulous elder world whose nature was becoming more and more hideously plain to us. In the end, however, we made the plunge; and scrambled up over the rubble into the gaping embrasure. The floor beyond was of great slate slabs, and seemed to form the outlet of a long, high corridor with sculptured walls.

Observing the many inner archways which led off from it, and realising the probable complexity of the nest of apartments within, we decided that we must begin our system of hare-and-hound trail-blazing. Hitherto our compasses, together with frequent glimpses of the vast mountain-range between the towers in our rear, had been enough to prevent our losing our way; but from now on, the artificial substitute would be necessary. Accordingly we reduced our extra paper to shreds of suitable size, placed these in a bag to be carried by Danforth, and prepared to use them as economically as safety would allow. This method would probably gain us immunity from straying, since there did not appear to be any strong air-currents inside the primordial masonry. If such should develop, or if our paper supply should give out, we could of course fall back on the more secure though more tedious and retarding method of rock-chipping.

Just how extensive a territory we had opened up, it was impossible to guess without a trial. The close and frequent connexion of the different buildings made it likely that we might cross from one to another on bridges underneath the ice except where impeded by local collapses and geologic rifts, for very little glaciation seemed to have entered the massive constructions. Almost all the areas of transparent ice had revealed the submerged windows as tightly shuttered, as if the town had been left in that uniform state until the glacial sheet came to crystallise the lower part for all succeeding time. Indeed, one gained a curious impression that this place had been deliberately closed and deserted in some dim, bygone aeon, rather than overwhelmed by any sudden calamity or even gradual decay. Had the coming of the ice been foreseen, and had a nameless population left en masse to seek a less doomed abode? The precise physiographic conditions attending the formation of the ice-sheet at this point would have to wait for later solution. It had not, very plainly, been a grinding drive. Perhaps the pressure of accumulated snows had been responsible; and perhaps some flood from the river, or from the bursting of some ancient glacial dam in the great range, had helped to create the special state now observable. Imagination could conceive almost anything in connexion with this place.

VI.

It would be cumbrous to give a detailed, consecutive account of our wanderings inside that cavernous, aeon-dead honeycomb of primal masonry; that monstrous lair of elder secrets which now echoed for the first time, after uncounted epochs, to the tread of human feet. This is especially true because so much of the horrible drama and revelation came from a mere study of the omnipresent mural carvings. Our flashlight photographs of those carvings will do much toward proving the truth of what we are now disclosing, and it is lamentable that we had not a larger film supply with us. As it was, we made crude notebook sketches of certain salient features after all our films were used up.

The building which we had entered was one of great size and elaborateness, and gave us an impressive notion of the architecture of that nameless geologic past. The inner partitions were less massive than the outer walls, but on the lower levels were excellently preserved. Labyrinthine complexity, involving curiously irregular differences in floor levels, characterised the entire arrangement; and we should certainly have been lost at the very outset but for the trail of torn paper left behind us. We decided to explore the more decrepit upper parts first of all, hence climbed aloft in the maze for a distance of some 100 feet, to where the topmost tier of chambers yawned snowily and ruinously open to the polar sky. Ascent was effected over the steep, transversely ribbed stone ramps or inclined planes which everywhere served in lieu of stairs. The rooms we encountered were of all imaginable shapes and proportions, ranging from five-pointed stars to triangles and perfect cubes. It might be safe to say that their general average was about 30 × 30 feet in floor area, and 20 feet in height; though many larger apartments existed. After thoroughly examining the upper regions and the glacial level we descended story by story into the submerged part, where indeed we soon saw we were in a continuous maze of connected chambers and passages probably leading over unlimited areas outside this particular building. The Cyclopean massiveness and giganticism of everything about us became curiously oppressive; and there was something vaguely but deeply unhuman in all the contours, dimensions, proportions, decorations, and constructional nuances of the blasphemously archaic stonework. We soon realised from what the carvings revealed that this monstrous city was many million years old.

We cannot yet explain the engineering principles used in the anomalous balancing and adjustment of the vast rock masses, though the function of the arch was clearly much relied on. The rooms we visited were wholly bare of all portable contents, a circumstance which sustained our belief in the city's deliberate desertion. The prime decorative feature was the almost universal system of mural sculpture; which tended to run in continuous horizontal bands three feet wide and arranged from floor to ceiling in alternation with bands of equal width given over to geometrical arabesques. There were exceptions to this rule of arrangement, but its preponderance was overwhelming. Often, however, a series of smooth cartouches containing oddly patterned groups of dots would be sunk along one of the arabesque bands.

The technique, we soon saw, was mature, accomplished, and aesthetically evolved to the highest degree of civilised

mastery; though utterly alien in every detail to any known art tradition of the human race. In delicacy of execution no sculpture I have ever seen could approach it. The minutest details of elaborate vegetation, or of animal life, were rendered with astonishing vividness despite the bold scale of the carvings; whilst the conventional designs were marvels of skilful intricacy. The arabesques displayed a profound use of mathematical principles, and were made up of obscurely symmetrical curves and angles based on the quantity of five. The pictorial bands followed a highly formalised tradition, and involved a peculiar treatment of perspective; but had an artistic force that moved us profoundly notwithstanding the intervening gulf of vast geologic periods. Their method of design hinged on a singular juxtaposition of the cross-section with the two-dimensional silhouette, and embodied an analytical psychology beyond that of any known race of antiquity. It is useless to try to compare this art with any represented in our museums. Those who see our photographs will probably find its closest analogue in certain grotesque conceptions of the most daring futurists.

The arabesque tracery consisted altogether of depressed lines whose depth on unweathered walls varied from one to two inches. When cartouches with dot-groups appeared—evidently as inscriptions in some unknown and primordial language and alphabet—the depression of the smooth surface was perhaps an inch and a half, and of the dots perhaps a half-inch more. The pictorial bands were in counter-sunk low relief, their background being depressed about two inches from the original wall surface. In some specimens marks of a former colouration could be detected, though for the most part the untold aeons had disintegrated and banished any pigments which may have been applied. The more one studied the marvellous technique the more one admired the things. Beneath their strict conventionalisation one could grasp the minute and accurate observation and graphic skill of the artists; and indeed, the very conventions themselves served to symbolise and accentuate the real essence or vital differentiation of every object delineated. We felt, too, that besides these recognisable excellences there were others lurking beyond the reach of our perceptions. Certain touches here and there gave vague hints of latent symbols and stimuli which another mental and emotional background, and a fuller or different sensory equipment, might have made of profound and poignant significance to us.

The subject-matter of the sculptures obviously came from the life of the vanished epoch of their creation, and contained a large proportion of evident history. It is this abnormal historic-mindedness of the primal race—a chance circumstance operating, through coincidence, miraculously in our favour—which made the carvings so awesomely informative to us, and which caused us to place their photography and transcription above all other considerations. In certain rooms the dominant arrangement was varied by the presence of maps, astronomical charts, and other scientific designs on an enlarged scale—these things giving a naive and terrible corroboration to what we gathered from the pictorial friezes and dadoes. In hinting at what the whole revealed, I can only hope that my account will not arouse a curiosity greater than sane caution on the part of those who believe me at all. It would be tragic if any were to be allured to that realm of death and horror by the very warning meant to discourage them.

Interrupting these sculptured walls were high windows

and massive twelve-foot doorways; both now and then retaining the petrified wooden planks—elaborately carved and polished—of the actual shutters and doors. All metal fixtures had long ago vanished, but some of the doors remained in place and had to be forced aside as we progressed from room to room. Window-frames with odd transparent panes—mostly elliptical—survived here and there, though in no considerable quantity. There were also frequent niches of great magnitude, generally empty, but once in a while containing some bizarre object carved from green soapstone which was either broken or perhaps held too inferior to warrant removal. Other apertures were undoubtedly connected with bygone mechanical facilities—heating, lighting, and the like— of a sort suggested in many of the carvings. Ceilings tended to be plain, but had sometimes been inlaid with green soapstone or other tiles, mostly fallen now. Floors were also paved with such tiles, though plain stonework predominated.

As I have said, all furniture and other moveables were absent; but the sculptures gave a clear idea of the strange devices which had once filled these tomb-like, echoing rooms. Above the glacial sheet the floors were generally thick with detritus, litter, and debris; but farther down this condition decreased. In some of the lower chambers and corridors there was little more than gritty dust or ancient incrustations, while occasional areas had an uncanny air of newly swept immaculateness. Of course, where rifts or collapses had occurred, the lower levels were as littered as the upper ones. A central court—as in other structures we had seen from the air—saved the inner regions from total darkness; so that we seldom had to use our electric torches in the upper rooms except when studying sculptured details. Below the ice-cap, however, the twilight deepened; and in many parts of the tangled ground level there was an approach to absolute blackness.

To form even a rudimentary idea of our thoughts and feelings as we penetrated this aeon-silent maze of unhuman masonry one must correlate a hopelessly bewildering chaos of fugitive moods, memories, and impressions. The sheer appalling antiquity and lethal desolation of the place were enough to overwhelm almost any sensitive person, but added to these elements were the recent unexplained horror at the camp, and the revelations all too soon effected by the terrible mural sculptures around us. The moment we came upon a perfect section of carving, where no ambiguity of interpretation could exist, it took only a brief study to give us the hideous truth—a truth which it would be naive to claim Danforth and I had not independently suspected before, though we had carefully refrained from even hinting it to each other. There could now be no further merciful doubt about the nature of the beings which had built and inhabited this monstrous dead city millions of years ago, when man's ancestors were primitive archaic mammals, and vast dinosaurs roamed the tropical steppes of Europe and Asia.

We had previously clung to a desperate alternative and insisted—each to himself—that the omnipresence of the five-pointed motif meant only some cultural or religious exaltation of the Archaean natural object which had so patently embodied the quality of five-pointedness; as the decorative motifs of Minoan Crete exalted the sacred bull, those of Egypt the scarabacus, those of Rome the wolf and the eagle, and those of various savage tribes some chosen totem-animal. But this lone refuge was now

stripped from us, and we were forced to face definitely the reason-shaking realisation which the reader of these pages has doubtless long ago anticipated. I can scarcely bear to write it down in black and white even now, but perhaps that will not be necessary.

The things once rearing and dwelling in this frightful masonry in the age of dinosaurs were not indeed dinosaurs, but far worse. Mere dinosaurs were new and almost brainless objects—but the builders of the city were wise and old, and had left certain traces in rocks even then laid down well-nigh a thousand million years . . . rocks laid down before the true life of earth had advanced beyond plastic groups of cells . . . rocks laid down before the true life of earth had existed at all. They were the makers and enslavers of that life, and above all doubt the originals of the fiendish elder myths which things like the Pnakotic Manuscripts and the Necronomicon affrightedly hint about. They were the Great Old Ones that had filtered down from the stars when earth was young—the beings whose substance an alien evolution had shaped, and whose powers were such as this planet had never bred. And to think that only the day before Danforth and I had actually looked upon fragments of their millennially fossilised substance . . . and that poor Lake and his party had seen their complete outlines. . . .

It is of course impossible for me to relate in proper order the stages by which we picked up what we know of that monstrous chapter of pre-human life. After the first shock of the certain revelation we had to pause a while to recuperate, and it was fully three o'clock before we got started on our actual tour of systematic research. The sculptures in the building we entered were of relatively late date—perhaps two million years ago—as checked up by geological, biological, and astronomical features; and embodied an art which would be called decadent in comparison with that of specimens we found in older buildings after crossing bridges under the glacial sheet. One edifice hewn from the solid rock seemed to go back forty or possibly even fifty million years—to the lower Eocene or upper Cretaceous—and contained bas-reliefs of an artistry surpassing anything else, with one tremendous exception, that we encountered. That was, we have since agreed, the oldest domestic structure we traversed.

Were it not for the support of those flashlights soon to be made public, I would refrain from telling what I found and inferred, lest I be confined as a madman. Of course, the infinitely early parts of the patchwork tale—representing the pre-terrestrial life of the star-headed beings on other planets, and in other galaxies, and in other universes—can readily be interpreted as the fantastic mythology of those beings themselves; yet such parts sometimes involved designs and diagrams so uncannily close to the latest findings of mathematics and astrophysics that I scarcely know what to think. Let others judge when they see the photographs I shall publish.

Naturally, no one set of carvings which we encountered told more than a fraction of any connected story; nor did we even begin to come upon the various stages of that story in their proper order. Some of the vast rooms were independent units so far as their designs were concerned, whilst in other cases a continuous chronicle would be carried through a series of rooms and corridors. The best of the maps and diagrams were on the walls of a frightful abyss below even the ancient ground level—a cavern perhaps 200 feet square and sixty feet high, which had

almost undoubtedly been an educational centre of some sort. There were many provoking repetitions of the same material in different rooms and buildings; since certain chapters of experience, and certain summaries or phases of racial history, had evidently been favourites with different decorators or dwellers. Sometimes, though, variant versions of the same theme proved useful in settling debatable points and filling in gaps.

I still wonder that we deduced so much in the short time at our disposal. Of course, we even now have only the barest outline; and much of that was obtained later on from a study of the photographs and sketches we made. It may be the effect of this later study—the revived memories and vague impressions acting in conjunction with his general sensitiveness and with that final supposed horror-glimpse whose essence he will not reveal even to me—which has been the immediate source of Danforth's present breakdown. But it had to be; for we could not issue our warning intelligently without the fullest possible information, and the issuance of that warning is a prime necessity. Certain lingering influences in that unknown antarctic world of disordered time and alien natural law make it imperative that further exploration be discouraged.

VII.

The full story, so far as deciphered, will shortly appear in an official bulletin of Miskatonic University. Here I shall sketch only the salient high lights in a formless, rambling way. Myth or otherwise, the sculptures told of the coming of those star-headed things to the nascent, lifeless earth out of cosmic space—their coming, and the coming of many other alien entities such as at certain times embark upon spatial pioneering. They seemed able to traverse the interstellar ether on their vast membraneous wings—thus oddly confirming some curious hill folklore long ago told me by an antiquarian colleague. They had lived under the sea a good deal, building fantastic cities and fighting terrific battles with nameless adversaries by means of intricate devices employing unknown principles of energy. Evidently their scientific and mechanical knowledge far surpassed man's today, though they made use of its more widespread and elaborate forms only when obliged to. Some of the sculptures suggested that they had passed through a stage of mechanised life on other planets, but had receded upon finding its effects emotionally unsatisfying. Their preternatural toughness of organisation and simplicity of natural wants made them peculiarly able to live on a high plane without the more specialised fruits of artificial manufacture, and even without garments except for occasional protection against the elements.

It was under the sea, at first for food and later for other purposes, that they first created earth-life—using available substances according to long-known methods. The more elaborate experiments came after the annihilation of various cosmic enemies. They had done the same thing on other planets; having manufactured not only necessary foods, but certain multicellular protoplasmic masses capable of moulding their tissues into all sorts of temporary organs under hypnotic influence and thereby forming ideal slaves to perform the

heavy work of the community. These viscous masses were without doubt what Abdul Alhazred whispered about as the "shoggoths" in his frightful Necronomicon, though even that mad Arab had not hinted that any existed on earth except in the dreams of those who had chewed a certain alkaloidal herb. When the star-headed Old Ones on this planet had synthesised their simple food forms and bred a good supply of shoggoths, they allowed other cell-groups to develop into other forms of animal and vegetable life for sundry purposes; extirpating any whose presence became troublesome.

With the aid of the shoggoths, whose expansions could be made to lift prodigious weights, the small, low cities under the sea grew to vast and imposing labyrinths of stone not unlike those which later rose on land. Indeed, the highly adaptable Old Ones had lived much on land in other parts of the universe, and probably retained many traditions of land construction. As we studied the architecture of all these sculptured palaeogean cities, including that whose aeon-dead corridors we were even then traversing, we were impressed by a curious coincidence which we have not yet tried to explain, even to ourselves. The tops of the buildings, which in the actual city around us had of course been weathered into shapeless ruins ages ago, were clearly displayed in the bas-reliefs; and shewed vast clusters of needle-like spires, delicate finials on certain cone and pyramid apexes, and tiers of thin, horizontal scalloped discs capping cylindrical shafts. This was exactly what we had seen in that monstrous and portentous mirage, cast by a dead city whence such skyline features had been absent for thousands and tens of thousands of years, which loomed on our ignorant eyes across the unfathomed mountains of madness as we first approached poor Lake's ill-fated camp.

Of the life of the Old Ones, both under the sea and after part of them migrated to land, volumes could be written. Those in shallow water had continued the fullest use of the eyes at the ends of their five main head tentacles, and had practiced the arts of sculpture and of writing in quite the usual way—the writing accomplished with a stylus on waterproof waxen surfaces. Those lower down in the ocean depths, though they used a curious phosphorescent organism to furnish light, pieced out their vision with obscure special senses operating through the prismatic cilia on their heads—senses which rendered all the Old Ones partly independent of light in emergencies. Their forms of sculpture and writing had changed curiously during the descent, embodying certain apparently chemical coating processes— probably to secure phosphorescence—which the bas-reliefs could not make clear to us. The beings moved in the sea partly by swimming—using the lateral crinoid arms—and partly by wriggling with the lower tier of tentacles containing the pseudo-feet. Occasionally they accomplished long swoops with the auxiliary use of two or more sets of their fan-like folding wings. On land they locally used the pseudo-feet, but now and then flew to great heights or over long distances with their wings. The many slender tentacles into which the crinoid arms branched were infinitely delicate, flexible, strong, and accurate in muscular-nervous coördination; ensuring the utmost skill and dexterity in all artistic and other manual operations.

The toughness of the things was almost incredible. Even the terrific pressures of the deepest sea-bottoms appeared powerless to harm them. Very few seemed to

die at all except by violence, and their burial-places were very limited. The fact that they covered their vertically inhumed dead with five-pointed inscribed mounds set up thoughts in Danforth and me which made a fresh pause and recuperation necessary after the sculptures revealed it. The beings multiplied by means of spores—like vegetable pteridophytes as Lake had suspected—but owing to their prodigious toughness and longevity, and consequent lack of replacement needs, they did not encourage the large-scale development of new prothalli except when they had new regions to colonise. The young matured swiftly, and received an education evidently beyond any standard we can imagine. The prevailing intellectual and aesthetic life was highly evolved, and produced a tenaciously enduring set of customs and institutions which I shall describe more fully in my coming monograph. These varied slightly according to sea or land residence, but had the same foundations and essentials.

Though able, like vegetables, to derive nourishment from inorganic substances; they vastly preferred organic and especially animal food. They ate uncooked marine life under the sea, but cooked their viands on land. They hunted game and raised meat herds—slaughtering with sharp weapons whose odd marks on certain fossil bones our expedition had noted. They resisted all ordinary temperatures marvellously; and in their natural state could live in water down to freezing. When the great chill of the Pleistocene drew on, however—nearly a million years ago—the land dwellers had to resort to special measures including artificial heating; until at last the deadly cold appears to have driven them back into the sea. For their prehistoric flights through cosmic space, legend said, they had absorbed certain chemicals and became almost independent of eating, breathing, or heat conditions; but by the time of the great cold they had lost track of the method. In any case they could not have prolonged the artificial state indefinitely without harm.

Being non-pairing and semi-vegetable in structure, the Old Ones had no biological basis for the family phase of mammal life; but seemed to organise large households on the principles of comfortable space-utility and—as we deduced from the pictured occupations and diversions of co-dwellers—congenial mental association. In furnishing their homes they kept everything in the centre of the huge rooms, leaving all the wall spaces free for decorative treatment. Lighting, in the case of the land inhabitants, was accomplished by a device probably electro-chemical in nature. Both on land and under water they used curious tables, chairs, and couches like cylindrical frames—for they rested and slept upright with folded-down tentacles—and racks for the hinged sets of dotted surfaces forming their books.

Government was evidently complex and probably socialistic, though no certainties in this regard could be deduced from the sculptures we saw. There was extensive commerce, both local and between different cities; certain small, flat counters, five-pointed and inscribed, serving as money. Probably the smaller of the various greenish soapstones found by our expedition were pieces of such currency. Though the culture was mainly urban, some agriculture and much stock-raising existed. Mining and a limited amount of manufacturing were also practiced. Travel was very frequent, but permanent migration seemed relatively rare except for the vast colonising movements by which the race expanded. For personal locomotion no external aid was used; since in land, air, and water movement alike the Old Ones seemed to possess

excessively vast capacities for speed. Loads, however, were drawn by beasts of burden—shoggoths under the sea, and a curious variety of primitive vertebrates in the later years of land existence.

These vertebrates, as well as an infinity of other life-forms—animal and vegetable, marine, terrestrial, and aërial—were the products of unguided evolution acting on life-cells made by the Old Ones but escaping beyond their radius of attention. They had been suffered to develop unchecked because they had not come in conflict with the dominant beings. Bothersome forms, of course, were mechanically exterminated. It interested us to see in some of the very last and most decadent sculptures a shambling primitive mammal, used sometimes for food and sometimes as an amusing buffoon by the land dwellers, whose vaguely simian and human foreshadowings were unmistakable. In the building of land cities the huge stone blocks of the high towers were generally lifted by vast-winged pterodactyls of a species heretofore unknown to palaeontology.

The persistence with which the Old Ones survived various geologic changes and convulsions of the earth's crust was little short of miraculous. Though few or none of their first cities seem to have remained beyond the Archaean age, there was no interruption in their civilisation or in the transmission of their records. Their original place of advent to the planet was the Antarctic Ocean, and it is likely that they came not long after the matter forming the moon was wrenched from the neighbouring South Pacific. According to one of the sculptured maps, the whole globe was then under water, with stone cities scattered farther and farther from the antarctic as aeons passed. Another map shews a vast bulk of dry land around the south pole, where it is evident that some of the beings made experimental settlements though their main centres were transferred to the nearest sea-bottom. Later maps, which display this land mass as cracking and drifting, and sending certain detached parts northward, uphold in a striking way the theories of continental drift lately advanced by Taylor, Wegener, and Joly.

With the upheaval of new land in the South Pacific tremendous events began. Some of the marine cities were hopelessly shattered, yet that was not the worst misfortune. Another race—a land race of beings shaped like octopi and probably corresponding to the fabulous pre-human spawn of Cthulhu—soon began filtering down from cosmic infinity and precipitated a monstrous war which for a time drove the Old Ones wholly back to the sea—a colossal blow in view of the increasing land settlements. Later peace was made, and the new lands were given to the Cthulhu spawn whilst the Old Ones held the sea and the older lands. New land cities were founded—the greatest of them in the antarctic, for this region of first arrival was sacred. From then on, as before, the antarctic remained the centre of the Old Ones' civilisation, and all the discoverable cities built there by the Cthulhu spawn were blotted out. Then suddenly the lands of the Pacific sank again, taking with them the frightful stone city of R'lyeh and all the cosmic octopi, so that the Old Ones were again supreme on the planet except for one shadowy fear about which they did not like to speak. At a rather later age their cities dotted all the land and water areas of the globe—hence the recommendation in my coming monograph that some archaeologist make systematic borings with Pabodie's type of apparatus in certain widely separated regions.

The steady trend down the ages was from water to land; a movement encouraged by the rise of new land masses, though the ocean was never wholly deserted. Another cause of the landward movement was the new difficulty in breeding and managing the shoggoths upon which successful sea-life depended. With the march of time, as the sculptures sadly confessed, the art of creating new life from inorganic matter had been lost; so that the Old Ones had to depend on the moulding of forms already in existence. On land the great reptiles proved highly tractable; but the shoggoths of the sea, reproducing by fission and acquiring a dangerous degree of accidental intelligence, presented for a time a formidable problem.

They had always been controlled through the hypnotic suggestion of the Old Ones, and had modelled their tough plasticity into various useful temporary limbs and organs; but now their self-modelling powers were sometimes exercised independently, and in various imitative forms implanted by past suggestion. They had, it seems, developed a semi-stable brain whose separate and occasionally stubborn volition echoed the will of the Old Ones without always obeying it. Sculptured images of these shoggoths filled Danforth and me with horror and loathing. They were normally shapeless entities composed of a viscous jelly which looked like an agglutination of bubbles; and each averaged about fifteen feet in diameter when a sphere. They had, however, a constantly shifting shape and volume; throwing out temporary developments or forming apparent organs of sight, hearing, and speech in imitation of their masters, either spontaneously or according to suggestion.

They seem to have become peculiarly intractable toward the middle of the Permian age, perhaps 150 million years ago, when a veritable war of re-subjugation was waged upon them by the marine Old Ones. Pictures of this war, and of the headless, slime-coated fashion in which the shoggoths typically left their slain victims, held a marvellously fearsome quality despite the intervening abyss of untold ages. The Old Ones had used curious weapons of molecular disturbance against the rebel entities, and in the end had achieved a complete victory. Thereafter the sculptures shewed a period in which shoggoths were tamed and broken by armed Old Ones as the wild horses of the American west were tamed by cowboys. Though during the rebellion the shoggoths had shewn an ability to live out of water, this transition was not encouraged; since their usefulness on land would hardly have been commensurate with the trouble of their management.

During the Jurassic age the Old Ones met fresh adversity in the form of a new invasion from outer space—this time by half-fungous, half-crustacean creatures from a planet identifiable as the remote and recently discovered Pluto; creatures undoubtedly the same as those figuring in certain whispered hill legends of the north, and remembered in the Himalayas as the Mi-Go, or Abominable Snow-Men. To fight these beings the Old Ones attempted, for the first time since their terrene advent, to sally forth again into the planetary ether; but despite all traditional preparations found it no longer possible to leave the earth's atmosphere. Whatever the old secret of interstellar travel had been, it was now definitely lost to the race. In the end the Mi-Go drove the Old Ones out of all the northern lands, though they were powerless to disturb those in the sea. Little by little the slow retreat of the elder race to their original antarctic habitat was beginning.

It was curious to note from the pictured battles that both the Cthulhu spawn and the Mi-Go seem to have been composed of matter more widely different from that which we know than was the substance of the Old Ones. They were able to undergo transformations and reintegrations impossible for their adversaries, and seem therefore to have originally come from even remoter gulfs of cosmic space. The Old Ones, but for their abnormal toughness and peculiar vital properties, were strictly material, and must have had their absolute origin within the known space-time continuum; whereas the first sources of the other beings can only be guessed at with bated breath. All this, of course, assuming that the non-terrestrial linkages and the anomalies ascribed to the invading foes are not pure mythology. Conceivably, the Old Ones might have invented a cosmic framework to account for their occasional defeats; since historical interest and pride obviously formed their chief psychological element. It is significant that their annals failed to mention many advanced and potent races of beings whose mighty cultures and towering cities figure persistently in certain obscure legends.

The changing state of the world through long geologic ages appeared with startling vividness in many of the sculptured maps and scenes. In certain cases existing science will require revision, while in other cases its bold deductions are magnificently confirmed. As I have said, the hypothesis of Taylor, Wegener, and Joly that all the continents are fragments of an original antarctic land mass which cracked from centrifugal force and drifted apart over a technically viscous lower surface—an hypothesis suggested by such things as the complementary outlines of Africa and South America, and the way the great mountain chains are rolled and shoved up—receives striking support from this uncanny source.

Maps evidently shewing the Carboniferous world of an hundred million or more years ago displayed significant rifts and chasms destined later to separate Africa from the once continuous realms of Europe (then the Valusia of hellish primal legend), Asia, the Americas, and the antarctic continent. Other charts—and most significantly one in connexion with the founding fifty million years ago of the vast dead city around us—shewed all the present continents well differentiated. And in the latest discoverable specimen—dating perhaps from the Pliocene age—the approximate world of today appeared quite clearly despite the linkage of Alaska with Siberia, of North America with Europe through Greenland, and of South America with the antarctic continent through Graham Land. In the Carboniferous map the whole globe—ocean floor and rifted land mass alike—bore symbols of the Old Ones' vast stone cities, but in the later charts the gradual recession toward the antarctic became very plain. The final Pliocene specimen shewed no land cities except on the antarctic continent and the tip of South America, nor any ocean cities north of the fiftieth parallel of South Latitude. Knowledge and interest in the northern world, save for a study of coast-lines probably made during long exploration flights on those fan-like membraneous wings, had evidently declined to zero among the Old Ones.

Destruction of cities through the upthrust of mountains, the centrifugal rending of continents, the seismic convulsions of land or sea-bottom, and other natural causes was a matter of common record; and it was

curious to observe how fewer and fewer replacements were made as the ages wore on. The vast dead megalopolis that yawned around us seemed to be the last general centre of the race; built early in the Cretaceous age after a titanic earth-buckling had obliterated a still vaster predecessor not far distant. It appeared that this general region was the most sacred spot of all, where reputedly the first Old Ones had settled on a primal sea-bottom. In the new city—many of whose features we could recognise in the sculptures, but which stretched fully an hundred miles along the mountain-range in each direction beyond the farthest limits of our aërial survey—there were reputed to be preserved certain sacred stones forming part of the first sea-bottom city, which were thrust up to light after long epochs in the course of the general crumpling of strata.

VIII.

Naturally, Danforth and I studied with especial interest and a peculiarly personal sense of awe everything pertaining to the immediate district in which we were. Of this local material there was naturally a vast abundance; and on the tangled ground level of the city we were lucky enough to find a house of very late date whose walls, though somewhat damaged by a neighbouring rift, contained sculptures of decadent workmanship carrying the story of the region much beyond the period of the Pliocene map whence we derived our last general glimpse of the pre-human world. This was the last place we examined in detail, since what we found there gave us a fresh immediate objective.

Certainly, we were in one of the strangest, weirdest, and most terrible of all the corners of earth's globe. Of all existing lands it was infinitely the most ancient; and the conviction grew upon us that this hideous upland must indeed be the fabled nightmare plateau of Leng which even the mad author of the Necronomicon was reluctant to discuss. The great mountain chain was tremendously long—starting as a low range at Luitpold Land on the coast of Weddell Sea and virtually crossing the entire continent. The really high part stretched in a mighty arc from about Latitude 82°, E. Longitude 60° to Latitude 70°, E. Longitude 115°, with its concave side toward our camp and its seaward end in the region of that long, ice-locked coast whose hills were glimpsed by Wilkes and Mawson at the Antarctic Circle.

Yet even more monstrous exaggerations of Nature seemed disturbingly close at hand. I have said that these peaks are higher than the Himalayas, but the sculptures forbid me to say that they are earth's highest. That grim honour is beyond doubt reserved for something which half the sculptures hesitated to record at all, whilst others approached it with obvious repugnance and trepidation. It seems that there was one part of the ancient land—the first part that ever rose from the waters after the earth had flung off the moon and the Old Ones had seeped down from the stars—which had come to be shunned as vaguely and namelessly evil. Cities built there had crumbled before their time, and had been found suddenly deserted. Then when the first great earth-buckling had convulsed the region in the Comanchian age, a frightful line of peaks had shot suddenly up amidst the most appalling din and chaos—and earth had received her loftiest and most terrible mountains.

If the scale of the carvings was correct, these abhorred things must have been much over 40,000 feet high—radically vaster than even the shocking mountains of madness we had crossed. They extended, it appeared, from about Latitude 77°, E. Longitude 70° to Latitude 70°, E. Longitude 100°—less than 300 miles away from the dead city, so that we would have spied their dreaded summits in the dim western distance had it not been for that vague opalescent haze. Their northern end must likewise be visible from the long Antarctic Circle coast-line at Queen Mary Land.

Some of the Old Ones, in the decadent days, had made strange prayers to those mountains; but none ever went near them or dared to guess what lay beyond. No human eye had ever seen them, and as I studied the emotions conveyed in the carvings I prayed that none ever might. There are protecting hills along the coast beyond them—Queen Mary and Kaiser Wilhelm Lands—and I thank heaven no one has been able to land and climb those hills. I am not as sceptical about old tales and fears as I used to be, and I do not laugh now at the pre-human sculptor's notion that lightning paused meaningfully now and then at each of the brooding crests, and that an unexplained glow shone from one of those terrible pinnacles all through the long polar night. There may be a very real and very monstrous meaning in the old Pnakotic whispers about Kadath in the Cold Waste.

But the terrain close at hand was hardly less strange, even if less namelessly accursed. Soon after the founding of the city the great mountain-range became the seat of the principal temples, and many carvings shewed what grotesque and fantastic towers had pierced the sky where now we saw only the curiously clinging cubes and ramparts. In the course of ages the caves had appeared, and had been shaped into adjuncts of the temples. With the advance of still later epochs all the limestone veins of the region were hollowed out by ground waters, so that the mountains, the foothills, and the plains below them were a veritable network of connected caverns and galleries. Many graphic sculptures told of explorations deep underground, and of the final discovery of the Stygian sunless sea that lurked at earth's bowels.

This vast nighted gulf had undoubtedly been worn by the great river which flowed down from the nameless and horrible westward mountains, and which had formerly turned at the base of the Old Ones' range and flowed beside that chain into the Indian Ocean between Budd and Totten Lands on Wilkes's coast-line. Little by little it had eaten away the limestone hill base at its turning, till at last its sapping currents reached the caverns of the ground waters and joined with them in digging a deeper abyss. Finally its whole bulk emptied into the hollow hills and left the old bed toward the ocean dry. Much of the later city as we now found it had been built over that former bed. The Old Ones, understanding what had happened, and exercising their always keen artistic sense, had carved into ornate pylons those headlands of the foothills where the great stream began its descent into eternal darkness.

This river, once crossed by scores of noble stone bridges, was plainly the one whose extinct course we had seen in our aëroplane survey. Its position in different carvings of the city helped us to orient ourselves to the scene as it had been at various stages of the region's age-long, aeon-dead history; so that we were able to sketch a hasty but careful map of the salient features—squares,

important buildings, and the like—for guidance in further explorations. We could soon reconstruct in fancy the whole stupendous thing as it was a million or ten million or fifty million years ago, for the sculptures told us exactly what the buildings and mountains and squares and suburbs and landscape setting and luxuriant Tertiary vegetation had looked like. It must have had a marvellous and mystic beauty, and as I thought of it I almost forgot the clammy sense of sinister oppression with which the city's inhuman age and massiveness and deadness and remoteness and glacial twilight had choked and weighed on my spirit. Yet according to certain carvings the denizens of that city had themselves known the clutch of oppressive terror; for there was a sombre and recurrent type of scene in which the Old Ones were shewn in the act of recoiling affrightedly from some object—never allowed to appear in the design—found in the great river and indicated as having been washed down through waving, vine-draped cycad-forests from those horrible westward mountains.

It was only in the one late-built house with the decadent carvings that we obtained any foreshadowing of the final calamity leading to the city's desertion. Undoubtedly there must have been many sculptures of the same age elsewhere, even allowing for the slackened energies and aspirations of a stressful and uncertain period; indeed, very certain evidence of the existence of others came to us shortly afterward. But this was the first and only set we directly encountered. We meant to look farther later on; but as I have said, immediate conditions dictated another present objective. There would, though, have been a limit—for after all hope of a long future occupancy of the place had perished among the Old Ones, there could not but have been a complete cessation of mural decoration. The ultimate blow, of course, was the coming of the great cold which once held most of the earth in thrall, and which has never departed from the ill-fated poles—the great cold that, at the world's other extremity, put an end to the fabled lands of Lomar and Hyperborea.

Just when this tendency began in the antarctic it would be hard to say in terms of exact years. Nowadays we set the beginning of the general glacial periods at a distance of about 500,000 years from the present, but at the poles the terrible scourge must have commenced much earlier. All quantitative estimates are partly guesswork; but it is quite likely that the decadent sculptures were made considerably less than a million years ago, and that the actual desertion of the city was complete long before the conventional opening of the Pleistocene—500,000 years ago—as reckoned in terms of the earth's whole surface.

In the decadent sculptures there were signs of thinner vegetation everywhere, and of a decreased country life on the part of the Old Ones. Heating devices were shewn in the houses, and winter travellers were represented as muffled in protective fabrics. Then we saw a series of cartouches (the continuous band arrangement being frequently interrupted in these late carvings) depicting a constantly growing migration to the nearest refuges of greater warmth—some fleeing to cities under the sea off the far-away coast, and some clambering down through networks of limestone caverns in the hollow hills to the neighbouring black abyss of subterrene waters.

In the end it seems to have been the neighbouring abyss which received the greatest colonisation. This was partly due, no doubt, to the traditional sacredness of this

especial region; but may have been more conclusively determined by the opportunities it gave for continuing the use of the great temples on the honeycombed mountains, and for retaining the vast land city as a place of summer residence and base of communication with various mines. The linkage of old and new abodes was made more effective by means of several gradings and improvements along the connecting routes, including the chiselling of numerous direct tunnels from the ancient metropolis to the black abyss—sharply down-pointing tunnels whose mouths we carefully drew, according to our most thoughtful estimates, on the guide map we were compiling. It was obvious that at least two of these tunnels lay within a reasonable exploring distance of where we were; both being on the mountainward edge of the city, one less than a quarter-mile toward the ancient river-course, and the other perhaps twice that distance in the opposite direction.

The abyss, it seems, had shelving shores of dry land at certain places; but the Old Ones built their new city under water—no doubt because of its greater certainty of uniform warmth. The depth of the hidden sea appears to have been very great, so that the earth's internal heat could ensure its habitability for an indefinite period. The beings seem to have had no trouble in adapting themselves to part-time—and eventually, of course, whole-time—residence under water; since they had never allowed their gill systems to atrophy. There were many sculptures which shewed how they had always frequently visited their submarine kinsfolk elsewhere, and how they had habitually bathed on the deep bottom of their great river. The darkness of inner earth could likewise have been no deterrent to a race accustomed to long antarctic nights.

Decadent though their style undoubtedly was, these latest carvings had a truly epic quality where they told of the building of the new city in the cavern sea. The Old Ones had gone about it scientifically; quarrying insoluble rocks from the heart of the honeycombed mountains, and employing expert workers from the nearest submarine city to perform the construction according to the best methods. These workers brought with them all that was necessary to establish the new venture—shoggoth-tissue from which to breed stone-lifters and subsequent beasts of burden for the cavern city, and other protoplasmic matter to mould into phosphorescent organisms for lighting purposes.

At last a mighty metropolis rose on the bottom of that Stygian sea; its architecture much like that of the city above, and its workmanship displaying relatively little decadence because of the precise mathematical element inherent in building operations. The newly bred shoggoths grew to enormous size and singular intelligence, and were represented as taking and executing orders with marvellous quickness. They seemed to converse with the Old Ones by mimicking their voices—a sort of musical piping over a wide range, if poor Lake's dissection had indicated aright—and to work more from spoken commands than from hypnotic suggestions as in earlier times. They were, however, kept in admirable control. The phosphorescent organisms supplied light with vast effectiveness, and doubtless atoned for the loss of the familiar polar auroras of the outer-world night.

Art and decoration were pursued, though of course with a certain decadence. The Old Ones seemed to realise this falling off themselves; and in many cases anticipated the policy of Constantine the Great by transplanting

especially fine blocks of ancient carving from their land city, just as the emperor, in a similar age of decline, stripped Greece and Asia of their finest art to give his new Byzantine capital greater splendours than its own people could create. That the transfer of sculptured blocks had not been more extensive, was doubtless owing to the fact that the land city was not at first wholly abandoned. By the time total abandonment did occur—and it surely must have occurred before the polar Pleistocene was far advanced—the Old Ones had perhaps become satisfied with their decadent art—or had ceased to recognise the superior merit of the older carvings. At any rate, the aeon-silent ruins around us had certainly undergone no wholesale sculptural denudation; though all the best separate statues, like other moveables, had been taken away.

The decadent cartouches and dadoes telling this story were, as I have said, the latest we could find in our limited search. They left us with a picture of the Old Ones shuttling back and forth betwixt the land city in summer and the sea-cavern city in winter, and sometimes trading with the sea-bottom cities off the antarctic coast. By this time the ultimate doom of the land city must have been recognised, for the sculptures shewed many signs of the cold's malign encroachments. Vegetation was declining, and the terrible snows of the winter no longer melted completely even in midsummer. The saurian livestock were nearly all dead, and the mammals were standing it none too well. To keep on with the work of the upper world it had become necessary to adapt some of the amorphous and curiously cold-resistant shoggoths to land life; a thing the Old Ones had formerly been reluctant to do. The great river was now lifeless, and the upper sea had lost most of its denizens except the seals and whales. All the birds had flown away, save only the great, grotesque penguins.

What had happened afterward we could only guess. How long had the new sea-cavern city survived? Was it still down there, a stony corpse in eternal blackness? Had the subterranean waters frozen at last? To what fate had the ocean-bottom cities of the outer world been delivered? Had any of the Old Ones shifted north ahead of the creeping ice-cap? Existing geology shews no trace of their presence. Had the frightful Mi-Go been still a menace in the outer land world of the north? Could one be sure of what might or might not linger even to this day in the lightless and unplumbed abysses of earth's deepest waters? Those things had seemingly been able to withstand any amount of pressure—and men of the sea have fished up curious objects at times. And has the killer-whale theory really explained the savage and mysterious scars on antarctic seals noticed a generation ago by Borchgrevingk?

The specimens found by poor Lake did not enter into these guesses, for their geologic setting proved them to have lived at what must have been a very early date in the land city's history. They were, according to their location, certainly not less than thirty million years old; and we reflected that in their day the sea-cavern city, and indeed the cavern itself, had no existence. They would have remembered an older scene, with lush Tertiary vegetation everywhere, a younger land city of flourishing arts around them, and a great river sweeping northward along the base of the mighty mountains toward a far-away tropic ocean.

And yet we could not help thinking about these

specimens—especially about the eight perfect ones that were missing from Lake's hideously ravaged camp. There was something abnormal about that whole business—the strange things we had tried so hard to lay to somebody's madness—those frightful graves—the amount and nature of the missing material—Gedney—the unearthly toughness of those archaic monstrosities, and the queer vital freaks the sculptures now shewed the race to have. . . . Danforth and I had seen a good deal in the last few hours, and were prepared to believe and keep silent about many appalling and incredible secrets of primal Nature.

IX.

I have said that our study of the decadent sculptures brought about a change in our immediate objective. This of course had to do with the chiselled avenues to the black inner world, of whose existence we had not known before, but which we were now eager to find and traverse. From the evident scale of the carvings we deduced that a steeply descending walk of about a mile through either of the neighbouring tunnels would bring us to the brink of the dizzy sunless cliffs above the great abyss; down whose side adequate paths, improved by the Old Ones, led to the rocky shore of the hidden and nighted ocean. To behold this fabulous gulf in stark reality was a lure which seemed impossible of resistance once we knew of the thing—yet we realised we must begin the quest at once if we expected to include it on our present flight.

It was now 8 P.M., and we had not enough battery replacements to let our torches burn on forever. We had done so much of our studying and copying below the glacial level that our battery supply had had at least five hours of nearly continuous use; and despite the special dry cell formula would obviously be good for only about four more—though by keeping one torch unused, except for especially interesting or difficult places, we might manage to eke out a safe margin beyond that. It would not do to be without a light in these Cyclopean catacombs, hence in order to make the abyss trip we must give up all further mural deciphering. Of course we intended to revisit the place for days and perhaps weeks of intensive study and photography—curiosity having long ago got the better of horror—but just now we must hasten. Our supply of trail-blazing paper was far from unlimited, and we were reluctant to sacrifice spare notebooks or sketching paper to augment it; but we did let one large notebook go. If worst came to worst, we could resort to rock-chipping—and of course it would be possible, even in case of really lost direction, to work up to full daylight by one channel or another if granted sufficient time for plentiful trial and error. So at last we set off eagerly in the indicated direction of the nearest tunnel.

According to the carvings from which we had made our map, the desired tunnel-mouth could not be much more than a quarter-mile from where we stood; the intervening space shewing solid-looking buildings quite likely to be penetrable still at a sub-glacial level. The opening itself would be in the basement—on the angle nearest the foothills—of a vast five-pointed structure of evidently public and perhaps ceremonial nature, which we tried to identify from our aërial survey of the ruins. No such structure came to our minds as we recalled our flight, hence we concluded that its upper parts had been greatly damaged, or that it had been totally shattered in an ice-rift we had noticed. In the latter case the tunnel

would probably turn out to be choked, so that we would have to try the next nearest one—the one less than a mile to the north. The intervening river-course prevented our trying any of the more southerly tunnels on this trip; and indeed, if both of the neighbouring ones were choked it was doubtful whether our batteries would warrant an attempt on the next northerly one—about a mile beyond our second choice.

As we threaded our dim way through the labyrinth with the aid of map and compass—traversing rooms and corridors in every stage of ruin or preservation, clambering up ramps, crossing upper floors and bridges and clambering down again, encountering choked doorways and piles of debris, hastening now and then along finely preserved and uncannily immaculate stretches, taking false leads and retracing our way (in such cases removing the blind paper trail we had left), and once in a while striking the bottom of an open shaft through which daylight poured or trickled down— we were repeatedly tantalised by the sculptured walls along our route. Many must have told tales of immense historical importance, and only the prospect of later visits reconciled us to the need of passing them by. As it was, we slowed down once in a while and turned on our second torch. If we had had more films we would certainly have paused briefly to photograph certain bas-reliefs, but time-consuming hand copying was clearly out of the question.

I come now once more to a place where the temptation to hesitate, or to hint rather than state, is very strong. It is necessary, however, to reveal the rest in order to justify my course in discouraging further exploration. We had wormed our way very close to the computed site of the tunnel's mouth—having crossed a second-story bridge to what seemed plainly the tip of a pointed wall, and descended to a ruinous corridor especially rich in decadently elaborate and apparently ritualistic sculptures of late workmanship—when, about 8:30 P.M., Danforth's keen young nostrils gave us the first hint of something unusual. If we had had a dog with us, I suppose we would have been warned before. At first we could not precisely say what was wrong with the formerly crystal-pure air, but after a few seconds our memories reacted only too definitely. Let me try to state the thing without flinching. There was an odour—and that odour was vaguely, subtly, and unmistakably akin to what had nauseated us upon opening the insane grave of the horror poor Lake had dissected.

Of course the revelation was not as clearly cut at the time as it sounds now. There were several conceivable explanations, and we did a good deal of indecisive whispering. Most important of all, we did not retreat without further investigation; for having come this far, we were loath to be balked by anything short of certain disaster. Anyway, what we must have suspected was altogether too wild to believe. Such things did not happen in any normal world. It was probably sheer irrational instinct which made us dim our single torch—tempted no longer by the decadent and sinister sculptures that leered menacingly from the oppressive walls—and which softened our progress to a cautious tiptoeing and crawling over the increasingly littered floor and heaps of debris.

Danforth's eyes as well as nose proved better than mine, for it was likewise he who first noticed the queer aspect of the debris after we had passed many half-choked arches leading to chambers and corridors on

the ground level. It did not look quite as it ought after countless thousands of years of desertion, and when we cautiously turned on more light we saw that a kind of swath seemed to have been lately tracked through it. The irregular nature of the litter precluded any definite marks, but in the smoother places there were suggestions of the dragging of heavy objects. Once we thought there was a hint of parallel tracks, as if of runners. This was what made us pause again.

It was during that pause that we caught—simultaneously this time—the other odour ahead. Paradoxically, it was both a less frightful and a more frightful odour—less frightful intrinsically, but infinitely appalling in this place under the known circumstances . . . unless, of course, Gedney. . . . For the odour was the plain and familiar one of common petrol—every-day gasoline.

Our motivation after that is something I will leave to psychologists. We knew now that some terrible extension of the camp horrors must have crawled into this nighted burial-place of the aeons, hence could not doubt any longer the existence of nameless conditions—present or at least recent—just ahead. Yet in the end we did let sheer burning curiosity—or anxiety—or auto-hypnotism—or vague thoughts of responsibility toward Gedney—or what not—drive us on. Danforth whispered again of the print he thought he had seen at the alley-turning in the ruins above; and of the faint musical piping—potentially of tremendous significance in the light of Lake's dissection report despite its close resemblance to the cave-mouth echoes of the windy peaks—which he thought he had shortly afterward half heard from unknown depths below. I, in my turn, whispered of how the camp was left—of what had disappeared, and of how the madness of a lone survivor might have conceived the inconceivable—a wild trip across the monstrous mountains and a descent into the unknown primal masonry—

But we could not convince each other, or even ourselves, of anything definite. We had turned off all light as we stood still, and vaguely noticed that a trace of deeply filtered upper day kept the blackness from being absolute. Having automatically begun to move ahead, we guided ourselves by occasional flashes from our torch. The disturbed debris formed an impression we could not shake off, and the smell of gasoline grew stronger. More and more ruin met our eyes and hampered our feet, until very soon we saw that the forward way was about to cease. We had been all too correct in our pessimistic guess about that rift glimpsed from the air. Our tunnel quest was a blind one, and we were not even going to be able to reach the basement out of which the abyssward aperture opened.

The torch, flashing over the grotesquely carven walls of the blocked corridor in which we stood, shewed several doorways in various states of obstruction; and from one of them the gasoline odour—quite submerging that other hint of odour—came with especial distinctness. As we looked more steadily, we saw that beyond a doubt there had been a slight and recent clearing away of debris from that particular opening. Whatever madness lurking horror might be, we believed the direct avenue toward it was now plainly manifest. I do not think anyone will wonder that we waited an appreciable time before making any further motion.

And yet, when we did venture inside that black arch,

our first impression was one of anticlimax. For amidst the littered expanse of that sculptured crypt—a perfect cube with sides of about twenty feet—there remained no recent object of instantly discernible size; so that we looked instinctively, though in vain, for a farther doorway. In another moment, however, Danforth's sharp vision had descried a place where the floor debris had been disturbed; and we turned on both torches full strength. Though what we saw in that light was actually simple and trifling, I am none the less reluctant to tell of it because of what it implied. It was a rough levelling of the debris, upon which several small objects lay carelessly scattered, and at one corner of which a considerable amount of gasoline must have been spilled lately enough to leave a strong odour even at this extreme super-plateau altitude. In other words, it could not be other than a sort of camp—a camp made by questing beings who like us had been turned back by the unexpectedly choked way to the abyss.

Let me be plain. The scattered objects were, so far as substance was concerned, all from Lake's camp; and consisted of tin cans as queerly opened as those we had seen at that ravaged place, many spent matches, three illustrated books more or less curiously smudged, an empty ink bottle with its pictorial and instructional carton, a broken fountain pen, some oddly snipped fragments of fur and tent-cloth, a used electric battery with circular of directions, a folder that came with our type of tent heater, and a sprinkling of crumpled papers. It was all bad enough, but when we smoothed out the papers and looked at what was on them we felt we had come to the worst. We had found certain inexplicably blotted papers at the camp which might have prepared us, yet the effect of the sight down there in the pre-human vaults of a nightmare city was almost too much to bear.

A mad Gedney might have made the groups of dots in imitation of those found on the greenish soapstones, just as the dots on those insane five-pointed grave-mounds might have been made; and he might conceivably have prepared rough, hasty sketches—varying in their accuracy or lack of it—which outlined the neighbouring parts of the city and traced the way from a circularly represented place outside our previous route—a place we identified as a great cylindrical tower in the carvings and as a vast circular gulf glimpsed in our aërial survey—to the present five-pointed structure and the tunnel-mouth therein. He might, I repeat, have prepared such sketches; for those before us were quite obviously compiled as our own had been from late sculptures somewhere in the glacial labyrinth, though not from the ones which we had seen and used. But what this art-blind bungler could never have done was to execute those sketches in a strange and assured technique perhaps superior, despite haste and carelessness, to any of the decadent carvings from which they were taken—the characteristic and unmistakable technique of the Old Ones themselves in the dead city's heyday.

There are those who will say Danforth and I were utterly mad not to flee for our lives after that; since our conclusions were now—notwithstanding their wildness—completely fixed, and of a nature I need not even mention to those who have read my account as far as this. Perhaps we were mad—for have I not said those horrible peaks were mountains of madness? But I think I can detect something of the same spirit—albeit in a less extreme form—in the men who stalk deadly beasts through African jungles to photograph them or study

their habits. Half-paralysed with terror though we were, there was nevertheless fanned within us a blazing flame of awe and curiosity which triumphed in the end.

Of course we did not mean to face that—or those—which we knew had been there, but we felt that they must be gone by now. They would by this time have found the other neighbouring entrance to the abyss, and have passed within to whatever night-black fragments of the past might await them in the ultimate gulf—the ultimate gulf they had never seen. Or if that entrance, too, was blocked, they would have gone on to the north seeking another. They were, we remembered, partly independent of light.

Looking back to that moment, I can scarcely recall just what precise form our new emotions took—just what change of immediate objective it was that so sharpened our sense of expectancy. We certainly did not mean to face what we feared—yet I will not deny that we may have had a lurking, unconscious wish to spy certain things from some hidden vantage-point. Probably we had not given up our zeal to glimpse the abyss itself, though there was interposed a new goal in the form of that great circular place shewn on the crumpled sketches we had found. We had at once recognised it as a monstrous cylindrical tower figuring in the very earliest carvings, but appearing only as a prodigious round aperture from above. Something about the impressiveness of its rendering, even in these hasty diagrams, made us think that its sub-glacial levels must still form a feature of peculiar importance. Perhaps it embodied architectural marvels as yet unencountered by us. It was certainly of incredible age according to the sculptures in which it figured—being indeed among the first things built in the city. Its carvings, if preserved, could not but be highly significant. Moreover, it might form a good present link with the upper world—a shorter route than the one we were so carefully blazing, and probably that by which those others had descended.

At any rate, the thing we did was to study the terrible sketches—which quite perfectly confirmed our own—and start back over the indicated course to the circular place; the course which our nameless predecessors must have traversed twice before us. The other neighbouring gate to the abyss would lie beyond that. I need not speak of our journey—during which we continued to leave an economical trail of paper—for it was precisely the same in kind as that by which we had reached the cul de sac; except that it tended to adhere more closely to the ground level and even descend to basement corridors. Every now and then we could trace certain disturbing marks in the debris or litter under foot; and after we had passed outside the radius of the gasoline scent we were again faintly conscious—spasmodically—of that more hideous and more persistent scent. After the way had branched from our former course we sometimes gave the rays of our single torch a furtive sweep along the walls; noting in almost every case the well-nigh omnipresent sculptures, which indeed seem to have formed a main aesthetic outlet for the Old Ones.

About 9:30 P.M., while traversing a vaulted corridor whose increasingly glaciated floor seemed somewhat below the ground level and whose roof grew lower as we advanced, we began to see strong daylight ahead and were able to turn off our torch. It appeared that we were coming to the vast circular place, and that our distance from the upper air could not be very great. The corridor ended in an arch surprisingly low for these megalithic

ruins, but we could see much through it even before we emerged. Beyond there stretched a prodigious round space—fully 200 feet in diameter—strown with debris and containing many choked archways corresponding to the one we were about to cross. The walls were—in available spaces—boldly sculptured into a spiral band of heroic proportions; and displayed, despite the destructive weathering caused by the openness of the spot, an artistic splendour far beyond anything we had encountered before. The littered floor was quite heavily glaciated, and we fancied that the true bottom lay at a considerably lower depth.

But the salient object of the place was the titanic stone ramp which, eluding the archways by a sharp turn outward into the open floor, wound spirally up the stupendous cylindrical wall like an inside counterpart of those once climbing outside the monstrous towers or ziggurats of antique Babylon. Only the rapidity of our flight, and the perspective which confounded the descent with the tower's inner wall, had prevented our noticing this feature from the air, and thus caused us to seek another avenue to the sub-glacial level. Pabodie might have been able to tell what sort of engineering held it in place, but Danforth and I could merely admire and marvel. We could see mighty stone corbels and pillars here and there, but what we saw seemed inadequate to the function performed. The thing was excellently preserved up to the present top of the tower—a highly remarkable circumstance in view of its exposure—and its shelter had done much to protect the bizarre and disturbing cosmic sculptures on the walls.

As we stepped out into the awesome half-daylight of this monstrous cylinder-bottom—fifty million years old, and without doubt the most primally ancient structure ever to meet our eyes—we saw that the ramp-traversed sides stretched dizzily up to a height of fully sixty feet. This, we recalled from our aërial survey, meant an outside glaciation of some forty feet; since the yawning gulf we had seen from the plane had been at the top of an approximately twenty-foot mound of crumbled masonry, somewhat sheltered for three-fourths of its circumference by the massive curving walls of a line of higher ruins. According to the sculptures the original tower had stood in the centre of an immense circular plaza; and had been perhaps 500 or 600 feet high, with tiers of horizontal discs near the top, and a row of needle-like spires along the upper rim. Most of the masonry had obviously toppled outward rather than inward—a fortunate happening, since otherwise the ramp might have been shattered and the whole interior choked. As it was, the ramp shewed sad battering; whilst the choking was such that all the archways at the bottom seemed to have been recently half-cleared.

It took us only a moment to conclude that this was indeed the route by which those others had descended, and that this would be the logical route for our own ascent despite the long trail of paper we had left elsewhere. The tower's mouth was no farther from the foothills and our waiting plane than was the great terraced building we had entered, and any further sub-glacial exploration we might make on this trip would lie in this general region. Oddly, we were still thinking about possible later trips—even after all we had seen and guessed. Then as we picked our way cautiously over the debris of the great floor, there came a sight which for the time excluded all other matters.

It was the neatly huddled array of three sledges in that farther angle of the ramp's lower and outward-projecting course which had hitherto been screened from our view. There they were—the three sledges missing from Lake's camp—shaken by a hard usage which must have included forcible dragging along great reaches of snowless masonry and debris, as well as much hand portage over utterly unnavigable places. They were carefully and intelligently packed and strapped, and contained things memorably familiar enough—the gasoline stove, fuel cans, instrument cases, provision tins, tarpaulins obviously bulging with books, and some bulging with less obvious contents—everything derived from Lake's equipment. After what we had found in that other room, we were in a measure prepared for this encounter. The really great shock came when we stepped over and undid one tarpaulin whose outlines had peculiarly disquieted us. It seems that others as well as Lake had been interested in collecting typical specimens; for there were two here, both stiffly frozen, perfectly preserved, patched with adhesive plaster where some wounds around the neck had occurred, and wrapped with patent care to prevent further damage. They were the bodies of young Gedney and the missing dog.

X.

Many people will probably judge us callous as well as mad for thinking about the northward tunnel and the abyss so soon after our sombre discovery, and I am not prepared to say that we would have immediately revived such thoughts but for a specific circumstance which broke in upon us and set up a whole new train of speculations.

We had replaced the tarpaulin over poor Gedney and were standing in a kind of mute bewilderment when the sounds finally reached our consciousness—the first sounds we had heard since descending out of the open where the mountain wind whined faintly from its unearthly heights. Well known and mundane though they were, their presence in this remote world of death was more unexpected and unnerving than any grotesque or fabulous tones could possibly have been—since they gave a fresh upsetting to all our notions of cosmic harmony.

Had it been some trace of that bizarre musical piping over a wide range which Lake's dissection report had led us to expect in those others—and which, indeed, our overwrought fancies had been reading into every wind-howl we had heard since coming on the camp horror—it would have had a kind of hellish congruity with the aeon-dead region around us. A voice from other epochs belongs in a graveyard of other epochs. As it was, however, the noise shattered all our profoundly seated adjustments—all our tacit acceptance of the inner antarctic as a waste as utterly and irrevocably void of every vestige of normal life as the sterile disc of the moon. What we heard was not the fabulous note of any buried blasphemy of elder earth from whose supernal toughness an age-denied polar sun had evoked a monstrous response. Instead, it was a thing so mockingly normal and so unerringly familiarised by our sea days off Victoria Land and our camp days at McMurdo Sound that we shuddered to think of it here, where such things ought not to be. To be brief—it was simply the raucous squawking of a penguin.

The muffled sound floated from sub-glacial recesses nearly opposite to the corridor whence we had come—regions manifestly in the direction of that other tunnel

to the vast abyss. The presence of a living water-bird in such a direction—in a world whose surface was one of age-long and uniform lifelessness—could lead to only one conclusion; hence our first thought was to verify the objective reality of the sound. It was, indeed, repeated; and seemed at times to come from more than one throat. Seeking its source, we entered an archway from which much debris had been cleared; resuming our trail-blazing—with an added paper-supply taken with curious repugnance from one of the tarpaulin bundles on the sledges—when we left daylight behind.

As the glaciated floor gave place to a litter of detritus, we plainly discerned some curious dragging tracks; and once Danforth found a distinct print of a sort whose description would be only too superfluous. The course indicated by the penguin cries was precisely what our map and compass prescribed as an approach to the more northerly tunnel-mouth, and we were glad to find that a bridgeless thoroughfare on the ground and basement levels seemed open. The tunnel, according to the chart, ought to start from the basement of a large pyramidal structure which we seemed vaguely to recall from our aërial survey as remarkably well preserved. Along our path the single torch shewed a customary profusion of carvings, but we did not pause to examine any of these.

Suddenly a bulky white shape loomed up ahead of us, and we flashed on the second torch. It is odd how wholly this new quest had turned our minds from earlier fears of what might lurk near. Those other ones, having left their supplies in the great circular place, must have planned to return after their scouting trip toward or into the abyss; yet we had now discarded all caution concerning them as completely as if they had never existed. This white, waddling thing was fully six feet high, yet we seemed to realise at once that it was not one of those others. They were larger and dark, and according to the sculptures their motion over land surfaces was a swift, assured matter despite the queerness of their sea-born tentacle equipment. But to say that the white thing did not profoundly frighten us would be vain. We were indeed clutched for an instant by a primitive dread almost sharper than the worst of our reasoned fears regarding those others. Then came a flash of anticlimax as the white shape sidled into a lateral archway to our left to join two others of its kind which had summoned it in raucous tones. For it was only a penguin—albeit of a huge, unknown species larger than the greatest of the known king penguins, and monstrous in its combined albinism and virtual eyelessness.

When we had followed the thing into the archway and turned both our torches on the indifferent and unheeding group of three we saw that they were all eyeless albinos of the same unknown and gigantic species. Their size reminded us of some of the archaic penguins depicted in the Old Ones' sculptures, and it did not take us long to conclude that they were descended from the same stock—undoubtedly surviving through a retreat to some warmer inner region whose perpetual blackness had destroyed their pigmentation and atrophied their eyes to mere useless slits. That their present habitat was the vast abyss we sought, was not for a moment to be doubted; and this evidence of the gulf's continued warmth and habitability filled us with the most curious and subtly perturbing fancies.

We wondered, too, what had caused these three birds to venture out of their usual domain. The state and

silence of the great dead city made it clear that it had at no time been an habitual seasonal rookery, whilst the manifest indifference of the trio to our presence made it seem odd that any passing party of those others should have startled them. Was it possible that those others had taken some aggressive action or tried to increase their meat supply? We doubted whether that pungent odour which the dogs had hated could cause an equal antipathy in these penguins; since their ancestors had obviously lived on excellent terms with the Old Ones—an amicable relationship which must have survived in the abyss below as long as any of the Old Ones remained. Regretting—in a flareup of the old spirit of pure science—that we could not photograph these anomalous creatures, we shortly left them to their squawking and pushed on toward the abyss whose openness was now so positively proved to us, and whose exact direction occasional penguin tracks made clear.

Not long afterward a steep descent in a long, low, doorless, and peculiarly sculptureless corridor led us to believe that we were approaching the tunnel-mouth at last. We had passed two more penguins, and heard others immediately ahead. Then the corridor ended in a prodigious open space which made us gasp involuntarily—a perfect inverted hemisphere, obviously deep underground; fully an hundred feet in diameter and fifty feet high, with low archways opening around all parts of the circumference but one, and that one yawning cavernously with a black arched aperture which broke the symmetry of the vault to a height of nearly fifteen feet. It was the entrance to the great abyss.

In this vast hemisphere, whose concave roof was impressively though decadently carved to a likeness of the primordial celestial dome, a few albino penguins waddled—aliens there, but indifferent and unseeing. The black tunnel yawned indefinitely off at a steep descending grade, its aperture adorned with grotesquely chiselled jambs and lintel. From that cryptical mouth we fancied a current of slightly warmer air and perhaps even a suspicion of vapour proceeded; and we wondered what living entities other than penguins the limitless void below, and the contiguous honeycombings of the land and the titan mountains, might conceal. We wondered, too, whether the trace of mountain-top smoke at first suspected by poor Lake, as well as the odd haze we had ourselves perceived around the rampart-crowned peak, might not be caused by the tortuous-channelled rising of some such vapour from the unfathomed regions of earth's core.

Entering the tunnel, we saw that its outline was—at least at the start—about fifteen feet each way; sides, floor, and arched roof composed of the usual megalithic masonry. The sides were sparsely decorated with cartouches of conventional designs in a late, decadent style; and all the construction and carving were marvellously well preserved. The floor was quite clear, except for a slight detritus bearing outgoing penguin tracks and the inward tracks of those others. The farther one advanced, the warmer it became; so that we were soon unbuttoning our heavy garments. We wondered whether there were any actually igneous manifestations below, and whether the waters of that sunless sea were hot. After a short distance the masonry gave place to solid rock, though the tunnel kept the same proportions and presented the same aspect of carved regularity. Occasionally its varying grade became so steep that grooves were cut in the floor. Several times we noted the mouths of small lateral galleries not recorded in our diagrams; none of them such as to

complicate the problem of our return, and all of them welcome as possible refuges in case we met unwelcome entities on their way back from the abyss. The nameless scent of such things was very distinct. Doubtless it was suicidally foolish to venture into that tunnel under the known conditions, but the lure of the unplumbed is stronger in certain persons than most suspect—indeed, it was just such a lure which had brought us to this unearthly polar waste in the first place. We saw several penguins as we passed along, and speculated on the distance we would have to traverse. The carvings had led us to expect a steep downhill walk of about a mile to the abyss, but our previous wanderings had shewn us that matters of scale were not wholly to be depended on.

After about a quarter of a mile that nameless scent became greatly accentuated, and we kept very careful track of the various lateral openings we passed. There was no visible vapour as at the mouth, but this was doubtless due to the lack of contrasting cooler air. The temperature was rapidly ascending, and we were not surprised to come upon a careless heap of material shudderingly familiar to us. It was composed of furs and tent-cloth taken from Lake's camp, and we did not pause to study the bizarre forms into which the fabrics had been slashed. Slightly beyond this point we noticed a decided increase in the size and number of the side-galleries, and concluded that the densely honeycombed region beneath the higher foothills must now have been reached. The nameless scent was now curiously mixed with another and scarcely less offensive odour—of what nature we could not guess, though we thought of decaying organisms and perhaps unknown subterrene fungi. Then came a startling expansion of the tunnel for which the carvings had not prepared us—a broadening and rising into a lofty, natural-looking elliptical cavern with a level floor; some 75 feet long and 50 broad, and with many immense side-passages leading away into cryptical darkness.

Though this cavern was natural in appearance, an inspection with both torches suggested that it had been formed by the artificial destruction of several walls between adjacent honeycombings. The walls were rough, and the high vaulted roof was thick with stalactites; but the solid rock floor had been smoothed off, and was free from all debris, detritus, or even dust to a positively abnormal extent. Except for the avenue through which we had come, this was true of the floors of all the great galleries opening off from it; and the singularity of the condition was such as to set us vainly puzzling. The curious new foetor which had supplemented the nameless scent was excessively pungent here; so much so that it destroyed all trace of the other. Something about this whole place, with its polished and almost glistening floor, struck us as more vaguely baffling and horrible than any of the monstrous things we had previously encountered.

The regularity of the passage immediately ahead, as well as the larger proportion of penguin-droppings there, prevented all confusion as to the right course amidst this plethora of equally great cave-mouths. Nevertheless we resolved to resume our paper trail-blazing if any further complexity should develop; for dust tracks, of course, could no longer be expected. Upon resuming our direct progress we cast a beam of torchlight over the tunnel walls—and stopped short in amazement at the supremely radical change which had come over the carvings in this part of the passage. We realised, of course, the great decadence of the Old Ones' sculpture at the time of the tunnelling; and had indeed noticed the inferior

workmanship of the arabesques in the stretches behind us. But now, in this deeper section beyond the cavern, there was a sudden difference wholly transcending explanation—a difference in basic nature as well as in mere quality, and involving so profound and calamitous a degradation of skill that nothing in the hitherto observed rate of decline could have led one to expect it.

This new and degenerate work was coarse, bold, and wholly lacking in delicacy of detail. It was counter-sunk with exaggerated depth in bands following the same general line as the sparse cartouches of the earlier sections, but the height of the reliefs did not reach the level of the general surface. Danforth had the idea that it was a second carving—a sort of palimpsest formed after the obliteration of a previous design. In nature it was wholly decorative and conventional; and consisted of crude spirals and angles roughly following the quintile mathematical tradition of the Old Ones, yet seeming more like a parody than a perpetuation of that tradition. We could not get it out of our minds that some subtly but profoundly alien element had been added to the aesthetic feeling behind the technique—an alien element, Danforth guessed, that was responsible for the manifestly laborious substitution. It was like, yet disturbingly unlike, what we had come to recognise as the Old Ones' art; and I was persistently reminded of such hybrid things as the ungainly Palmyrene sculptures fashioned in the Roman manner. That others had recently noticed this belt of carving was hinted by the presence of a used torch battery on the floor in front of one of the most characteristic designs.

Since we could not afford to spend any considerable time in study, we resumed our advance after a cursory look; though frequently casting beams over the walls to see if any further decorative changes developed. Nothing of the sort was perceived, though the carvings were in places rather sparse because of the numerous mouths of smooth-floored lateral tunnels. We saw and heard fewer penguins, but thought we caught a vague suspicion of an infinitely distant chorus of them somewhere deep within the earth. The new and inexplicable odour was abominably strong, and we could detect scarcely a sign of that other nameless scent. Puffs of visible vapour ahead bespoke increasing contrasts in temperature, and the relative nearness of the sunless sea-cliffs of the great abyss. Then, quite unexpectedly, we saw certain obstructions on the polished floor ahead—obstructions which were quite definitely not penguins—and turned on our second torch after making sure that the objects were quite stationary.

XI.

Still another time have I come to a place where it is very difficult to proceed. I ought to be hardened by this stage; but there are some experiences and intimations which scar too deeply to permit of healing, and leave only such an added sensitiveness that memory reinspires all the original horror. We saw, as I have said, certain obstructions on the polished floor ahead; and I may add that our nostrils were assailed almost simultaneously by a very curious intensification of the strange prevailing foetor, now quite plainly mixed with the nameless stench of those others which had gone before us. The light of the second torch left no doubt of what the obstructions were, and we dared approach them only because we could see, even from a distance, that they were quite as past

all harming power as had been the six similar specimens unearthed from the monstrous star-mounded graves at poor Lake's camp.

They were, indeed, as lacking in completeness as most of those we had unearthed—though it grew plain from the thick, dark-green pool gathering around them that their incompleteness was of infinitely greater recency. There seemed to be only four of them, whereas Lake's bulletins would have suggested no less than eight as forming the group which had preceded us. To find them in this state was wholly unexpected, and we wondered what sort of monstrous struggle had occurred down here in the dark.

Penguins, attacked in a body, retaliate savagely with their beaks; and our ears now made certain the existence of a rookery far beyond. Had those others disturbed such a place and aroused murderous pursuit? The obstructions did not suggest it, for penguin beaks against the tough tissues Lake had dissected could hardly account for the terrible damage our approaching glance was beginning to make out. Besides, the huge blind birds we had seen appeared to be singularly peaceful.

Had there, then, been a struggle among those others, and were the absent four responsible? If so, where were they? Were they close at hand and likely to form an immediate menace to us? We glanced anxiously at some of the smooth-floored lateral passages as we continued our slow and frankly reluctant approach. Whatever the conflict was, it had clearly been that which had frightened the penguins into their unaccustomed wandering. It must, then, have arisen near that faintly heard rookery in the incalculable gulf beyond, since there were no signs that any birds had normally dwelt here. Perhaps, we reflected, there had been a hideous running fight, with the weaker party seeking to get back to the cached sledges when their pursuers finished them. One could picture the daemoniac fray between namelessly monstrous entities as it surged out of the black abyss with great clouds of frantic penguins squawking and scurrying ahead.

I say that we approached those sprawling and incomplete obstructions slowly and reluctantly. Would to heaven we had never approached them at all, but had run back at top speed out of that blasphemous tunnel with the greasily smooth floors and the degenerate murals aping and mocking the things they had superseded—run back, before we had seen what we did see, and before our minds were burned with something which will never let us breathe easily again!

Both of our torches were turned on the prostrate objects, so that we soon realised the dominant factor in their incompleteness. Mauled, compressed, twisted, and ruptured as they were, their chief common injury was total decapitation. From each one the tentacled starfish-head had been removed; and as we drew near we saw that the manner of removal looked more like some hellish tearing or suction than like any ordinary form of cleavage. Their noisome dark-green ichor formed a large, spreading pool; but its stench was half overshadowed by that newer and stranger stench, here more pungent than at any other point along our route. Only when we had come very close to the sprawling obstructions could we trace that second, unexplainable foetor to any immediate source—and the instant we did so Danforth, remembering certain very vivid sculptures of the Old Ones' history in the Permian age 150 million years ago, gave vent to a nerve-tortured

cry which echoed hysterically through that vaulted and archaic passage with the evil palimpsest carvings.

I came only just short of echoing his cry myself; for I had seen those primal sculptures, too, and had shudderingly admired the way the nameless artist had suggested that hideous slime-coating found on certain incomplete and prostrate Old Ones—those whom the frightful shoggoths had characteristically slain and sucked to a ghastly headlessness in the great war of re-subjugation. They were infamous, nightmare sculptures even when telling of age-old, bygone things; for shoggoths and their work ought not to be seen by human beings or portrayed by any beings. The mad author of the Necronomicon had nervously tried to swear that none had been bred on this planet, and that only drugged dreamers had ever conceived them. Formless protoplasm able to mock and reflect all forms and organs and processes—viscous agglutinations of bubbling cells—rubbery fifteen-foot spheroids infinitely plastic and ductile—slaves of suggestion, builders of cities—more and more sullen, more and more intelligent, more and more amphibious, more and more imitative—Great God! What madness made even those blasphemous Old Ones willing to use and to carve such things?

And now, when Danforth and I saw the freshly glistening and reflectively iridescent black slime which clung thickly to those headless bodies and stank obscenely with that new unknown odour whose cause only a diseased fancy could envisage—clung to those bodies and sparkled less voluminously on a smooth part of the accursedly re-sculptured wall in a series of grouped dots—we understood the quality of cosmic fear to its uttermost depths. It was not fear of those four missing others—for all too well did we suspect they would do no harm again. Poor devils! After all, they were not evil things of their kind. They were the men of another age and another order of being. Nature had played a hellish jest on them—as it will on any others that human madness, callousness, or cruelty may hereafter drag up in that hideously dead or sleeping polar waste—and this was their tragic homecoming.

They had not been even savages—for what indeed had they done? That awful awakening in the cold of an unknown epoch—perhaps an attack by the furry, frantically barking quadrupeds, and a dazed defence against them and the equally frantic white simians with the queer wrappings and paraphernalia . . . poor Lake, poor Gedney . . . and poor Old Ones! Scientists to the last—what had they done that we would not have done in their place? God, what intelligence and persistence! What a facing of the incredible, just as those carven kinsmen and forbears had faced things only a little less incredible! Radiates, vegetables, monstrosities, star-spawn—whatever they had been, they were men!

They had crossed the icy peaks on whose templed slopes they had once worshipped and roamed among the tree-ferns. They had found their dead city brooding under its curse, and had read its carven latter days as we had done. They had tried to reach their living fellows in fabled depths of blackness they had never seen—and what had they found? All this flashed in unison through the thoughts of Danforth and me as we looked from those headless, slime-coated shapes to the loathsome palimpsest sculptures and the diabolical dot-groups of fresh slime on the wall beside them—looked and understood what must have triumphed and survived

down there in the Cyclopean water-city of that nighted, penguin-fringed abyss, whence even now a sinister curling mist had begun to belch pallidly as if in answer to Danforth's hysterical scream.

The shock of recognising that monstrous slime and headlessness had frozen us into mute, motionless statues, and it is only through later conversations that we have learned of the complete identity of our thoughts at that moment. It seemed aeons that we stood there, but actually it could not have been more than ten or fifteen seconds. That hateful, pallid mist curled forward as if veritably driven by some remoter advancing bulk—and then came a sound which upset much of what we had just decided, and in so doing broke the spell and enabled us to run like mad past squawking, confused penguins over our former trail back to the city, along ice-sunken megalithic corridors to the great open circle, and up that archaic spiral ramp in a frenzied automatic plunge for the sane outer air and light of day.

The new sound, as I have intimated, upset much that we had decided; because it was what poor Lake's dissection had led us to attribute to those we had just judged dead. It was, Danforth later told me, precisely what he had caught in infinitely muffled form when at that spot beyond the alley-corner above the glacial level; and it certainly had a shocking resemblance to the wind-pipings we had both heard around the lofty mountain caves. At the risk of seeming puerile I will add another thing, too; if only because of the surprising way Danforth's impression chimed with mine. Of course common reading is what prepared us both to make the interpretation, though Danforth has hinted at queer notions about unsuspected and forbidden sources to which Poe may have had access when writing his Arthur Gordon Pym a century ago. It will be remembered that in that fantastic tale there is a word of unknown but terrible and prodigious significance connected with the antarctic and screamed eternally by the gigantic, spectrally snowy birds of that malign region's core. "Tekeli-li! Tekeli-li!" That, I may admit, is exactly what we thought we heard conveyed by that sudden sound behind the advancing white mist—that insidious musical piping over a singularly wide range.

We were in full flight before three notes or syllables had been uttered, though we knew that the swiftness of the Old Ones would enable any scream-roused and pursuing survivor of the slaughter to overtake us in a moment if it really wished to do so. We had a vague hope, however, that non-aggressive conduct and a display of kindred reason might cause such a being to spare us in case of capture; if only from scientific curiosity. After all, if such an one had nothing to fear for itself it would have no motive in harming us. Concealment being futile at this juncture, we used our torch for a running glance behind, and perceived that the mist was thinning. Would we see, at last, a complete and living specimen of those others? Again came that insidious musical piping—"Tekeli-li! Tekeli-li!"

Then, noting that we were actually gaining on our pursuer, it occurred to us that the entity might be wounded. We could take no chances, however, since it was very obviously approaching in answer to Danforth's scream rather than in flight from any other entity. The timing was too close to admit of doubt. Of the whereabouts of that less conceivable and less mentionable nightmare—that foetid, unglimpsed mountain of slime-spewing protoplasm whose race had conquered the abyss

and sent land pioneers to re-carve and squirm through the burrows of the hills—we could form no guess; and it cost us a genuine pang to leave this probably crippled Old One—perhaps a lone survivor—to the peril of recapture and a nameless fate.

Thank heaven we did not slacken our run. The curling mist had thickened again, and was driving ahead with increased speed; whilst the straying penguins in our rear were squawking and screaming and displaying signs of a panic really surprising in view of their relatively minor confusion when we had passed them. Once more came that sinister, wide-ranged piping—"Tekeli-li! Tekeli-li!" We had been wrong. The thing was not wounded, but had merely paused on encountering the bodies of its fallen kindred and the hellish slime inscription above them. We could never know what that daemon message was—but those burials at Lake's camp had shewn how much importance the beings attached to their dead. Our recklessly used torch now revealed ahead of us the large open cavern where various ways converged, and we were glad to be leaving those morbid palimpsest sculptures—almost felt even when scarcely seen—behind.

Another thought which the advent of the cave inspired was the possibility of losing our pursuer at this bewildering focus of large galleries. There were several of the blind albino penguins in the open space, and it seemed clear that their fear of the oncoming entity was extreme to the point of unaccountability. If at that point we dimmed our torch to the very lowest limit of travelling need, keeping it strictly in front of us, the frightened squawking motions of the huge birds in the mist might muffle our footfalls, screen our true course, and somehow set up a false lead. Amidst the churning, spiralling fog the littered and unglistening floor of the main tunnel beyond this point, as differing from the other morbidly polished burrows, could hardly form a highly distinguishing feature; even, so far as we could conjecture, for those indicated special senses which made the Old Ones partly though imperfectly independent of light in emergencies. In fact, we were somewhat apprehensive lest we go astray ourselves in our haste. For we had, of course, decided to keep straight on toward the dead city; since the consequences of loss in those unknown foothill honeycombings would be unthinkable.

The fact that we survived and emerged is sufficient proof that the thing did take a wrong gallery whilst we providentially hit on the right one. The penguins alone could not have saved us, but in conjunction with the mist they seem to have done so. Only a benign fate kept the curling vapours thick enough at the right moment, for they were constantly shifting and threatening to vanish. Indeed, they did lift for a second just before we emerged from the nauseously re-sculptured tunnel into the cave; so that we actually caught one first and only half-glimpse of the oncoming entity as we cast a final, desperately fearful glance backward before dimming the torch and mixing with the penguins in the hope of dodging pursuit. If the fate which screened us was benign, that which gave us the half-glimpse was infinitely the opposite; for to that flash of semi-vision can be traced a full half of the horror which has ever since haunted us.

Our exact motive in looking back again was perhaps no more than the immemorial instinct of the pursued to gauge the nature and course of its pursuer; or perhaps it was an automatic attempt to answer a subconscious question raised by one of our senses. In the midst of our

flight, with all our faculties centred on the problem of escape, we were in no condition to observe and analyse details; yet even so our latent brain-cells must have wondered at the message brought them by our nostrils. Afterward we realised what it was—that our retreat from the foetid slime-coating on those headless obstructions, and the coincident approach of the pursuing entity, had not brought us the exchange of stenches which logic called for. In the neighbourhood of the prostrate things that new and lately unexplainable foetor had been wholly dominant; but by this time it ought to have largely given place to the nameless stench associated with those others. This it had not done—for instead, the newer and less bearable smell was now virtually undiluted, and growing more and more poisonously insistent each second.

So we glanced back—simultaneously, it would appear; though no doubt the incipient motion of one prompted the imitation of the other. As we did so we flashed both torches full strength at the momentarily thinned mist; either from sheer primitive anxiety to see all we could, or in a less primitive but equally unconscious effort to dazzle the entity before we dimmed our light and dodged among the penguins of the labyrinth-centre ahead. Unhappy act! Not Orpheus himself, or Lot's wife, paid much more dearly for a backward glance. And again came that shocking, wide-ranged piping—"Tekeli-li! Tekeli-li!"

I might as well be frank—even if I cannot bear to be quite direct—in stating what we saw; though at the time we felt that it was not to be admitted even to each other. The words reaching the reader can never even suggest the awfulness of the sight itself. It crippled our consciousness so completely that I wonder we had the residual sense to dim our torches as planned, and to strike the right tunnel toward the dead city. Instinct alone must have carried us through—perhaps better than reason could have done; though if that was what saved us, we paid a high price. Of reason we certainly had little enough left. Danforth was totally unstrung, and the first thing I remember of the rest of the journey was hearing him light-headedly chant an hysterical formula in which I alone of mankind could have found anything but insane irrelevance. It reverberated in falsetto echoes among the squawks of the penguins; reverberated through the vaultings ahead, and—thank God—through the now empty vaultings behind. He could not have begun it at once—else we would not have been alive and blindly racing. I shudder to think of what a shade of difference in his nervous reactions might have brought.

"South Station Under—Washington Under—Park Street Under—Kendall—Central—Harvard. . . ." The poor fellow was chanting the familiar stations of the Boston-Cambridge tunnel that burrowed through our peaceful native soil thousands of miles away in New England, yet to me the ritual had neither irrelevance nor home-feeling. It had only horror, because I knew unerringly the monstrous, nefandous analogy that had suggested it. We had expected, upon looking back, to see a terrible and incredibly moving entity if the mists were thin enough; but of that entity we had formed a clear idea. What we did see—for the mists were indeed all too malignly thinned—was something altogether different, and immeasurably more hideous and detestable. It was the utter, objective embodiment of the fantastic novelist's 'thing that should not be'; and its nearest comprehensible analogue is a vast, onrushing subway train as one sees it from a station platform—the great black front looming colossally out of infinite subterranean distance,

constellated with strangely coloured lights and filling the prodigious burrow as a piston fills a cylinder.

But we were not on a station platform. We were on the track ahead as the nightmare plastic column of foetid black iridescence oozed tightly onward through its fifteen-foot sinus; gathering unholy speed and driving before it a spiral, re-thickening cloud of the pallid abyss-vapour. It was a terrible, indescribable thing vaster than any subway train—a shapeless congeries of protoplasmic bubbles, faintly self-luminous, and with myriads of temporary eyes forming and unforming as pustules of greenish light all over the tunnel-filling front that bore down upon us, crushing the frantic penguins and slithering over the glistening floor that it and its kind had swept so evilly free of all litter. Still came that eldritch, mocking cry—"Tekeli-li! Tekeli-li!" And at last we remembered that the daemoniac shoggoths—given life, thought, and plastic organ patterns solely by the Old Ones, and having no language save that which the dot-groups expressed—had likewise no voice save the imitated accents of their bygone masters.

XII.

Danforth and I have recollections of emerging into the great sculptured hemisphere and of threading our back trail through the Cyclopean rooms and corridors of the dead city; yet these are purely dream-fragments involving no memory of volition, details, or physical exertion. It was as if we floated in a nebulous world or dimension without time, causation, or orientation. The grey half-daylight of the vast circular space sobered us somewhat;

but we did not go near those cached sledges or look again at poor Gedney and the dog. They have a strange and titanic mausoleum, and I hope the end of this planet will find them still undisturbed.

It was while struggling up the colossal spiral incline that we first felt the terrible fatigue and short breath which our race through the thin plateau air had produced; but not even the fear of collapse could make us pause before reaching the normal outer realm of sun and sky. There was something vaguely appropriate about our departure from those buried epochs; for as we wound our panting way up the sixty-foot cylinder of primal masonry we glimpsed beside us a continuous procession of heroic sculptures in the dead race's early and undecayed technique—a farewell from the Old Ones, written fifty million years ago.

Finally scrambling out at the top, we found ourselves on a great mound of tumbled blocks; with the curved walls of higher stonework rising westward, and the brooding peaks of the great mountains shewing beyond the more crumbled structures toward the east. The low antarctic sun of midnight peered redly from the southern horizon through rifts in the jagged ruins, and the terrible age and deadness of the nightmare city seemed all the starker by contrast with such relatively known and accustomed things as the features of the polar landscape. The sky above was a churning and opalescent mass of tenuous ice-vapours, and the cold clutched at our vitals. Wearily resting the outfit-bags to which we had instinctively clung throughout our desperate flight, we rebuttoned our heavy garments for the stumbling climb down the mound and the walk through the aeon-old stone maze to the foothills where our aëroplane waited. Of what had set

us fleeing from the darkness of earth's secret and archaic gulfs we said nothing at all.

In less than a quarter of an hour we had found the steep grade to the foothills—the probable ancient terrace—by which we had descended, and could see the dark bulk of our great plane amidst the sparse ruins on the rising slope ahead. Half way uphill toward our goal we paused for a momentary breathing-spell, and turned to look again at the fantastic palaeogean tangle of incredible stone shapes below us—once more outlined mystically against an unknown west. As we did so we saw that the sky beyond had lost its morning haziness; the restless ice-vapours having moved up to the zenith, where their mocking outlines seemed on the point of settling into some bizarre pattern which they feared to make quite definite or conclusive.

There now lay revealed on the ultimate white horizon behind the grotesque city a dim, elfin line of pinnacled violet whose needle-pointed heights loomed dream-like against the beckoning rose-colour of the western sky. Up toward this shimmering rim sloped the ancient table-land, the depressed course of the bygone river traversing it as an irregular ribbon of shadow. For a second we gasped in admiration of the scene's unearthly cosmic beauty, and then vague horror began to creep into our souls. For this far violet line could be nothing else than the terrible mountains of the forbidden land—highest of earth's peaks and focus of earth's evil; harbourers of nameless horrors and Archaean secrets; shunned and prayed to by those who feared to carve their meaning; untrodden by any living thing of earth, but visited by the sinister lightnings and sending strange beams across the plains in the polar night—beyond doubt the unknown archetype of that dreaded Kadath in the Cold Waste beyond abhorrent Leng, whereof unholy primal legends hint evasively. We were the first human beings ever to see them—and I hope to God we may be the last.

If the sculptured maps and pictures in that pre-human city had told truly, these cryptic violet mountains could not be much less than 300 miles away; yet none the less sharply did their dim elfin essence jut above that remote and snowy rim, like the serrated edge of a monstrous alien planet about to rise into unaccustomed heavens. Their height, then, must have been tremendous beyond all known comparison—carrying them up into tenuous atmospheric strata peopled by such gaseous wraiths as rash flyers have barely lived to whisper of after unexplainable falls. Looking at them, I thought nervously of certain sculptured hints of what the great bygone river had washed down into the city from their accursed slopes—and wondered how much sense and how much folly had lain in the fears of those Old Ones who carved them so reticently. I recalled how their northerly end must come near the coast at Queen Mary Land, where even at that moment Sir Douglas Mawson's expedition was doubtless working less than a thousand miles away; and hoped that no evil fate would give Sir Douglas and his men a glimpse of what might lie beyond the protecting coastal range. Such thoughts formed a measure of my overwrought condition at the time—and Danforth seemed to be even worse.

Yet long before we had passed the great star-shaped ruin and reached our plane our fears had become transferred to the lesser but vast enough range whose re-crossing lay ahead of us. From these foothills the black, ruin-crusted slopes reared up starkly and hideously against the east,

again reminding us of those strange Asian paintings of Nicholas Roerich; and when we thought of the damnable honeycombs inside them, and of the frightful amorphous entities that might have pushed their foetidly squirming way even to the topmost hollow pinnacles, we could not face without panic the prospect of again sailing by those suggestive skyward cave-mouths where the wind made sounds like an evil musical piping over a wide range. To make matters worse, we saw distinct traces of local mist around several of the summits—as poor Lake must have done when he made that early mistake about volcanism—and thought shiveringly of that kindred mist from which we had just escaped; of that, and of the blasphemous, horror-fostering abyss whence all such vapours came.

All was well with the plane, and we clumsily hauled on our heavy flying furs. Danforth got the engine started without trouble, and we made a very smooth takeoff over the nightmare city. Below us the primal Cyclopean masonry spread out as it had done when first we saw it—so short, yet infinitely long, a time ago—and we began rising and turning to test the wind for our crossing through the pass. At a very high level there must have been great disturbance, since the ice-dust clouds of the zenith were doing all sorts of fantastic things; but at 24,000 feet, the height we needed for the pass, we found navigation quite practicable. As we drew close to the jutting peaks the wind's strange piping again became manifest, and I could see Danforth's hands trembling at the controls. Rank amateur though I was, I thought at that moment that I might be a better navigator than he in effecting the dangerous crossing between pinnacles; and when I made motions to change seats and take over his duties he did not protest. I tried to keep all my skill and self-possession about me, and stared at the sector of reddish farther sky betwixt the walls of the pass—resolutely refusing to pay attention to the puffs of mountain-top vapour, and wishing that I had wax-stopped ears like Ulysses' men off the Sirens' coast to keep that disturbing wind-piping from my consciousness.

But Danforth, released from his piloting and keyed up to a dangerous nervous pitch, could not keep quiet. I felt him turning and wriggling about as he looked back at the terrible receding city, ahead at the cave-riddled, cube-barnacled peaks, sidewise at the bleak sea of snowy, rampart-strown foothills, and upward at the seething, grotesquely clouded sky. It was then, just as I was trying to steer safely through the pass, that his mad shrieking brought us so close to disaster by shattering my tight hold on myself and causing me to fumble helplessly with the controls for a moment. A second afterward my resolution triumphed and we made the crossing safely—yet I am afraid that Danforth will never be the same again.

I have said that Danforth refused to tell me what final horror made him scream out so insanely—a horror which, I feel sadly sure, is mainly responsible for his present breakdown. We had snatches of shouted conversation above the wind's piping and the engine's buzzing as we reached the safe side of the range and swooped slowly down toward the camp, but that had mostly to do with the pledges of secrecy we had made as we prepared to leave the nightmare city. Certain things, we had agreed, were not for people to know and discuss lightly—and I would not speak of them now but for the need of heading off that Starkweather-Moore Expedition, and others, at any cost. It is absolutely necessary, for the peace and safety of mankind, that some of earth's dark, dead corners and unplumbed depths be let alone; lest sleeping

abnormalities wake to resurgent life, and blasphemously surviving nightmares squirm and splash out of their black lairs to newer and wider conquests.

All that Danforth has ever hinted is that the final horror was a mirage. It was not, he declares, anything connected with the cubes and caves of echoing, vaporous, wormily honeycombed mountains of madness which we crossed; but a single fantastic, daemoniac glimpse, among the churning zenith-clouds, of what lay back of those other violet westward mountains which the Old Ones had shunned and feared. It is very probable that the thing was a sheer delusion born of the previous stresses we had passed through, and of the actual though unrecognised mirage of the dead transmontane city experienced near Lake's camp the day before; but it was so real to Danforth that he suffers from it still.

He has on rare occasions whispered disjointed and irresponsible things about "the black pit", "the carven rim", "the proto-shoggoths", "the windowless solids with five dimensions", "the nameless cylinder", "the elder pharos", "Yog-Sothoth", "the primal white jelly", "the colour out of space", "the wings", "the eyes in darkness", "the moon-ladder", "the original, the eternal, the undying", and other bizarre conceptions; but when he is fully himself he repudiates all this and attributes it to his curious and macabre reading of earlier years. Danforth, indeed, is known to be among the few who have ever dared go completely through that worm-riddled copy of the Necronomicon kept under lock and key in the college library.

The higher sky, as we crossed the range, was surely vaporous and disturbed enough; and although I did not see the zenith I can well imagine that its swirls of ice-dust may have taken strange forms. Imagination, knowing how vividly distant scenes can sometimes be reflected, refracted, and magnified by such layers of restless cloud, might easily have supplied the rest—and of course Danforth did not hint any of those specific horrors till after his memory had had a chance to draw on his bygone reading. He could never have seen so much in one instantaneous glance.

At the time his shrieks were confined to the repetition of a single mad word of all too obvious source:

"Tekeli-li! Tekeli-li!"

'Tekeli-li! Tekeli-li!'

A WARNING TO THE CURIOUS

BY M. R. JAMES

The place on the east coast which the reader is asked to consider is Scaburgh. It is not very different now from what I remember it to have been when I was a child. Marshes intersected by dykes to the south, recalling the early chapters of Great Expectations; flat fields to the north, merging into heath; heath, fir woods, and, above all, gorse, inland. A long sea-front and a street: behind that a spacious church of flint, with a broad, solid western tower and a peal of six bells. How well I remember their sound on a hot Sunday in August, as our party went slowly up the white, dusty slope of road towards them, for the church stands at the top of a short, steep incline. They rang with a flat clacking sort of sound on those hot days, but when the air was softer they were mellower too. The railway ran down to its little terminus farther along the same road. There was a gay white windmill just before you came to the station, and another down near the shingle at the south end the town, and yet others on higher ground to the north. There were cottages of bright red brick with slate roofs... but why do I encumber you with these commonplace details? The fact is that they come crowding to the point of the pencil when it begins to write of Seaburgh. I should like to be sure that I had allowed the right ones to get on to the paper. But I forgot. I have not quite done with the word-painting business yet.

Walk away from the sea and the town, pass the station,

and turn up the road on the right. It is a sandy road, parallel with the railway, and if you follow it, it climbs to somewhat higher ground. On your left (you are now going northward) is heath, on your right (the side towards the sea) is a belt of old firs, wind-beaten, thick at the top, with the slope that old seaside trees have; seen on the skyline from the train they would tell you in an instant, if you did not know it, that you were approaching a windy coast. Well, at the top of my little hill, a line of these firs strikes out and runs towards the sea, for there is a ridge that goes that way; and the ridge ends in a rather well-defined mound commanding the level fields of rough grass, and a little knot of fir trees crowns it. And here you may sit on a hot spring day, very well content to look at blue sea, white windmills, red cottages bright green grass, church tower, and distant martello tower on the south.

As I have said, I began to know Seaburgh as a child; but a gap of a good many years separates my early knowledge from that which is more recent. Still it keeps its place in my affections, and any tales of it that I pick up have an interest for me. One such tale is this: it came to me in a place very remote from Seaburgh, and quite accidentally, from a man whom I had been able to oblige--enough in his opinion to justify his making me his confidant to this extent.

I know all that country more or less (he said). I used to go to Scaburgh pretty regularly for golf in the spring. I generally put up at the 'Bear', with a friend--Henry Long it was, you knew him perhaps--('Slightly,' I said) and we used to take a sitting-room and be very happy there. Since he died I haven't cared to go there. And I don't know that I should anyhow after the particular thing that happened on our last visit.

It was in April, 19--, we were there, and by some chance we were almost the only people in the hotel. So the ordinary public rooms were practically empty, and we were the more surprised when, after dinner, our sitting-room door opened, and a young man put his head in. We were aware of this young man. He was rather a rabbity anaemic subject--light hair and light eyes--but not unpleasing. So when he said: 'I beg your pardon, is this a private room?' we did not growl and say: 'Yes, it is,' but Long said, or I did--no matter which: 'Please come in.' 'Oh, may I?' he said, and seemed relieved. Of course it was obvious that he wanted company; and as he was a reasonable kind of person--not the sort to bestow his whole family history on you--we urged him to make himself at home. 'I dare say you find the other rooms rather bleak,' I said. Yes, he did: but it was really too good of us, and so on. That being got over, he made some pretence of reading a book. Long was playing Patience, I was writing. It became plain to me after a few minutes that this visitor of ours was in rather a state of fidgets or nerves, which communicated itself to me, and so I put away my writing and turned to at engaging him in talk.

After some remarks, which I forget, he became rather confidential. 'You'll think it very odd of me' (this was the sort of way he began), 'but the fact is I've had something of a shock.' Well, I recommended a drink of some cheering kind, and we had it. The waiter coming in made an interruption (and I thought our young man seemed very jumpy when the door opened), but after a while he got back to his woes again. There was nobody he knew in the place, and he did happen to know who we both were (it turned out there was some common acquaintance in town), and really he did want a word of advice, if we didn't mind. Of course we both said: 'By all means,' or 'Not at all,' and Long put away his cards. And we settled down to hear what his difficulty was.

'It began,' he said, 'more than a week ago, when I bicycled over to Froston, only about five or six miles, to see the church; I'm very much interested in architecture, 'and it's got one of those pretty porches with niches and shields. I took a photograph of it, and then an old man who was tidying up in the churchyard came and asked if I'd care to look into the church. I said yes, and he produced a key and let me in. There wasn't much inside, but I told him it was a nice little church, and he kept it very clean, "But," I said, "the porch is the best part of it." We were just outside the porch then, and he said, "Ah, yes, that is a nice porch; and do you know, sir, what's the meanin' of that coat of arms there?"

'It was the one with the three crowns, and though. I'm not much of a herald, I was able to say yes, I thought it was the old arms of the kingdom of East Anglia.

"'That's right, sir," he said, "and do you know the meanin' of them three crowns that's on it?"

'I said I'd no doubt it was known, but I couldn't recollect to have heard it myself.

"'Well, then," he said, "for all you're a scholard, I can tell you something you don't know. Them's the three 'oly crowns what was buried in the ground near by the coast to keep the Germans from landing--ah, I can see you don't believe that. But I tell you, if it hadn't have been for one of them 'oly crowns bein' there still, them Germans would a landed here time and again, they would. Land-

ed with their ships, and killed man, woman and child in their beds. Now then, that's the truth what I'm telling you, that is; and if you don't believe me, you ast the rector. There he comes: you ast him, I says."

'I looked round, and there was the rector, a nice-looking old man, coming up the path; and before I could begin assuring my old man, who was getting quite excited, that I didn't disbelieve him, the rector struck in, and said:

"What's all this about, John? Good day to you, sir. Have you been looking at our little church?"'

'So then there was a little talk which allowed the old man to calm down, and then the rector asked him again what was the matter.

"'Oh," he said, "it warn't nothink, only I was telling this gentleman he'd ought to ast you about them 'oly crowns."

"'Ah, yes, to be sure," said the rector, "that's a very curious matter, isn't it? But I don't know whether the gentleman is interested in our old stories, eh?"

"'Oh, he'll be interested fast enough," says the old man, "he'll put his confidence in what you tells him, sir; why, you known William Ager yourself, father and son too."

'Then I put in a word to say how much I should like to hear all about it, and before many minutes I was walking up the village street with the rector, who had one or two words to say to parishioners, and then to the rectory, where he took me into his study. He had made out, on the way, that I really was capable of taking an intelligent interest in a piece of folklore, and not quite the ordinary

150

tripper. So he was very willing to talk, and it is rather surprising to me that the particular legend he told me has not made its way into print before. His account of it was this: "There has always been a belief in these parts in the three holy crowns. The old people say they were buried in different places near the coast to keep off the Danes or the French or the Germans. And they say that one of the three was dug up a long time ago, and another has disappeared by the encroaching of the sea, and one's still left doing its work, keeping off invaders. Well, now, if you have read the ordinary guides and histories of this county, you will remember perhaps that in 1687 a crown, which was said to be the crown of Redwald, King of the East Angles, was dug up at Rendlesham, and alas! alas! melted down before it was even properly described or drawn. Well, Rendlesham isn't on the coast, but it isn't so very far inland, and it's on a very important line of access. And I believe that is the crown which the people mean when they say that one has been dug up. Then on the south you don't want me to tell you where there was a Saxon royal palace which is now under the sea, eh? Well, there was the second crown, I take it. And up beyond these two, they say, lies the third."

'"Do they say where it is?" of course I asked.

'He said, "Yes, indeed, they do, but they don't tell," and his manner did not encourage me to put the obvious question. Instead of that I waited a moment, and said: "What did the old man mean when he said you knew William Ager, as if that had something to do with the crowns?"

'"To be sure," he said, "now that's another curious story. These Agers it's a very old name in these parts, but

I can't find that they were ever people of quality or big owners these Agers say, or said, that their branch of the family were the guardians of the last crown. A certain old Nathaniel Ager was the first one I knew--I was born and brought up quite near here--and he, I believe, camped out at the place during the whole of the war of 1870. William, his son, did the same, I know, during the South African War. And young William, his son, who has only died fairly recently, took lodgings at the cottage nearest the spot; and I've no doubt hastened his end, for he was a consumptive, by exposure and night watching. And he was the last of that branch. It was a dreadful grief to him to think that he was the last, but he could do nothing, the only relations at all near to him were in the colonies. I wrote letters for him to them imploring them to come over on business very important to the family, but there has been no answer. So the last of the holy crowns, if it's there, has no guardian now."

'That was what the rector told me, and you can fancy how interesting I found it. The only thing I could think of when I left him was how to hit upon the spot where the crown was supposed to be. I wish I'd left it alone.

'But there was a sort of fate in it, for as I bicycled back past the churchyard wall my eye caught a fairly new gravestone, and on it was the name of William Ager. Of course I got off and read it. It said "of this parish, died at Seaburgh, 19--, aged 28." There it was, you see. A little judicious questioning in the right place, and I should at least find the cottage nearest the spot. Only I didn't quite know what was the right place to begin my questioning at. Again there was fate: it took me to the curiosity-shop down that way--you know--and I turned over some old books, and, if you please, one was a prayer-book of 1740 odd, in a rather handsome binding--I'll just go and get it, it's in my room.'

He left us in a state of some surprise, but we had hardly time to exchange any remarks when he was back, panting, and handed us the book opened at the fly-leaf, on which was, in a straggly hand:

'Nathaniel Ager is my name and England is my nation,

Seaburgh is my dwelling-place and Christ is my Salvation,

When I am dead and in my Grave, and all my bones are rotton,

I hope the lord will think on me when I am quite forgotten.'

This poem was dated 1754, and there were many more entries of Agers, Nathaniel, Frederick, William, and so on, ending with William, 19--.

'You see,' he said, 'anybody would call it the greatest bit of luck. I did, but I don't now. Of course I asked the shopman about William Ager, and of course he happened to remember that he lodged in a cottage in the North Field and died there. This was just chalking the road for me. I knew which the cottage must be: there is only one sizable one about there. The next thing was to scrape some sort of acquaintance with the people, and I took a walk that way at once. A dog did the business for me: he made at me so fiercely that they had to run out and beat him off, and then naturally begged my pardon, and we got into talk. I had only to bring up Ager's name, and pretend I

knew, or thought I knew something of him, and then the woman said how sad it was him dying so young, and she was sure it came of him spending the night out of doors in the cold weather. Then I had to say: "Did he go out on the sea at night?" and she said: "Oh, no, it was on the hillock yonder with the trees on it." And there I was.

'I know something about digging in these barrows: I've opened many of them in the down country. But that was with owner's leave, and in broad daylight and with men to help. I had to prospect very carefully here before I put a spade in: I couldn't trench across the mound, and with those old firs growing there I knew there would be awkward tree loots. Still the soil was very light and sandy and easy, and there was a rabbit hole or so that might be developed into a sort of tunnel. The going out and coming back at odd hours to the hotel was going to be the awkward part. When I made up my mind about the way to excavate I told the people that I was called away for a night, and I spent it out there. I made my tunnel: I won't bore you with the details of how I supported it and filled it in when I'd done, but the main thing is that I got the crown.'

Naturally we both broke out into exclamations of surprise and interest. I for one had long known about the finding of the crown at Rendlesham and had often lamented its fate. No one has ever seen an Anglo-Saxon crown--at least no one had. But our man gazed at us with a rueful eye. 'Yes,' he said, 'and the worst of it is I don't know how to put it back.'

'Put it back?' we cried out. 'Why, my dear sir, you've made one of the most exciting finds ever heard of in this country. Of course it ought to go to the Jewel House at the Tower. What's your difficulty? If you're thinking about the owner of the land, and treasure-trove, and all that, we can certainly help you through. Nobody's going to make a fuss about technicalities in a case of this kind.'

Probably more was said, but all he did was to put his face in his hands, and mutter: 'I don't know how to put it back.'

At last Long said: 'You'll forgive me, I hope, if I seem impertinent, but are you quite sure you've got it?' I was wanting to ask much the same question myself, for of course the story did seem a lunatic's dream when one thought over it. But I hadn't quite dared to say what might hurt the poor young man's feelings. However, he took it quite calmly--really, with the calm of despair, you might say. He sat up and said: 'Oh, yes, there's no doubt of that: I have it here, in my loom, locked up in my bag. You can come and look at it if you like: I won't offer to bring it here.'

We were not likely to let the chance slip. We went with him; his room was only a few doors off. The boots was just collecting shoes in the passage: or so we thought: afterwards we were not sure. Our visitor--his name was Paxton--was in a worse state of shivers than before, and went hurriedly into the room, and beckoned us after him, turned on the light, and shut the door carefully. Then he unlocked his kit-bag, and produced a bundle of clean pocket-handkerchief in which something was wrapped, laid it on the bed, and undid it. I can now say I have seen an actual Anglo-Saxon crown. It was of silver--as the Rendlesham one is always said to have been--it was set with some gems, mostly antique intaglios and cameos, and was of rather plain, almost rough workmanship. In

fact, it was like those you see on the coins and in the man-uscripts. I found no reason to think it was later than the ninth century. I was intensely interested, of course, and I wanted to turn it over in my hands, but Paxton prevented me. 'Don't you touch it,' he said, 'I'll do that.' And with a sigh that was, I declare to you, dreadful to hear, he took it up and turned it about so that we could see every part of it. 'Seen enough?' he said at last, and we nodded. He wrapped it up and locked it in his bag, and stood looking at us dumbly. 'Come back to our room,' Long said, 'and tell us what the trouble is.' He thanked us, and said: 'Will you go first and see if--if the coast is clear?' That wasn't very intelligible, for our proceedings hadn't been, after all, very suspicious, and the hotel, as I said, was practical-ly empty. However, we were beginning to have inklings of--we didn't know what, and anyhow nerves are infec-tious. So we did go, first peering out as we opened the door, and fancying (I found we both had the fancy) that a shadow, or more than a shadow--but it made no sound--passed from before us to one side as we came out into the passage. 'It's all right,' we whispered to Paxton--whis-pering seemed the proper tone--and we went, with him between us, back to our sitting-room. I was preparing, when we got there, to be ecstatic about the unique inter-est of what we had seen, but when I looked at Paxton I saw that would be terribly out of place, and I left it to him to begin.

'What is to be done?' was his opening. Long thought it right (as he explained to me afterwards) to be obtuse, and said: 'Why not find out who the owner of the land is, and inform--' Oh, no, no!' Paxton broke in impatient-ly, 'I beg your pardon: you've been very kind, but don't you see it's got to go back, and I daren't be there at night, and daytime's impossible. Perhaps, though, you don't see:

well, then, the truth is that I've never been alone since I touched it.' I was beginning some fairly stupid comment, but Long caught my eye, and I stopped. Long said: 'I think I do see, perhaps: but wouldn't it be a relief--to tell us a little more clearly what the situation is?'

Then it all came out: Paxton looked over his shoulder and beckoned to us to come nearer to him, and began speaking in a low voice: we listened most intently, of course, and compared notes afterwards, and I wrote down our version, so I am confident I have what he told us almost word for word. He said: 'It began when I was first prospecting, and put me off again and again. There was always somebody--a man--standing by one of the firs. This was in daylight, you know. He was never in front of me. I always saw him with the tail of my eye on the left or the right, and he was never there when I looked straight for him. I would lie down for quite a long time and take careful observations, and make sure there was no one, and then when I got up and began prospecting again, there he was. And he began to give me hints, besides; for wherever I put that prayer-book--short of locking it up, which I did at last--when I came back to my room it was always out on my table open at the fly-leaf where the names are, and one of my razors across it to keep it open. I'm sure he just can't open my bag, or something more would have happened. You see, he's light and weak, but all the same I daren't face him. Well, then, when I was making the tunnel, of course it was worse, and if I hadn't been so keen I should have dropped the whole thing and run. It was like someone scraping at my back all the time: I thought for a long time it was only soil dropping on me, but as I got nearer the--the crown, it was unmistakable. And when I actually laid it bare and got my fingers into the ring of it and pulled it out, there came a sort of cry behind me--oh, I can't tell you how desolate it was! And horribly threatening too. It spoilt all my pleasure in my find--cut it off that moment. And if I hadn't been the wretched fool I am, I should have put the thing back and left it. But I didn't. The rest of the time was just awful. I had hours to get through before I could decently come back to the hotel. First I spent time filling up my tunnel and covering my tracks, and all the while he was there trying to thwart me. Sometimes, you know, you see him, and sometimes you don't, just as he pleases, I think: he's there, but he has some power over your eyes. Well, I wasn't off the spot very long before sunrise, and then I had to get to the junction for Seaburgh, and take a train back. And though it was daylight fairly soon, I don't know if that made it much better. There were always hedges, or gorse-bushes, or park fences along the road--some sort of cover, I mean--and I was never easy for a second. And then when I began to meet people going to work, they always looked behind me very strangely: it might have been that they were surprised at seeing anyone so early; but I didn't think it was only that, and I don't now: they didn't look exactly at me. And the porter at the train was like that too. And the guard held open the door after I'd got into the carriage--just as he would if there was somebody else coming, you know. Oh, you may be very sure it isn't my fancy,' he said with a dull sort of laugh. Then he went on: 'And even if I do get it put back, he won't forgive me: I can tell that. And I was so happy a fortnight ago.' He dropped into a chair, and I believe he began to cry.

We didn't know what to say, but we felt we must come to the rescue somehow, and so--it really seemed the only thing--we said if he was so set on putting the crown back in its place, we would help him. And I must say that after what we had heard it did seem the right thing. If these horrid consequences had come on this poor man, might there not really be something in the original idea of the crown having some curious power bound up with it, to guard the coast? At least, that was my feeling, and I think it was Long's too. Our offer was very welcome to Paxton, anyhow. When could we do it? It was nearing half-past ten. Could we contrive to make a late walk plausible to the hotel people that very night? We looked out of the window: there was a brilliant full moon--the Paschal moon. Long undertook to tackle the boots and propitiate him. He was to say that we should not be much over the hour, and if we did find it so pleasant that we stopped out a bit longer we would see that he didn't lose by sitting up. Well, we were pretty regular customers of the hotel, and did not give much trouble, and were considered by the servants to be not under the mark in the way of tips; and so the boots was propitiated, and let us out on to the sea-front, and remained, as we heard later, looking after us. Paxton had a large coat over his arm, under which was the wrapped-up crown.

So we were off on this strange errand before we had time to think how very much out of the way it was. I have told this part quite shortly on purpose, for it really does represent the haste with which we settled our plan and took action. 'The shortest way is up the hill and through the churchyard,' Paxton said, as we stood a moment before, the hotel looking up and down the front. There was nobody about--nobody at all. Seaburgh out of the season is an early, quiet place. 'We can't go along the dyke by the cottage, because of the dog,' Paxton also said, when I pointed to what I thought a shorter way along the front and across two fields. The reason he gave was good enough. We went up the road to the church, and turned

in at the churchyard gate. I confess to having thought that there might be some lying there who might be conscious of our business: but if it was so, they were also conscious that one who was on their side, so to say, had us under surveillance, and we saw no sign of them. But under observation we felt we were, as I have never felt it at another time. Specially was it so when we passed out of the churchyard into a narrow path with close high hedges, through which we hurried as Christian did through that Valley; and so got out into open fields. Then along hedges, though I would sooner have been in the open, where I could see if anyone was visible behind me; over a gate or two, and then a swerve to the left, taking us up on to the ridge which ended in that mound.

As we neared it, Henry Long felt, and I felt too, that there were what I can only call dim presences waiting for us, as well as a far more actual one attending us. Of Paxton's agitation all this time I can give you no adequate picture: he breathed like a hunted beast, and we could not either of us look at his face. How he would manage when we got to the very place we had not troubled to think: he had seemed so sure that that would not be difficult. Nor was it. I never saw anything like the dash with which he flung himself at a particular spot in the side of the mound, and tore at it, so that in a very few minutes the greater part of his body was out of sight. We stood holding the coat and that bundle of handkerchief, and looking, very fearfully, I must admit, about us. There was nothing to be seen: a line of dark firs behind us made one skyline, more trees and the church tower half a mile off on the right, cottages and a windmill on the horizon on the left, calm sea dead in front, faint barking of a dog at a cottage on a gleaming dyke between us and it: full moon making that path we know across the sea: the eternal whisper of the Scotch firs just above us, and of the sea in front. Yet, in all this quiet, an acute, an acrid consciousness of a restrained hostility very near us, like a dog on a leash that might be let go at any moment.

Paxton pulled himself out of the hole, and stretched a hand back to us. 'Give it to me,' he whispered, 'unwrapped.' We pulled off the handkerchiefs, and he took the crown. The moonlight just fell on it as he snatched it. We had not ourselves touched that bit of metal, and I have thought since that it was just as well. In another moment Paxton was out of the hole again and busy shovelling back the soil with hands that were already bleeding He would have none of our help though It was much the longest part of the job to get the place to look undisturbed yet--I don't know how--he made a wonderful success of it. At last he was satisfied and we turned back.

We were a couple of hundred yards from the hill when Long suddenly said to him: 'I say you've left your coat there. That won't do See?' And I certainly did see it--the long dark overcoat lying where the tunnel had been. Paxton had not stopped, however: he only shook his head, and held up the coat on his arm. And when we joined him, he said, without any excitement, but as if nothing mattered any more: 'That wasn't my coat.' And, indeed, when we looked back again, that dark thing was not to be seen.

Well, we got out on to the road, and came rapidly back that way. It was well before twelve when we got in, trying to put a good face on it, and saying--Long and I--what a lovely night it was for a walk. The boots was on the look-out for us, and we made remarks like that for his edification as we entered the hotel. He gave another look up and

down the sea-front before he locked the front door, and said: 'You didn't meet many people about, I s'pose, sir?' 'No, indeed, not a soul,' I said; at which I remember Paxton looked oddly at me. 'Only I thought I see someone turn up the station road after you gentlemen,' said the boots. 'Still, you was three together, and I don't suppose he meant mischief.' I didn't know what to say; Long merely said 'Good night,' and we went off upstairs, promising to turn put all lights, and to go to bed in a few minutes.

Back in our room, we did our very best to make Paxton take a cheerful view. 'There's the crown safe back,' we said; 'very likely you'd have done better not to touch it' (and he heavily assented to that), 'but no real harm has been done, and we shall never give this away to anyone who would be so mad as to go near it. Besides, don't you feel better yourself? I don't mind confessing,' I said, 'that on the way there I was very much inclined to take your view about--well, about being followed; but going back, it wasn't at all the same thing, was it?' No, it wouldn't do: 'You've nothing to trouble yourselves about,' he said, 'but I'm not forgiven. I've got to pay for that miserable sacrilege still. I know what you are going to say. The Church might help. Yes, but it's the body that has to suffer. It's true I'm not feeling that he's waiting outside for me just now. But-' Then he stopped. Then he turned to thanking us, and we put him off as soon as we could. And naturally we pressed him to use our sitting-room next day, and said we should be glad to go out with him. Or did he play golf, perhaps? Yes, he did, but he didn't think he should care about that tomorrow. Well, we recommended him to get up late and sit in our room in the morning while we were playing, and we would have a walk later in the day. He was very submissive and piano about it all: ready to do just what we thought best, but clearly quite certain in his own mind that what was coming could not be averted or palliated. You'll wonder why we didn't insist on accompanying him to his home and seeing him safe into the care of brothers or someone. The fact was he had nobody. He had had a flat in town, but lately he had made up his mind to settle for a time in Sweden, and he had dismantled his flat and shipped off his belongings, and was whiling away a fortnight or three weeks before he made a start. Anyhow, we didn't see what we could do better than sleep on it--or not sleep very much, as was my case and see what we felt like tomorrow morning.

We felt very different, Long and I, on as beautiful an April morning as you could desire; and Paxton also looked very different when we saw him at breakfast. 'The first approach to a decent night I seem ever to have had,' was what he said. But he was going to do as we had settled: stay in probably all the morning, and come out with us later. We went to the links; we met some other men and played with them in the morning, and had lunch there rather early, so as not to be late back. All the same, the snares of death overtook him.

Whether it could have been prevented, I don't know. I think he would have been got at somehow, do what we might. Anyhow, this is what happened.

We went straight up to our room. Paxton was there, reading quite peaceably. 'Ready to come out shortly?' said Long, 'say in half an hour's time?' 'Certainly,' he said: and I said we would change first, and perhaps have baths, and call for him in half an hour. I had my bath first, and went and lay down on my bed, and slept for about ten minutes. We came out of our rooms at the same time, and went together to the sitting-room. Paxton wasn't there--only

his book. Nor was he in his room, nor in the downstair rooms. We shouted for him. A servant came out and said: 'Why, I thought you gentlemen was gone out already, and so did the other gentleman. He heard you a-calling from the path there, and run out in a hurry, and I looked out of the coffee-room window, but I didn't see you. 'Owever, he run off down the beach that way.'

Without a word we ran that way too--it was the opposite direction to that of last night's expedition. It wasn't quite four o'clock, and the day was fair, though not so fair as it had been, so that was really no reason, you'd say, for anxiety: with people about, surely a man couldn't come to much harm.

But something in our look as we ran out must have struck the servant, for she came out on the steps, and pointed, and said, 'Yes, that's the way he went.' We ran on as far as the top of the shingle bank, and there pulled up. There was a choice of ways: past the houses on the sea-front, or along the sand at the bottom of the beach, which, the tide being now out, was fairly broad. Or of course we might keep along the shingle between these two tracks and have some view of both of them; only that was heavy going. We chose the sand, for that was the loneliest, and someone might come to harm there without being seen from the public path.

Long said he saw Paxton some distance ahead, running and waving his stick, as if he wanted to signal to people who were on ahead of him. I couldn't be sure: one of these sea-mists was coming up very quickly from the south. There was someone, that's all I could say. And there were tracks on the sand as of someone running who wore shoes; and there were other tracks made before those--

for the shoes sometimes trod in them and interfered with them--of someone not in shoes. Oh, of course, it's only my word you've got to take for all this: Long's dead, we'd no time or means to make sketches or take casts, and the next tide washed everything away. All we could do was to notice these marks as we hurried on. But there they were over and over again, and we had no doubt whatever that what we saw was the track of a bare foot, and one that showed more bones than flesh.

The notion of Paxton running after--after anything like this, and supposing it to be the friends he was looking for, was very dreadful to us. You can guess what we fancied: how the thing he was following might stop suddenly and turn round on him, and what sort of face it would show, half-seen at first in the mist--which all the while was getting thicker and thicker. And as I ran on wondering how the poor wretch could have been lured into mistaking that other thing for us, I remembered his saying, 'He has some power over your eyes.' And then I wondered what the end would be, for I had no hope now that the end could be averted, and--well, there is no need to tell all the dismal and horrid thoughts that flitted through my head as we ran on into the mist. It was uncanny, too, that the sun should still be bright in the sky and we could see nothing. We could only tell that we were now past the houses and had reached that gap there is between them and the old martello tower. When you are past the tower, you know, there is nothing but shingle for a long way-- not a house, not a human creature; just that spit of land, or rather shingle, with the river on your right and the sea on your left.

But just before that, just by the martello tower, you re- member there is the old battery, close to the sea. I believe

there are only a few blocks of concrete left now: the rest has all been washed away, but at this time there was a lot more, though the place was a ruin. Well, when we got there, we clambered to the top as quick as we could to take breath and look over the shingle in front if by chance the mist would let us see anything. But a moment's rest we must have. We had run a mile at least. Nothing whatever was visible ahead of us, and we were just turning by common consent to get down and run hopelessly on, when we heard what I can only call a laugh: and if you can understand what I mean by a breathless, a lungless laugh, you have it: but I don't suppose you can. It came from below, and swerved away into the mist. That was enough. We bent over the wall. Paxton was there at the bottom.

You don't need to be told that he was dead. His tracks showed that he had run along the side of the battery, had turned sharp round the corner of it, and, small doubt of it, must have dashed straight into the open arms of someone who was waiting there. His mouth was full of sand and stones, and his teeth and jaws were broken to bits. I only glanced once at his face.

At the same moment, just as we were scrambling down from the battery to get to the body, we heard a shout, and saw a man running down the bank of the martello tower. He was the caretaker stationed there, and his keen old eyes had managed to descry through the mist that something was wrong. He had seen Paxton fall, and had seen us a moment after, running up--fortunate this, for otherwise we could hardly have escaped suspicion of being concerned in the dreadful business. Had he, we asked, caught sight of anybody attacking our friend? He could not be sure.

We sent him off for help, and stayed by the dead man till they came with the stretcher. It was then that we traced out how he had come, on the narrow fringe of sand under the battery wall. The rest was shingle, and it was hopelessly impossible to tell whither the other had gone.

What were we to say at the inquest? It was a duty, we felt, not to give up, there and then, the secret of the crown, to be published in every paper. I don't know how much you would have told; but what we did agree upon was this: to say that we had only made acquaintance with Paxton the day before, and that he had told us he was under some apprehension of danger at the hands of a man called William Ager. Also that we had seen some other tracks besides Paxton's when we followed him along the beach. But of course by that time everything was gone from the sands.

No one had any knowledge, fortunately, of any William Ager living in the district. The evidence of the man at the martello tower freed us from all suspicion. All that could be done was to return a verdict of wilful murder by some person or persons unknown.

Paxton was so totally without connections that all the inquiries that were subsequently made ended in a No Thoroughfare. And I have never been at Seaburgh, or even near it, since.

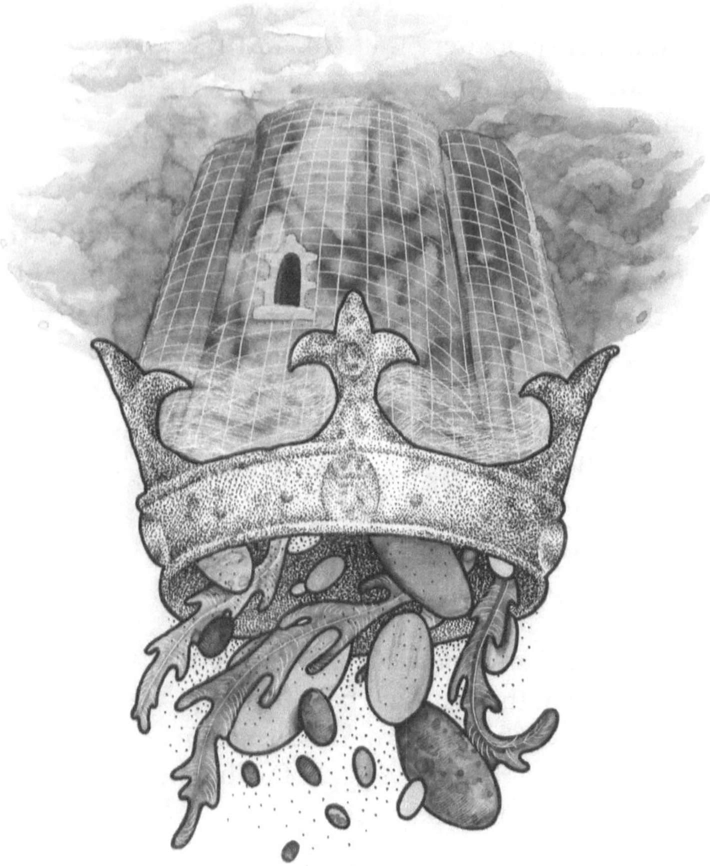

'I don't know how to put it back.'

Cool Air

by H. P. Lovecraft

You ask me to explain why I am afraid of a draught of cool air; why I shiver more than others upon entering a cold room, and seem nauseated and repelled when the chill of evening creeps through the heat of a mild autumn day. There are those who say I respond to cold as others do to a bad odour, and I am the last to deny the impression. What I will do is to relate the most horrible circumstance I ever encountered, and leave it to you to judge whether or not this forms a suitable explanation of my peculiarity.

It is a mistake to fancy that horror is associated inextricably with darkness, silence, and solitude. I found it in the glare of mid-afternoon, in the clangour of a metropolis, and in the teeming midst of a shabby and commonplace rooming-house with a prosaic landlady and two stalwart men by my side. In the spring of 1923 I had secured some dreary and unprofitable magazine work in the city of New York; and being unable to pay any substantial rent, began drifting from one cheap boarding establishment to another in search of a room which might combine the qualities of decent cleanliness, endurable furnishings, and very reasonable price. It soon developed that I had only a choice between different evils, but after a time I came upon a house in West Fourteenth Street which disgusted me much less than the others I had sampled.

The place was a four-story mansion of brownstone, dating apparently from the late forties, and fitted with woodwork and marble whose stained and sullied splendour argued a descent from high levels of tasteful opulence. In the rooms, large and lofty, and decorated with impossible paper and ridiculously ornate stucco cornices, there lingered a depressing mustiness and hint of obscure cookery; but the floors were clean, the linen tolerably regular, and the hot water not too often cold or turned off, so that I came to regard it as at least a bearable place to hibernate till one might really live again. The landlady, a slatternly, almost bearded Spanish woman named Herrero, did not annoy me with gossip or with criticisms of the late-burning electric light in my third-floor front hall room; and my fellow-lodgers were as quiet and uncommunicative as one might desire, being mostly Spaniards a little above the coarsest and crudest grade. Only the din of street cars in the thoroughfare below proved a serious annoyance.

I had been there about three weeks when the first odd incident occurred. One evening at about eight I heard a spattering on the floor and became suddenly aware that I had been smelling the pungent odour of ammonia for some time. Looking about, I saw that the ceiling was wet and dripping; the soaking apparently proceeding from a corner on the side toward the street. Anxious to stop the matter at its source, I hastened to the basement to tell the landlady; and was assured by her that the trouble would quickly be set right.

"Doctair Muñoz," she cried as she rushed upstairs ahead of me, "he have speel hees chemicals. He ees too seeck for doctair heemself—seecker and seecker all the time—but he weel not have no othair for help. He ees vairy queer in hees seeckness—all day he take funnee-smelling baths, and he cannot get excite or warm. All hees own housework he do—hees leetle room are full of bottles and machines, and he do not work as doctair. But he was great once—my fathair in Barcelona have hear of heem—and only joost now he feex a arm of the plumber that get hurt of sudden. He nevair go out, only on roof, and my boy Esteban he breeng heem hees food and laundry and mediceens and chemicals. My Gawd, the sal-ammoniac that man use for keep heem cool!"

Mrs. Herrero disappeared up the staircase to the fourth floor, and I returned to my room. The ammonia ceased to drip, and as I cleaned up what had spilled and opened the window for air, I heard the landlady's heavy footsteps above me. Dr. Muñoz I had never heard, save for certain sounds as of some gasoline-driven mechanism; since his step was soft and gentle. I wondered for a moment what the strange affliction of this man might be, and whether his obstinate refusal of outside aid were not the result of a rather baseless eccentricity. There is, I reflected tritely, an infinite deal of pathos in the state of an eminent person who has come down in the world.

I might never have known Dr. Muñoz had it not been for the heart attack that suddenly seized me one forenoon as I sat writing in my room. Physicians had told me of the danger of those spells, and I knew there was no time to be lost; so remembering what the landlady had said about the invalid's help of the injured workman, I dragged myself upstairs and knocked feebly at the door above mine. My knock was answered in good English by a curious voice some distance to the right, asking my name and business; and these things being stated, there came an opening of the door next to the one I had sought.

A rush of cool air greeted me; and though the day was one of the hottest of late June, I shivered as I crossed the threshold into a large apartment whose rich and tasteful decoration surprised me in this nest of squalor and seediness. A folding couch now filled its diurnal role of sofa, and the mahogany furniture, sumptuous hangings, old paintings, and mellow bookshelves all bespoke a gentleman's study rather than a boarding-house bedroom. I now saw that the hall room above mine—the "leetle room" of bottles and machines which Mrs. Herrero had mentioned—was merely the laboratory of the doctor; and that his main living quarters lay in the spacious adjoining room whose convenient alcoves and large contiguous bathroom permitted him to hide all dressers and obtrusive utilitarian devices. Dr. Muñoz, most certainly, was a man of birth, cultivation, and discrimination.

The figure before me was short but exquisitely proportioned, and clad in somewhat formal dress of perfect cut and fit. A high-bred face of masterful though not arrogant expression was adorned by a short iron-grey full beard, and an old-fashioned pince-nez shielded the full, dark eyes and surmounted an aquiline nose which gave a Moorish touch to a physiognomy otherwise dominantly Celtiberian. Thick, well-trimmed hair that argued the punctual calls of a barber was parted gracefully above a high forehead; and the whole picture was one of striking intelligence and superior blood and breeding.

Nevertheless, as I saw Dr. Muñoz in that blast of cool air, I felt a repugnance which nothing in his aspect could justify. Only his lividly inclined complexion and coldness of touch could have afforded a physical basis

for this feeling, and even these things should have been excusable considering the man's known invalidism. It might, too, have been the singular cold that alienated me; for such chilliness was abnormal on so hot a day, and the abnormal always excites aversion, distrust, and fear.

But repugnance was soon forgotten in admiration, for the strange physician's extreme skill at once became manifest despite the ice-coldness and shakiness of his bloodless-looking hands. He clearly understood my needs at a glance, and ministered to them with a master's deftness; the while reassuring me in a finely modulated though oddly hollow and timbreless voice that he was the bitterest of sworn enemies to death, and had sunk his fortune and lost all his friends in a lifetime of bizarre experiment devoted to its bafflement and extirpation. Something of the benevolent fanatic seemed to reside in him, and he rambled on almost garrulously as he sounded my chest and mixed a suitable draught of drugs fetched from the smaller laboratory room. Evidently he found the society of a well-born man a rare novelty in this dingy environment, and was moved to unaccustomed speech as memories of better days surged over him.

His voice, if queer, was at least soothing; and I could not even perceive that he breathed as the fluent sentences rolled urbanely out. He sought to distract my mind from my own seizure by speaking of his theories and experiments; and I remember his tactfully consoling me about my weak heart by insisting that will and consciousness are stronger than organic life itself, so that if a bodily frame be but originally healthy and carefully preserved, it may through a scientific enhancement of these qualities retain a kind of nervous animation despite the most serious impairments, defects, or even absences in the battery of specific organs. He might, he half jestingly said, some day teach me to live—or at least to possess some kind of conscious existence—without any heart at all! For his part, he was afflicted with a complication of maladies requiring a very exact regimen which included constant cold. Any marked rise in temperature might, if prolonged, affect him fatally; and the frigidity of his habitation—some 55 or 56 degrees Fahrenheit—was maintained by an absorption system of ammonia cooling, the gasoline engine of whose pumps I had often heard in my own room below.

Relieved of my seizure in a marvellously short while, I left the shivery place a disciple and devotee of the gifted recluse. After that I paid him frequent overcoated calls; listening while he told of secret researches and almost ghastly results, and trembling a bit when I examined the unconventional and astonishingly ancient volumes on his shelves. I was eventually, I may add, almost cured of my disease for all time by his skilful ministrations. It seems that he did not scorn the incantations of the mediaevalists, since he believed these cryptic formulae to contain rare psychological stimuli which might conceivably have singular effects on the substance of a nervous system from which organic pulsations had fled. I was touched by his account of the aged Dr. Torres of Valencia, who had shared his earlier experiments with him through the great illness of eighteen years before, whence his present disorders proceeded. No sooner had the venerable practitioner saved his colleague than he himself succumbed to the grim enemy he had fought. Perhaps the strain had been too great; for Dr. Muñoz made it whisperingly clear—though not in detail—that the methods of healing had been most extraordinary, involving scenes and processes not welcomed by elderly

and conservative Galens.

As the weeks passed, I observed with regret that my new friend was indeed slowly but unmistakably losing ground physically, as Mrs. Herrero had suggested. The livid aspect of his countenance was intensified, his voice became more hollow and indistinct, his muscular motions were less perfectly coördinated, and his mind and will displayed less resilience and initiative. Of this sad change he seemed by no means unaware, and little by little his expression and conversation both took on a gruesome irony which restored in me something of the subtle repulsion I had originally felt.

He developed strange caprices, acquiring a fondness for exotic spices and Egyptian incense till his room smelled like the vault of a sepulchred Pharaoh in the Valley of Kings. At the same time his demands for cold air increased, and with my aid he amplified the ammonia piping of his room and modified the pumps and feed of his refrigerating machine till he could keep the temperature as low as 34° or 40° and finally even 28°; the bathroom and laboratory, of course, being less chilled, in order that water might not freeze, and that chemical processes might not be impeded. The tenant adjoining him complained of the icy air from around the connecting door, so I helped him fit heavy hangings to obviate the difficulty. A kind of growing horror, of outré and morbid cast, seemed to possess him. He talked of death incessantly, but laughed hollowly when such things as burial or funeral arrangements were gently suggested.

All in all, he became a disconcerting and even gruesome companion; yet in my gratitude for his healing I could not well abandon him to the strangers around him, and was careful to dust his room and attend to his needs each day, muffled in a heavy ulster which I bought especially for the purpose. I likewise did much of his shopping, and gasped in bafflement at some of the chemicals he ordered from druggists and laboratory supply houses.

An increasing and unexplained atmosphere of panic seemed to rise around his apartment. The whole house, as I have said, had a musty odour; but the smell in his room was worse—and in spite of all the spices and incense, and the pungent chemicals of the now incessant baths which he insisted on taking unaided. I perceived that it must be connected with his ailment, and shuddered when I reflected on what that ailment might be. Mrs. Herrero crossed herself when she looked at him, and gave him up unreservedly to me; not even letting her son Esteban continue to run errands for him. When I suggested other physicians, the sufferer would fly into as much of a rage as he seemed to dare to entertain. He evidently feared the physical effect of violent emotion, yet his will and driving force waxed rather than waned, and he refused to be confined to his bed. The lassitude of his earlier ill days gave place to a return of his fiery purpose, so that he seemed about to hurl defiance at the death-daemon even as that ancient enemy seized him. The pretence of eating, always curiously like a formality with him, he virtually abandoned; and mental power alone appeared to keep him from total collapse.

He acquired a habit of writing long documents of some sort, which he carefully sealed and filled with injunctions that I transmit them after his death to certain persons whom he named—for the most part lettered East Indians, but including a once celebrated French physician now generally thought dead, and about whom the most inconceivable things had been whispered. As it happened, I burned all these papers undelivered and unopened. His aspect and voice became utterly frightful, and his presence almost unbearable. One September day an unexpected glimpse of him induced an epileptic fit in a man who had come to repair his electric desk lamp; a fit for which he prescribed effectively whilst keeping himself well out of sight. That man, oddly enough, had been through the terrors of the Great War without having incurred any fright so thorough.

Then, in the middle of October, the horror of horrors came with stupefying suddenness. One night about eleven the pump of the refrigerating machine broke down, so that within three hours the process of ammonia cooling became impossible. Dr. Muñoz summoned me by thumping on the floor, and I worked desperately to repair the injury while my host cursed in a tone whose lifeless, rattling hollowness surpassed description. My amateur efforts, however, proved of no use; and when I had brought in a mechanic from a neighbouring all-night garage we learned that nothing could be done till morning, when a new piston would have to be obtained. The moribund hermit's rage and fear, swelling to grotesque proportions, seemed likely to shatter what remained of his failing physique; and once a spasm caused him to clap his hands to his eyes and rush into the bathroom. He groped his way out with face tightly bandaged, and I never saw his eyes again.

The frigidity of the apartment was now sensibly diminishing, and at about 5 a.m. the doctor retired to the bathroom, commanding me to keep him supplied with all the ice I could obtain at all-night drug stores and cafeterias. As I would return from my sometimes discouraging trips and lay my spoils before the closed bathroom door, I could hear a restless splashing within, and a thick voice croaking out the order for "More— more!" At length a warm day broke, and the shops opened one by one. I asked Esteban either to help with the ice-fetching whilst I obtained the pump piston, or to order the piston while I continued with the ice; but instructed by his mother, he absolutely refused.

Finally I hired a seedy-looking loafer whom I encountered on the corner of Eighth Avenue to keep the patient supplied with ice from a little shop where I introduced him, and applied myself diligently to the task of finding a pump piston and engaging workmen competent to install it. The task seemed interminable, and I raged almost as violently as the hermit when I saw the hours slipping by in a breathless, foodless round of vain telephoning, and a hectic quest from place to place, hither and thither by subway and surface car. About noon I encountered a suitable supply house far downtown, and at approximately 1:30 p.m. arrived at my boarding-place with the necessary paraphernalia and two sturdy and intelligent mechanics. I had done all I could, and hoped I was in time.

Black terror, however, had preceded me. The house was in utter turmoil, and above the chatter of awed voices I heard a man praying in a deep basso. Fiendish things were in the air, and lodgers told over the beads of their rosaries as they caught the odour from beneath the doctor's closed door. The lounger I had hired, it seems, had fled screaming and mad-eyed not long after his second delivery of ice; perhaps as a result of excessive curiosity. He could not, of course, have locked the door

behind him; yet it was now fastened, presumably from the inside. There was no sound within save a nameless sort of slow, thick dripping.

Briefly consulting with Mrs. Herrero and the workmen despite a fear that gnawed my inmost soul, I advised the breaking down of the door; but the landlady found a way to turn the key from the outside with some wire device. We had previously opened the doors of all the other rooms on that hall, and flung all the windows to the very top. Now, noses protected by handkerchiefs, we tremblingly invaded the accursed south room which blazed with the warm sun of early afternoon.

A kind of dark, slimy trail led from the open bathroom door to the hall door, and thence to the desk, where a terrible little pool had accumulated. Something was scrawled there in pencil in an awful, blind hand on a piece of paper hideously smeared as though by the very claws that traced the hurried last words. Then the trail led to the couch and ended unutterably.

What was, or had been, on the couch I cannot and dare not say here. But this is what I shiveringly puzzled out on the stickily smeared paper before I drew a match and burned it to a crisp; what I puzzled out in terror as the landlady and two mechanics rushed frantically from that hellish place to babble their incoherent stories at the nearest police station. The nauseous words seemed well-nigh incredible in that yellow sunlight, with the clatter of cars and motor trucks ascending clamorously from crowded Fourteenth Street, yet I confess that I believed them then. Whether I believe them now I honestly do not know. There are things about which it is better not to speculate, and all that I can say is that I hate the smell of ammonia, and grow faint at a draught of unusually cool air.

"The end," ran that noisome scrawl, "is here. No more ice—the man looked and ran away. Warmer every minute, and the tissues can't last. I fancy you know—what I said about the will and the nerves and the preserved body after the organs ceased to work. It was good theory, but couldn't keep up indefinitely. There was a gradual deterioration I had not foreseen. Dr. Torres knew, but the shock killed him. He couldn't stand what he had to do— he had to get me in a strange, dark place when he minded my letter and nursed me back. And the organs never would work again. It had to be done my way—artificial preservation—for you see I died that time eighteen years ago."

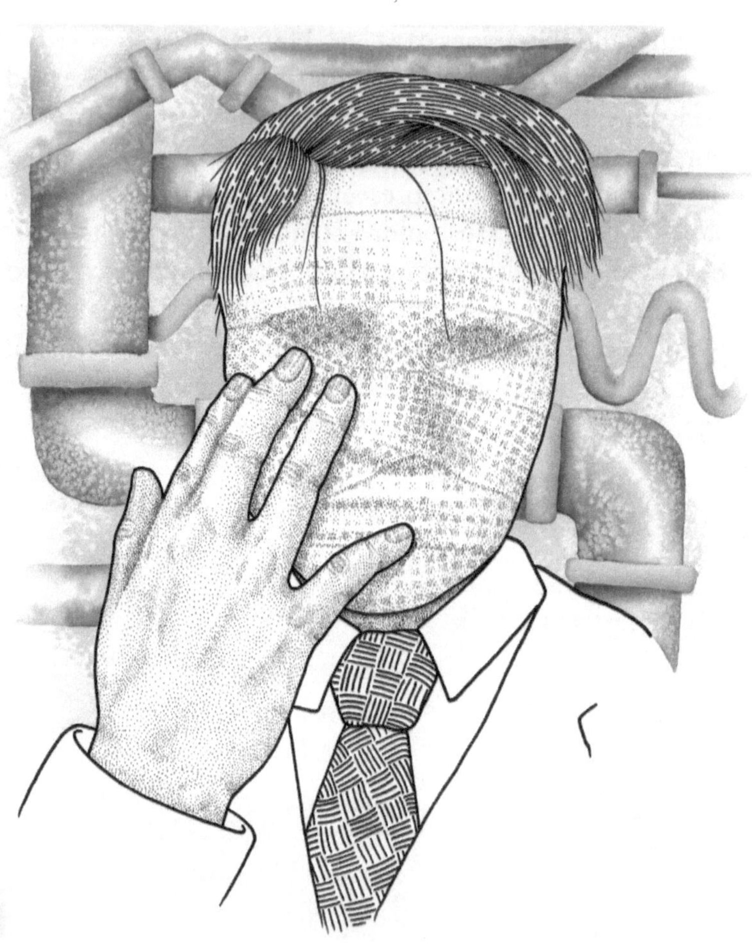

'I died that time eighteen years ago.'

Cool Air

The Rose Garden

by M. R. James

Mr. and Mrs. Anstruther were at breakfast in the parlour of Westfield Hall, in the county of Essex. They were arranging plans for the day.

'George,' said Mrs. Anstruther, 'I think you had better take the car to Maldon and see if you can get any of those knitted things I was speaking about which would do for my stall at the bazaar.'

'Oh well, if you wish it, Mary, of course I can do that, but I had half arranged to play a round with Geoffrey Williamson this morning. The bazaar isn't till Thursday of next week, is it?'

'What has that to do with it, George? I should have thought you would have guessed that if I can't get the things I want in Maldon I shall have to write to all manner of shops in town: and they are certain to send something quite unsuitable in price or quality the first time. If you have actually made an appointment with Mr. Williamson, you had better keep it, but I must say I think you might have let me know.'

'Oh no, no, it wasn't really an appointment. I quite see what you mean. I'll go. And what shall you do yourself?'

'Why, when the work of the house is arranged for, I must see about laying out my new rose garden. By the way, before you start for Maldon I wish you would just take Collins to look at the place I fixed upon. You know it, of course.'

'Well, I'm not quite sure that I do, Mary. Is it at the upper end, towards the village?'

'Good gracious no, my dear George; I thought I had made that quite clear. No, it's that small clearing just off the shrubbery path that goes towards the church.'

'Oh yes, where we were saying there must have been a summer-house once: the place with the old seat and the posts. But do you think there's enough sun there?'

'My dear George, do allow me some common sense, and don't credit me with all your ideas about summer-houses. Yes, there will be plenty of sun when we have got rid of some of those box-bushes. I know what you are going to say, and I have as little wish as you to strip the place bare. All I want Collins to do is to clear away the old seats and the posts and things before I come out in an hour's time. And I hope you will manage to get off fairly soon. After luncheon I think I shall go on with my sketch of the church; and if you please you can go over to the links, or—'

'Ah, a good idea—very good! Yes, you finish that sketch, Mary, and I should be glad of a round.'

'I was going to say, you might call on the Bishop; but I suppose it is no use my making any suggestion. And now do be getting ready, or half the morning will be gone.'

Mr. Anstruther's face, which had shown symptoms of lengthening, shortened itself again, and he hurried from the room, and was soon heard giving orders in the passage. Mrs. Anstruther, a stately dame of some fifty summers, proceeded, after a second consideration of the morning's letters, to her housekeeping.

Within a few minutes Mr. Anstruther had discovered Collins in the greenhouse, and they were on their way to the site of the projected rose garden. I do not know much about the conditions most suitable to these nurseries, but I am inclined to believe that Mrs. Anstruther, though in the habit of describing herself as 'a great gardener', had not been well advised in the selection of a spot for the purpose. It was a small, dank clearing, bounded on one side by a path, and on the other by thick box-bushes, laurels, and other evergreens. The ground was almost bare of grass and dark of aspect. Remains of rustic seats and an old and corrugated oak post somewhere near the middle of the clearing had given rise to Mr. Anstruther's conjecture that a summer-house had once stood there.

Clearly Collins had not been put in possession of his mistress's intentions with regard to this plot of ground: and when he learnt them from Mr. Anstruther he displayed no enthusiasm.

'Of course I could clear them seats away soon enough,' he said. 'They aren't no ornament to the place, Mr. Anstruther, and rotten too. Look 'ere, sir,'—and he broke off a large piece—'rotten right through. Yes, clear them away, to be sure we can do that.'

'And the post,' said Mr. Anstruther, 'that's got to go too.'

Collins advanced, and shook the post with both hands: then he rubbed his chin.

'That's firm in the ground, that post is,' he said. 'That's been there a number of years, Mr. Anstruther. I doubt I shan't get that up not quite so soon as what I can do with them seats.'

'But your mistress specially wishes it to be got out of the way in an hour's time,' said Mr. Anstruther.

Collins smiled and shook his head slowly. 'You'll excuse me, sir, but you feel of it for yourself. No, sir, no one can't do what's impossible to 'em, can they, sir? I could git that post up by after tea-time, sir, but that'll want a lot of digging. What you require, you see, sir, if you'll excuse me naming of it, you want the soil loosening round this post 'ere, and me and the boy we shall take a little time doing of that. But now, these 'ere seats,' said Collins, appearing to appropriate this portion of the scheme as due to his own resourcefulness, 'why, I can get the barrer round and 'ave them cleared away in, why less than an hour's time from now, if you'll permit of it. Only—'

'Only what, Collins?'

'Well now, ain't for me to go against orders no more than what it is for you yourself—or anyone else' (this was added somewhat hurriedly), 'but if you'll pardon me, sir, this ain't the place I should have picked out for no rose garden myself. Why look at them box and laurestinus, 'ow they reg'lar preclude the light from—'

'Ah yes, but we've got to get rid of some of them, of course.'

'Oh, indeed, get rid of them! Yes, to be sure, but—I beg your pardon, Mr. Anstruther—'

'I'm sorry, Collins, but I must be getting on now. I hear the car at the door. Your mistress will explain exactly what she wishes. I'll tell her, then, that you can see your way to clearing away the seats at once, and the post this afternoon. Good morning.'

Collins was left rubbing his chin. Mrs. Anstruther received the report with some discontent, but did not insist upon any change of plan.

By four o'clock that afternoon she had dismissed her husband to his golf, had dealt faithfully with Collins and with the other duties of the day, and, having sent a campstool and umbrella to the proper spot, had just settled down to her sketch of the church as seen from the shrubbery, when a maid came hurrying down the path to report that Miss Wilkins had called.

Miss Wilkins was one of the few remaining members of the family from whom the Anstruthers had bought the Westfield estate some few years back. She had been staying in the neighbourhood, and this was probably a farewell visit. 'Perhaps you could ask Miss Wilkins to join me here,' said Mrs. Anstruther, and soon Miss Wilkins, a person of mature years, approached.

'Yes, I'm leaving the Ashes tomorrow, and I shall be able to tell my brother how tremendously you have improved the place. Of course he can't help regretting the old house just a little—as I do myself—but the garden is really delightful now.'

'I am so glad you can say so. But you mustn't think we've finished our improvements. Let me show you where I mean to put a rose garden. It's close by here.'

The details of the project were laid before Miss Wilkins at some length; but her thoughts were evidently elsewhere.

'Yes, delightful,' she said at last rather absently. 'But do you know, Mrs. Anstruther, I'm afraid I was thinking of old times. I'm very glad to have seen just this spot again before you altered it. Frank and I had quite a romance about this place.'

'Yes?' said Mrs. Anstruther smilingly; 'do tell me what it was. Something quaint and charming, I'm sure.'

'Not so very charming, but it has always seemed to me curious. Neither of us would ever be here alone when we were children, and I'm not sure that I should care about it now in certain moods. It is one of those things that can hardly be put into words—by me at least— and that sound rather foolish if they are not properly expressed. I can tell you after a fashion what it was that gave us —well, almost a horror of the place when we were alone. It was towards the evening of one very hot autumn day, when Frank had disappeared mysteriously about the grounds, and I was looking for him to fetch him to tea, and going down this path I suddenly saw him, not hiding in the bushes, as I rather expected, but sitting on the bench in the old summer-house—there was a wooden summer-house here, you know—up in the corner, asleep, but with such a dreadful look on his face that I really thought he must be ill or even dead. I rushed at him and shook him, and told him to wake up; and wake up he did, with a scream. I assure you the poor boy seemed almost beside himself with fright. He hurried me away to the house, and was in a terrible state all that night, hardly sleeping. Someone had to sit up with him, as far as I remember. He was better very soon, but for days I couldn't get him to say why he had been in such a condition. It came out at last that he had really been asleep and had had a very odd disjointed sort of dream. He never saw much of what was around him, but he felt the scenes most vividly. First he made out that he was standing in a large room with a number of people in it, and that someone was opposite to him who was 'very powerful', and he was being asked questions which he felt to be very important, and, whenever he answered them, someone—either the person opposite to him, or someone else in the room—seemed to be, as he said, making something up against him. All the voices sounded to him very distant, but he remembered bits of the things that were said: 'Where were you on the 19th of October?' and 'Is this your handwriting?' and so on. I can see now, of course, that he was dreaming of some trial: but we were never allowed to see the papers, and it was odd that a boy of eight should have such a vivid idea of what went on in a court. All the time he felt, he said, the most intense anxiety and oppression and hopelessness (though I don't suppose he used such words as that to me). Then, after that, there was an interval in which he remembered being dreadfully restless and miserable, and then there came another sort of picture, when he was aware that he had come out of doors on a dark raw morning with a little snow about. It was in a street, or at any rate among houses, and he felt that there were numbers and numbers of people there too, and that he was taken up some creaking wooden steps and stood on a sort of platform, but the only thing he could actually see was a small fire burning somewhere near him. Someone who had been holding his arm left hold of it and went towards this fire, and then he said the fright he was in was worse than at any other part of his dream, and if I had not wakened him up he didn't know what would have become of him. A curious dream for a child to have, wasn't it? Well, so much for that. It must have been later in the year that Frank and I were here, and I was sitting in the arbour just about sunset. I noticed the sun was going down, and told Frank to run in and see if tea was ready while I finished a chapter in the book I was reading. Frank was away longer than I expected, and the light was going so fast that I had to bend over my book to make it out. All at once I became conscious that someone was whispering to me inside the arbour. The only words I could distinguish, or thought I could, were something like 'Pull, pull. I'll push, you pull.'

'I started up in something of a fright. The voice—it was little more than a whisper—sounded so hoarse and angry, and yet as if it came from a long, long way off—just as it had done in Frank's dream. But, though I was startled, I had enough courage to look round and try to make out where the sound came from. And—this sounds very foolish, I know, but still it is the fact—I made sure that it was strongest when I put my ear to an old post which was part of the end of the seat. I was so certain of this that I remember making some marks on the post—as deep as I could with the scissors out of my work-basket. I don't know why. I wonder, by the way, whether that isn't the very post itself.... Well, yes, it might be: there are marks and scratches on it—but one can't be sure. Anyhow, it was just like that post you have there. My father got to know that both of us had had a fright in the arbour, and he went down there himself one evening after dinner, and the arbour was pulled down at very short notice. I recollect hearing my father talking about it to an old man who used to do odd jobs in the place, and the old man saying, 'Don't you fear for that, sir: he's fast enough in there without no one don't take and let him out.' But when I asked who it was, I could get no satisfactory answer. Possibly my father or mother might have told me more about it when I grew up, but, as you know, they both died when we were still quite children. I must say it has always seemed very odd to me, and I've often asked the older people in the village whether they knew of anything strange: but either they knew nothing or they wouldn't tell me. Dear, dear, how I have been boring you with my childish remembrances! but indeed that arbour did absorb our thoughts quite remarkably for a time. You can fancy, can't you, the kind of stories that we made up for ourselves. Well, dear Mrs. Anstruther, I must be leaving you now. We shall meet in town this winter, I hope, shan't we?' etc., etc.

The seats and the post were cleared away and uprooted respectively by that evening. Late summer weather is proverbially treacherous, and during dinner-time Mrs. Collins sent up to ask for a little brandy, because her husband had took a nasty chill and she was afraid he would not be able to do much next day.

Mrs. Anstruther's morning reflections were not wholly placid. She was sure some roughs had got into the plantation during the night. 'And another thing, George: the moment that Collins is about again, you must tell him to do something about the owls. I never heard anything like them, and I'm positive one came and perched somewhere just outside our window. If it had come in I should have been out of my wits: it must have been a very large bird, from its voice. Didn't you hear it? No, of course not, you were sound asleep as usual. Still, I must say, George, you don't look as if your night had done you much good.'

'My dear, I feel as if another of the same would turn me silly. You have no idea of the dreams I had. I couldn't speak of them when I woke up, and if this room wasn't so bright and sunny I shouldn't care to think of them even now.'

'Well, really, George, that isn't very common with you, I must say. You must have—no, you only had what I had yesterday—unless you had tea at that wretched club house: did you?'

'No, no; nothing but a cup of tea and some bread and butter. I should really like to know how I came to put my dream together—as I suppose one does put one's dreams together from a lot of little things one has been seeing or reading. Look here, Mary, it was like this—if I shan't be boring you—'

'I wish to hear what it was, George. I will tell you when I have had enough.'

'All right. I must tell you that it wasn't like other nightmares in one way, because I didn't really see anyone who spoke to me or touched me, and yet I was most fearfully impressed with the reality of it all. First I was sitting, no, moving about, in an old-fashioned sort of panelled room. I remember there was a fireplace and a lot of burnt papers in it, and I was in a great state of anxiety about something. There was someone else—a servant, I suppose, because I remember saying to him, 'Horses, as quick as you can,' and then waiting a bit: and next I heard several people coming upstairs and a noise like spurs on a boarded floor, and then the door opened and whatever it was that I was expecting happened.'

'Yes, but what was that?'

'You see, I couldn't tell: it was the sort of shock that upsets you in a dream. You either wake up or else everything goes black. That was what happened to me. Then I was in a big dark-walled room, panelled, I think, like the other, and a number of people, and I was evidently—'

'Standing your trial, I suppose, George.'

'Goodness! yes, Mary, I was; but did you dream that too? How very odd!'

'No, no; I didn't get enough sleep for that. Go on, George, and I will tell you afterwards.'

'Yes; well, I was being tried, for my life, I've no doubt, from the state I was in. I had no one speaking for me, and somewhere there was a most fearful fellow—on the bench I should have said, only that he seemed to be pitching into me most unfairly, and twisting everything I said, and asking most abominable questions.'

'What about?'

'Why, dates when I was at particular places, and letters I was supposed to have written, and why I had destroyed some papers; and I recollect his laughing at answers I made in a way that quite daunted me. It doesn't sound much, but I can tell you, Mary, it was really appalling at the time. I am quite certain there was such a man once, and a most horrible villain he must have been. The things he said—'

'Thank you, I have no wish to hear them. I can go to the links any day myself. How did it end?'

'Oh, against me; he saw to that. I do wish, Mary, I could give you a notion of the strain that came after that, and seemed to me to last for days: waiting and waiting, and sometimes writing things I knew to be enormously important to me, and waiting for answers and none coming, and after that I came out—'

'Ah!'

'What makes you say that? Do you know what sort of thing I saw?'

'Was it a dark cold day, and snow in the streets, and a

fire burning somewhere near you?'

'By George, it was! You have had the same nightmare! Really not? Well, it is the oddest thing! Yes; I've no doubt it was an execution for high treason. I know I was laid on straw and jolted along most wretchedly, and then had to go up some steps, and someone was holding my arm, and I remember seeing a bit of a ladder and hearing a sound of a lot of people. I really don't think I could bear now to go into a crowd of people and hear the noise they make talking. However, mercifully, I didn't get to the real business. The dream passed off with a sort of thunder inside my head. But, Mary—'

'I know what you are going to ask. I suppose this is an instance of a kind of thought-reading. Miss Wilkins called yesterday and told me of a dream her brother had as a child when they lived here, and something did no doubt make me think of that when I was awake last night listening to those horrible owls and those men talking and laughing in the shrubbery (by the way, I wish you would see if they have done any damage, and speak to the police about it); and so, I suppose, from my brain it must have got into yours while you were asleep. Curious, no doubt, and I am sorry it gave you such a bad night. You had better be as much in the fresh air as you can today.'

'Oh, it's all right now; but I think I will go over to the Lodge and see if I can get a game with any of them. And you?'

'I have enough to do for this morning; and this afternoon, if I am not interrupted, there is my drawing.'

'To be sure—I want to see that finished very much.'

No damage was discoverable in the shrubbery. Mr. Anstruther surveyed with faint interest the site of the rose garden, where the uprooted post still lay, and the hole it had occupied remained unfilled. Collins, upon inquiry made, proved to be better, but quite unable to come to his work. He expressed, by the mouth of his wife, a hope that he hadn't done nothing wrong clearing away them things. Mrs. Collins added that there was a lot of talking people in Westfield, and the hold ones was the worst: seemed to think everything of them having been in the parish longer than what other people had. But as to what they said no more could then be ascertained than that it had quite upset Collins, and was a lot of nonsense.

Recruited by lunch and a brief period of slumber, Mrs. Anstruther settled herself comfortably upon her sketching chair in the path leading through the shrubbery to the side-gate of the churchyard. Trees and buildings were among her favourite subjects, and here she had good studies of both. She worked hard, and the drawing was becoming a really pleasant thing to look upon by the time that the wooded hills to the west had shut off the sun. Still she would have persevered, but the light changed rapidly, and it became obvious that the last touches must be added on the morrow. She rose and turned towards the house, pausing for a time to take delight in the limpid green western sky. Then she passed on between the dark box-bushes, and, at a point just before the path debouched on the lawn, she stopped once again and considered the quiet evening landscape, and made a mental note that that must be the tower of one of the Roothing churches that one caught on the sky-line. Then a bird (perhaps) rustled in the box-bush on her left, and she turned and started at seeing what at first she took to be a Fifth of November mask peeping out among the branches. She looked closer.

It was not a mask. It was a face—large, smooth, and pink. She remembers the minute drops of perspiration which were starting from its forehead: she remembers how the jaws were clean-shaven and the eyes shut. She remembers also, and with an accuracy which makes the thought intolerable to her, how the mouth was open and a single tooth appeared below the upper lip. As she looked the face receded into the darkness of the bush. The shelter of the house was gained and the door shut before she collapsed.

Mr. and Mrs. Anstruther had been for a week or more recruiting at Brighton before they received a circular from the Essex Archaeological Society, and a query as to whether they possessed certain historical portraits which it was desired to include in the forthcoming work on Essex Portraits, to be published under the Society's auspices. There was an accompanying letter from the Secretary which contained the following passage: 'We are specially anxious to know whether you possess the original of the engraving of which I enclose a photograph. It represents Sir————, Lord Chief Justice under Charles II, who, as you doubtless know, retired after his disgrace to Westfield, and is supposed to have died there of remorse. It may interest you to hear that a curious entry has recently been found in the registers, not of Westfield but of Priors Roothing to the effect that the parish was so much troubled after his death that the rector of Westfield summoned the parsons of all the Roothings to come and lay him; which they did. The entry ends by saying: 'The stake is in a field adjoining to the churchyard of Westfield, on the west side.' Perhaps you can let us know if any tradition to this effect is current in your parish.'

The incidents which the 'enclosed photograph' recalled were productive of a severe shock to Mrs. Anstruther. It was decided that she must spend the winter abroad.

Mr. Anstruther, when he went down to Westfield to make the necessary arrangements, not unnaturally told his story to the rector (an old gentleman), who showed little surprise.

'Really I had managed to piece out for myself very much what must have happened, partly from old people's talk and partly from what I saw in your grounds. Of course we have suffered to some extent also. Yes, it was bad at first: like owls, as you say, and men talking sometimes. One night it was in this garden, and at other times about several of the cottages. But lately there has been very little: I think it will die out. There is nothing in our registers except the entry of the burial, and what I for a long time took to be the family motto: but last time I looked at it I noticed that it was added in a later hand and had the initials of one of our rectors quite late in the seventeenth century, A. C.—Augustine Crompton. Here it is, you see—quieta non movere. I suppose—Well, it is rather hard to say exactly what I do suppose.'

PULL, PULL.
I'LL
PUSH YOU PULL.

The Lurking Fear

by H. P. Lovecraft

I. The Shadow on the Chimney

There was thunder in the air on the night I went to the deserted mansion atop Tempest Mountain to find the lurking fear. I was not alone, for foolhardiness was not then mixed with that love of the grotesque and the terrible which has made my career a series of quests for strange horrors in literature and in life. With me were two faithful and muscular men for whom I had sent when the time came; men long associated with me in my ghastly explorations because of their peculiar fitness.

We had started quietly from the village because of the reporters who still lingered about after the eldritch panic of a month before—the nightmare creeping death. Later, I thought, they might aid me; but I did not want them then. Would to God I had let them share the search, that I might not have had to bear the secret alone so long; to bear it alone for fear the world would call me mad or go mad itself at the daemon implications of the thing. Now that I am telling it anyway, lest the brooding make me a maniac, I wish I had never concealed it. For I, and I only, know what manner of fear lurked on that spectral and desolate mountain.

In a small motor-car we covered the miles of primeval forest and hill until the wooded ascent checked it. The country bore an aspect more than usually sinister as we viewed it by night and without the accustomed crowds of investigators, so that we were often tempted to use the acetylene headlight despite the attention it might attract. It was not a wholesome landscape after dark, and I believe I would have noticed its morbidity even had I been ignorant of the terror that stalked there. Of wild creatures there were none—they are wise when death leers close. The ancient lightning-scarred trees seemed unnaturally large and twisted, and the other vegetation unnaturally thick and feverish, while curious mounds and hummocks in the weedy, fulgurite-pitted earth reminded me of snakes and dead men's skulls swelled to gigantic proportions.

Fear had lurked on Tempest Mountain for more than a century. This I learned at once from newspaper accounts of the catastrophe which first brought the region to the world's notice. The place is a remote, lonely elevation in that part of the Catskills where Dutch civilisation once feebly and transiently penetrated, leaving behind as it receded only a few ruined mansions and a degenerate squatter population inhabiting pitiful hamlets on isolated slopes. Normal beings seldom visited the locality till the state police were formed, and even now only infrequent troopers patrol it. The fear, however, is an old tradition throughout the neighbouring villages; since it is a prime topic in the simple discourse of the poor mongrels who sometimes leave their valleys to trade hand-woven baskets for such primitive necessities as they cannot shoot, raise, or make.

The lurking fear dwelt in the shunned and deserted

Martense mansion, which crowned the high but gradual eminence whose liability to frequent thunderstorms gave it the name of Tempest Mountain. For over a hundred years the antique, grove-circled stone house had been the subject of stories incredibly wild and monstrously hideous; stories of a silent colossal creeping death which stalked abroad in summer. With whimpering insistence the squatters told tales of a daemon which seized lone wayfarers after dark, either carrying them off or leaving them in a frightful state of gnawed dismemberment; while sometimes they whispered of blood-trails toward the distant mansion. Some said the thunder called the lurking fear out of its habitation, while others said the thunder was its voice.

No one outside the backwoods had believed these varying and conflicting stories, with their incoherent, extravagant descriptions of the half-glimpsed fiend; yet not a farmer or villager doubted that the Martense mansion was ghoulishly haunted. Local history forbade such a doubt, although no ghostly evidence was ever found by such investigators as had visited the building after some especially vivid tale of the squatters. Grandmothers told strange myths of the Martense spectre; myths concerning the Martense family itself, its queer hereditary dissimilarity of eyes, its long, unnatural annals, and the murder which had cursed it.

The terror which brought me to the scene was a sudden and portentous confirmation of the mountaineers' wildest legends. One summer night, after a thunderstorm of unprecedented violence, the countryside was aroused by a squatter stampede which no mere delusion could create. The pitiful throngs of natives shrieked and whined of the unnamable horror which had descended upon them, and they were not doubted. They had not seen it, but had heard such cries from one of their hamlets that they knew a creeping death had come.

In the morning citizens and state troopers followed the shuddering mountaineers to the place where they said the death had come. Death was indeed there. The ground under one of the squatters' villages had caved in after a lightning stroke, destroying several of the malodorous shanties; but upon this property damage was superimposed an organic devastation which paled it to insignificance. Of a possible 75 natives who had inhabited this spot, not one living specimen was visible. The disordered earth was covered with blood and human debris bespeaking too vividly the ravages of daemon teeth and talons; yet no visible trail led away from the carnage. That some hideous animal must be the cause, everyone quickly agreed; nor did any tongue now revive the charge that such cryptic deaths formed merely the sordid murders common in decadent communities. That charge was revived only when about 25 of the estimated population were found missing from the dead; and even then it was hard to explain the murder of fifty by half that number. But the fact remained that on a summer night a bolt had come out of the heavens and left a dead village whose corpses were horribly mangled, chewed, and clawed.

The excited countryside immediately connected the horror with the haunted Martense mansion, though the localities were over three miles apart. The troopers were more sceptical; including the mansion only casually in their investigations, and dropping it altogether when they found it thoroughly deserted. Country and village people, however, canvassed the place with infinite care;

overturning everything in the house, sounding ponds and brooks, beating down bushes, and ransacking the nearby forests. All was in vain; the death that had come had left no trace save destruction itself.

By the second day of the search the affair was fully treated by the newspapers, whose reporters overran Tempest Mountain. They described it in much detail, and with many interviews to elucidate the horror's history as told by local grandams. I followed the accounts languidly at first, for I am a connoisseur in horrors; but after a week I detected an atmosphere which stirred me oddly, so that on August 5th, 1921, I registered among the reporters who crowded the hotel at Lefferts Corners, nearest village to Tempest Mountain and acknowledged headquarters of the searchers. Three weeks more, and the dispersal of the reporters left me free to begin a terrible exploration based on the minute inquiries and surveying with which I had meanwhile busied myself.

So on this summer night, while distant thunder rumbled, I left a silent motor-car and tramped with two armed companions up the last mound-covered reaches of Tempest Mountain, casting the beams of an electric torch on the spectral grey walls that began to appear through giant oaks ahead. In this morbid night solitude and feeble shifting illumination, the vast box-like pile displayed obscure hints of terror which day could not uncover; yet I did not hesitate, since I had come with fierce resolution to test an idea. I believed that the thunder called the death-daemon out of some fearsome secret place; and be that daemon solid entity or vaporous pestilence, I meant to see it.

I had thoroughly searched the ruin before, hence

knew my plan well; choosing as the seat of my vigil the old room of Jan Martense, whose murder looms so great in the rural legends. I felt subtly that the apartment of this ancient victim was best for my purposes. The chamber, measuring about twenty feet square, contained like the other rooms some rubbish which had once been furniture. It lay on the second story, on the southeast corner of the house, and had an immense east window and narrow south window, both devoid of panes or shutters. Opposite the large window was an enormous Dutch fireplace with scriptural tiles representing the prodigal son, and opposite the narrow window was a spacious bed built into the wall.

As the tree-muffled thunder grew louder, I arranged my plan's details. First I fastened side by side to the ledge of the large window three rope ladders which I had brought with me. I knew they reached a suitable spot on the grass outside, for I had tested them. Then the three of us dragged from another room a wide four-poster bedstead, crowding it laterally against the window. Having strown it with fir boughs, all now rested on it with drawn automatics, two relaxing while the third watched. From whatever direction the daemon might come, our potential escape was provided. If it came from within the house, we had the window ladders; if from outside, the door and the stairs. We did not think, judging from precedent, that it would pursue us far even at worst.

I watched from midnight to one o'clock, when in spite of the sinister house, the unprotected window, and the approaching thunder and lightning, I felt singularly drowsy. I was between my two companions, George Bennett being toward the window and William Tobey toward the fireplace. Bennett was asleep, having apparently felt the same anomalous drowsiness which affected me, so I designated Tobey for the next watch although even he was nodding. It is curious how intently I had been watching that fireplace.

The increasing thunder must have affected my dreams, for in the brief time I slept there came to me apocalyptic visions. Once I partly awaked, probably because the sleeper toward the window had restlessly flung an arm across my chest. I was not sufficiently awake to see whether Tobey was attending to his duties as sentinel, but felt a distinct anxiety on that score. Never before had the presence of evil so poignantly oppressed me. Later I must have dropped asleep again, for it was out of a phantasmal chaos that my mind leaped when the night grew hideous with shrieks beyond anything in my former experience or imagination.

In that shrieking the inmost soul of human fear and agony clawed hopelessly and insanely at the ebony gates of oblivion. I awoke to red madness and the mockery of diabolism, as farther and farther down inconceivable vistas that phobic and crystalline anguish retreated and reverberated. There was no light, but I knew from the empty space at my right that Tobey was gone, God alone knew whither. Across my chest still lay the heavy arm of the sleeper at my left.

Then came the devastating stroke of lightning which shook the whole mountain, lit the darkest crypts of the hoary grove, and splintered the patriarch of the twisted trees. In the daemon flash of a monstrous fireball the sleeper started up suddenly while the glare from beyond the window threw his shadow vividly upon the chimney above the fireplace from which my eyes had never strayed.

That I am still alive and sane, is a marvel I cannot fathom. I cannot fathom it, for the shadow on that chimney was not that of George Bennett or of any other human creature, but a blasphemous abnormality from hell's nethermost craters; a nameless, shapeless abomination which no mind could fully grasp and no pen even partly describe. In another second I was alone in the accursed mansion, shivering and gibbering. George Bennett and William Tobey had left no trace, not even of a struggle. They were never heard of again.

II. A Passer in the Storm

For days after that hideous experience in the forest-swathed mansion I lay nervously exhausted in my hotel room at Lefferts Corners. I do not remember exactly how I managed to reach the motor-car, start it, and slip unobserved back to the village; for I retain no distinct impression save of wild-armed titan trees, daemoniac mutterings of thunder, and Charonian shadows athwart the low mounds that dotted and streaked the region.

As I shivered and brooded on the casting of that brain-blasting shadow, I knew that I had at last pried out one of earth's supreme horrors—one of those nameless blights of outer voids whose faint daemon scratchings we sometimes hear on the farthest rim of space, yet from which our own finite vision has given us a merciful immunity. The shadow I had seen, I hardly dared to analyse or identify. Something had lain between me and the window that night, but I shuddered whenever I could not cast off the instinct to classify it. If it had only snarled, or bayed, or laughed titteringly—even that would have

relieved the abysmal hideousness. But it was so silent. It had rested a heavy arm or fore leg on my chest. . . . Obviously it was organic, or had once been organic. . . . Jan Martense, whose room I had invaded, was buried in the graveyard near the mansion. . . . I must find Bennett and Tobey, if they lived . . . why had it picked them, and left me for the last? . . . Drowsiness is so stifling, and dreams are so horrible. . . .

In a short time I realised that I must tell my story to someone or break down completely. I had already decided not to abandon the quest for the lurking fear, for in my rash ignorance it seemed to me that uncertainty was worse than enlightenment, however terrible the latter might prove to be. Accordingly I resolved in my mind the best course to pursue; whom to select for my confidences, and how to track down the thing which had obliterated two men and cast a nightmare shadow.

My chief acquaintances at Lefferts Corners had been the affable reporters, of whom several still remained to collect final echoes of the tragedy. It was from these that I determined to choose a colleague, and the more I reflected the more my preference inclined toward one Arthur Munroe, a dark, lean man of about thirty-five, whose education, taste, intelligence, and temperament all seemed to mark him as one not bound to conventional ideas and experiences.

On an afternoon in early September Arthur Munroe listened to my story. I saw from the beginning that he was both interested and sympathetic, and when I had finished he analysed and discussed the thing with the greatest shrewdness and judgment. His advice, moreover, was eminently practical; for he recommended a postponement of operations at the Martense mansion until we might become fortified with more detailed historical and geographical data. On his initiative we combed the countryside for information regarding the terrible Martense family, and discovered a man who possessed a marvellously illuminating ancestral diary. We also talked at length with such of the mountain mongrels as had not fled from the terror and confusion to remoter slopes, and arranged to precede our culminating task—the exhaustive and definitive examination of the mansion in the light of its detailed history—with an equally exhaustive and definitive examination of spots associated with the various tragedies of squatter legend.

The results of this examination were not at first very enlightening, though our tabulation of them seemed to reveal a fairly significant trend; namely, that the number of reported horrors was by far the greatest in areas either comparatively near the avoided house or connected with it by stretches of the morbidly overnourished forest. There were, it is true, exceptions; indeed, the horror which had caught the world's ear had happened in a treeless space remote alike from the mansion and from any connecting woods.

As to the nature and appearance of the lurking fear, nothing could be gained from the scared and witless shanty-dwellers. In the same breath they called it a snake and a giant, a thunder-devil and a bat, a vulture and a walking tree. We did, however, deem ourselves justified in assuming that it was a living organism highly susceptible to electrical storms; and although certain of the stories suggested wings, we believed that its aversion for open spaces made land locomotion a more probable theory. The only thing really incompatible with the latter

view was the rapidity with which the creature must have travelled in order to perform all the deeds attributed to it.

When we came to know the squatters better, we found them curiously likeable in many ways. Simple animals they were, gently descending the evolutionary scale because of their unfortunate ancestry and stultifying isolation. They feared outsiders, but slowly grew accustomed to us; finally helping vastly when we beat down all the thickets and tore out all the partitions of the mansion in our search for the lurking fear. When we asked them to help us find Bennett and Tobey they were truly distressed; for they wanted to help us, yet knew that these victims had gone as wholly out of the world as their own missing people. That great numbers of them had actually been killed and removed, just as the wild animals had long been exterminated, we were of course thoroughly convinced; and we waited apprehensively for further tragedies to occur.

By the middle of October we were puzzled by our lack of progress. Owing to the clear nights no daemoniac aggressions had taken place, and the completeness of our vain searches of house and country almost drove us to regard the lurking fear as a non-material agency. We feared that the cold weather would come on and halt our explorations, for all agreed that the daemon was generally quiet in winter. Thus there was a kind of haste and desperation in our last daylight canvass of the horror-visited hamlet; a hamlet now deserted because of the squatters' fears.

The ill-fated squatter hamlet had borne no name, but had long stood in a sheltered though treeless cleft between two elevations called respectively Cone

Mountain and Maple Hill. It was closer to Maple Hill than to Cone Mountain, some of the crude abodes indeed being dugouts on the side of the former eminence. Geographically it lay about two miles northwest of the base of Tempest Mountain, and three miles from the oak-girt mansion. Of the distance between the hamlet and the mansion, fully two miles and a quarter on the hamlet's side was entirely open country; the plain being of fairly level character save for some of the low snake-like mounds, and having as vegetation only grass and scattered weeds. Considering this topography, we had finally concluded that the daemon must have come by way of Cone Mountain, a wooded southern prolongation of which ran to within a short distance of the westernmost spur of Tempest Mountain. The upheaval of ground we traced conclusively to a landslide from Maple Hill, a tall lone splintered tree on whose side had been the striking point of the thunderbolt which summoned the fiend.

As for the twentieth time or more Arthur Munroe and I went minutely over every inch of the violated village, we were filled with a certain discouragement coupled with vague and novel fears. It was acutely uncanny, even when frightful and uncanny things were common, to encounter so blankly clueless a scene after such overwhelming occurrences; and we moved about beneath the leaden, darkening sky with that tragic directionless zeal which results from a combined sense of futility and necessity of action. Our care was gravely minute; every cottage was again entered, every hillside dugout again searched for bodies, every thorny foot of adjacent slope again scanned for dens and caves, but all without result. And yet, as I have said, vague new fears hovered menacingly over us; as if giant bat-winged gryphons squatted invisibly on the mountain-tops and leered with Abaddon-eyes that had

looked on trans-cosmic gulfs.

As the afternoon advanced, it became increasingly difficult to see; and we heard the rumble of a thunderstorm gathering over Tempest Mountain. This sound in such a locality naturally stirred us, though less than it would have done at night. As it was, we hoped desperately that the storm would last until well after dark; and with that hope turned from our aimless hillside searching toward the nearest inhabited hamlet to gather a body of squatters as helpers in the investigation. Timid as they were, a few of the younger men were sufficiently inspired by our protective leadership to promise such help.

We had hardly more than turned, however, when there descended such a blinding sheet of torrential rain that shelter became imperative. The extreme, almost nocturnal darkness of the sky caused us to stumble sadly, but guided by the frequent flashes of lightning and by our minute knowledge of the hamlet we soon reached the least porous cabin of the lot; an heterogeneous combination of logs and boards whose still existing door and single tiny window both faced Maple Hill. Barring the door after us against the fury of the wind and rain, we put in place the crude window shutter which our frequent searches had taught us where to find. It was dismal sitting there on rickety boxes in the pitchy darkness, but we smoked pipes and occasionally flashed our pocket lamps about. Now and then we could see the lightning through the cracks in the wall; the afternoon was so incredibly dark that each flash was extremely vivid.

The stormy vigil reminded me shudderingly of my ghastly night on Tempest Mountain. My mind turned to that odd question which had kept recurring ever since the nightmare thing had happened; and again I wondered why the daemon, approaching the three watchers either from the window or the interior, had begun with the men on each side and left the middle man till the last, when the titan fireball had scared it away. Why had it not taken its victims in natural order, with myself second, from whichever direction it had approached? With what manner of far-reaching tentacles did it prey? Or did it know that I was the leader, and save me for a fate worse than that of my companions?

In the midst of these reflections, as if dramatically arranged to intensify them, there fell near by a terrific bolt of lightning followed by the sound of sliding earth. At the same time the wolfish wind rose to daemoniac crescendoes of ululation. We were sure that the lone tree on Maple Hill had been struck again, and Munroe rose from his box and went to the tiny window to ascertain the damage. When he took down the shutter the wind and rain howled deafeningly in, so that I could not hear what he said; but I waited while he leaned out and tried to fathom Nature's pandemonium.

Gradually a calming of the wind and dispersal of the unusual darkness told of the storm's passing. I had hoped it would last into the night to help our quest, but a furtive sunbeam from a knothole behind me removed the likelihood of such a thing. Suggesting to Munroe that we had better get some light even if more showers came, I unbarred and opened the crude door. The ground outside was a singular mass of mud and pools, with fresh heaps of earth from the slight landslide; but I saw nothing to justify the interest which kept my companion silently leaning out the window. Crossing to where he leaned, I touched his shoulder; but he did not move. Then, as I

playfully shook him and turned him around, I felt the strangling tendrils of a cancerous horror whose roots reached into illimitable pasts and fathomless abysms of the night that broods beyond time.

For Arthur Munroe was dead. And on what remained of his chewed and gouged head there was no longer a face.

III. What the Red Glare Meant

On the tempest-racked night of November 8, 1921, with a lantern which cast charnel shadows, I stood digging alone and idiotically in the grave of Jan Martense. I had begun to dig in the afternoon, because a thunderstorm was brewing, and now that it was dark and the storm had burst above the maniacally thick foliage I was glad.

I believe that my mind was partly unhinged by events since August 5th; the daemon shadow in the mansion, the general strain and disappointment, and the thing that occurred at the hamlet in an October storm. After that thing I had dug a grave for one whose death I could not understand. I knew that others could not understand either, so let them think Arthur Munroe had wandered away. They searched, but found nothing. The squatters might have understood, but I dared not frighten them more. I myself seemed strangely callous. That shock at the mansion had done something to my brain, and I could think only of the quest for a horror now grown to cataclysmic stature in my imagination; a quest which the fate of Arthur Munroe made me vow to keep silent and solitary.

216

The scene of my excavations would alone have been enough to unnerve any ordinary man. Baleful primal trees of unholy size, age, and grotesqueness leered above me like the pillars of some hellish Druidic temple; muffling the thunder, hushing the clawing wind, and admitting but little rain. Beyond the scarred trunks in the background, illumined by faint flashes of filtered lightning, rose the damp ivied stones of the deserted mansion, while somewhat nearer was the abandoned Dutch garden whose walks and beds were polluted by a white, fungous, foetid, overnourished vegetation that never saw full daylight. And nearest of all was the graveyard, where deformed trees tossed insane branches as their roots displaced unhallowed slabs and sucked venom from what lay below. Now and then, beneath the brown pall of leaves that rotted and festered in the antediluvian forest darkness, I could trace the sinister outlines of some of those low mounds which characterised the lightning-pierced region.

History had led me to this archaic grave. History, indeed, was all I had after everything else ended in mocking Satanism. I now believed that the lurking fear was no material thing, but a wolf-fanged ghost that rode the midnight lightning. And I believed, because of the masses of local tradition I had unearthed in my search with Arthur Munroe, that the ghost was that of Jan Martense, who died in 1762. That is why I was digging idiotically in his grave.

The Martense mansion was built in 1670 by Gerrit Martense, a wealthy New-Amsterdam merchant who disliked the changing order under British rule, and had constructed this magnificent domicile on a remote

woodland summit whose untrodden solitude and unusual scenery pleased him. The only substantial disappointment encountered in this site was that which concerned the prevalence of violent thunderstorms in summer. When selecting the hill and building his mansion, Mynheer Martense had laid these frequent natural outbursts to some peculiarity of the year; but in time he perceived that the locality was especially liable to such phenomena. At length, having found these storms injurious to his health, he fitted up a cellar into which he could retreat from their wildest pandemonium.

Of Gerrit Martense's descendants less is known than of himself; since they were all reared in hatred of the English civilisation, and trained to shun such of the colonists as accepted it. Their life was exceedingly secluded, and people declared that their isolation had made them heavy of speech and comprehension. In appearance all were marked by a peculiar inherited dissimilarity of eyes; one generally being blue and the other brown. Their social contacts grew fewer and fewer, till at last they took to intermarrying with the numerous menial class about the estate. Many of the crowded family degenerated, moved across the valley, and merged with the mongrel population which was later to produce the pitiful squatters. The rest had stuck sullenly to their ancestral mansion, becoming more and more clannish and taciturn, yet developing a nervous responsiveness to the frequent thunderstorms.

Most of this information reached the outside world through young Jan Martense, who from some kind of restlessness joined the colonial army when news of the Albany Convention reached Tempest Mountain. He was the first of Gerrit's descendants to see much of the world; and when he returned in 1760 after six years of campaigning, he was hated as an outsider by his father, uncles, and brothers, in spite of his dissimilar Martense eyes. No longer could he share the peculiarities and prejudices of the Martenses, while the very mountain thunderstorms failed to intoxicate him as they had before. Instead, his surroundings depressed him; and he frequently wrote to a friend in Albany of plans to leave the paternal roof.

In the spring of 1763 Jonathan Gifford, the Albany friend of Jan Martense, became worried by his correspondent's silence; especially in view of the conditions and quarrels at the Martense mansion. Determined to visit Jan in person, he went into the mountains on horseback. His diary states that he reached Tempest Mountain on September 20, finding the mansion in great decrepitude. The sullen, odd-eyed Martenses, whose unclean animal aspect shocked him, told him in broken gutturals that Jan was dead. He had, they insisted, been struck by lightning the autumn before; and now lay buried behind the neglected sunken gardens. They shewed the visitor the grave, barren and devoid of markers. Something in the Martenses' manner gave Gifford a feeling of repulsion and suspicion, and a week later he returned with spade and mattock to explore the sepulchral spot. He found what he expected—a skull crushed cruelly as if by savage blows—so returning to Albany he openly charged the Martenses with the murder of their kinsman.

Legal evidence was lacking, but the story spread rapidly round the countryside; and from that time the Martenses were ostracised by the world. No one would deal with them, and their distant manor was shunned as an accursed place. Somehow they managed to live on independently by the products of their estate, for occasional lights glimpsed from far-away hills attested their continued presence. These lights were seen as late as 1810, but toward the last they became very infrequent.

Meanwhile there grew up about the mansion and the mountain a body of diabolic legendry. The place was avoided with doubled assiduousness, and invested with every whispered myth tradition could supply. It remained unvisited till 1816, when the continued absence of lights was noticed by the squatters. At that time a party made investigations, finding the house deserted and partly in ruins.

There were no skeletons about, so that departure rather than death was inferred. The clan seemed to have left several years before, and improvised penthouses shewed how numerous it had grown prior to its migration. Its cultural level had fallen very low, as proved by decaying furniture and scattered silverware which must have been long abandoned when its owners left. But though the dreaded Martenses were gone, the fear of the haunted house continued; and grew very acute when new and strange stories arose among the mountain decadents. There it stood; deserted, feared, and linked with the vengeful ghost of Jan Martense. There it still stood on the night I dug in Jan Martense's grave.

I have described my protracted digging as idiotic, and such it indeed was in object and method. The coffin of Jan Martense had soon been unearthed—it now held only dust and nitre—but in my fury to exhume his ghost I delved irrationally and clumsily down beneath where he had lain. God knows what I expected to find—I only felt that I was digging in the grave of a man whose ghost stalked by night.

It is impossible to say what monstrous depth I had attained when my spade, and soon my feet, broke through the ground beneath. The event, under the circumstances, was tremendous; for in the existence of a subterranean space here, my mad theories had terrible confirmation. My slight fall had extinguished the lantern, but I produced an electric pocket lamp and viewed the small horizontal tunnel which led away indefinitely in both directions. It was amply large enough for a man to wriggle through; and though no sane person would have tried it at that time, I forgot danger, reason, and cleanliness in my single-minded fever to unearth the lurking fear. Choosing the direction toward the house, I scrambled recklessly into the narrow burrow; squirming ahead blindly and rapidly, and flashing but seldom the lamp I kept before me.

What language can describe the spectacle of a man lost in infinitely abysmal earth; pawing, twisting, wheezing; scrambling madly through sunken convolutions of immemorial blackness without an idea of time, safety, direction, or definite object? There is something hideous in it, but that is what I did. I did it for so long that life faded to a far memory, and I became one with the moles and grubs of nighted depths. Indeed, it was only by accident that after interminable writhings I jarred my forgotten electric lamp alight, so that it shone eerily along the burrow of caked loam that stretched and curved ahead.

I had been scrambling in this way for some time, so that my battery had burned very low, when the passage suddenly inclined sharply upward, altering my mode of progress. And as I raised my glance it was

without preparation that I saw glistening in the distance two daemoniac reflections of my expiring lamp; two reflections glowing with a baneful and unmistakable effulgence, and provoking maddeningly nebulous memories. I stopped automatically, though lacking the brain to retreat. The eyes approached, yet of the thing that bore them I could distinguish only a claw. But what a claw! Then far overhead I heard a faint crashing which I recognised. It was the wild thunder of the mountain, raised to hysteric fury—I must have been crawling upward for some time, so that the surface was now quite near. And as the muffled thunder clattered, those eyes still stared with vacuous viciousness.

Thank God I did not then know what it was, else I should have died. But I was saved by the very thunder that had summoned it, for after a hideous wait there burst from the unseen outside sky one of those frequent mountainward bolts whose aftermath I had noticed here and there as gashes of disturbed earth and fulgurites of various sizes. With Cyclopean rage it tore through the soil above that damnable pit, blinding and deafening me, yet not wholly reducing me to a coma.

In the chaos of sliding, shifting earth I clawed and floundered helplessly till the rain on my head steadied me and I saw that I had come to the surface in a familiar spot; a steep unforested place on the southwest slope of the mountain. Recurrent sheet lightnings illumed the tumbled ground and the remains of the curious low hummock which had stretched down from the wooded higher slope, but there was nothing in the chaos to shew my place of egress from the lethal catacomb. My brain was as great a chaos as the earth, and as a distant red glare burst on the landscape from the south I hardly realised the horror I had been through.

But when two days later the squatters told me what the red glare meant, I felt more horror than that which the mould-burrow and the claw and eyes had given; more horror because of the overwhelming implications. In a hamlet twenty miles away an orgy of fear had followed the bolt which brought me above ground, and a nameless thing had dropped from an overhanging tree into a weak-roofed cabin. It had done a deed, but the squatters had fired the cabin in frenzy before it could escape. It had been doing that deed at the very moment the earth caved in on the thing with the claw and eyes.

IV. The Horror in the Eyes

There can be nothing normal in the mind of one who, knowing what I knew of the horrors of Tempest Mountain, would seek alone for the fear that lurked there. That at least two of the fear's embodiments were destroyed, formed but a slight guarantee of mental and physical safety in this Acheron of multiform diabolism; yet I continued my quest with even greater zeal as events and revelations became more monstrous.

When, two days after my frightful crawl through that crypt of the eyes and claw, I learned that a thing had malignly hovered twenty miles away at the same instant the eyes were glaring at me, I experienced virtual convulsions of fright. But that fright was so mixed with wonder and alluring grotesqueness, that it was almost a pleasant sensation. Sometimes, in the throes of a nightmare when unseen powers whirl one over the roofs

of strange dead cities toward the grinning chasm of Nis, it is a relief and even a delight to shriek wildly and throw oneself voluntarily along with the hideous vortex of dream-doom into whatever bottomless gulf may yawn. And so it was with the waking nightmare of Tempest Mountain; the discovery that two monsters had haunted the spot gave me ultimately a mad craving to plunge into the very earth of the accursed region, and with bare hands dig out the death that leered from every inch of the poisonous soil.

As soon as possible I visited the grave of Jan Martense and dug vainly where I had dug before. Some extensive cave-in had obliterated all trace of the underground passage, while the rain had washed so much earth back into the excavation that I could not tell how deeply I had dug that other day. I likewise made a difficult trip to the distant hamlet where the death-creature had been burnt, and was little repaid for my trouble. In the ashes of the fateful cabin I found several bones, but apparently none of the monster's. The squatters said the thing had had only one victim; but in this I judged them inaccurate, since besides the complete skull of a human being, there was another bony fragment which seemed certainly to have belonged to a human skull at some time. Though the rapid drop of the monster had been seen, no one could say just what the creature was like; those who had glimpsed it called it simply a devil. Examining the great tree where it had lurked, I could discern no distinctive marks. I tried to find some trail into the black forest, but on this occasion could not stand the sight of those morbidly large boles, or of those vast serpent-like roots that twisted so malevolently before they sank into the earth.

My next step was to re-examine with microscopic care the deserted hamlet where death had come most abundantly, and where Arthur Munroe had seen something he never lived to describe. Though my vain previous searches had been exceedingly minute, I now had new data to test; for my horrible grave-crawl convinced me that at least one of the phases of the monstrosity had been an underground creature. This time, on the fourteenth of November, my quest concerned itself mostly with the slopes of Cone Mountain and Maple Hill where they overlook the unfortunate hamlet, and I gave particular attention to the loose earth of the landslide region on the latter eminence.

The afternoon of my search brought nothing to light, and dusk came as I stood on Maple Hill looking down at the hamlet and across the valley to Tempest Mountain. There had been a gorgeous sunset, and now the moon came up, nearly full and shedding a silver flood over the plain, the distant mountainside, and the curious low mounds that rose here and there. It was a peaceful Arcadian scene, but knowing what it hid I hated it. I hated the mocking moon, the hypocritical plain, the festering mountain, and those sinister mounds. Everything seemed to me tainted with a loathsome contagion, and inspired by a noxious alliance with distorted hidden powers.

Presently, as I gazed abstractedly at the moonlit panorama, my eye became attracted by something singular in the nature and arrangement of a certain topographical element. Without having any exact knowledge of geology, I had from the first been interested in the odd mounds and hummocks of the region. I had noticed that they were pretty widely distributed around Tempest Mountain, though less numerous on the plain

than near the hill-top itself, where prehistoric glaciation had doubtless found feebler opposition to its striking and fantastic caprices. Now, in the light of that low moon which cast long weird shadows, it struck me forcibly that the various points and lines of the mound system had a peculiar relation to the summit of Tempest Mountain. That summit was undeniably a centre from which the lines or rows of points radiated indefinitely and irregularly, as if the unwholesome Martense mansion had thrown visible tentacles of terror. The idea of such tentacles gave me an unexplained thrill, and I stopped to analyse my reason for believing these mounds glacial phenomena.

The more I analysed the less I believed, and against my newly opened mind there began to beat grotesque and horrible analogies based on superficial aspects and upon my experience beneath the earth. Before I knew it I was uttering frenzied and disjointed words to myself: "My God! . . . Molehills . . . the damned place must be honeycombed . . . how many . . . that night at the mansion . . . they took Bennett and Tobey first . . . on each side of us. . . ." Then I was digging frantically into the mound which had stretched nearest me; digging desperately, shiveringly, but almost jubilantly; digging and at last shrieking aloud with some unplaced emotion as I came upon a tunnel or burrow just like the one through which I had crawled on that other daemoniac night.

After that I recall running, spade in hand; a hideous run across moon-litten, mound-marked meadows and through diseased, precipitous abysses of haunted hillside forest; leaping, screaming, panting, bounding toward the terrible Martense mansion. I recall digging unreasoningly in all parts of the brier-choked cellar; digging to find the core and centre of that malignant universe of mounds.

And then I recall how I laughed when I stumbled on the passageway; the hole at the base of the old chimney, where the thick weeds grew and cast queer shadows in the light of the lone candle I had happened to have with me. What still remained down in that hell-hive, lurking and waiting for the thunder to arouse it, I did not know. Two had been killed; perhaps that had finished it. But still there remained that burning determination to reach the innermost secret of the fear, which I had once more come to deem definite, material, and organic.

My indecisive speculation whether to explore the passage alone and immediately with my pocket-light or to try to assemble a band of squatters for the quest, was interrupted after a time by a sudden rush of wind from outside which blew out the candle and left me in stark blackness. The moon no longer shone through the chinks and apertures above me, and with a sense of fateful alarm I heard the sinister and significant rumble of approaching thunder. A confusion of associated ideas possessed my brain, leading me to grope back toward the farthest corner of the cellar. My eyes, however, never turned away from the horrible opening at the base of the chimney; and I began to get glimpses of the crumbling bricks and unhealthy weeds as faint glows of lightning penetrated the woods outside and illumined the chinks in the upper wall. Every second I was consumed with a mixture of fear and curiosity. What would the storm call forth—or was there anything left for it to call? Guided by a lightning flash I settled myself down behind a dense clump of vegetation, through which I could see the opening without being seen.

If heaven is merciful, it will some day efface from my consciousness the sight that I saw, and let me live

my last years in peace. I cannot sleep at night now, and have to take opiates when it thunders. The thing came abruptly and unannounced; a daemon, rat-like scurrying from pits remote and unimaginable, a hellish panting and stifled grunting, and then from that opening beneath the chimney a burst of multitudinous and leprous life—a loathsome night-spawned flood of organic corruption more devastatingly hideous than the blackest conjurations of mortal madness and morbidity. Seething, stewing, surging, bubbling like serpents' slime it rolled up and out of that yawning hole, spreading like a septic contagion and streaming from the cellar at every point of egress—streaming out to scatter through the accursed midnight forests and strew fear, madness, and death.

God knows how many there were—there must have been thousands. To see the stream of them in that faint, intermittent lightning was shocking. When they had thinned out enough to be glimpsed as separate organisms, I saw that they were dwarfed, deformed hairy devils or apes—monstrous and diabolic caricatures of the monkey tribe. They were so hideously silent; there was hardly a squeal when one of the last stragglers turned with the skill of long practice to make a meal in accustomed fashion on a weaker companion. Others snapped up what it left and ate with slavering relish. Then, in spite of my daze of fright and disgust, my morbid curiosity triumphed; and as the last of the monstrosities oozed up alone from that nether world of unknown nightmare, I drew my automatic pistol and shot it under cover of the thunder.

Shrieking, slithering, torrential shadows of red viscous madness chasing one another through endless, ensanguined corridors of purple fulgurous sky...formless phantasms and kaleidoscopic mutations of a ghoulish, remembered scene; forests of monstrous overnourished oaks with serpent roots twisting and sucking unnamable juices from an earth verminous with millions of cannibal devils; mound-like tentacles groping from underground nuclei of polypous perversion . . . insane lightning over malignant ivied walls and daemon arcades choked with fungous vegetation. . . . Heaven be thanked for the instinct which led me unconscious to places where men dwell; to the peaceful village that slept under the calm stars of clearing skies.

I had recovered enough in a week to send to Albany for a gang of men to blow up the Martense mansion and the entire top of Tempest Mountain with dynamite, stop up all the discoverable mound-burrows, and destroy certain overnourished trees whose very existence seemed an insult to sanity. I could sleep a little after they had done this, but true rest will never come as long as I remember that nameless secret of the lurking fear. The thing will haunt me, for who can say the extermination is complete, and that analogous phenomena do not exist all over the world? Who can, with my knowledge, think of the earth's unknown caverns without a nightmare dread of future possibilities? I cannot see a well or a subway entrance without shuddering . . . why cannot the doctors give me something to make me sleep, or truly calm my brain when it thunders?

What I saw in the glow of my flashlight after I shot the unspeakable straggling object was so simple that almost a minute elapsed before I understood and went delirious. The object was nauseous; a filthy whitish gorilla thing with sharp yellow fangs and matted fur. It was the ultimate product of mammalian degeneration; the frightful outcome of isolated spawning, multiplication,

and cannibal nutrition above and below the ground; the embodiment of all the snarling chaos and grinning fear that lurk behind life. It had looked at me as it died, and its eyes had the same odd quality that marked those other eyes which had stared at me underground and excited cloudy recollections. One eye was blue, the other brown. They were the dissimilar Martense eyes of the old legends, and I knew in one inundating cataclysm of voiceless horror what had become of that vanished family; the terrible and thunder-crazed house of Martense.

'...the deserted mansion atop Tempest Mountain...'

THE TRACTATE MIDDOTH

BY M. R. JAMES

Towards the end of an autumn afternoon an elderly man with a thin face and grey Piccadilly weepers pushed open the swing-door leading into the vestibule of a certain famous library, and addressing himself to an attendant, stated that he believed he was entitled to use the library, and inquired if he might take a book out. Yes, if he were on the list of those to whom that privilege was given. He produced his card—Mr. John Eldred—and, the register being consulted, a favourable answer was given. 'Now, another point,' said he. 'It is a long time since I was here, and I do not know my way about your building; besides, it is near closing-time, and it is bad for me to hurry up and down stairs. I have here the title of the book I want: is there anyone at liberty who could go and find it for me?' After a moment's thought the doorkeeper beckoned to a young man who was passing. 'Mr. Garrett,' he said, 'have you a minute to assist this gentleman?' 'With pleasure,' was Mr. Garrett's answer. The slip with the title was handed to him. 'I think I can put my hand on this; it happens to be in the class I inspected last quarter, but I'll just look it up in the catalogue to make sure. I suppose it is that particular edition that you require, sir?' 'Yes, if you please; that, and no other,' said Mr. Eldred; 'I am exceedingly obliged to you.' 'Don't mention it I beg, sir,' said Mr. Garrett, and hurried off.

'I thought so,' he said to himself, when his finger, travelling down the pages of the catalogue, stopped at a particular entry. 'Talmud: Tractate Middoth, with the commentary of Nachmanides, Amsterdam, 1707. 11.3.34. Hebrew class, of course. Not a very difficult job this.'

Mr. Eldred, accommodated with a chair in the vestibule, awaited anxiously the return of his messenger—and his disappointment at seeing an empty-handed Mr. Garrett running down the staircase was very evident. 'I'm sorry to disappoint you, sir,' said the young man, 'but the book is out.' 'Oh dear!' said Mr. Eldred, 'is that so? You are sure there can be no mistake?' 'I don't think there is much chance of it, sir: but it's possible, if you like to wait a minute, that you might meet the very gentleman that's got it. He must be leaving the library soon, and I think I saw him take that particular book out of the shelf.' 'Indeed! You didn't recognize him, I suppose? Would it be one of the professors or one of the students?' 'I don't think so: certainly not a professor. I should have known him; but the light isn't very good in that part of the library at this time of day, and I didn't see his face. I should have said he was a shortish old gentleman, perhaps a clergyman, in a cloak. If you could wait, I can easily find out whether he wants the book very particularly.'

'No, no,' said Mr. Eldred, 'I won't—I can't wait now, thank you—no. I must be off. But I'll call again tomorrow if I may, and perhaps you could find out who has it.'

'Certainly, sir, and I'll have the book ready for you if we—' But Mr. Eldred was already off, and hurrying more than one would have thought wholesome for him.

Garrett had a few moments to spare; and, thought he, 'I'll go back to that case and see if I can find the old man. Most likely he could put off using the book for a few days. I dare say the other one doesn't want to keep it for long.' So off with him to the Hebrew class. But when he got there it was unoccupied, and the volume marked 11.3.34 was in its place on the shelf. It was vexatious to Garrett's self-respect to have disappointed an inquirer with so little reason: and he would have liked, had it not been against library rules, to take the book down to the vestibule then and there, so that it might be ready for Mr. Eldred when he called. However, next morning he would be on the look out for him, and he begged the doorkeeper to send and let him know when the moment came. As a matter of fact, he was himself in the vestibule when Mr. Eldred arrived, very soon after the library opened and when hardly anyone besides the staff were in the building.

'I'm very sorry,' he said; 'it's not often that I make such a stupid mistake, but I did feel sure that the old gentleman I saw took out that very book and kept it in his hand without opening it, just as people do, you know, sir, when they mean to take a book out of the library and not merely refer to it. But, however, I'll run up now at once and get it for you this time.'

And here intervened a pause. Mr. Eldred paced the entry, read all the notices, consulted his watch, sat and gazed up the staircase, did all that a very impatient man could, until some twenty minutes had run out. At last he addressed himself to the doorkeeper and inquired if it was a very long way to that part of the library to which Mr. Garrett had gone.

'Well, I was thinking it was funny, sir: he's a quick man as a rule, but to be sure he might have been sent for by the librarian, but even so I think he'd have mentioned to him that you was waiting. I'll just speak him up on the toob and see.' And to the tube he addressed himself. As he absorbed the reply to his question his face changed, and he made one or two supplementary inquiries which were shortly answered. Then he came forward to his counter and spoke in a lower tone. 'I'm sorry to hear, sir, that something seems to have 'appened a little awkward. Mr. Garrett has been took poorly, it appears, and the librarian sent him 'ome in a cab the other way. Something of an attack, by what I can hear.' 'What, really? Do you mean that someone has injured him?' 'No, sir, not violence 'ere, but, as I should judge, attacked with an attack, what you might term it, of illness. Not a strong constitootion, Mr. Garrett. But as to your book, sir, perhaps you might be able to find it for yourself. It's too bad you should be disappointed this way twice over—' 'Er—well, but I'm so sorry that Mr. Garrett should have been taken ill in this way while he was obliging me. I think I must leave the book, and call and inquire after him. You can give me his address, I suppose.' That was easily done: Mr. Garrett, it appeared, lodged in rooms not far from the station. 'And one other question. Did you happen to notice if an old gentleman, perhaps a clergyman, in a—yes—in a black cloak, left the library after I did yesterday. I think he may have been a—I think, that is, that he may be staying—or rather that I may have known him.'

'Not in a black cloak, sir; no. There were only two

gentlemen left later than what you done, sir, both of them youngish men. There was Mr. Carter took out a music-book and one of the prefessors with a couple o' novels. That's the lot, sir; and then I went off to me tea, and glad to get it. Thank you, sir, much obliged.'

Mr. Eldred, still a prey to anxiety, betook himself in a cab to Mr. Garrett's address, but the young man was not yet in a condition to receive visitors. He was better, but his landlady considered that he must have had a severe shock. She thought most likely from what the doctor said that he would be able to see Mr. Eldred tomorrow. Mr. Eldred returned to his hotel at dusk and spent, I fear, but a dull evening.

On the next day he was able to see Mr. Garrett. When in health Mr. Garrett was a cheerful and pleasant-looking young man. Now he was a very white and shaky being, propped up in an arm-chair by the fire, and inclined to shiver and keep an eye on the door. If however, there were visitors whom he was not prepared to welcome, Mr. Eldred was not among them. 'It really is I who owe you an apology, and I was despairing of being able to pay it, for I didn't know your address. But I am very glad you have called. I do dislike and regret giving all this trouble, but you know I could not have foreseen this— this attack which I had.'

'Of course not; but now, I am something of a doctor. You'll excuse my asking; you have had, I am sure, good advice. Was it a fall you had?'

'No. I did fall on the floor—but not from any height. It was, really, a shock.'

'You mean something startled you. Was it anything you thought you saw?'

'Not much thinking in the case, I'm afraid. Yes, it was something I saw. You remember when you called the first time at the library?'

'Yes, of course. Well, now, let me beg you not to try to describe it—it will not be good for you to recall it, I'm sure.'

'But indeed it would be a relief to me to tell anyone like yourself: you might be able to explain it away. It was just when I was going into the class where your book is—'

'Indeed, Mr. Garrett, I insist; besides, my watch tells me I have but very little time left in which to get my things together and take the train. No—not another word—it would be more distressing to you than you imagine, perhaps. Now there is just one thing I want to say. I feel that I am really indirectly responsible for this illness of yours, and I think I ought to defray the expense which it has—eh?'

But this offer was quite distinctly declined. Mr. Eldred, not pressing it, left almost at once: not, however, before Mr. Garrett had insisted upon his taking a note of the class-mark of the Tractate Middoth, which, as he said, Mr. Eldred could at leisure get for himself. But Mr. Eldred did not reappear at the library.

William Garrett had another visitor that day in the person of a contemporary and colleague from the library, one George Earle. Earle had been one of those who found Garrett lying insensible on the floor just inside the 'class' or cubicle (opening upon the central alley of a spacious gallery) in which the Hebrew books were placed, and Earle had naturally been very anxious about his friend's condition. So as soon as library hours were over he appeared at the lodgings. 'Well,' he said (after other conversation), 'I've no notion what it was that put you wrong, but I've got the idea that there's something wrong in the atmosphere of the library. I know this, that just before we found you I was coming along the gallery with Davis, and I said to him, 'Did ever you know such a musty smell anywhere as there is about here? It can't be wholesome.' Well now, if one goes on living a long time with a smell of that kind (I tell you it was worse than I ever knew it) it must get into the system and break out some time, don't you think?'

Garrett shook his head. 'That's all very well about the smell—but it isn't always there, though I've noticed it the last day or two—a sort of unnaturally strong smell of dust. But no—that's not what did for me. It was something I saw. And I want to tell you about it. I went into that Hebrew class to get a book for a man that was inquiring for it down below. Now that same book I'd made a mistake about the day before. I'd been for it, for the same man, and made sure that I saw an old parson in a cloak taking it out. I told my man it was out: off he went, to call again next day. I went back to see if I could get it out of the parson: no parson there, and the book on the shelf. Well, yesterday, as I say, I went again. This time, if you please—ten o'clock in the morning, remember, and as much light as ever you get in those classes, and there was my parson again, back to me, looking at the books on the shelf I wanted. His hat was on the table, and he had a bald head. I waited a second or two looking at him rather particularly. I tell you, he had a very nasty bald head. It looked to me dry, and it looked dusty, and the streaks of hair across it were much less like hair than cobwebs. Well, I made a bit of a noise on purpose, coughed and moved my feet. He turned round and let me see his face—which I hadn't seen before. I tell you again, I'm not mistaken. Though, for one reason or another I didn't take in the lower part of his face, I did see the upper part; and it was perfectly dry, and the eyes were very deep-sunk; and over them, from the eyebrows to the cheek-bone, there were cobwebs—thick. Now that closed me up, as they say, and I can't tell you anything more.'

What explanations were furnished by Earle of this phenomenon it does not very much concern us to inquire; at all events they did not convince Garrett that he had not seen what he had seen.

Before William Garrett returned to work at the library, the librarian insisted upon his taking a week's rest and change of air. Within a few days' time, therefore, he was at the station with his bag, looking for a desirable smoking compartment in which to travel to Burnstow-on-Sea, which he had not previously visited. One compartment and one only seemed to be suitable. But, just as he approached it, he saw, standing in front of the door, a figure so like one bound up with recent unpleasant associations that, with a sickening qualm, and hardly knowing what he did, he tore open the door of the next compartment and pulled himself into it as quickly as if death were at his heels. The train moved off, and he must have turned quite faint, for he was next conscious of a smelling-bottle being put to his nose. His physician was a nice-looking old lady, who, with her daughter, was the only passenger in the carriage.

But for this incident it is not very likely that he would have made any overtures to his fellow-travellers. As it was, thanks and inquiries and general conversation supervened inevitably; and Garrett found himself provided before the journey's end not only with a physician, but with a landlady: for Mrs. Simpson had apartments to let at Burnstow, which seemed in all ways suitable. The place was empty at that season, so that Garrett was thrown a good deal into the society of the mother and daughter. He found them very acceptable company. On the third evening of his stay he was on such terms with them as to be asked to spend the evening in their private sitting-room.

During their talk it transpired that Garrett's work lay in a library. 'Ah, libraries are fine places,' said Mrs. Simpson, putting down her work with a sigh; 'but for all that, books have played me a sad turn, or rather a book has.'

'Well, books give me my living, Mrs. Simpson, and I should be sorry to say a word against them: I don't like to hear that they have been bad for you.'

'Perhaps Mr. Garrett could help us to solve our puzzle,

mother,' said Miss Simpson.

'I don't want to set Mr. Garrett off on a hunt that might waste a lifetime, my dear, nor yet to trouble him with our private affairs.'

'But if you think it in the least likely that I could be of use, I do beg you to tell me what the puzzle is, Mrs. Simpson. If it is finding out anything about a book, you see, I am in rather a good position to do it.'

'Yes, I do see that, but the worst of it is that we don't know the name of the book.'

'Nor what it is about?'

'No, nor that either.'

'Except that we don't think it's in English, mother— and that is not much of a clue.'

'Well, Mr. Garrett,' said Mrs. Simpson, who had not yet resumed her work, and was looking at the fire thoughtfully, 'I shall tell you the story. You will please keep it to yourself, if you don't mind? Thank you. Now it is just this. I had an old uncle, a Dr. Rant. Perhaps you may have heard of him. Not that he was a distinguished man, but from the odd way he chose to be buried.'

'I rather think I have seen the name in some guidebook.'

'That would be it,' said Miss Simpson. 'He left directions—horrid old man!—that he was to be put, sitting at a table in his ordinary clothes, in a brick room that he'd had made underground in a field near his house. Of course the country people say he's been seen about there in his old black cloak.'

'Well, dear, I don't know much about such things,' Mrs. Simpson went on, 'but anyhow he is dead, these twenty years and more. He was a clergyman, though I'm sure I can't imagine how he got to be one: but he did no duty for the last part of his life, which I think was a good thing; and he lived on his own property: a very nice estate not a great way from here. He had no wife or family; only one niece, who was myself, and one nephew, and he had no particular liking for either of us—nor for anyone else, as far as that goes. If anything, he liked my cousin better than he did me—for John was much more like him in his temper, and, I'm afraid I must say, his very mean sharp ways. It might have been different if I had not married; but I did, and that he very much resented. Very well: here he was with this estate and a good deal of money, as it turned out, of which he had the absolute disposal, and it was understood that we—my cousin and I—would share it equally at his death. In a certain winter, over twenty years back, as I said, he was taken ill, and I was sent for to nurse him. My husband was alive then, but the old man would not hear of his coming. As I drove up to the house I saw my cousin John driving away from it in an open fly and looking, I noticed, in very good spirits. I went up and did what I could for my uncle, but I was very soon sure that this would be his last illness; and he was convinced of it too. During the day before he died he got me to sit by him all the time, and I could see there was something, and probably something unpleasant, that he was saving up to tell me, and putting it off as long as he felt he could afford the strength—I'm afraid purposely in order to keep me on the stretch. But, at last, out it came. 'Mary,' he said,—'Mary, I've made my will in John's favour: he has everything, Mary.' Well, of course that came as a bitter shock to me, for we—my husband and I—were not rich people, and if he could have managed to live a little easier than he was obliged to do, I felt it might be the prolonging of his life. But I said little or nothing to my uncle, except that he had a right to do what he pleased: partly because I couldn't think of anything to say, and partly because I was sure there was more to come: and so there was. 'But, Mary,' he said, 'I'm not very fond of John, and I've made another will in your favour. You can have everything. Only you've got to find the will, you see: and I don't mean to tell you where it is.' Then he chuckled to himself, and I waited, for again I was sure he hadn't finished. 'That's a good girl,' he said after a time,—'you wait, and I'll tell you as much as I told John. But just let me remind you, you can't go into court with what I'm saying to you, for you won't be able to produce any collateral evidence beyond your own word, and John's a man that can do a little hard swearing if necessary. Very well then, that's understood. Now, I had the fancy that I wouldn't write this will quite in the common way, so I wrote it in a book, Mary, a printed book. And there's several thousand books in this house. But there! you needn't trouble yourself with them, for it isn't one of them. It's in safe keeping elsewhere: in a place where John can go and find it any day, if he only knew, and you can't. A good will it is: properly signed and witnessed, but I don't think you'll find the witnesses in a hurry.'

'Still I said nothing: if I had moved at all I must have taken hold of the old wretch and shaken him. He lay there laughing to himself, and at last he said:

' 'Well, well, you've taken it very quietly, and as I want to start you both on equal terms, and John has a bit of a purchase in being able to go where the book is, I'll tell you just two other things which I didn't tell him. The will's in English, but you won't know that if ever you see it. That's one thing, and another is that when I'm gone you'll find an envelope in my desk directed to you, and inside it something that would help you to find it, if only you have the wits to use it.'

'In a few hours from that he was gone, and though I made an appeal to John Eldred about it—'

'John Eldred? I beg your pardon, Mrs. Simpson—I think I've seen a Mr. John Eldred. What is he like to look at?'

'It must be ten years since I saw him: he would be a thin elderly man now, and unless he has shaved them off, he has that sort of whiskers which people used to call Dundreary or Piccadilly something.'

'—weepers. Yes, that is the man.'

'Where did you come across him, Mr. Garrett?'

'I don't know if I could tell you,' said Garrett mendaciously, 'in some public place. But you hadn't finished.'

'Really I had nothing much to add, only that John Eldred, of course, paid no attention whatever to my letters, and has enjoyed the estate ever since, while my daughter and I have had to take to the lodging-house business here, which I must say has not turned out by any means so unpleasant as I feared it might.'

'But about the envelope.'

'To be sure! Why, the puzzle turns on that. Give Mr. Garrett the paper out of my desk.'

It was a small slip, with nothing whatever on it but five numerals, not divided or punctuated in any way: 11334.

Mr. Garrett pondered, but there was a light in his eye. Suddenly he 'made a face', and then asked, 'Do you suppose that Mr. Eldred can have any more clue than you have to the title of the book?'

'I have sometimes thought he must,' said Mrs. Simpson, 'and in this way: that my uncle must have made the will not very long before he died (that, I think, he said himself), and got rid of the book immediately afterwards. But all his books were very carefully catalogued: and John has the catalogue: and John was most particular that no books whatever should be sold out of the house. And I'm told that he is always journeying about to booksellers and libraries; so I fancy that he must have found out just which books are missing from my uncle's library of those which are entered in the catalogue, and must be hunting for them.'

'Just so, just so,' said Mr. Garrett, and relapsed into thought.

No later than next day he received a letter which, as he told Mrs. Simpson with great regret, made it absolutely necessary for him to cut short his stay at Burnstow.

Sorry as he was to leave them (and they were at least as sorry to part with him), he had begun to feel that a crisis, all-important to Mrs. (and shall we add, Miss?) Simpson, was very possibly supervening.

In the train Garrett was uneasy and excited. He racked his brains to think whether the press mark of the book which Mr. Eldred had been inquiring after was one in any way corresponding to the numbers on Mrs. Simpson's little bit of paper. But he found to his dismay that the shock of the previous week had really so upset him that he could neither remember any vestige of the title or nature of the book, or even of the locality to which he had gone to seek it. And yet all other parts of library topography and work were clear as ever in his mind.

And another thing—he stamped with annoyance as he thought of it—he had at first hesitated, and then had forgotten, to ask Mrs. Simpson for the name of the place where Eldred lived. That, however, he could write about.

At least he had his clue in the figures on the paper. If they referred to a press mark in his library, they were only susceptible of a limited number of interpretations. They might be divided into 1.13.34, 11.33.4, or 11.3.34. He could try all these in the space of a few minutes, and if any one were missing he had every means of tracing it. He got very quickly to work, though a few minutes had to be spent in explaining his early return to his landlady and his colleagues. 1.13.34. was in place and contained no extraneous writing. As he drew near to Class 11 in the same gallery, its association struck him like a chill. But he must go on. After a cursory glance at 11.33.4 (which first confronted him, and was a perfectly new book) he ran his eye along the line of quartos which fills 11.3. The gap he feared was there: 34 was out. A moment was spent in making sure that it had not been misplaced, and then he was off to the vestibule.

'Has 11.3.34 gone out? Do you recollect noticing that number?'

'Notice the number? What do you take me for, Mr. Garrett? There, take and look over the tickets for yourself, if you've got a free day before you.'

'Well then, has a Mr. Eldred called again?—the old gentleman who came the day I was taken ill. Come! you'd remember him.'

'What do you suppose? Of course I recollect of him: no, he haven't been in again, not since you went off for your 'oliday. And yet I seem to—there now. Roberts'll know. Roberts, do you recollect of the name of Heldred?'

'Not arf,' said Roberts. 'You mean the man that sent a bob over the price for the parcel, and I wish they all did.'

'Do you mean to say you've been sending books to Mr. Eldred? Come, do speak up! Have you?'

'Well now, Mr. Garrett, if a gentleman sends the ticket

all wrote correct and the secketry says this book may go and the box ready addressed sent with the note, and a sum of money sufficient to deefray the railway charges, what would be your action in the matter, Mr. Garrett, if I may take the liberty to ask such a question? Would you or would you not have taken the trouble to oblige, or would you have chucked the 'ole thing under the counter and—'

'You were perfectly right, of course, Hodgson—perfectly right: only, would you kindly oblige me by showing me the ticket Mr. Eldred sent, and letting me know his address?'

'To be sure, Mr. Garrett; so long as I'm not 'ectored about and informed that I don't know my duty, I'm willing to oblige in every way feasible to my power. There is the ticket on the file. J. Eldred, 11.3.34. Title of work: T-a-l-m—well, there, you can make what you like of it—not a novel, I should 'azard the guess. And here is Mr. Heldred's note applying for the book in question, which I see he terms it a track.'

'Thanks, thanks: but the address? There's none on the note.'

'Ah, indeed; well, now... stay now, Mr. Garrett, I 'ave it. Why, that note come inside of the parcel, which was directed very thoughtful to save all trouble, ready to be sent back with the book inside; and if I have made any mistake in this 'ole transaction, it lays just in the one point that I neglected to enter the address in my little book here what I keep. Not but what I dare say there was good reasons for me not entering of it: but there, I haven't the time, neither have you, I dare say, to go into 'em just now. And—no, Mr. Garrett, I do not carry it in my 'ed, else what would be the use of me keeping this little book here—just a ordinary common notebook, you see, which I make a practice of entering all such names and addresses in it as I see fit to do?'

'Admirable arrangement, to be sure—but—all right, thank you. When did the parcel go off?'

'Half-past ten, this morning.'

'Oh, good; and it's just one now.'

Garrett went upstairs in deep thought. How was he to get the address? A telegram to Mrs. Simpson: he might miss a train by waiting for the answer. Yes, there was one other way. She had said that Eldred lived on his uncle's estate. If this were so, he might find that place entered in the donation-book. That he could run through quickly, now that he knew the title of the book. The register was soon before him, and, knowing that the old man had died more than twenty years ago, he gave him a good margin, and turned back to 1870. There was but one entry possible. 1875, August 14th. Talmud: Tractatus Middoth cum comm. R. Nachmanidae. Amstelod. 1707. Given by J. Rant, D.D., of Bretfield Manor.

A gazetteer showed Bretfield to be three miles from a small station on the main line. Now to ask the doorkeeper whether he recollected if the name on the parcel had been anything like Bretfield.

'No, nothing like. It was, now you mention it, Mr.

Garrett, either Bredfield or Britfield, but nothing like that other name what you coated.'

So far well. Next, a time-table. A train could be got in twenty minutes—taking two hours over the journey. The only chance, but one not to be missed; and the train was taken.

If he had been fidgety on the journey up, he was almost distracted on the journey down. If he found Eldred, what could he say? That it had been discovered that the book was a rarity and must be recalled? An obvious untruth. Or that it was believed to contain important manuscript notes? Eldred would of course show him the book, from which the leaf would already have been removed. He might, perhaps, find traces of the removal—a torn edge of a fly-leaf probably—and who could disprove, what Eldred was certain to say, that he too had noticed and regretted the mutilation? Altogether the chase seemed very hopeless. The one chance was this. The book had left the library at 10.30: it might not have been put into the first possible train, at 11.20. Granted that, then he might be lucky enough to arrive simultaneously with it and patch up some story which would induce Eldred to give it up.

It was drawing towards evening when he got out upon the platform of his station, and, like most country stations, this one seemed unnaturally quiet. He waited about till the one or two passengers who got out with him had drifted off, and then inquired of the station-master whether Mr. Eldred was in the neighbourhood.

'Yes, and pretty near too, I believe. I fancy he means

calling here for a parcel he expects. Called for it once today already, didn't he, Bob?' (to the porter).

'Yes, sir, he did; and appeared to think it was all along of me that it didn't come by the two o'clock. Anyhow, I've got it for him now,' and the porter flourished a square parcel, which—a glance assured Garrett—contained all that was of any importance to him at that particular moment.

'Bretfield, sir? Yes—three miles just about. Short cut across these three fields brings it down by half a mile. There: there's Mr. Eldred's trap.'

A dog-cart drove up with two men in it, of whom Garrett, gazing back as he crossed the little station yard, easily recognized one. The fact that Eldred was driving was slightly in his favour—for most likely he would not open the parcel in the presence of his servant. On the other hand, he would get home quickly, and unless Garrett were there within a very few minutes of his arrival, all would be over. He must hurry; and that he did. His short cut took him along one side of a triangle, while the cart had two sides to traverse; and it was delayed a little at the station, so that Garrett was in the third of the three fields when he heard the wheels fairly near. He had made the best progress possible, but the pace at which the cart was coming made him despair. At this rate it must reach home ten minutes before him, and ten minutes would more than suffice for the fulfilment of Mr. Eldred's project.

It was just at this time that the luck fairly turned. The evening was still, and sounds came clearly. Seldom has any sound given greater relief than that which he now heard: that of the cart pulling up. A few words were exchanged, and it drove on. Garrett, halting in the utmost anxiety, was able to see as it drove past the stile (near which he now stood) that it contained only the servant and not Eldred; further, he made out that Eldred was following on foot. From behind the tall hedge by the stile leading into the road he watched the thin wiry figure pass quickly by with the parcel beneath its arm, and feeling in its pockets. Just as he passed the stile something fell out of a pocket upon the grass, but with so little sound that Eldred was not conscious of it. In a moment more it was safe for Garrett to cross the stile into the road and pick up—a box of matches. Eldred went on, and, as he went, his arms made hasty movements, difficult to interpret in the shadow of the trees that overhung the road. But, as Garrett followed cautiously, he found at various points the key to them—a piece of string, and then the wrapper of the parcel—meant to be thrown over the hedge, but sticking in it.

Now Eldred was walking slower, and it could just be made out that he had opened the book and was turning over the leaves. He stopped, evidently troubled by the failing light. Garrett slipped into a gate-opening, but still watched. Eldred, hastily looking around, sat down on a felled tree-trunk by the roadside and held the open book up close to his eyes. Suddenly he laid it, still open, on his knee, and felt in all his pockets: clearly in vain, and clearly to his annoyance. 'You would be glad of your matches now,' thought Garrett. Then he took hold of a leaf, and was carefully tearing it out, when two things happened. First, something black seemed to drop upon the white leaf and run down it, and then as Eldred started and was turning to look behind him, a little dark form appeared to rise out of the shadow behind the tree-trunk and from it two arms enclosing a mass of blackness came before Eldred's face and covered his head and neck. His legs and arms were wildly flourished, but no sound came. Then, there was no more movement. Eldred was alone. He had fallen back into the grass behind the tree-trunk. The book was cast into the roadway. Garrett, his anger and suspicion gone for the moment at the sight of this horrid struggle, rushed up with loud cries of 'Help!' and so too, to his enormous relief, did a labourer who had just emerged from a field opposite. Together they bent over and supported Eldred, but to no purpose. The conclusion that he was dead was inevitable. 'Poor gentleman!' said Garrett to the labourer, when they had laid him down, 'what happened to him, do you think?' 'I wasn't two hundred yards away,' said the man, 'when I see Squire Eldred setting reading in his book, and to my thinking he was took with one of these fits—face seemed to go all over black.' 'Just so,' said Garrett. 'You didn't see anyone near him? It couldn't have been an assault?' 'Not possible—no one couldn't have got away without you or me seeing them.' 'So I thought. Well, we must get some help, and the doctor and the policeman; and perhaps I had better give them this book.'

It was obviously a case for an inquest, and obvious also that Garrett must stay at Bretfield and give his evidence. The medical inspection showed that, though some black dust was found on the face and in the mouth of the deceased, the cause of death was a shock to a weak heart, and not asphyxiation. The fateful book was produced, a respectable quarto printed wholly in Hebrew, and not of an aspect likely to excite even the most sensitive.

'You say, Mr. Garrett, that the deceased gentleman appeared at the moment before his attack to be tearing a leaf out of this book?'

'Yes; I think one of the fly-leaves.'

'There is here a fly-leaf partially torn through. It has Hebrew writing on it. Will you kindly inspect it?'

'There are three names in English, sir, also, and a date. But I am sorry to say I cannot read Hebrew writing.'

'Thank you. The names have the appearance of being signatures. They are John Rant, Walter Gibson, and James Frost, and the date is 20 July, 1875. Does anyone here know any of these names?'

The Rector, who was present, volunteered a statement that the uncle of the deceased, from whom he inherited, had been named Rant.

The book being handed to him, he shook a puzzled head. 'This is not like any Hebrew I ever learnt.'

'You are sure that it is Hebrew?'

'What? Yes—I suppose.... No—my dear sir, you are perfectly right—that is, your suggestion is exactly to the point. Of course—it is not Hebrew at all. It is English, and it is a will.'

It did not take many minutes to show that here was indeed a will of Dr. John Rant, bequeathing the whole of the property lately held by John Eldred to Mrs. Mary Simpson. Clearly the discovery of such a document would amply justify Mr. Eldred's agitation. As to the partial tearing of the leaf, the coroner pointed out that no useful purpose could be attained by speculations whose correctness it would never be possible to establish.

The Tractate Middoth was naturally taken in charge by the coroner for further investigation, and Mr. Garrett explained privately to him the history of it, and the position of events so far as he knew or guessed them.

He returned to his work next day, and on his walk to the station passed the scene of Mr. Eldred's catastrophe. He could hardly leave it without another look, though the recollection of what he had seen there made him shiver, even on that bright morning. He walked round, with some misgivings, behind the felled tree. Something dark that still lay there made him start back for a moment: but it hardly stirred. Looking closer, he saw that it was a thick black mass of cobwebs; and, as he stirred it gingerly with his stick, several large spiders ran out of it into the grass.

There is no great difficulty in imagining the steps by which William Garrett, from being an assistant in a great library, attained to his present position of prospective owner of Bretfield Manor, now in the occupation of his mother-inlaw, Mrs. Mary Simpson.

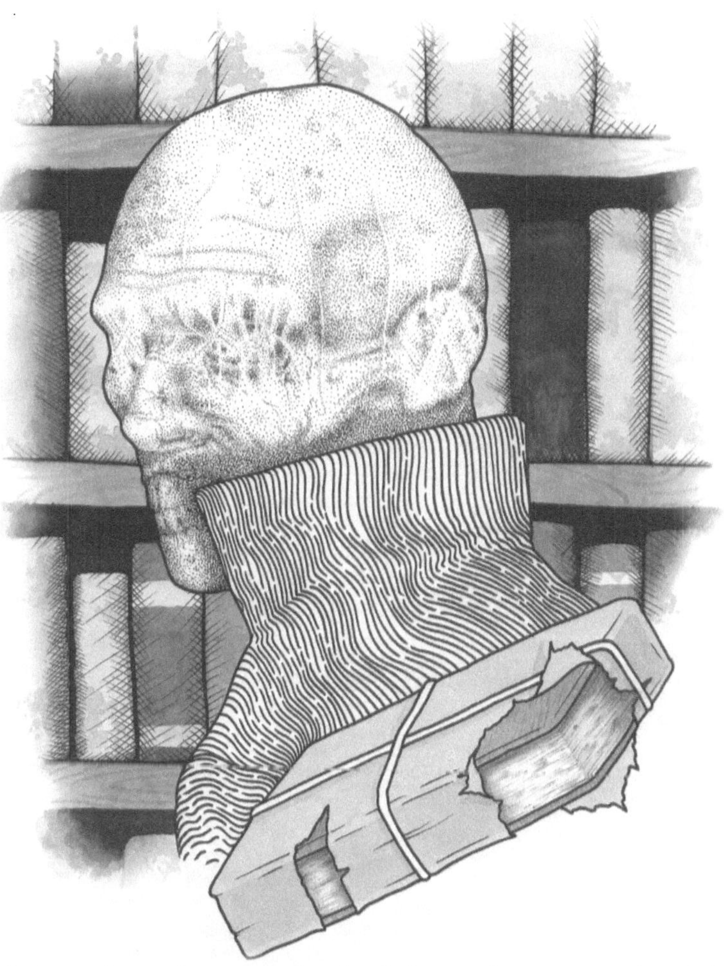

'...from the eyebrows to the cheek-bone, there were cobwebs.'

The Colour Out of Space

by H. P. Lovecraft

West of Arkham the hills rise wild, and there are valleys with deep woods that no axe has ever cut. There are dark narrow glens where the trees slope fantastically, and where thin brooklets trickle without ever having caught the glint of sunlight. On the gentler slopes there are farms, ancient and rocky, with squat, moss-coated cottages brooding eternally over old New England secrets in the lee of great ledges; but these are all vacant now, the wide chimneys crumbling and the shingled sides bulging perilously beneath low gambrel roofs.

The old folk have gone away, and foreigners do not like to live there. French-Canadians have tried it, Italians have tried it, and the Poles have come and departed. It is not because of anything that can be seen or heard or handled, but because of something that is imagined. The place is not good for the imagination, and does not bring restful dreams at night. It must be this which keeps the foreigners away, for old Ammi Pierce has never told them of anything he recalls from the strange days. Ammi, whose head has been a little queer for years, is the only one who still remains, or who ever talks of the strange days; and he dares to do this because his house is so near the open fields and the travelled roads around Arkham.

There was once a road over the hills and through the valleys, that ran straight where the blasted heath is now; but people ceased to use it and a new road was laid curving far toward the south. Traces of the old one can still be found amidst the weeds of a returning wilderness, and some of them will doubtless linger even when half the hollows are flooded for the new reservoir. Then the dark woods will be cut down and the blasted heath will slumber far below blue waters whose surface will mirror the sky and ripple in the sun. And the secrets of the strange days will be one with the deep's secrets; one with the hidden lore of old ocean, and all the mystery of primal earth.

When I went into the hills and vales to survey for the new reservoir they told me the place was evil. They told me this in Arkham, and because that is a very old town full of witch legends I thought the evil must be something which grandams had whispered to children through centuries. The name "blasted heath" seemed to me very odd and theatrical, and I wondered how it had come into the folklore of a Puritan people. Then I saw that dark westward tangle of glens and slopes for myself, and ceased to wonder at anything besides its own elder mystery. It was morning when I saw it, but shadow lurked always there. The trees grew too thickly, and their trunks were too big for any healthy New England wood. There was too much silence in the dim alleys between them, and the floor was too soft with the dank moss and mattings of infinite years of decay.

In the open spaces, mostly along the line of the old road, there were little hillside farms; sometimes with all the buildings standing, sometimes with only one or two, and sometimes with only a lone chimney or fast-filling cellar. Weeds and briers reigned, and furtive wild things rustled in the undergrowth. Upon everything was a haze

of restlessness and oppression; a touch of the unreal and the grotesque, as if some vital element of perspective or chiaroscuro were awry. I did not wonder that the foreigners would not stay, for this was no region to sleep in. It was too much like a landscape of Salvator Rosa; too much like some forbidden woodcut in a tale of terror.

But even all this was not so bad as the blasted heath. I knew it the moment I came upon it at the bottom of a spacious valley; for no other name could fit such a thing, or any other thing fit such a name. It was as if the poet had coined the phrase from having seen this one particular region. It must, I thought as I viewed it, be the outcome of a fire; but why had nothing new ever grown over those five acres of grey desolation that sprawled open to the sky like a great spot eaten by acid in the woods and fields? It lay largely to the north of the ancient road line, but encroached a little on the other side. I felt an odd reluctance about approaching, and did so at last only because my business took me through and past it. There was no vegetation of any kind on that broad expanse, but only a fine grey dust or ash which no wind seemed ever to blow about. The trees near it were sickly and stunted, and many dead trunks stood or lay rotting at the rim. As I walked hurriedly by I saw the tumbled bricks and stones of an old chimney and cellar on my right, and the yawning black maw of an abandoned well whose stagnant vapours played strange tricks with the hues of the sunlight. Even the long, dark woodland climb beyond seemed welcome in contrast, and I marvelled no more at the frightened whispers of Arkham people. There had been no house or ruin near; even in the old days the place must have been lonely and remote. And at twilight, dreading to repass that ominous spot, I walked circuitously back to the town by the curving road on the south. I vaguely wished some clouds would gather, for an odd timidity about the deep skyey voids above had crept into my soul.

In the evening I asked old people in Arkham about the blasted heath, and what was meant by that phrase "strange days" which so many evasively muttered. I could not, however, get any good answers, except that all the mystery was much more recent than I had dreamed. It was not a matter of old legendry at all, but something within the lifetime of those who spoke. It had happened in the 'eighties, and a family had disappeared or was killed. Speakers would not be exact; and because they all told me to pay no attention to old Ammi Pierce's crazy tales, I sought him out the next morning, having heard that he lived alone in the ancient tottering cottage where the trees first begin to get very thick. It was a fearsomely archaic place, and had begun to exude the faint miasmal odour which clings about houses that have stood too long. Only with persistent knocking could I rouse the aged man, and when he shuffled timidly to the door I could tell he was not glad to see me. He was not so feeble as I had expected; but his eyes drooped in a curious way, and his unkempt clothing and white beard made him seem very worn and dismal. Not knowing just how he could best be launched on his tales, I feigned a matter of business; told him of my surveying, and asked vague questions about the district. He was far brighter and more educated than I had been led to think, and before I knew it had grasped quite as much of the subject as any man I had talked with in Arkham. He was not like other rustics I had known in the sections where reservoirs were to be. From him there were no protests at the miles of old wood and farmland to be blotted out, though perhaps there would have been had not his home lain outside the

bounds of the future lake. Relief was all that he shewed; relief at the doom of the dark ancient valleys through which he had roamed all his life. They were better under water now—better under water since the strange days. And with this opening his husky voice sank low, while his body leaned forward and his right forefinger began to point shakily and impressively.

It was then that I heard the story, and as the rambling voice scraped and whispered on I shivered again and again despite the summer day. Often I had to recall the speaker from ramblings, piece out scientific points which he knew only by a fading parrot memory of professors' talk, or bridge over gaps where his sense of logic and continuity broke down. When he was done I did not wonder that his mind had snapped a trifle, or that the folk of Arkham would not speak much of the blasted heath. I hurried back before sunset to my hotel, unwilling to have the stars come out above me in the open; and the next day returned to Boston to give up my position. I could not go into that dim chaos of old forest and slope again, or face another time that grey blasted heath where the black well yawned deep beside the tumbled bricks and stones. The reservoir will soon be built now, and all those elder secrets will be safe forever under watery fathoms. But even then I do not believe I would like to visit that country by night—at least, not when the sinister stars are out; and nothing could bribe me to drink the new city water of Arkham.

It all began, old Ammi said, with the meteorite. Before that time there had been no wild legends at all since the witch trials, and even then these western woods were not feared half so much as the small island in the Miskatonic where the devil held court beside a curious stone altar older than the Indians. These were not haunted woods, and their fantastic dusk was never terrible till the strange days. Then there had come that white noontide cloud, that string of explosions in the air, and that pillar of smoke from the valley far in the wood. And by night all Arkham had heard of the great rock that fell out of the sky and bedded itself in the ground beside the well at the Nahum Gardner place. That was the house which had stood where the blasted heath was to come—the trim white Nahum Gardner house amidst its fertile gardens and orchards.

Nahum had come to town to tell people about the stone, and had dropped in at Ammi Pierce's on the way. Ammi was forty then, and all the queer things were fixed very strongly in his mind. He and his wife had gone with the three professors from Miskatonic University who hastened out the next morning to see the weird visitor from unknown stellar space, and had wondered why Nahum had called it so large the day before. It had shrunk, Nahum said as he pointed out the big brownish mound above the ripped earth and charred grass near the archaic well-sweep in his front yard; but the wise men answered that stones do not shrink. Its heat lingered persistently, and Nahum declared it had glowed faintly in the night. The professors tried it with a geologist's hammer and found it was oddly soft. It was, in truth, so soft as to be almost plastic; and they gouged rather than chipped a specimen to take back to the college for testing. They took it in an old pail borrowed from Nahum's kitchen, for even the small piece refused to grow cool. On the trip back they stopped at Ammi's to rest, and seemed thoughtful when Mrs. Pierce remarked that the fragment was growing smaller and burning the bottom of the pail. Truly, it was not large, but perhaps they had taken less than they thought.

The day after that—all this was in June of '82—the professors had trooped out again in a great excitement. As they passed Ammi's they told him what queer things the specimen had done, and how it had faded wholly away when they put it in a glass beaker. The beaker had gone, too, and the wise men talked of the strange stone's affinity for silicon. It had acted quite unbelievably in that well-ordered laboratory; doing nothing at all and shewing no occluded gases when heated on charcoal, being wholly negative in the borax bead, and soon proving itself absolutely non-volatile at any producible temperature, including that of the oxy-hydrogen blowpipe. On an anvil it appeared highly malleable, and in the dark its luminosity was very marked. Stubbornly refusing to grow cool, it soon had the college in a state of real excitement; and when upon heating before the spectroscope it displayed shining bands unlike any known colours of the normal spectrum there was much breathless talk of new elements, bizarre optical properties, and other things which puzzled men of science are wont to say when faced by the unknown.

Hot as it was, they tested it in a crucible with all the proper reagents. Water did nothing. Hydrochloric acid was the same. Nitric acid and even aqua regia merely hissed and spattered against its torrid invulnerability. Ammi had difficulty in recalling all these things, but recognised some solvents as I mentioned them in the usual order of use. There were ammonia and caustic soda, alcohol and ether, nauseous carbon disulphide and a dozen others; but although the weight grew steadily less as time passed, and the fragment seemed to be slightly cooling, there was no change in the solvents to shew that they had attacked the substance at all. It was a metal, though, beyond a doubt. It was magnetic, for one thing; and after its immersion in the acid solvents there seemed to be faint traces of the Widmannstätten figures found on meteoric iron. When the cooling had grown very considerable, the testing was carried on in glass; and it was in a glass beaker that they left all the chips made of the original fragment during the work. The next morning both chips and beaker were gone without trace, and only a charred spot marked the place on the wooden shelf where they had been.

All this the professors told Ammi as they paused at his door, and once more he went with them to see the stony messenger from the stars, though this time his wife did not accompany him. It had now most certainly shrunk, and even the sober professors could not doubt the truth of what they saw. All around the dwindling brown lump near the well was a vacant space, except where the earth had caved in; and whereas it had been a good seven feet across the day before, it was now scarcely five. It was still hot, and the sages studied its surface curiously as they detached another and larger piece with hammer and chisel. They gouged deeply this time, and as they pried away the smaller mass they saw that the core of the thing was not quite homogeneous.

They had uncovered what seemed to be the side of a large coloured globule imbedded in the substance. The colour, which resembled some of the bands in the meteor's strange spectrum, was almost impossible to describe; and it was only by analogy that they called it colour at all. Its texture was glossy, and upon tapping it appeared to promise both brittleness and hollowness. One of the professors gave it a smart blow with a hammer, and

it burst with a nervous little pop. Nothing was emitted, and all trace of the thing vanished with the puncturing. It left behind a hollow spherical space about three inches across, and all thought it probable that others would be discovered as the enclosing substance wasted away.

Conjecture was vain; so after a futile attempt to find additional globules by drilling, the seekers left again with their new specimen—which proved, however, as baffling in the laboratory as its predecessor had been. Aside from being almost plastic, having heat, magnetism, and slight luminosity, cooling slightly in powerful acids, possessing an unknown spectrum, wasting away in air, and attacking silicon compounds with mutual destruction as a result, it presented no identifying features whatsoever; and at the end of the tests the college scientists were forced to own that they could not place it. It was nothing of this earth, but a piece of the great outside; and as such dowered with outside properties and obedient to outside laws.

That night there was a thunderstorm, and when the professors went out to Nahum's the next day they met with a bitter disappointment. The stone, magnetic as it had been, must have had some peculiar electrical property; for it had "drawn the lightning", as Nahum said, with a singular persistence. Six times within an hour the farmer saw the lightning strike the furrow in the front yard, and when the storm was over nothing remained but a ragged pit by the ancient well-sweep, half-choked with caved-in earth. Digging had borne no fruit, and the scientists verified the fact of the utter vanishment. The failure was total; so that nothing was left to do but go back to the laboratory and test again the disappearing fragment left carefully cased in lead. That fragment lasted a week, at the end of which nothing of value had been learned of it. When it had gone, no residue was left behind, and in time the professors felt scarcely sure they had indeed seen with waking eyes that cryptic vestige of the fathomless gulfs outside; that lone, weird message from other universes and other realms of matter, force, and entity.

As was natural, the Arkham papers made much of the incident with its collegiate sponsoring, and sent reporters to talk with Nahum Gardner and his family. At least one Boston daily also sent a scribe, and Nahum quickly became a kind of local celebrity. He was a lean, genial person of about fifty, living with his wife and three sons on the pleasant farmstead in the valley. He and Ammi exchanged visits frequently, as did their wives; and Ammi had nothing but praise for him after all these years. He seemed slightly proud of the notice his place had attracted, and talked often of the meteorite in the succeeding weeks. That July and August were hot, and Nahum worked hard at his haying in the ten-acre pasture across Chapman's Brook; his rattling wain wearing deep ruts in the shadowy lanes between. The labour tired him more than it had in other years, and he felt that age was beginning to tell on him.

Then fell the time of fruit and harvest. The pears and apples slowly ripened, and Nahum vowed that his orchards were prospering as never before. The fruit was growing to phenomenal size and unwonted gloss, and in such abundance that extra barrels were ordered to handle the future crop. But with the ripening came sore disappointment; for of all that gorgeous array of specious lusciousness not one single jot was fit to eat. Into the fine flavour of the pears and apples had crept a stealthy bitterness and sickishness, so that even the smallest of

bites induced a lasting disgust. It was the same with the melons and tomatoes, and Nahum sadly saw that his entire crop was lost. Quick to connect events, he declared that the meteorite had poisoned the soil, and thanked heaven that most of the other crops were in the upland lot along the road.

Winter came early, and was very cold. Ammi saw Nahum less often than usual, and observed that he had begun to look worried. The rest of his family, too, seemed to have grown taciturn; and were far from steady in their churchgoing or their attendance at the various social events of the countryside. For this reserve or melancholy no cause could be found, though all the household confessed now and then to poorer health and a feeling of vague disquiet. Nahum himself gave the most definite statement of anyone when he said he was disturbed about certain footprints in the snow. They were the usual winter prints of red squirrels, white rabbits, and foxes, but the brooding farmer professed to see something not quite right about their nature and arrangement. He was never specific, but appeared to think that they were not as characteristic of the anatomy and habits of squirrels and rabbits and foxes as they ought to be. Ammi listened without interest to this talk until one night when he drove past Nahum's house in his sleigh on the way back from Clark's Corners. There had been a moon, and a rabbit had run across the road, and the leaps of that rabbit were longer than either Ammi or his horse liked. The latter, indeed, had almost run away when brought up by a firm rein. Thereafter Ammi gave Nahum's tales more respect, and wondered why the Gardner dogs seemed so cowed and quivering every morning. They had, it developed, nearly lost the spirit to bark.

In February the McGregor boys from Meadow Hill were out shooting woodchucks, and not far from the Gardner place bagged a very peculiar specimen. The proportions of its body seemed slightly altered in a queer way impossible to describe, while its face had taken on an expression which no one ever saw in a woodchuck before. The boys were genuinely frightened, and threw the thing away at once, so that only their grotesque tales of it ever reached the people of the countryside. But the shying of the horses near Nahum's house had now become an acknowledged thing, and all the basis for a cycle of whispered legend was fast taking form.

People vowed that the snow melted faster around Nahum's than it did anywhere else, and early in March there was an awed discussion in Potter's general store at Clark's Corners. Stephen Rice had driven past Gardner's in the morning, and had noticed the skunk-cabbages coming up through the mud by the woods across the road. Never were things of such size seen before, and they held strange colours that could not be put into any words. Their shapes were monstrous, and the horse had snorted at an odour which struck Stephen as wholly unprecedented. That afternoon several persons drove past to see the abnormal growth, and all agreed that plants of that kind ought never to sprout in a healthy world. The bad fruit of the fall before was freely mentioned, and it went from mouth to mouth that there was poison in Nahum's ground. Of course it was the meteorite; and remembering how strange the men from the college had found that stone to be, several farmers spoke about the matter to them.

One day they paid Nahum a visit; but having no love of wild tales and folklore were very conservative in

what they inferred. The plants were certainly odd, but all skunk-cabbages are more or less odd in shape and odour and hue. Perhaps some mineral element from the stone had entered the soil, but it would soon be washed away. And as for the footprints and frightened horses—of course this was mere country talk which such a phenomenon as the aërolite would be certain to start. There was really nothing for serious men to do in cases of wild gossip, for superstitious rustics will say and believe anything. And so all through the strange days the professors stayed away in contempt. Only one of them, when given two phials of dust for analysis in a police job over a year and a half later, recalled that the queer colour of that skunk-cabbage had been very like one of the anomalous bands of light shewn by the meteor fragment in the college spectroscope, and like the brittle globule found imbedded in the stone from the abyss. The samples in this analysis case gave the same odd bands at first, though later they lost the property.

The trees budded prematurely around Nahum's, and at night they swayed ominously in the wind. Nahum's second son Thaddeus, a lad of fifteen, swore that they swayed also when there was no wind; but even the gossips would not credit this. Certainly, however, restlessness was in the air. The entire Gardner family developed the habit of stealthy listening, though not for any sound which they could consciously name. The listening was, indeed, rather a product of moments when consciousness seemed half to slip away. Unfortunately such moments increased week by week, till it became common speech that "something was wrong with all Nahum's folks". When the early saxifrage came out it had another strange colour; not quite like that of the skunk-cabbage, but plainly related and equally unknown to anyone who saw it. Nahum took some blossoms to Arkham and shewed them to the editor of the Gazette, but that dignitary did no more than write a humorous article about them, in which the dark fears of rustics were held up to polite ridicule. It was a mistake of Nahum's to tell a stolid city man about the way the great, overgrown mourning-cloak butterflies behaved in connexion with these saxifrages.

April brought a kind of madness to the country folk, and began that disuse of the road past Nahum's which led to its ultimate abandonment. It was the vegetation. All the orchard trees blossomed forth in strange colours, and through the stony soil of the yard and adjacent pasturage there sprang up a bizarre growth which only a botanist could connect with the proper flora of the region. No sane wholesome colours were anywhere to be seen except in the green grass and leafage; but everywhere those hectic and prismatic variants of some diseased, underlying primary tone without a place among the known tints of earth. The Dutchman's breeches became a thing of sinister menace, and the bloodroots grew insolent in their chromatic perversion. Ammi and the Gardners thought that most of the colours had a sort of haunting familiarity, and decided that they reminded one of the brittle globule in the meteor. Nahum ploughed and sowed the ten-acre pasture and the upland lot, but did nothing with the land around the house. He knew it would be of no use, and hoped that the summer's strange growths would draw all the poison from the soil. He was prepared for almost anything now, and had grown used to the sense of something near him waiting to be heard. The shunning of his house by neighbours told on him, of course; but it told on his wife more. The boys were better off, being at school each day; but they could not help being frightened by the gossip. Thaddeus, an especially sensitive youth, suffered the most.

In May the insects came, and Nahum's place became a nightmare of buzzing and crawling. Most of the creatures seemed not quite usual in their aspects and motions, and their nocturnal habits contradicted all former experience. The Gardners took to watching at night—watching in all directions at random for something . . . they could not tell what. It was then that they all owned that Thaddeus had been right about the trees. Mrs. Gardner was the next to see it from the window as she watched the swollen boughs of a maple against a moonlit sky. The boughs surely moved, and there was no wind. It must be the sap. Strangeness had come into everything growing now. Yet it was none of Nahum's family at all who made the next discovery. Familiarity had dulled them, and what they could not see was glimpsed by a timid windmill salesman from Bolton who drove by one night in ignorance of the country legends. What he told in Arkham was given a short paragraph in the Gazette; and it was there that all the farmers, Nahum included, saw it first. The night had been dark and the buggy-lamps faint, but around a farm in the valley which everyone knew from the account must be Nahum's the darkness had been less thick. A dim though distinct luminosity seemed to inhere in all the vegetation, grass, leaves, and blossoms alike, while at one moment a detached piece of the phosphorescence appeared to stir furtively in the yard near the barn.

The grass had so far seemed untouched, and the cows were freely pastured in the lot near the house, but toward the end of May the milk began to be bad. Then Nahum had the cows driven to the uplands, after which the trouble ceased. Not long after this the change in grass and leaves became apparent to the eye. All the verdure was going grey, and was developing a highly singular quality of brittleness. Ammi was now the only person who ever visited the place, and his visits were becoming fewer and fewer. When school closed the Gardners were virtually cut off from the world, and sometimes let Ammi do their errands in town. They were failing curiously both physically and mentally, and no one was surprised when the news of Mrs. Gardner's madness stole around.

It happened in June, about the anniversary of the meteor's fall, and the poor woman screamed about things in the air which she could not describe. In her raving there was not a single specific noun, but only verbs and pronouns. Things moved and changed and fluttered, and ears tingled to impulses which were not wholly sounds. Something was taken away—she was being drained of something—something was fastening itself on her that ought not to be—someone must make it keep off—nothing was ever still in the night—the walls and windows shifted. Nahum did not send her to the county asylum, but let her wander about the house as long as she was harmless to herself and others. Even when her expression changed he did nothing. But when the boys grew afraid of her, and Thaddeus nearly fainted at the way she made faces at him, he decided to keep her locked in the attic. By July she had ceased to speak and crawled on all fours, and before that month was over Nahum got the mad notion that she was slightly luminous in the dark, as he now clearly saw was the case with the nearby vegetation.

It was a little before this that the horses had stampeded. Something had aroused them in the night, and their neighing and kicking in their stalls had been terrible. There seemed virtually nothing to do to calm them, and when Nahum opened the stable door they

all bolted out like frightened woodland deer. It took a week to track all four, and when found they were seen to be quite useless and unmanageable. Something had snapped in their brains, and each one had to be shot for its own good. Nahum borrowed a horse from Ammi for his haying, but found it would not approach the barn. It shied, balked, and whinnied, and in the end he could do nothing but drive it into the yard while the men used their own strength to get the heavy wagon near enough the hayloft for convenient pitching. And all the while the vegetation was turning grey and brittle. Even the flowers whose hues had been so strange were greying now, and the fruit was coming out grey and dwarfed and tasteless. The asters and goldenrod bloomed grey and distorted, and the roses and zinneas and hollyhocks in the front yard were such blasphemous-looking things that Nahum's oldest boy Zenas cut them down. The strangely puffed insects died about that time, even the bees that had left their hives and taken to the woods.

By September all the vegetation was fast crumbling to a greyish powder, and Nahum feared that the trees would die before the poison was out of the soil. His wife now had spells of terrific screaming, and he and the boys were in a constant state of nervous tension. They shunned people now, and when school opened the boys did not go. But it was Ammi, on one of his rare visits, who first realised that the well water was no longer good. It had an evil taste that was not exactly foetid nor exactly salty, and Ammi advised his friend to dig another well on higher ground to use till the soil was good again. Nahum, however, ignored the warning, for he had by that time become calloused to strange and unpleasant things. He and the boys continued to use the tainted supply, drinking it as listlessly and mechanically as they ate their meagre and ill-cooked meals and did their thankless and monotonous chores through the aimless days. There was something of stolid resignation about them all, as if they walked half in another world between lines of nameless guards to a certain and familiar doom.

Thaddeus went mad in September after a visit to the well. He had gone with a pail and had come back empty-handed, shrieking and waving his arms, and sometimes lapsing into an inane titter or a whisper about "the moving colours down there". Two in one family was pretty bad, but Nahum was very brave about it. He let the boy run about for a week until he began stumbling and hurting himself, and then he shut him in an attic room across the hall from his mother's. The way they screamed at each other from behind their locked doors was very terrible, especially to little Merwin, who fancied they talked in some terrible language that was not of earth. Merwin was getting frightfully imaginative, and his restlessness was worse after the shutting away of the brother who had been his greatest playmate.

Almost at the same time the mortality among the livestock commenced. Poultry turned greyish and died very quickly, their meat being found dry and noisome upon cutting. Hogs grew inordinately fat, then suddenly began to undergo loathsome changes which no one could explain. Their meat was of course useless, and Nahum was at his wit's end. No rural veterinary would approach his place, and the city veterinary from Arkham was openly baffled. The swine began growing grey and brittle and falling to pieces before they died, and their eyes and muzzles developed singular alterations. It was very inexplicable, for they had never been fed from the tainted vegetation. Then something struck the cows. Certain

areas or sometimes the whole body would be uncannily shrivelled or compressed, and atrocious collapses or disintegrations were common. In the last stages—and death was always the result—there would be a greying and turning brittle like that which beset the hogs. There could be no question of poison, for all the cases occurred in a locked and undisturbed barn. No bites of prowling things could have brought the virus, for what live beast of earth can pass through solid obstacles? It must be only natural disease—yet what disease could wreak such results was beyond any mind's guessing. When the harvest came there was not an animal surviving on the place, for the stock and poultry were dead and the dogs had run away. These dogs, three in number, had all vanished one night and were never heard of again. The five cats had left some time before, but their going was scarcely noticed since there now seemed to be no mice, and only Mrs. Gardner had made pets of the graceful felines.

On the nineteenth of October Nahum staggered into Ammi's house with hideous news. The death had come to poor Thaddeus in his attic room, and it had come in a way which could not be told. Nahum had dug a grave in the railed family plot behind the farm, and had put therein what he found. There could have been nothing from outside, for the small barred window and locked door were intact; but it was much as it had been in the barn. Ammi and his wife consoled the stricken man as best they could, but shuddered as they did so. Stark terror seemed to cling round the Gardners and all they touched, and the very presence of one in the house was a breath from regions unnamed and unnamable. Ammi accompanied Nahum home with the greatest reluctance, and did what he might to calm the hysterical sobbing of little Merwin. Zenas needed no calming. He had come of late to do nothing but stare into space and obey what his father told him; and Ammi thought that his fate was very merciful. Now and then Merwin's screams were answered faintly from the attic, and in response to an inquiring look Nahum said that his wife was getting very feeble. When night approached, Ammi managed to get away; for not even friendship could make him stay in that spot when the faint glow of the vegetation began and the trees may or may not have swayed without wind. It was really lucky for Ammi that he was not more imaginative. Even as things were, his mind was bent ever so slightly; but had he been able to connect and reflect upon all the portents around him he must inevitably have turned a total maniac. In the twilight he hastened home, the screams of the mad woman and the nervous child ringing horribly in his ears.

Three days later Nahum lurched into Ammi's kitchen in the early morning, and in the absence of his host stammered out a desperate tale once more, while Mrs. Pierce listened in a clutching fright. It was little Merwin this time. He was gone. He had gone out late at night with a lantern and pail for water, and had never come back. He'd been going to pieces for days, and hardly knew what he was about. Screamed at everything. There had been a frantic shriek from the yard then, but before the father could get to the door, the boy was gone. There was no glow from the lantern he had taken, and of the child himself no trace. At the time Nahum thought the lantern and pail were gone too; but when dawn came, and the man had plodded back from his all-night search of the woods and fields, he had found some very curious things near the well. There was a crushed and apparently somewhat melted mass of iron which had certainly been the lantern; while a bent bail and twisted iron hoops

beside it, both half-fused, seemed to hint at the remnants of the pail. That was all. Nahum was past imagining, Mrs. Pierce was blank, and Ammi, when he had reached home and heard the tale, could give no guess. Merwin was gone, and there would be no use in telling the people around, who shunned all Gardners now. No use, either, in telling the city people at Arkham who laughed at everything. Thad was gone, and now Merwin was gone. Something was creeping and creeping and waiting to be seen and felt and heard. Nahum would go soon, and he wanted Ammi to look after his wife and Zenas if they survived him. It must all be a judgment of some sort; though he could not fancy what for, since he had always walked uprightly in the Lord's ways so far as he knew.

For over two weeks Ammi saw nothing of Nahum; and then, worried about what might have happened, he overcame his fears and paid the Gardner place a visit. There was no smoke from the great chimney, and for a moment the visitor was apprehensive of the worst. The aspect of the whole farm was shocking—greyish withered grass and leaves on the ground, vines falling in brittle wreckage from archaic walls and gables, and great bare trees clawing up at the grey November sky with a studied malevolence which Ammi could not but feel had come from some subtle change in the tilt of the branches. But Nahum was alive, after all. He was weak, and lying on a couch in the low-ceiled kitchen, but perfectly conscious and able to give simple orders to Zenas. The room was deadly cold; and as Ammi visibly shivered, the host shouted huskily to Zenas for more wood. Wood, indeed, was sorely needed; since the cavernous fireplace was unlit and empty, with a cloud of soot blowing about in the chill wind that came down the chimney. Presently Nahum asked him if the extra wood had made him any more comfortable, and then Ammi saw what had happened. The stoutest cord had broken at last, and the hapless farmer's mind was proof against more sorrow.

Questioning tactfully, Ammi could get no clear data at all about the missing Zenas. "In the well—he lives in the well—" was all that the clouded father would say. Then there flashed across the visitor's mind a sudden thought of the mad wife, and he changed his line of inquiry. "Nabby? Why, here she is!" was the surprised response of poor Nahum, and Ammi soon saw that he must search for himself. Leaving the harmless babbler on the couch, he took the keys from their nail beside the door and climbed the creaking stairs to the attic. It was very close and noisome up there, and no sound could be heard from any direction. Of the four doors in sight, only one was locked, and on this he tried various keys on the ring he had taken. The third key proved the right one, and after some fumbling Ammi threw open the low white door.

It was quite dark inside, for the window was small and half-obscured by the crude wooden bars; and Ammi could see nothing at all on the wide-planked floor. The stench was beyond enduring, and before proceeding further he had to retreat to another room and return with his lungs filled with breathable air. When he did enter he saw something dark in the corner, and upon seeing it more clearly he screamed outright. While he screamed he thought a momentary cloud eclipsed the window, and a second later he felt himself brushed as if by some hateful current of vapour. Strange colours danced before his eyes; and had not a present horror numbed him he would have thought of the globule in the meteor that the geologist's hammer had shattered, and of the morbid vegetation that

had sprouted in the spring. As it was he thought only of the blasphemous monstrosity which confronted him, and which all too clearly had shared the nameless fate of young Thaddeus and the livestock. But the terrible thing about this horror was that it very slowly and perceptibly moved as it continued to crumble.

Ammi would give me no added particulars to this scene, but the shape in the corner does not reappear in his tale as a moving object. There are things which cannot be mentioned, and what is done in common humanity is sometimes cruelly judged by the law. I gathered that no moving thing was left in that attic room, and that to leave anything capable of motion there would have been a deed so monstrous as to damn any accountable being to eternal torment. Anyone but a stolid farmer would have fainted or gone mad, but Ammi walked conscious through that low doorway and locked the accursed secret behind him. There would be Nahum to deal with now; he must be fed and tended, and removed to some place where he could be cared for.

Commencing his descent of the dark stairs, Ammi heard a thud below him. He even thought a scream had been suddenly choked off, and recalled nervously the clammy vapour which had brushed by him in that frightful room above. What presence had his cry and entry started up? Halted by some vague fear, he heard still further sounds below. Indubitably there was a sort of heavy dragging, and a most detestably sticky noise as of some fiendish and unclean species of suction. With an associative sense goaded to feverish heights, he thought unaccountably of what he had seen upstairs. Good God! What eldritch dream-world was this into which he had blundered? He dared move neither backward nor forward, but stood there trembling at the black curve of the boxed-in staircase. Every trifle of the scene burned itself into his brain. The sounds, the sense of dread expectancy, the darkness, the steepness of the narrow steps—and merciful heaven! . . . the faint but unmistakable luminosity of all the woodwork in sight; steps, sides, exposed laths, and beams alike!

Then there burst forth a frantic whinny from Ammi's horse outside, followed at once by a clatter which told of a frenzied runaway. In another moment horse and buggy had gone beyond earshot, leaving the frightened man on the dark stairs to guess what had sent them. But that was not all. There had been another sound out there. A sort of liquid splash—water—it must have been the well. He had left Hero untied near it, and a buggy-wheel must have brushed the coping and knocked in a stone. And still the pale phosphorescence glowed in that detestably ancient woodwork. God! how old the house was! Most of it built before 1670, and the gambrel roof not later than 1730.

A feeble scratching on the floor downstairs now sounded distinctly, and Ammi's grip tightened on a heavy stick he had picked up in the attic for some purpose. Slowly nerving himself, he finished his descent and walked boldly toward the kitchen. But he did not complete the walk, because what he sought was no longer there. It had come to meet him, and it was still alive after a fashion. Whether it had crawled or whether it had been dragged by any external force, Ammi could not say; but the death had been at it. Everything had happened in the last half-hour, but collapse, greying, and disintegration were already far advanced. There was a horrible brittleness, and dry fragments were scaling off. Ammi could not touch it, but looked horrifiedly into

the distorted parody that had been a face. "What was it, Nahum—what was it?" he whispered, and the cleft, bulging lips were just able to crackle out a final answer.

"Nothin' . . . nothin' . . . the colour . . . it burns . . . cold an' wet . . . but it burns . . . it lived in the well . . . I seen it . . . a kind o' smoke . . . jest like the flowers last spring . . . the well shone at night . . . Thad an' Mernie an' Zenas . . . everything alive . . . suckin' the life out of everything . . . in that stone . . . it must a' come in that stone . . . pizened the whole place . . . dun't know what it wants . . . that round thing them men from the college dug outen the stone . . . they smashed it . . . it was that same colour . . . jest the same, like the flowers an' plants . . . must a' ben more of 'em . . . seeds . . . seeds . . . they growed . . . I seen it the fust time this week . . . must a' got strong on Zenas . . . he was a big boy, full o' life . . . it beats down your mind an' then gits ye . . . burns ye up . . . in the well water . . . you was right about that . . . evil water . . . Zenas never come back from the well . . . can't git away . . . draws ye . . . ye know summ'at's comin', but 'tain't no use . . . I seen it time an' agin senct Zenas was took . . . whar's Nabby, Ammi? . . . my head's no good . . . dun't know how long senct I fed her . . . it'll git her ef we ain't keerful . . . jest a colour . . . her face is gettin' to hev that colour sometimes towards night . . . an' it burns an' sucks . . . it come from some place whar things ain't as they is here . . . one o' them professors said so . . . he was right . . . look out, Ammi, it'll do suthin' more . . . sucks the life out. . . ."

But that was all. That which spoke could speak no more because it had completely caved in. Ammi laid a red checked tablecloth over what was left and reeled out the back door into the fields. He climbed the slope to the ten-acre pasture and stumbled home by the north road and the woods. He could not pass that well from which his horse had run away. He had looked at it through the window, and had seen that no stone was missing from the rim. Then the lurching buggy had not dislodged anything after all—the splash had been something else— something which went into the well after it had done with poor Nahum. . . .

When Ammi reached his house the horse and buggy had arrived before him and thrown his wife into fits of anxiety. Reassuring her without explanations, he set out at once for Arkham and notified the authorities that the Gardner family was no more. He indulged in no details, but merely told of the deaths of Nahum and Nabby, that of Thaddeus being already known, and mentioned that the cause seemed to be the same strange ailment which had killed the livestock. He also stated that Merwin and Zenas had disappeared. There was considerable questioning at the police station, and in the end Ammi was compelled to take three officers to the Gardner farm, together with the coroner, the medical examiner, and the veterinary who had treated the diseased animals. He went much against his will, for the afternoon was advancing and he feared the fall of night over that accursed place, but it was some comfort to have so many people with him.

The six men drove out in a democrat-wagon, following Ammi's buggy, and arrived at the pest-ridden farmhouse about four o'clock. Used as the officers were to gruesome experiences, not one remained unmoved at what was found in the attic and under the red checked tablecloth on the floor below. The whole aspect of the farm with its grey desolation was terrible enough, but those two crumbling objects were beyond all bounds. No one could look long at them, and even the medical

examiner admitted that there was very little to examine. Specimens could be analysed, of course, so he busied himself in obtaining them—and here it develops that a very puzzling aftermath occurred at the college laboratory where the two phials of dust were finally taken. Under the spectroscope both samples gave off an unknown spectrum, in which many of the baffling bands were precisely like those which the strange meteor had yielded in the previous year. The property of emitting this spectrum vanished in a month, the dust thereafter consisting mainly of alkaline phosphates and carbonates.

Ammi would not have told the men about the well if he had thought they meant to do anything then and there. It was getting toward sunset, and he was anxious to be away. But he could not help glancing nervously at the stony curb by the great sweep, and when a detective questioned him he admitted that Nahum had feared something down there—so much so that he had never even thought of searching it for Merwin or Zenas. After that nothing would do but that they empty and explore the well immediately, so Ammi had to wait trembling while pail after pail of rank water was hauled up and splashed on the soaking ground outside. The men sniffed in disgust at the fluid, and toward the last held their noses against the foetor they were uncovering. It was not so long a job as they had feared it would be, since the water was phenomenally low. There is no need to speak too exactly of what they found. Merwin and Zenas were both there, in part, though the vestiges were mainly skeletal. There were also a small deer and a large dog in about the same state, and a number of bones of smaller animals. The ooze and slime at the bottom seemed inexplicably porous and bubbling, and a man who descended on hand-holds with a long pole found that he could sink the wooden shaft to any depth in the mud of the floor without meeting any solid obstruction.

Twilight had now fallen, and lanterns were brought from the house. Then, when it was seen that nothing further could be gained from the well, everyone went indoors and conferred in the ancient sitting-room while the intermittent light of a spectral half-moon played wanly on the grey desolation outside. The men were frankly nonplussed by the entire case, and could find no convincing common element to link the strange vegetable conditions, the unknown disease of livestock and humans, and the unaccountable deaths of Merwin and Zenas in the tainted well. They had heard the common country talk, it is true; but could not believe that anything contrary to natural law had occurred. No doubt the meteor had poisoned the soil, but the illness of persons and animals who had eaten nothing grown in that soil was another matter. Was it the well water? Very possibly. It might be a good idea to analyse it. But what peculiar madness could have made both boys jump into the well? Their deeds were so similar—and the fragments shewed that they had both suffered from the grey brittle death. Why was everything so grey and brittle?

It was the coroner, seated near a window overlooking the yard, who first noticed the glow about the well. Night had fully set in, and all the abhorrent grounds seemed faintly luminous with more than the fitful moonbeams; but this new glow was something definite and distinct, and appeared to shoot up from the black pit like a softened ray from a searchlight, giving dull reflections in the little ground pools where the water had been emptied. It had a very queer colour, and as all the men clustered round the window Ammi gave a violent start.

For this strange beam of ghastly miasma was to him of no unfamiliar hue. He had seen that colour before, and feared to think what it might mean. He had seen it in the nasty brittle globule in that aërolite two summers ago, had seen it in the crazy vegetation of the springtime, and had thought he had seen it for an instant that very morning against the small barred window of that terrible attic room where nameless things had happened. It had flashed there a second, and a clammy and hateful current of vapour had brushed past him—and then poor Nahum had been taken by something of that colour. He had said so at the last—said it was the globule and the plants. After that had come the runaway in the yard and the splash in the well—and now that well was belching forth to the night a pale insidious beam of the same daemoniac tint.

It does credit to the alertness of Ammi's mind that he puzzled even at that tense moment over a point which was essentially scientific. He could not but wonder at his gleaning of the same impression from a vapour glimpsed in the daytime, against a window opening on the morning sky, and from a nocturnal exhalation seen as a phosphorescent mist against the black and blasted landscape. It wasn't right—it was against Nature—and he thought of those terrible last words of his stricken friend, "It come from some place whar things ain't as they is here . . . one o' them professors said so. . . ."

All three horses outside, tied to a pair of shrivelled saplings by the road, were now neighing and pawing frantically. The wagon driver started for the door to do something, but Ammi laid a shaky hand on his shoulder. "Dun't go out thar," he whispered. "They's more to this nor what we know. Nahum said somethin' lived in the well that sucks your life out. He said it must be some'at growed from a round ball like one we all seen in the meteor stone that fell a year ago June. Sucks an' burns, he said, an' is jest a cloud of colour like that light out thar now, that ye can hardly see an' can't tell what it is. Nahum thought it feeds on everything livin' an' gits stronger all the time. He said he seen it this last week. It must be somethin' from away off in the sky like the men from the college last year says the meteor stone was. The way it's made an' the way it works ain't like no way o' God's world. It's some'at from beyond."

So the men paused indecisively as the light from the well grew stronger and the hitched horses pawed and whinnied in increasing frenzy. It was truly an awful moment; with terror in that ancient and accursed house itself, four monstrous sets of fragments—two from the house and two from the well—in the woodshed behind, and that shaft of unknown and unholy iridescence from the slimy depths in front. Ammi had restrained the driver on impulse, forgetting how uninjured he himself was after the clammy brushing of that coloured vapour in the attic room, but perhaps it is just as well that he acted as he did. No one will ever know what was abroad that night; and though the blasphemy from beyond had not so far hurt any human of unweakened mind, there is no telling what it might not have done at that last moment, and with its seemingly increased strength and the special signs of purpose it was soon to display beneath the half-clouded moonlit sky.

All at once one of the detectives at the window gave a short, sharp gasp. The others looked at him, and then quickly followed his own gaze upward to the point at which its idle straying had been suddenly arrested. There was no need for words. What had been disputed in

country gossip was disputable no longer, and it is because of the thing which every man of that party agreed in whispering later on that the strange days are never talked about in Arkham. It is necessary to premise that there was no wind at that hour of the evening. One did arise not long afterward, but there was absolutely none then. Even the dry tips of the lingering hedge-mustard, grey and blighted, and the fringe on the roof of the standing democrat-wagon were unstirred. And yet amid that tense, godless calm the high bare boughs of all the trees in the yard were moving. They were twitching morbidly and spasmodically, clawing in convulsive and epileptic madness at the moonlit clouds; scratching impotently in the noxious air as if jerked by some alien and bodiless line of linkage with subterrene horrors writhing and struggling below the black roots.

Not a man breathed for several seconds. Then a cloud of darker depth passed over the moon, and the silhouette of clutching branches faded out momentarily. At this there was a general cry; muffled with awe, but husky and almost identical from every throat. For the terror had not faded with the silhouette, and in a fearsome instant of deeper darkness the watchers saw wriggling at that treetop height a thousand tiny points of faint and unhallowed radiance, tipping each bough like the fire of St. Elmo or the flames that came down on the apostles' heads at Pentecost. It was a monstrous constellation of unnatural light, like a glutted swarm of corpse-fed fireflies dancing hellish sarabands over an accursed marsh; and its colour was that same nameless intrusion which Ammi had come to recognise and dread. All the while the shaft of phosphorescence from the well was getting brighter and brighter, bringing to the minds of the huddled men a sense of doom and abnormality which far outraced any image their conscious minds could form. It was no longer shining out, it was pouring out; and as the shapeless stream of unplaceable colour left the well it seemed to flow directly into the sky.

The veterinary shivered, and walked to the front door to drop the heavy extra bar across it. Ammi shook no less, and had to tug and point for lack of a controllable voice when he wished to draw notice to the growing luminosity of the trees. The neighing and stamping of the horses had become utterly frightful, but not a soul of that group in the old house would have ventured forth for any earthly reward. With the moments the shining of the trees increased, while their restless branches seemed to strain more and more toward verticality. The wood of the well-sweep was shining now, and presently a policeman dumbly pointed to some wooden sheds and bee-hives near the stone wall on the west. They were commencing to shine, too, though the tethered vehicles of the visitors seemed so far unaffected. Then there was a wild commotion and clopping in the road, and as Ammi quenched the lamp for better seeing they realised that the span of frantic greys had broke their sapling and run off with the democrat-wagon.

The shock served to loosen several tongues, and embarrassed whispers were exchanged. "It spreads on everything organic that's been around here," muttered the medical examiner. No one replied, but the man who had been in the well gave a hint that his long pole must have stirred up something intangible. "It was awful," he added. "There was no bottom at all. Just ooze and bubbles and the feeling of something lurking under there." Ammi's horse still pawed and screamed deafeningly in the road outside, and nearly drowned its owner's faint quaver

as he mumbled his formless reflections. "It come from that stone . . . it growed down thar . . . it got everything livin' . . . it fed itself on 'em, mind and body . . . Thad an' Mernie, Zenas an' Nabby . . . Nahum was the last . . . they all drunk the water . . . it got strong on 'em . . . it come from beyond, whar things ain't like they be here . . . now it's goin' home. . . ."

At this point, as the column of unknown colour flared suddenly stronger and began to weave itself into fantastic suggestions of shape which each spectator later described differently, there came from poor tethered Hero such a sound as no man before or since ever heard from a horse. Every person in that low-pitched sitting room stopped his ears, and Ammi turned away from the window in horror and nausea. Words could not convey it—when Ammi looked out again the hapless beast lay huddled inert on the moonlit ground between the splintered shafts of the buggy. That was the last of Hero till they buried him next day. But the present was no time to mourn, for almost at this instant a detective silently called attention to something terrible in the very room with them. In the absence of the lamplight it was clear that a faint phosphorescence had begun to pervade the entire apartment. It glowed on the broad-planked floor and the fragment of rag carpet, and shimmered over the sashes of the small-paned windows. It ran up and down the exposed corner-posts, coruscated about the shelf and mantel, and infected the very doors and furniture. Each minute saw it strengthen, and at last it was very plain that healthy living things must leave that house.

Ammi shewed them the back door and the path up through the fields to the ten-acre pasture. They walked and stumbled as in a dream, and did not dare look back till they were far away on the high ground. They were glad of the path, for they could not have gone the front way, by that well. It was bad enough passing the glowing barn and sheds, and those shining orchard trees with their gnarled, fiendish contours; but thank heaven the branches did their worst twisting high up. The moon went under some very black clouds as they crossed the rustic bridge over Chapman's Brook, and it was blind groping from there to the open meadows.

When they looked back toward the valley and the distant Gardner place at the bottom they saw a fearsome sight. All the farm was shining with the hideous unknown blend of colour; trees, buildings, and even such grass and herbage as had not been wholly changed to lethal grey brittleness. The boughs were all straining skyward, tipped with tongues of foul flame, and lambent tricklings of the same monstrous fire were creeping about the ridgepoles of the house, barn, and sheds. It was a scene from a vision of Fuseli, and over all the rest reigned that riot of luminous amorphousness, that alien and undimensioned rainbow of cryptic poison from the well—seething, feeling, lapping, reaching, scintillating, straining, and malignly bubbling in its cosmic and unrecognisable chromaticism.

Then without warning the hideous thing shot vertically up toward the sky like a rocket or meteor, leaving behind no trail and disappearing through a round and curiously regular hole in the clouds before any man could gasp or cry out. No watcher can ever forget that sight, and Ammi stared blankly at the stars of Cygnus, Deneb twinkling above the others, where the unknown colour had melted into the Milky Way. But his gaze was the next moment called swiftly to earth by the crackling in the valley. It was just that. Only a wooden ripping and crackling, and not an

explosion, as so many others of the party vowed. Yet the outcome was the same, for in one feverish, kaleidoscopic instant there burst up from that doomed and accursed farm a gleamingly eruptive cataclysm of unnatural sparks and substance; blurring the glance of the few who saw it, and sending forth to the zenith a bombarding cloudburst of such coloured and fantastic fragments as our universe must needs disown. Through quickly re-closing vapours they followed the great morbidity that had vanished, and in another second they had vanished too. Behind and below was only a darkness to which the men dared not return, and all about was a mounting wind which seemed to sweep down in black, frore gusts from interstellar space. It shrieked and howled, and lashed the fields and distorted woods in a mad cosmic frenzy, till soon the trembling party realised it would be no use waiting for the moon to shew what was left down there at Nahum's.

Too awed even to hint theories, the seven shaking men trudged back toward Arkham by the north road. Ammi was worse than his fellows, and begged them to see him inside his own kitchen, instead of keeping straight on to town. He did not wish to cross the nighted, wind-whipped woods alone to his home on the main road. For he had had an added shock that the others were spared, and was crushed forever with a brooding fear he dared not even mention for many years to come. As the rest of the watchers on that tempestuous hill had stolidly set their faces toward the road, Ammi had looked back an instant at the shadowed valley of desolation so lately sheltering his ill-starred friend. And from that stricken, far-away spot he had seen something feebly rise, only to sink down again upon the place from which the great shapeless horror had shot into the sky. It was just a colour—but not any colour of our earth or heavens. And because Ammi recognised that colour, and knew that this last faint remnant must still lurk down there in the well, he has never been quite right since.

Ammi would never go near the place again. It is over half a century now since the horror happened, but he has never been there, and will be glad when the new reservoir blots it out. I shall be glad, too, for I do not like the way the sunlight changed colour around the mouth of that abandoned well I passed. I hope the water will always be very deep—but even so, I shall never drink it. I do not think I shall visit the Arkham country hereafter. Three of the men who had been with Ammi returned the next morning to see the ruins by daylight, but there were not any real ruins. Only the bricks of the chimney, the stones of the cellar, some mineral and metallic litter here and there, and the rim of that nefandous well. Save for Ammi's dead horse, which they towed away and buried, and the buggy which they shortly returned to him, everything that had ever been living had gone. Five eldritch acres of dusty grey desert remained, nor has anything ever grown there since. To this day it sprawls open to the sky like a great spot eaten by acid in the woods and fields, and the few who have ever dared glimpse it in spite of the rural tales have named it "the blasted heath".

The rural tales are queer. They might be even queerer if city men and college chemists could be interested enough to analyse the water from that disused well, or the grey dust that no wind seems ever to disperse. Botanists, too, ought to study the stunted flora on the borders of that spot, for they might shed light on the country notion that the blight is spreading—little by little, perhaps an inch a year. People say the colour of the neighbouring herbage is not quite right in the spring, and that wild things leave

queer prints in the light winter snow. Snow never seems quite so heavy on the blasted heath as it is elsewhere. Horses—the few that are left in this motor age—grow skittish in the silent valley; and hunters cannot depend on their dogs too near the splotch of greyish dust.

They say the mental influences are very bad, too. Numbers went queer in the years after Nahum's taking, and always they lacked the power to get away. Then the stronger-minded folk all left the region, and only the foreigners tried to live in the crumbling old homesteads. They could not stay, though; and one sometimes wonders what insight beyond ours their wild, weird stores of whispered magic have given them. Their dreams at night, they protest, are very horrible in that grotesque country; and surely the very look of the dark realm is enough to stir a morbid fancy. No traveller has ever escaped a sense of strangeness in those deep ravines, and artists shiver as they paint thick woods whose mystery is as much of the spirit as of the eye. I myself am curious about the sensation I derived from my one lone walk before Ammi told me his tale. When twilight came I had vaguely wished some clouds would gather, for an odd timidity about the deep skyey voids above had crept into my soul.

Do not ask me for my opinion. I do not know—that is all. There was no one but Ammi to question; for Arkham people will not talk about the strange days, and all three professors who saw the aërolite and its coloured globule are dead. There were other globules—depend upon that. One must have fed itself and escaped, and probably there was another which was too late. No doubt it is still down the well—I know there was something wrong with the sunlight I saw above that miasmal brink. The rustics say the blight creeps an inch a year, so perhaps there is a kind of growth or nourishment even now. But whatever daemon hatchling is there, it must be tethered to something or else it would quickly spread. Is it fastened to the roots of those trees that claw the air? One of the current Arkham tales is about fat oaks that shine and move as they ought not to do at night.

What it is, only God knows. In terms of matter I suppose the thing Ammi described would be called a gas, but this gas obeyed laws that are not of our cosmos. This was no fruit of such worlds and suns as shine on the telescopes and photographic plates of our observatories. This was no breath from the skies whose motions and dimensions our astronomers measure or deem too vast to measure. It was just a colour out of space—a frightful messenger from unformed realms of infinity beyond all Nature as we know it; from realms whose mere existence stuns the brain and numbs us with the black extra-cosmic gulfs it throws open before our frenzied eyes.

I doubt very much if Ammi consciously lied to me, and I do not think his tale was all a freak of madness as the townfolk had forewarned. Something terrible came to the hills and valleys on that meteor, and something terrible—though I know not in what proportion—still remains. I shall be glad to see the water come. Meanwhile I hope nothing will happen to Ammi. He saw so much of the thing—and its influence was so insidious. Why has he never been able to move away? How clearly he recalled those dying words of Nahum's—"can't git away . . . draws ye . . . ye know summ'at's comin', but 'tain't no use. . . ." Ammi is such a good old man—when the reservoir gang gets to work I must write the chief engineer to keep a sharp watch on him. I would hate to think of him as the grey, twisted, brittle monstrosity which persists more and

more in troubling my sleep.

'...the black well yawned deep beside the tumbled bricks...'

Lost Hearts

by M. R. James

It was, as far as I can ascertain, in September of the year 1811 that a postchaise drew up before the door of Aswarby Hall, in the heart of Lincolnshire. The little boy who was the only passenger in the chaise, and who jumped out as soon as it had stopped, looked about him with the keenest curiosity during the short interval that elapsed between the ringing of the bell and the opening of the hall door. He saw a tall, square, red-brick house, built in the reign of Anne; a stone-pillared porch had been added in the purer classical style of 1790; the windows of the house were many, tall and narrow, with small panes and thick white woodwork. A pediment, pierced with a round window, crowned the front. There were wings to right and left, connected by curious glazed galleries, supported by colonnades, with the central block. These wings plainly contained the stables and offices of the house. Each was surmounted by an ornamental cupola with a gilded vane.

An evening light shone on the building, making the window-panes glow like so many fires. Away from the Hall in front stretched a flat park studded with oaks and fringed with firs, which stood out against the sky. The clock in the church-tower, buried in trees on the edge of the park, only its golden weather-cock catching the light, was striking six, and the sound came gently beating down the wind. It was altogether a pleasant impression, though tinged with the sort of melancholy appropriate to an evening in early autumn, that was conveyed to the mind of the boy who was standing in the porch waiting for the door to open to him.

He had just come from Warwickshire, and some six months ago had been left an orphan. Now, owing to the generous and unexpected offer of his elderly cousin, Mr. Abney, he had come to live at Aswarby. The offer was unexpected, because all who knew anything of Mr. Abney looked upon him as a somewhat austere recluse, into whose steady-going household the advent of a small boy would import a new and, it seemed, incongruous element. The truth is that very little was known of Mr. Abney's pursuits or temper. The Professor of Greek at Cambridge had been heard to say that no one knew more of the religious beliefs of the later pagans than did the owner of Aswarby. Certainly his library contained all the then available books bearing on the Mysteries, the Orphic poems, the worship of Mithras, and the Neo-Platonists. In the marble-paved hall stood a fine group of Mithras slaying a bull, which had been imported from the Levant at great expense by the owner. He had contributed a description of it to the Gentleman's Magazine, and he had written a remarkable series of articles in the Critical Museum on the superstitions of the Romans of the Lower Empire. He was looked upon, in fine, as a man wrapped up in his books, and it was a matter of great surprise among his neighbours that he should ever have heard of his orphan cousin, Stephen Elliott, much more that he should have volunteered to make him an inmate of Aswarby Hall.

Whatever may have been expected by his neighbours, it is certain that Mr. Abney—the tall, the thin, the austere—

seemed inclined to give his young cousin a kindly reception. The moment the front-door was opened he darted out of his study, rubbing his hands with delight.

'How are you, my boy?—how are you? How old are you?' said he—'that is, you are not too much tired, I hope, by your journey to eat your supper?'

'No, thank you, sir,' said Master Elliott; 'I am pretty well.'

'That's a good lad,' said Mr. Abney. 'And how old are you, my boy?'

It seemed a little odd that he should have asked the question twice in the first two minutes of their acquaintance.

'I'm twelve years old next birthday, sir,' said Stephen.

'And when is your birthday, my dear boy? Eleventh of September, eh? That's well—that's very well. Nearly a year hence, isn't it? I like—ha, ha!—I like to get these things down in my book. Sure it's twelve? Certain?'

'Yes, quite sure, sir.'

'Well, well! Take him to Mrs. Bunch's room, Parkes, and let him have his tea—supper—whatever it is.'

'Yes, sir,' answered the staid Mr. Parkes; and conducted Stephen to the lower regions.

Mrs. Bunch was the most comfortable and human person whom Stephen had as yet met in Aswarby. She made him completely at home; they were great friends

in a quarter of an hour: and great friends they remained. Mrs. Bunch had been born in the neighbourhood some fifty-five years before the date of Stephen's arrival, and her residence at the Hall was of twenty years' standing. Consequently, if anyone knew the ins and outs of the house and the district, Mrs. Bunch knew them; and she was by no means disinclined to communicate her information.

Certainly there were plenty of things about the Hall and the Hall gardens which Stephen, who was of an adventurous and inquiring turn, was anxious to have explained to him. 'Who built the temple at the end of the laurel walk? Who was the old man whose picture hung on the staircase, sitting at a table, with a skull under his hand?' These and many similar points were cleared up by the resources of Mrs. Bunch's powerful intellect. There were others, however, of which the explanations furnished were less satisfactory.

One November evening Stephen was sitting by the fire in the housekeeper's room reflecting on his surroundings.

'Is Mr. Abney a good man, and will he go to heaven?' he suddenly asked, with the peculiar confidence which children possess in the ability of their elders to settle these questions, the decision of which is believed to be reserved for other tribunals.

'Good?—bless the child!' said Mrs. Bunch. 'Master's as kind a soul as ever I see! Didn't I never tell you of the little boy as he took in out of the street, as you may say, this seven years back? and the little girl, two years after I first come here?'

'No. Do tell me all about them, Mrs. Bunch—now this minute!'

'Well,' said Mrs. Bunch, 'the little girl I don't seem to recollect so much about. I know master brought her back with him from his walk one day, and give orders to Mrs. Ellis, as was housekeeper then, as she should be took every care with. And the pore child hadn't no one belonging to her—she told me so her own self—and here she lived with us a matter of three weeks it might be; and then, whether she were somethink of a gipsy in her blood or what not, but one morning she out of her bed afore any of us had opened a eye and neither track nor yet trace of her have I set eyes on since. Master was wonderful put about, and had all the ponds dragged; but it's my belief she was had away by them gipsies, for there was singing round the house for as much as an hour the night she went, and Parkes, he declare as he heard them a-calling in the woods all that afternoon. Dear, dear! a hodd child she was, so silent in her ways and all, but I was wonderful taken up with her, so domesticated she was—surprising.'

'And what about the little boy?' said Stephen.

'Ah, that pore boy!' sighed Mrs. Bunch. 'He were a foreigner—Jevanny he called hisself—and he come a-tweaking his 'urdy-gurdy round and about the drive one winter day, and master 'ad him in that minute, and ast all about where he came from, and how old he was, and how he made his way, and where was his relatives, and all as kind as heart could wish. But it went the same way with him. They're a hunruly lot, them foreign nations, I do suppose, and he was off one fine morning just the same as the girl. Why he went and what he done was our

question for as much as a year after; for he never took his 'urdy-gurdy, and there it lays on the shelf.'

The remainder of the evening was spent by Stephen in miscellaneous cross-examination of Mrs. Bunch and in efforts to extract a tune from the hurdy-gurdy.

That night he had a curious dream. At the end of the passage at the top of the house, in which his bedroom was situated, there was an old disused bathroom. It was kept locked, but the upper half of the door was glazed, and, since the muslin curtains which used to hang there had long been gone, you could look in and see the lead-lined bath affixed to the wall on the right hand, with its head towards the window.

On the night of which I am speaking, Stephen Elliott found himself, as he thought, looking through the glazed door. The moon was shining through the window, and he was gazing at a figure which lay in the bath.

His description of what he saw reminds me of what I once beheld myself in the famous vaults of St. Michan's Church in Dublin, which possess the horrid property of preserving corpses from decay for centuries. A figure inexpressibly thin and pathetic, of a dusty leaden colour, enveloped in a shroud-like garment, the thin lips crooked into a faint and dreadful smile, the hands pressed tightly over the region of the heart.

As he looked upon it, a distant, almost inaudible moan seemed to issue from its lips, and the arms began to stir. The terror of the sight forced Stephen backwards, and he awoke to the fact that he was indeed standing on the cold boarded floor of the passage in the full light of the moon. With a courage which I do not think can be common among boys of his age, he went to the door of the bathroom to ascertain if the figure of his dream were really there. It was not, and he went back to bed.

Mrs. Bunch was much impressed next morning by his story, and went so far as to replace the muslin curtain over the glazed door of the bathroom. Mr. Abney, moreover, to whom he confided his experiences at breakfast, was greatly interested, and made notes of the matter in what he called 'his book.'

The spring equinox was approaching, as Mr. Abney frequently reminded his cousin, adding that this had been always considered by the ancients to be a critical time for the young: that Stephen would do well to take care of himself, and to shut his bedroom window at night; and that Censorinus had some valuable remarks on the subject. Two incidents that occurred about this time made an impression upon Stephen's mind.

The first was after an unusually uneasy and oppressed night that he had passed—though he could not recall any particular dream that he had had.

The following evening Mrs. Bunch was occupying herself in mending his nightgown.

'Gracious me, Master Stephen!' she broke forth rather irritably, 'how do you manage to tear your nightdress all to flinders this way? Look here, sir, what trouble you do give to poor servants that have to darn and mend after you!'

There was indeed a most destructive and apparently

wanton series of slits or scorings in the garment, which would undoubtedly require a skilful needle to make good. They were confined to the left side of the chest—long, parallel slits, about six inches in length, some of them not quite piercing the texture of the linen. Stephen could only express his entire ignorance of their origin: he was sure they were not there the night before.

'But,' he said, 'Mrs. Bunch, they are just the same as the scratches on the outside of my bedroom door; and I'm sure I never had anything to do with making them.'

Mrs. Bunch gazed at him open-mouthed, then snatched up a candle, departed hastily from the room, and was heard making her way upstairs. In a few minutes she came down.

'Well,' she said, 'Master Stephen, it's a funny thing to me how them marks and scratches can 'a' come there—too high up for any cat or dog to 'ave made 'em, much less a rat: for all the world like a Chinaman's fingernails, as my uncle in the tea-trade used to tell us of when we was girls together. I wouldn't say nothing to master, not if I was you, Master Stephen, my dear; and just turn the key of the door when you go to your bed.'

'I always do, Mrs. Bunch, as soon as I've said my prayers.'

'Ah, that's a good child: always say your prayers, and then no one can't hurt you.'

Herewith Mrs. Bunch addressed herself to mending the injured nightgown, with intervals of meditation, until bed-time. This was on a Friday night in March, 1812.

On the following evening the usual duet of Stephen and Mrs. Bunch was augmented by the sudden arrival of Mr. Parkes, the butler, who as a rule kept himself rather to himself in his own pantry. He did not see that Stephen was there: he was, moreover, flustered and less slow of speech than was his wont.

'Master may get up his own wine, if he likes, of an evening,' was his first remark. 'Either I do it in the daytime or not at all, Mrs. Bunch. I don't know what it may be: very like it's the rats, or the wind got into the cellars; but I'm not so young as I was, and I can't go through with it as I have done.'

'Well, Mr. Parkes, you know it is a surprising place for the rats, is the Hall.'

'I'm not denying that, Mrs. Bunch; and, to be sure, many a time I've heard the tale from the men in the shipyards about the rat that could speak. I never laid no confidence in that before; but to-night, if I'd demeaned myself to lay my ear to the door of the further bin, I could pretty much have heard what they was saying.'

'Oh, there, Mr. Parkes, I've no patience with your fancies! Rats talking in the wine-cellar indeed!'

'Well, Mrs. Bunch, I've no wish to argue with you: all I say is, if you choose to go to the far bin, and lay your ear to the door, you may prove my words this minute.'

'What nonsense you do talk, Mr. Parkes—not fit for children to listen to! Why, you'll be frightening Master Stephen there out of his wits.'

'What! Master Stephen?' said Parkes, awaking to the consciousness of the boy's presence. 'Master Stephen knows well enough when I'm a-playing a joke with you, Mrs. Bunch.'

In fact, Master Stephen knew much too well to suppose that Mr. Parkes had in the first instance intended a joke. He was interested, not altogether pleasantly, in the situation; but all his questions were unsuccessful in inducing the butler to give any more detailed account of his experiences in the wine-cellar.

We have now arrived at March 24, 1812. It was a day of curious experiences for Stephen: a windy, noisy day, which filled the house and the gardens with a restless impression. As Stephen stood by the fence of the grounds, and looked out into the park, he felt as if an endless procession of unseen people were sweeping past him on the wind, borne on resistlessly and aimlessly, vainly striving to stop themselves, to catch at something that might arrest their flight and bring them once again into contact with the living world of which they had formed a part. After luncheon that day Mr. Abney said:

'Stephen, my boy, do you think you could manage to come to me to-night as late as eleven o'clock in my study? I shall be busy until that time, and I wish to show you something connected with your future life which it is most important that you should know. You are not to mention this matter to Mrs. Bunch nor to anyone else in the house; and you had better go to your room at the usual time.'

Here was a new excitement added to life: Stephen

eagerly grasped at the opportunity of sitting up till eleven o'clock. He looked in at the library door on his way upstairs that evening, and saw a brazier, which he had often noticed in the corner of the room, moved out before the fire; an old silver-gilt cup stood on the table, filled with red wine, and some written sheets of paper lay near it. Mr. Abney was sprinkling some incense on the brazier from a round silver box as Stephen passed, but did not seem to notice his step.

The wind had fallen, and there was a still night and a full moon. At about ten o'clock Stephen was standing at the open window of his bedroom, looking out over the country. Still as the night was, the mysterious population of the distant moonlit woods was not yet lulled to rest. From time to time strange cries as of lost and despairing wanderers sounded from across the mere. They might be the notes of owls or water-birds, yet they did not quite resemble either sound. Were not they coming nearer? Now they sounded from the nearer side of the water, and in a few moments they seemed to be floating about among the shrubberies. Then they ceased; but just as Stephen was thinking of shutting the window and resuming his reading of 'Robinson Crusoe,' he caught sight of two figures standing on the gravelled terrace that ran along the garden side of the Hall—the figures of a boy and girl, as it seemed; they stood side by side, looking up at the windows. Something in the form of the girl recalled irresistibly his dream of the figure in the bath. The boy inspired him with more acute fear.

Whilst the girl stood still, half smiling, with her hands clasped over her heart, the boy, a thin shape, with black hair and ragged clothing, raised his arms in the air with an appearance of menace and of unappeasable hunger and longing. The moon shone upon his almost transparent hands, and Stephen saw that the nails were fearfully long and that the light shone through them. As he stood with his arms thus raised, he disclosed a terrifying spectacle. On the left side of his chest there opened a black and gaping rent; and there fell upon Stephen's brain, rather than upon his ear, the impression of one of those hungry and desolate cries that he had heard resounding over the woods of Aswarby all that evening. In another moment this dreadful pair had moved swiftly and noiselessly over the dry gravel, and he saw them no more.

Inexpressibly frightened as he was, he determined to take his candle and go down to Mr. Abney's study, for the hour appointed for their meeting was near at hand. The study or library opened out of the front-hall on one side, and Stephen, urged on by his terrors, did not take long in getting there. To effect an entrance was not so easy. It was not locked, he felt sure, for the key was on the outside of the door as usual. His repeated knocks produced no answer. Mr. Abney was engaged: he was speaking. What! why did he try to cry out? and why was the cry choked in his throat? Had he, too, seen the mysterious children? But now everything was quiet, and the door yielded to Stephen's terrified and frantic pushing.

On the table in Mr. Abney's study certain papers were found which explained the situation to Stephen Elliott when he was of an age to understand them. The most important sentences were as follows:

'It was a belief very strongly and generally held by the ancients—of whose wisdom in these matters I have had such experience as induces me to place confidence in their assertions—that by enacting certain processes, which to us moderns have something of a barbaric complexion, a very remarkable enlightenment of the spiritual faculties in man may be attained: that, for example, by absorbing the personalities of a certain number of his fellow-creatures, an individual may gain a complete ascendancy over those orders of spiritual beings which control the elemental forces of our universe.

'It is recorded of Simon Magus that he was able to fly in the air, to become invisible, or to assume any form he pleased, by the agency of the soul of a boy whom, to use the libellous phrase employed by the author of the "Clementine Recognitions," he had "murdered." I find it set down, moreover, with considerable detail in the writings of Hermes Trismegistus, that similar happy results may be produced by the absorption of the hearts of not less than three human beings below the age of twenty-one years. To the testing of the truth of this receipt I have devoted the greater part of the last twenty years, selecting as the corpora vilia of my experiment such persons as could conveniently be removed without occasioning a sensible gap in society. The first step I effected by the removal of one Phœbe Stanley, a girl of gipsy extraction, on March 24, 1792. The second, by the removal of a wandering Italian lad, named Giovanni Paoli, on the night of March 23, 1805. The final "victim"—to employ a word repugnant in the highest degree to my feelings—must be my cousin, Stephen Elliott. His day must be this March 24, 1812.

'The best means of effecting the required absorption is to remove the heart from the living subject, to reduce it to ashes, and to mingle them with about a pint of some

red wine, preferably port. The remains of the first two subjects, at least, it will be well to conceal: a disused bath-room or wine-cellar will be found convenient for such a purpose. Some annoyance may be experienced from the psychic portion of the subjects, which popular language dignifies with the name of ghosts. But the man of philosophic temperament—to whom alone the experiment is appropriate—will be little prone to attach importance to the feeble efforts of these beings to wreak their vengeance on him. I contemplate with the liveliest satisfaction the enlarged and emancipated existence which the experiment, if successful, will confer on me; not only placing me beyond the reach of human justice (so-called), but eliminating to a great extent the prospect of death itself.'

Mr. Abney was found in his chair, his head thrown back, his face stamped with an expression of rage, fright, and mortal pain. In his left side was a terrible lacerated wound, exposing the heart. There was no blood on his hands, and a long knife that lay on the table was perfectly clean. A savage wild-cat might have inflicted the injuries. The window of the study was open, and it was the opinion of the coroner that Mr. Abney had met his death by the agency of some wild creature. But Stephen Elliott's study of the papers I have quoted led him to a very different conclusion.

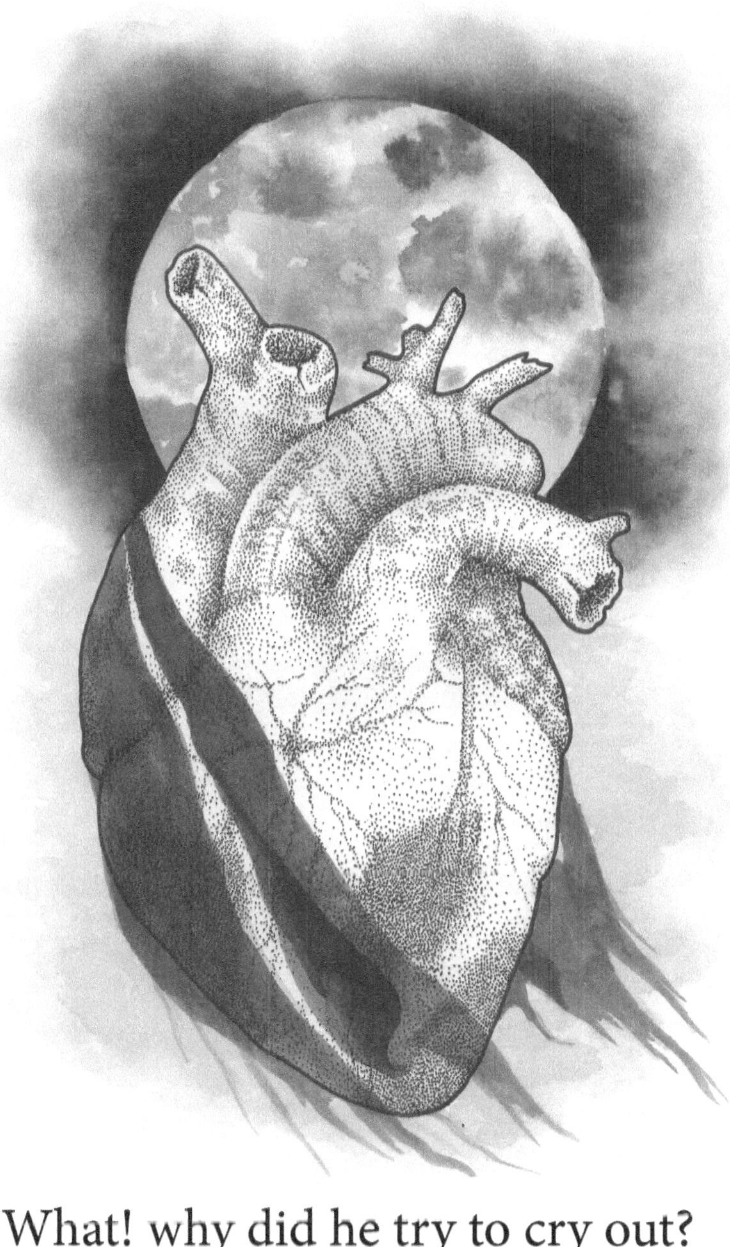

What! why did he try to cry out?

M. R. James

DAGON

BY H. P. LOVECRAFT

I am writing this under an appreciable mental strain, since by tonight I shall be no more. Penniless, and at the end of my supply of the drug which alone makes life endurable, I can bear the torture no longer; and shall cast myself from this garret window into the squalid street below. Do not think from my slavery to morphine that I am a weakling or a degenerate. When you have read these hastily scrawled pages you may guess, though never fully realise, why it is that I must have forgetfulness or death.

It was in one of the most open and least frequented parts of the broad Pacific that the packet of which I was supercargo fell a victim to the German sea-raider. The great war was then at its very beginning, and the ocean forces of the Hun had not completely sunk to their later degradation; so that our vessel was made a legitimate prize, whilst we of her crew were treated with all the fairness and consideration due us as naval prisoners. So liberal, indeed, was the discipline of our captors, that five days after we were taken I managed to escape alone in a small boat with water and provisions for a good length of time.

When I finally found myself adrift and free, I had but little idea of my surroundings. Never a competent navigator, I could only guess vaguely by the sun and stars that I was somewhat south of the equator. Of the longitude I knew nothing, and no island or coast-line was in sight. The weather kept fair, and for uncounted days I drifted aimlessly beneath the scorching sun; waiting either for some passing ship, or to be cast on the shores of some habitable land. But neither ship nor land appeared, and I began to despair in my solitude upon the heaving vastnesses of unbroken blue.

The change happened whilst I slept. Its details I shall never know; for my slumber, though troubled and dream-infested, was continuous. When at last I awaked, it was to discover myself half sucked into a slimy expanse of hellish black mire which extended about me in monotonous undulations as far as I could see, and in which my boat lay grounded some distance away.

Though one might well imagine that my first sensation would be of wonder at so prodigious and unexpected a transformation of scenery, I was in reality more horrified than astonished; for there was in the air and in the rotting soil a sinister quality which chilled me to the very core. The region was putrid with the carcasses of decaying fish, and of other less describable things which I saw protruding from the nasty mud of the unending plain. Perhaps I should not hope to convey in mere words the unutterable hideousness that can dwell in absolute silence and barren immensity. There was nothing within hearing, and nothing in sight save a vast reach of black slime; yet the very completeness of the stillness and the homogeneity of the landscape oppressed me with a nauseating fear.

The sun was blazing down from a sky which seemed to me almost black in its cloudless cruelty; as though reflecting the inky marsh beneath my feet. As I crawled into the stranded boat I realised that only one theory could explain my position. Through some unprecedented volcanic upheaval, a portion of the ocean floor must have been thrown to the surface, exposing regions which for innumerable millions of years had lain hidden under unfathomable watery depths. So great was the extent of the new land which had risen beneath me, that I could not detect the faintest noise of the surging ocean, strain my ears as I might. Nor were there any sea-fowl to prey upon the dead things.

For several hours I sat thinking or brooding in the boat, which lay upon its side and afforded a slight shade as the sun moved across the heavens. As the day progressed, the ground lost some of its stickiness, and seemed likely to dry sufficiently for travelling purposes in a short time. That night I slept but little, and the next day I made for myself a pack containing food and water, preparatory to an overland journey in search of the vanished sea and possible rescue.

On the third morning I found the soil dry enough to walk upon with ease. The odour of the fish was maddening; but I was too much concerned with graver things to mind so slight an evil, and set out boldly for an unknown goal. All day I forged steadily westward, guided by a far-away hummock which rose higher than any other elevation on the rolling desert. That night I encamped, and on the following day still travelled toward the hummock, though that object seemed scarcely nearer than when I had first espied it. By the fourth evening I attained the base of the mound, which turned out to be much higher than it had appeared from a distance; an intervening valley setting it out in sharper relief from the general surface. Too weary to ascend, I slept in the

shadow of the hill.

I know not why my dreams were so wild that night; but ere the waning and fantastically gibbous moon had risen far above the eastern plain, I was awake in a cold perspiration, determined to sleep no more. Such visions as I had experienced were too much for me to endure again. And in the glow of the moon I saw how unwise I had been to travel by day. Without the glare of the parching sun, my journey would have cost me less energy; indeed, I now felt quite able to perform the ascent which had deterred me at sunset. Picking up my pack, I started for the crest of the eminence.

I have said that the unbroken monotony of the rolling plain was a source of vague horror to me; but I think my horror was greater when I gained the summit of the mound and looked down the other side into an immeasurable pit or canyon, whose black recesses the moon had not yet soared high enough to illumine. I felt myself on the edge of the world; peering over the rim into a fathomless chaos of eternal night. Through my terror ran curious reminiscences of Paradise Lost, and of Satan's hideous climb through the unfashioned realms of darkness.

As the moon climbed higher in the sky, I began to see that the slopes of the valley were not quite so perpendicular as I had imagined. Ledges and outcroppings of rock afforded fairly easy foot-holds for a descent, whilst after a drop of a few hundred feet, the declivity became very gradual. Urged on by an impulse which I cannot definitely analyse, I scrambled with difficulty down the rocks and stood on the gentler slope beneath, gazing into the Stygian deeps where no light had yet penetrated.

All at once my attention was captured by a vast and singular object on the opposite slope, which rose steeply about an hundred yards ahead of me; an object that gleamed whitely in the newly bestowed rays of the ascending moon. That it was merely a gigantic piece of stone, I soon assured myself; but I was conscious of a distinct impression that its contour and position were not altogether the work of Nature. A closer scrutiny filled me with sensations I cannot express; for despite its enormous magnitude, and its position in an abyss which had yawned at the bottom of the sea since the world was young, I perceived beyond a doubt that the strange object was a well-shaped monolith whose massive bulk had known the workmanship and perhaps the worship of living and thinking creatures.

Dazed and frightened, yet not without a certain thrill of the scientist's or archaeologist's delight, I examined my surroundings more closely. The moon, now near the zenith, shone weirdly and vividly above the towering steeps that hemmed in the chasm, and revealed the fact that a far-flung body of water flowed at the bottom, winding out of sight in both directions, and almost lapping my feet as I stood on the slope. Across the chasm, the wavelets washed the base of the Cyclopean monolith; on whose surface I could now trace both inscriptions and crude sculptures. The writing was in a system of hieroglyphics unknown to me, and unlike anything I had ever seen in books; consisting for the most part of conventionalised aquatic symbols such as fishes, eels, octopi, crustaceans, molluscs, whales, and the like. Several characters obviously represented marine things which are unknown to the modern world, but whose decomposing forms I had observed on the ocean-risen

plain.

It was the pictorial carving, however, that did most to hold me spellbound. Plainly visible across the intervening water on account of their enormous size, were an array of bas-reliefs whose subjects would have excited the envy of a Doré. I think that these things were supposed to depict men—at least, a certain sort of men; though the creatures were shewn disporting like fishes in the waters of some marine grotto, or paying homage at some monolithic shrine which appeared to be under the waves as well. Of their faces and forms I dare not speak in detail; for the mere remembrance makes me grow faint. Grotesque beyond the imagination of a Poe or a Bulwer, they were damnably human in general outline despite webbed hands and feet, shockingly wide and flabby lips, glassy, bulging eyes, and other features less pleasant to recall. Curiously enough, they seemed to have been chiselled badly out of proportion with their scenic background; for one of the creatures was shewn in the act of killing a whale represented as but little larger than himself. I remarked, as I say, their grotesqueness and strange size; but in a moment decided that they were merely the imaginary gods of some primitive fishing or seafaring tribe; some tribe whose last descendant had perished eras before the first ancestor of the Piltdown or Neanderthal Man was born. Awestruck at this unexpected glimpse into a past beyond the conception of the most daring anthropologist, I stood musing whilst the moon cast queer reflections on the silent channel before me.

Then suddenly I saw it. With only a slight churning to mark its rise to the surface, the thing slid into view above the dark waters. Vast, Polyphemus-like, and loathsome, it darted like a stupendous monster of nightmares to the monolith, about which it flung its gigantic scaly arms, the while it bowed its hideous head and gave vent to certain measured sounds. I think I went mad then.

Of my frantic ascent of the slope and cliff, and of my delirious journey back to the stranded boat, I remember little. I believe I sang a great deal, and laughed oddly when I was unable to sing. I have indistinct recollections of a great storm some time after I reached the boat; at any rate, I know that I heard peals of thunder and other tones which Nature utters only in her wildest moods.

When I came out of the shadows I was in a San Francisco hospital; brought thither by the captain of the American ship which had picked up my boat in mid-ocean. In my delirium I had said much, but found that my words had been given scant attention. Of any land upheaval in the Pacific, my rescuers knew nothing; nor did I deem it necessary to insist upon a thing which I knew they could not believe. Once I sought out a celebrated ethnologist, and amused him with peculiar questions regarding the ancient Philistine legend of Dagon, the Fish-God; but soon perceiving that he was hopelessly conventional, I did not press my inquiries.

It is at night, especially when the moon is gibbous and waning, that I see the thing. I tried morphine; but the drug has given only transient surcease, and has drawn me into its clutches as a hopeless slave. So now I am to end it all, having written a full account for the information or the contemptuous amusement of my fellow-men. Often I ask myself if it could not all have been a pure phantasm—a mere freak of fever as I lay sun-stricken and raving in the open boat after my escape from the German man-of-war. This I ask myself, but ever does there come

before me a hideously vivid vision in reply. I cannot think of the deep sea without shuddering at the nameless things that may at this very moment be crawling and floundering on its slimy bed, worshipping their ancient stone idols and carving their own detestable likenesses on submarine obelisks of water-soaked granite. I dream of a day when they may rise above the billows to drag down in their reeking talons the remnants of puny, war-exhausted mankind—of a day when the land shall sink, and the dark ocean floor shall ascend amidst universal pandemonium.

The end is near. I hear a noise at the door, as of some immense slippery body lumbering against it. It shall not find me. God, that hand! The window! The window!

'...it bowed its hideous head...'

H. P. LOVECRAFT

COUNT MAGNUS

BY M. R. JAMES

By what means the papers out of which I have made a connected story came into my hands is the last point which the reader will learn from these pages. But it is necessary to prefix to my extracts from them a statement of the form in which I possess them.

They consist, then, partly of a series of collections for a book of travels, such a volume as was a common product of the forties and fifties. Horace Marryat's Journal of a Residence in Jutland and the Danish Isles is a fair specimen of the class to which I allude. These books usually treated of some unknown district on the Continent. They were illustrated with woodcuts or steel plates. They gave details of hotel accommodation, and of means of communication, such as we now expect to find in any well-regulated guide-book, and they dealt largely in reported conversations with intelligent foreigners, racy innkeepers, and garrulous peasants. In a word, they were chatty.

Begun with the idea of furnishing material for such a book, my papers as they progressed assumed the character of a record of one single personal experience, and this record was continued up to the very eve, almost, of its termination.

The writer was a Mr. Wraxall. For my knowledge

of him I have to depend entirely on the evidence his writings afford, and from these I deduce that he was a man past middle age, possessed of some private means, and very much alone in the world. He had, it seems, no settled abode in England, but was a denizen of hotels and boarding-houses. It is probable that he entertained the idea of settling down at some future time which never came; and I think it also likely that the Pantechnicon fire in the early seventies must have destroyed a great deal that would have thrown light on his antecedents, for he refers once or twice to property of his that was warehoused at that establishment.

It is further apparent that Mr. Wraxall had published a book, and that it treated of a holiday he had once taken in Brittany. More than this I cannot say about his work, because a diligent search in bibliographical works has convinced me that it must have appeared either anonymously or under a pseudonym.

As to his character, it is not difficult to form some superficial opinion. He must have been an intelligent and cultivated man. It seems that he was near being a Fellow of his college at OxfordBrasenose, as I judge from the Calendar. His besetting fault was pretty clearly that of over-inquisitiveness, possibly a good fault in a traveller, certainly a fault for which this traveller paid dearly enough in the end.

On what proved to be his last expedition, he was plotting another book. Scandinavia, a region not widely known to Englishmen forty years ago, had struck him as an interesting field. He must have alighted on some old books of Swedish history or memoirs, and the idea had struck him that there was room for a book descriptive of travel in Sweden, interspersed with episodes from the history of some of the great Swedish families. He procured letters of introduction, therefore, to some persons of quality in Sweden, and set out thither in the early summer of 1863.

Of his travels in the North there is no need to speak, nor of his residence of some weeks in Stockholm. I need only mention that some savant resident there put him on the track of an important collection of family papers belonging to the proprietors of an ancient manor-house in Vestergothland, and obtained for him permission to examine them.

The manor-house, or herrgård, in question is to be called Råbäck (pronounced something like Roebeck), though that is not its name. It is one of the best buildings of its kind in all the country, and the picture of it in Dahlenberg's Suecia antiqua et moderna, engraved in 1694, shows it very much as the tourist may see it today. It was built soon after 1600, and is, roughly speaking, very much like an English house of that period in respect of material---red-brick with stone facings---and style. The man who built it was a scion of the great house of De la Gardie, and his descendants possess it still. De la Gardie is the name by which I will designate them when mention of them becomes necessary.

They received Mr. Wraxall with great kindness and courtesy, and pressed him to stay in the house as long as his researches lasted. But, preferring to be independent, and mistrusting his powers of conversing in Swedish, he settled himself at the village inn, which turned out quite sufficiently comfortable, at any rate during the summer months. This arrangement would entail a short walk daily to and from the manor-house of something under a mile. The house itself stood in a park, and was protected---we should say grown up---with large old timber. Near it you found the walled garden, and then entered a close wood fringing one of the small lakes with which the whole country is pitted. Then came the wall of the demesne, and you climbed a steep knoll---a knob of rock lightly covered with soil---and on the top of this stood the church, fenced in with tall dark trees. It was a curious building to English eyes. The nave and aisles were low, and filled with pews and galleries. In the western gallery stood the handsome old organ, gaily painted, and with silver pipes. The ceiling was flat, and had been adorned by a seventeenth-century artist with a strange and hideous 'Last Judgement', full of lurid flames, falling cities, burning ships, crying souls, and brown and smiling demons. Handsome brass coronae hung from the roof; the pulpit was like a doll's-house covered with little painted wooden cherubs and saints; a stand with three hour-glasses was hinged to the preacher's desk. Such sights as these may be seen in many a church in Sweden now, but what distinguished this one was an addition to the original building. At the eastern end of the north aisle the builder of the manor-house had erected a mausoleum for himself and his family. It was a largish eight-sided building, lighted by a series of oval windows, and it had a domed roof, topped by a kind of pumpkin-shaped object rising into a spire, a form in which Swedish architects greatly delighted. The roof was of copper externally, and was painted black, while the walls, in common with those of the church, were staringly white. To this mausoleum there was no access from the church. It had a portal and steps of its own on the northern side.

Past the churchyard the path to the village goes, and

not more than three or four minutes bring you to the inn door.

On the first day of his stay at Råbäck Mr. Wraxall found the church door open, and made those notes of the interior which I have epitomized. Into the mausoleum, however, he could not make his way. He could by looking through the keyhole just descry that there were fine marble effigies and sarcophagi of copper, and a wealth of armorial ornament, which made him very anxious to spend some time in investigation.

The papers he had come to examine at the manor-house proved to be of just the kind he wanted for his book. There were family correspondence, journals, and account-books of the earliest owners of the estate, very carefully kept and clearly written, full of amusing and picturesque detail. The first De la Gardie appeared in them as a strong and capable man. Shortly after the building of the mansion there had been a period of distress in the district, and the peasants had risen and attacked several chateaux and done some damage. The owner of Råbäck took a leading part in suppressing the trouble, and there was reference to executions of ring-leaders and severe punishments inflicted with no sparing hand.

The portrait of this Magnus de la Gardie was one of the best in the house, and Mr. Wraxall studied it with no little interest after his day's work. He gives no detailed description of it, but I gather that the face impressed him rather by its power than by its beauty or goodness; in fact, he writes that Count Magnus was an almost phenomenally ugly man.

On this day Mr. Wraxall took his supper with the family,

and walked back in the late but still bright evening.

'I must remember,' he writes, 'to ask the sexton if he can let me into the mausoleum at the church. He evidently has access to it himself, for I saw him tonight standing on the steps, and, as I thought, locking or unlocking the door.'

I find that early on the following day Mr. Wraxall had some conversation with his landlord. His setting it down at such length as he does surprised me at first; but I soon realized that the papers I was reading were, at least in their beginning, the materials for the book he was meditating, and that it was to have been one of those quasi-journalistic productions which admit of the introduction of an admixture of conversational matter.

His object, he says, was to find out whether any traditions of Count Magnus de la Gardie lingered on in the scenes of that gentleman's activity, and whether the popular estimate of him were favourable or not. He found that the Count was decidedly not a favourite. If his tenants came late to their work on the days which they owed to him as Lord of the Manor, they were set on the wooden horse, or flogged and branded in the manor-house yard. One or two cases there were of men who had occupied lands which encroached on the lord's domain, and whose houses had been mysteriously burnt on a winters night, with the whole family inside. But what seemed to dwell on the innkeeper's mind most---for he returned to the subject more than once---was that the Count had been on the Black Pilgrimage, and had brought something or someone back with him.

You will naturally inquire, as Mr. Wraxall did, what the

Black Pilgrimage may have been. But your curiosity on the point must remain unsatisfied for the time being, just as his did. The landlord was evidently unwilling to give a full answer, or indeed any answer, on the point, and, being called out for a moment, trotted out with obvious alacrity, only putting his head in at the door a few minutes afterwards to say that he was called away to Skara, and should not be back till evening.

So Mr. Wraxall had to go unsatisfied to his day's work at the manor-house. The papers on which he was just then engaged soon put his thoughts into another channel, for he had to occupy himself with glancing over the correspondence between Sophia Albertina in Stockholm and her married cousin Ulrica Leonora at Råbäck in the years 1705-1710. The letters were of exceptional interest from the light they threw upon the culture of that period in Sweden, as anyone can testify who has read the full edition of them in the publications of the Swedish Historical Manuscripts Commission.

In the afternoon he had done with these, and after returning the boxes in which they were kept to their places on the shelf, he proceeded, very naturally, to take down some of the volumes nearest to them, in order to determine which of them had best be his principal subject of investigation next day. The shelf he had hit upon was occupied mostly by a collection of account-books in the writing of the first Count Magnus. But one among them was not an account-book, but a book of alchemical and other tracts in another sixteenth-century hand. Not being very familiar with alchemical literature, Mr. Wraxall spends much space which he might have spared in setting out the names and beginnings of the various treatises: The book of the Phoenix, book of the

Thirty Words, book of the Toad, book of Miriam, Turba philosophorum, and so forth; and then he announces with a good deal of circumstance his delight at finding, on a leaf originally left blank near the middle of the book, some writing of Count Magnus himself headed 'Liber nigrae peregrinationis.' It is true that only a few lines were written, but there was quite enough to show that the landlord had that morning been referring to a belief at least as old as the time of Count Magnus, and probably shared by him. This is the English of what was written:

'If any man desires to obtain a long life, if he would obtain a faithful messenger and see the blood of his enemies, it is necessary that he should first go into the city of Chorazin, and there salute the prince....' Here there was an erasure of one word, not very thoroughly done, so that Mr. Wraxall felt pretty sure that he was right in reading it as aëris (of the air). But there was no more of the text copied, only a line in Latin: 'Quaere reliqua hujus materiei inter secretiora.' (See the rest of this matter among the more private things.)

It could not be denied that this threw a rather lurid light upon the tastes and beliefs of the Count; but to Mr. Wraxall, separated from him by nearly three centuries, the thought that he might have added to his general forcefulness alchemy, and to alchemy something like magic, only made him a more picturesque figure; and when, after a rather prolonged contemplation of his picture in the hall, Mr. Wraxall set out on his homeward way, his mind was full of the thought of Count Magnus. He had no eyes for his surroundings, no perception of the evening scents of the woods or the evening light on the lake; and when all of a sudden he pulled up short, he was astonished to find himself already at the gate of the churchyard, and within a few minutes of his dinner. His eyes fell on the mausoleum.

'Ah,' he said, 'Count Magnus, there you are. I should dearly like to see you.'

'Like many solitary men,' he writes, 'I have a habit of talking to myself aloud; and, unlike some of the Greek and Latin particles, I do not expect an answer. Certainly, and perhaps fortunately in this case, there was neither voice nor any that regarded: only the woman who, I suppose, was cleaning up the church, dropped some metallic object on the floor, whose clang startled me. Count Magnus, I think, sleeps sound enough.'

That same evening the landlord of the inn, who had heard Mr. Wraxall say that he wished to see the clerk or deacon (as he would be called in Sweden) of the parish, introduced him to that official in the inn parlour. A visit to the De la Gardie tomb-house was soon arranged for the next day, and a little general conversation ensued.

Mr. Wraxall, remembering that one function of Scandinavian deacons is to teach candidates for Confirmation, thought he would refresh his own memory on a Biblical point.

'Can you tell me, he said, anything about Chorazin?'

The deacon seemed startled, but readily reminded him how that village had once been denounced.

'To be sure,' said Mr Wraxall; 'it is, I suppose, quite a ruin now?'

'So I expect,' replied the deacon. 'I have heard some of our old priests say that Antichrist is to be born there; and there are tales---'

'Ah! what tales are those?' Mr. Wraxall put in.

'Tales, I was going to say, which I have forgotten,' said the deacon; and soon after that he said good night.

The landlord was now alone, and at Mr. Wraxall's mercy; and that inquirer was not inclined to spare him.

'Herr Nielsen,' he said, 'I have found out something about the Black Pilgrimage. You may as well tell me what you know. What did the Count bring back with him?'

Swedes are habitually slow, perhaps, in answering, or perhaps the landlord was an exception. I am not sure; but Mr. Wraxall notes that the landlord spent at least one minute in looking at him before he said anything at all. Then he came close up to his guest, and with a good deal of effort he spoke:

'Mr. Wraxall, I can tell you this one little tale, and no more---not any more. You must not ask anything when I have done. In my grandfather's time---that is, ninety-two years ago---there were two men who said: "The Count is dead; we do not care for him. We will go tonight and have a free hunt in his wood"---the long wood on the hill that you have seen behind Råbäck. Well, those that heard them say this, they said: "No, do not go; we are sure you will meet with persons walking who should not be walking. They should be resting, not walking." These men laughed. There were no forest-men to keep the wood, because no one wished to live there. The family were not

340

here at the house. These men could do what they wished.

'Very well, they go to the wood that night. My grandfather was sitting here in this room. It was the summer, and a light night. With the window open, he could see out to the wood, and hear.

'So he sat there, and two or three men with him, and they listened. At first they hear nothing at all; then they hear someone---you know how far away it is---they hear someone scream, just as if the most inside part of his soul was twisted out of him. All of them in the room caught hold of each other, and they sat so for three-quarters of an hour. Then they hear someone else, only about three hundred ells off. They hear him laugh out loud: it was not one of those two men that laughed, and, indeed, they have all of them said that it was not any man at all. After that they hear a great door shut.

'Then, when it was just light with the sun, they all went to the priest. They said to him:

'"Father, put on your gown and your ruff, and come to bury these men, Anders Bjornsen and Hans Thorbjorn."

'You understand that they were sure these men were dead. So they went to the wood---my grandfather never forgot this. He said they were all like so many dead men themselves. The priest, too, he was in a white fear. He said when they came to him:

'"I heard one cry in the night, and I heard one laugh afterwards. If I cannot forget that, I shall not be able to sleep again."

'So they went to the wood, and they found these men on the edge of the wood. Hans Thorbjorn was standing with his back against a tree, and all the time he was pushing with his hands---pushing something away from him which was not there. So he was not dead. And they led him away, and took him to the house at Nykjoping, and he died before the winter; but he went on pushing with his hands. Also Anders Bjornsen was there; but he was dead. And I tell you this about Anders Bjornsen, that he was once a beautiful man, but now his face was not there, because the flesh of it was sucked away off the bones. You understand that? My grandfather did not forget that. And they laid him on the bier which they brought, and they put a cloth over his head, and the priest walked before; and they began to sing the psalm for the dead as well as they could. So, as they were singing the end of the first verse, one fell down, who was carrying the head of the bier, and the others looked back, and they saw that the cloth had fallen off, and the eyes of Anders Bjornsen were looking up, because there was nothing to close over them. And this they could not bear. Therefore the priest laid the cloth upon him, and sent for a spade, and they buried him in that place.'

The next day Mr. Wraxall records that the deacon called for him soon after his breakfast, and took him to the church and mausoleum. He noticed that the key of the latter was hung on a nail just by the pulpit, and it occurred to him that, as the church door seemed to be left unlocked as a rule, it would not be difficult for him to pay a second and more private visit to the monuments if there proved to be more of interest among them than could be digested at first. The building, when he entered it, he found not unimposing. The monuments, mostly large erections of the seventeenth and eighteenth centuries, were dignified if luxuriant, and the epitaphs and heraldry were copious. The central space of the domed room was occupied by three copper sarcophagi, covered with finely-engraved ornament. Two of them had, as is commonly the case in Denmark and Sweden, a large metal crucifix on the lid. The third, that of Count Magnus, as it appeared, had, instead of that, a full-length effigy engraved upon it, and round the edge were several bands of similar ornament representing various scenes. One was a battle, with cannon belching out smoke, and walled towns, and troops of pikemen. Another showed an execution. In a third, among trees, was a man running at full speed, with flying hair and outstretched hands. After him followed a strange form; it would be hard to say whether the artist had intended it for a man, and was unable to give the requisite similitude, or whether it was intentionally made as monstrous as it looked. In view of the skill with which the rest of the drawing was done, Mr. Wraxall felt inclined to adopt the latter idea. The figure was unduly short, and was for the most part muffled in a hooded garment which swept the ground. The only part of the form which projected from that shelter was not shaped like any hand or arm. Mr. Wraxall compares it to the tentacle of a devil-fish, and continues: 'On seeing this, I said to myself, "This, then, which is evidently an allegorical representation of some kind---a fiend pursuing a hunted soul---may be the origin of the story of Count Magnus and his mysterious companion. Let us see how the huntsman is pictured: doubtless it will be a demon blowing his horn."' But, as it turned out, there was no such sensational figure, only the semblance of a cloaked man on a hillock, who stood leaning on a stick, and watching the hunt with an interest which the engraver had tried to express in his attitude.

Mr. Wraxall noted the finely-worked and massive steel padlocks---three in number---which secured the sarcophagus. One of them, he saw, was detached, and lay on the pavement. And then, unwilling to delay the deacon longer or to waste his own working-time, he made his way onward to the manor-house.

'It is curious', he notes, 'how, on retracing a familiar path, ones thoughts engross one to the absolute exclusion of surrounding objects. Tonight, for the second time, I had entirely failed to notice where I was going (I had planned a private visit to the tomb-house to copy the epitaphs), when I suddenly, as it were, awoke to consciousness, and found myself (as before) turning in at the churchyard gate, and, I believe, singing or chanting some such words as, "Are you awake, Count Magnus? Are you asleep, Count Magnus?" and then something more which I have failed to recollect. It seemed to me that I must have been behaving in this nonsensical way for some time.'

He found the key of the mausoleum where he had expected to find it, and copied the greater part of what he wanted; in fact, he stayed until the light began to fail him.

'I must have been wrong,' he writes, 'in saying that one of the padlocks of my Counts sarcophagus was unfastened; I see tonight that two are loose. I picked both up, and laid them carefully on the window-ledge, after trying unsuccessfully to close them. The remaining one is still firm, and, though I take it to be a spring lock, I cannot guess how it is opened. Had I succeeded in undoing it, I am almost afraid I should have taken the liberty of opening the sarcophagus. It is strange, the interest I feel in the personality of this, I fear, somewhat ferocious and grim old noble.'

The day following was, as it turned out, the last of Mr. Wraxall's stay at Råbäck. He received letters connected with certain investments which made it desirable that he should return to England; his work among the papers was practically done, and travelling was slow. He decided, therefore, to make his farewells, put some finishing touches to his notes, and be off.

These finishing touches and farewells, as it turned out, took more time than he had expected. The hospitable family insisted on his staying to dine with them---they dined at three---and it was verging on half-past six before he was outside the iron gates of Råbäck. He dwelt on every step of his walk by the lake, determined to saturate himself, now that he trod it for the last time, in the sentiment of the place and hour. And when he reached the summit of the churchyard knoll, he lingered for many minutes, gazing at the limitless prospect of woods near and distant, all dark beneath a sky of liquid green. When at last he turned to go, the thought struck him that surely he must bid farewell to Count Magnus as well as the rest of the De la Gardies. The church was but twenty yards away, and he knew where the key of the mausoleum hung. It was not long before he was standing over the great copper coffin, and, as usual, talking to himself aloud. 'You may have been a bit of a rascal in your time, Magnus,' he was saying, 'but for all that I should like to see you, or, rather---'

'Just at that instant,' he says, 'I felt a blow on my foot. Hastily enough I drew it back, and something fell on the pavement with a clash. It was the third, the last of the three padlocks which had fastened the sarcophagus. I stooped to pick it up, and---Heaven is my witness that

I am writing only the bare truth---before I had raised myself there was a sound of metal hinges creaking, and I distinctly saw the lid shifting upwards. I may have behaved like a coward, but I could not for my life stay for one moment. I was outside that dreadful building in less time than I can write---almost as quickly as I could have said---the words; and what frightens me yet more, I could not turn the key in the lock. As I sit here in my room noting these facts, I ask myself (it was not twenty minutes ago) whether that noise of creaking metal continued, and I cannot tell whether it did or not. I only know that there was something more than I have written that alarmed me, but whether it was sound or sight I am not able to remember. What is this that I have done?'

Poor Mr. Wraxall! He set out on his journey to England on the next day, as he had planned, and he reached England in safety; and yet, as I gather from his changed hand and inconsequent jottings, a broken man. One of several small note-books that have come to me with his papers gives, not a key to, but a kind of inkling of, his experiences. Much of his journey was made by canal-boat, and I find not less than six painful attempts to enumerate and describe his fellow-passengers. The entries are of this kind:

24. Pastor of village in Skåne. Usual black coat and soft black hat.

25. Commercial traveller from Stockholm going to Trollhttan. Black cloak, brown hat.

26. Man in long black cloak, broad-leafed hat, very old-fashioned.

This entry is lined out, and a note added: 'Perhaps identical with No. 13. Have not yet seen his face.' On referring to No. 13, I find that he is a Roman priest in a cassock.

The net result of the reckoning is always the same. Twenty-eight people appear in the enumeration, one being always a man in a long black cloak and broad hat, and the other a 'short figure in dark cloak and hood.' On the other hand, it is always noted that only twenty-six passengers appear at meals, and that the man in the cloak is perhaps absent, and the short figure is certainly absent.

On reaching England, it appears that Mr. Wraxall landed at Harwich, and that he resolved at once to put himself out of the reach of some person or persons whom he never specifies, but whom he had evidently come to regard as his pursuers. Accordingly he took a vehicle---it was a closed fly---not trusting the railway and drove across country to the village of Belchamp St Paul. It was about nine o'clock on a moonlight August night when he neared the place. He was sitting forward, and looking out of the window at the fields and thickets---there was little else to be seen---racing past him. Suddenly he came to a cross-road. At the corner two figures were standing motionless; both were in dark cloaks; the taller one wore a hat, the shorter a hood. He had no time to see their faces, nor did they make any motion that he could discern. Yet the horse shied violently and broke into a gallop, and Mr. Wraxall sank back into his seat in something like desperation. He had seen them before.

Arrived at Belchamp St Paul, he was fortunate enough to find a decent furnished lodging, and for the next twenty-four hours he lived, comparatively speaking, in peace. His last notes were written on this day. They are too disjointed and ejaculatory to be given here in full, but the substance of them is clear enough. He is expecting a visit from his pursuers---how or when he knows not---and his constant cry is 'What has he done?' and 'Is there no hope?' Doctors, he knows, would call him mad, policemen would laugh at him. The parson is away. What can he do but lock his door and cry to God?

People still remembered last year at Belchamp St Paul how a strange gentleman came one evening in August years back; and how the next morning but one he was found dead, and there was an inquest; and the jury that viewed the body fainted, seven of 'em did, and none of 'em wouldn't speak to what they see, and the verdict was visitation of God; and how the people as kep' the 'ouse moved out that same week, and went away from that part. But they do not, I think, know that any glimmer of light has ever been thrown, or could be thrown, on the mystery. It so happened that last year the little house came into my hands as part of a legacy. It had stood empty since 1863, and there seemed no prospect of letting it; so I had it pulled down, and the papers of which I have given you an abstract were found in a forgotten cupboard under the window in the best bedroom.

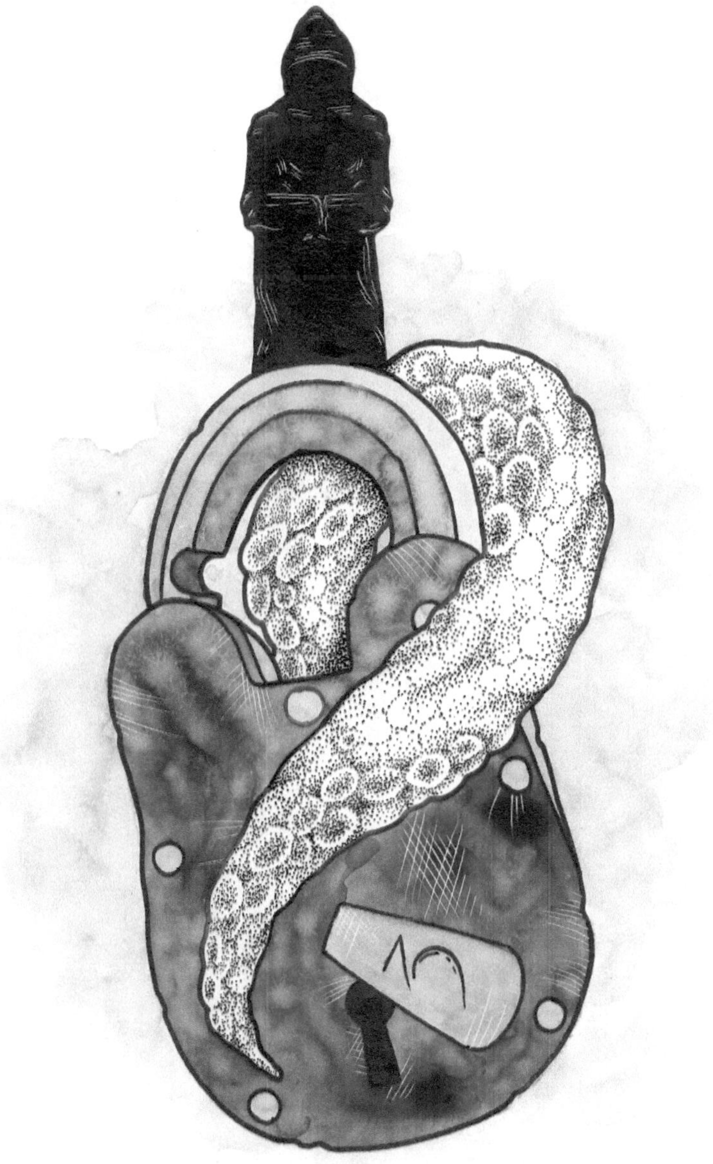

'Are you asleep, Count Magnus?'

M. R. James

THE TEMPLE

BY H. P. LOVECRAFT

(Manuscript found on the coast of Yucatan.)

On August 20, 1917, I, Karl Heinrich, Graf von Altberg-Ehrenstein, Lieutenant-Commander in the Imperial German Navy and in charge of the submarine U-29, deposit this bottle and record in the Atlantic Ocean at a point to me unknown but probably about N. Latitude 20°, W. Longitude 35°, where my ship lies disabled on the ocean floor. I do so because of my desire to set certain unusual facts before the public; a thing I shall not in all probability survive to accomplish in person, since the circumstances surrounding me are as menacing as they are extraordinary, and involve not only the hopeless crippling of the U-29, but the impairment of my iron German will in a manner most disastrous.

On the afternoon of June 18, as reported by wireless to the U-61, bound for Kiel, we torpedoed the British freighter Victory, New York to Liverpool, in N. Latitude 45° 16', W. Longitude 28° 34'; permitting the crew to leave in boats in order to obtain a good cinema view for the admiralty records. The ship sank quite picturesquely, bow first, the stern rising high out of the water whilst the hull shot down perpendicularly to the bottom of the sea. Our camera missed nothing, and I regret that so fine a reel of film should never reach Berlin. After that we sank

the lifeboats with our guns and submerged.

When we rose to the surface about sunset a seaman's body was found on the deck, hands gripping the railing in curious fashion. The poor fellow was young, rather dark, and very handsome; probably an Italian or Greek, and undoubtedly of the Victory's crew. He had evidently sought refuge on the very ship which had been forced to destroy his own—one more victim of the unjust war of aggression which the English pig-dogs are waging upon the Fatherland. Our men searched him for souvenirs, and found in his coat pocket a very odd bit of ivory carved to represent a youth's head crowned with laurel. My fellow-officer, Lieut. Klenze, believed that the thing was of great age and artistic value, so took it from the men for himself. How it had ever come into the possession of a common sailor, neither he nor I could imagine.

As the dead man was thrown overboard there occurred two incidents which created much disturbance amongst the crew. The fellow's eyes had been closed; but in the dragging of his body to the rail they were jarred open, and many seemed to entertain a queer delusion that they gazed steadily and mockingly at Schmidt and Zimmer, who were bent over the corpse. The Boatswain Müller, an elderly man who would have known better had he not been a superstitious Alsatian swine, became so excited by this impression that he watched the body in the water; and swore that after it sank a little it drew its limbs into a swimming position and sped away to the south under the waves. Klenze and I did not like these displays of peasant ignorance, and severely reprimanded the men, particularly Müller.

The next day a very troublesome situation was

created by the indisposition of some of the crew. They were evidently suffering from the nervous strain of our long voyage, and had had bad dreams. Several seemed quite dazed and stupid; and after satisfying myself that they were not feigning their weakness, I excused them from their duties. The sea was rather rough, so we descended to a depth where the waves were less troublesome. Here we were comparatively calm, despite a somewhat puzzling southward current which we could not identify from our oceanographic charts. The moans of the sick men were decidedly annoying; but since they did not appear to demoralise the rest of the crew, we did not resort to extreme measures. It was our plan to remain where we were and intercept the liner Dacia, mentioned in information from agents in New York.

In the early evening we rose to the surface, and found the sea less heavy. The smoke of a battleship was on the northern horizon, but our distance and ability to submerge made us safe. What worried us more was the talk of Boatswain Müller, which grew wilder as night came on. He was in a detestably childish state, and babbled of some illusion of dead bodies drifting past the undersea portholes; bodies which looked at him intensely, and which he recognised in spite of bloating as having seen dying during some of our victorious German exploits. And he said that the young man we had found and tossed overboard was their leader. This was very gruesome and abnormal, so we confined Müller in irons and had him soundly whipped. The men were not pleased at his punishment, but discipline was necessary. We also denied the request of a delegation headed by Seaman Zimmer, that the curious carved ivory head be cast into the sea.

On June 20, Seamen Bohm and Schmidt, who had been ill the day before, became violently insane. I regretted that no physician was included in our complement of officers, since German lives are precious; but the constant ravings of the two concerning a terrible curse were most subversive of discipline, so drastic steps were taken. The crew accepted the event in a sullen fashion, but it seemed to quiet Müller; who thereafter gave us no trouble. In the evening we released him, and he went about his duties silently.

In the week that followed we were all very nervous, watching for the Dacia. The tension was aggravated by the disappearance of Müller and Zimmer, who undoubtedly committed suicide as a result of the fears which had seemed to harass them, though they were not observed in the act of jumping overboard. I was rather glad to be rid of Müller, for even his silence had unfavourably affected the crew. Everyone seemed inclined to be silent now, as though holding a secret fear. Many were ill, but none made a disturbance. Lieut. Klenze chafed under the strain, and was annoyed by the merest trifles—such as the school of dolphins which gathered about the U-29 in increasing numbers, and the growing intensity of that southward current which was not on our chart.

It at length became apparent that we had missed the Dacia altogether. Such failures are not uncommon, and we were more pleased than disappointed; since our return to Wilhelmshaven was now in order. At noon June 28 we turned northeastward, and despite some rather comical entanglements with the unusual masses of dolphins were soon under way.

The explosion in the engine room at 2 P.M. was wholly

a surprise. No defect in the machinery or carelessness in the men had been noticed, yet without warning the ship was racked from end to end with a colossal shock. Lieut. Klenze hurried to the engine room, finding the fuel-tank and most of the mechanism shattered, and Engineers Raabe and Schneider instantly killed. Our situation had suddenly become grave indeed; for though the chemical air regenerators were intact, and though we could use the devices for raising and submerging the ship and opening the hatches as long as compressed air and storage batteries might hold out, we were powerless to propel or guide the submarine. To seek rescue in the lifeboats would be to deliver ourselves into the hands of enemies unreasonably embittered against our great German nation, and our wireless had failed ever since the Victory affair to put us in touch with a fellow U-boat of the Imperial Navy.

From the hour of the accident till July 2 we drifted constantly to the south, almost without plans and encountering no vessel. Dolphins still encircled the U-29, a somewhat remarkable circumstance considering the distance we had covered. On the morning of July 2 we sighted a warship flying American colours, and the men became very restless in their desire to surrender. Finally Lieut. Klenze had to shoot a seaman named Traube, who urged this un-German act with especial violence. This quieted the crew for the time, and we submerged unseen.

The next afternoon a dense flock of sea-birds appeared from the south, and the ocean began to heave ominously. Closing our hatches, we awaited developments until we realised that we must either submerge or be swamped in the mounting waves. Our air pressure and electricity were diminishing, and we wished to avoid all unnecessary use of our slender mechanical resources; but in this case there

was no choice. We did not descend far, and when after several hours the sea was calmer, we decided to return to the surface. Here, however, a new trouble developed; for the ship failed to respond to our direction in spite of all that the mechanics could do. As the men grew more frightened at this undersea imprisonment, some of them began to mutter again about Lieut. Klenze's ivory image, but the sight of an automatic pistol calmed them. We kept the poor devils as busy as we could, tinkering at the machinery even when we knew it was useless.

Klenze and I usually slept at different times; and it was during my sleep, about 5 A.M., July 4, that the general mutiny broke loose. The six remaining pigs of seamen, suspecting that we were lost, had suddenly burst into a mad fury at our refusal to surrender to the Yankee battleship two days before; and were in a delirium of cursing and destruction. They roared like the animals they were, and broke instruments and furniture indiscriminately; screaming about such nonsense as the curse of the ivory image and the dark dead youth who looked at them and swam away. Lieut. Klenze seemed paralysed and inefficient, as one might expect of a soft, womanish Rhinelander. I shot all six men, for it was necessary, and made sure that none remained alive.

We expelled the bodies through the double hatches and were alone in the U-29. Klenze seemed very nervous, and drank heavily. It was decided that we remain alive as long as possible, using the large stock of provisions and chemical supply of oxygen, none of which had suffered from the crazy antics of those swine-hound seamen. Our compasses, depth gauges, and other delicate instruments were ruined; so that henceforth our only reckoning would be guesswork, based on our watches, the calendar, and our apparent drift as judged by any objects we might spy through the portholes or from the conning tower. Fortunately we had storage batteries still capable of long use, both for interior lighting and for the searchlight. We often cast a beam around the ship, but saw only dolphins, swimming parallel to our own drifting course. I was scientifically interested in those dolphins; for though the ordinary Delphinus delphis is a cetacean mammal, unable to subsist without air, I watched one of the swimmers closely for two hours, and did not see him alter his submerged condition.

With the passage of time Klenze and I decided that we were still drifting south, meanwhile sinking deeper and deeper. We noted the marine fauna and flora, and read much on the subject in the books I had carried with me for spare moments. I could not help observing, however, the inferior scientific knowledge of my companion. His mind was not Prussian, but given to imaginings and speculations which have no value. The fact of our coming death affected him curiously, and he would frequently pray in remorse over the men, women, and children we had sent to the bottom; forgetting that all things are noble which serve the German state. After a time he became noticeably unbalanced, gazing for hours at his ivory image and weaving fanciful stories of the lost and forgotten things under the sea. Sometimes, as a psychological experiment, I would lead him on in these wanderings, and listen to his endless poetical quotations and tales of sunken ships. I was very sorry for him, for I dislike to see a German suffer; but he was not a good man to die with. For myself I was proud, knowing how the Fatherland would revere my memory and how my sons would be taught to be men like me.

On August 9, we espied the ocean floor, and sent a powerful beam from the searchlight over it. It was a vast undulating plain, mostly covered with seaweed, and strown with the shells of small molluscs. Here and there were slimy objects of puzzling contour, draped with weeds and encrusted with barnacles, which Klenze declared must be ancient ships lying in their graves. He was puzzled by one thing, a peak of solid matter, protruding above the ocean bed nearly four feet at its apex; about two feet thick, with flat sides and smooth upper surfaces which met at a very obtuse angle. I called the peak a bit of outcropping rock, but Klenze thought he saw carvings on it. After a while he began to shudder, and turned away from the scene as if frightened; yet could give no explanation save that he was overcome with the vastness, darkness, remoteness, antiquity, and mystery of the oceanic abysses. His mind was tired, but I am always a German, and was quick to notice two things; that the U-29 was standing the deep-sea pressure splendidly, and that the peculiar dolphins were still about us, even at a depth where the existence of high organisms is considered impossible by most naturalists. That I had previously overestimated our depth, I was sure; but none the less we must still be deep enough to make these phenomena remarkable. Our southward speed, as gauged by the ocean floor, was about as I had estimated from the organisms passed at higher levels.

It was at 3:15 P.M., August 12, that poor Klenze went wholly mad. He had been in the conning tower using the searchlight when I saw him bound into the library compartment where I sat reading, and his face at once betrayed him. I will repeat here what he said, underlining the words he emphasised: "He is calling! He is calling! I hear him! We must go!" As he spoke he took his ivory image from the table, pocketed it, and seized my arm in an effort to drag me up the companionway to the deck. In a moment I understood that he meant to open the hatch and plunge with me into the water outside, a vagary of suicidal and homicidal mania for which I was scarcely prepared. As I hung back and attempted to soothe him he grew more violent, saying: "Come now—do not wait until later; it is better to repent and be forgiven than to defy and be condemned." Then I tried the opposite of the soothing plan, and told him he was mad—pitifully demented. But he was unmoved, and cried: "If I am mad, it is mercy! May the gods pity the man who in his callousness can remain sane to the hideous end! Come and be mad whilst he still calls with mercy!"

This outburst seemed to relieve a pressure in his brain; for as he finished he grew much milder, asking me to let him depart alone if I would not accompany him. My course at once became clear. He was a German, but only a Rhinelander and a commoner; and he was now a potentially dangerous madman. By complying with his suicidal request I could immediately free myself from one who was no longer a companion but a menace. I asked him to give me the ivory image before he went, but this request brought from him such uncanny laughter that I did not repeat it. Then I asked him if he wished to leave any keepsake or lock of hair for his family in Germany in case I should be rescued, but again he gave me that strange laugh. So as he climbed the ladder I went to the levers, and allowing proper time-intervals operated the machinery which sent him to his death. After I saw that he was no longer in the boat I threw the searchlight around the water in an effort to obtain a last glimpse of him; since I wished to ascertain whether the water-pressure would flatten him as it theoretically should, or whether the body

would be unaffected, like those extraordinary dolphins. I did not, however, succeed in finding my late companion, for the dolphins were massed thickly and obscuringly about the conning tower.

That evening I regretted that I had not taken the ivory image surreptitiously from poor Klenze's pocket as he left, for the memory of it fascinated me. I could not forget the youthful, beautiful head with its leafy crown, though I am not by nature an artist. I was also sorry that I had no one with whom to converse. Klenze, though not my mental equal, was much better than no one. I did not sleep well that night, and wondered exactly when the end would come. Surely, I had little enough chance of rescue.

The next day I ascended to the conning tower and commenced the customary searchlight explorations. Northward the view was much the same as it had been all the four days since we had sighted the bottom, but I perceived that the drifting of the U-29 was less rapid. As I swung the beam around to the south, I noticed that the ocean floor ahead fell away in a marked declivity, and bore curiously regular blocks of stone in certain places, disposed as if in accordance with definite patterns. The boat did not at once descend to match the greater ocean depth, so I was soon forced to adjust the searchlight to cast a sharply downward beam. Owing to the abruptness of the change a wire was disconnected, which necessitated a delay of many minutes for repairs; but at length the light streamed on again, flooding the marine valley below me.

I am not given to emotion of any kind, but my amazement was very great when I saw what lay revealed in that electrical glow. And yet as one reared in the best Kultur of Prussia I should not have been amazed, for geology and tradition alike tell us of great transpositions in oceanic and continental areas. What I saw was an extended and elaborate array of ruined edifices; all of magnificent though unclassified architecture, and in various stages of preservation. Most appeared to be of marble, gleaming whitely in the rays of the searchlight, and the general plan was of a large city at the bottom of a narrow valley, with numerous isolated temples and villas on the steep slopes above. Roofs were fallen and columns were broken, but there still remained an air of immemorially ancient splendour which nothing could efface.

Confronted at last with the Atlantis I had formerly deemed largely a myth, I was the most eager of explorers. At the bottom of that valley a river once had flowed; for as I examined the scene more closely I beheld the remains of stone and marble bridges and sea-walls, and terraces and embankments once verdant and beautiful. In my enthusiasm I became nearly as idiotic and sentimental as poor Klenze, and was very tardy in noticing that the southward current had ceased at last, allowing the U-29 to settle slowly down upon the sunken city as an aëroplane settles upon a town of the upper earth. I was slow, too, in realising that the school of unusual dolphins had vanished.

In about two hours the boat rested in a paved plaza close to the rocky wall of the valley. On one side I could view the entire city as it sloped from the plaza down to the old river-bank; on the other side, in startling proximity, I was confronted by the richly ornate and perfectly preserved facade of a great building, evidently a temple, hollowed from the solid rock. Of the original workmanship of this titanic thing I can only make conjectures. The facade,

of immense magnitude, apparently covers a continuous hollow recess; for its windows are many and widely distributed. In the centre yawns a great open door, reached by an impressive flight of steps, and surrounded by exquisite carvings like the figures of Bacchanals in relief. Foremost of all are the great columns and frieze, both decorated with sculptures of inexpressible beauty; obviously portraying idealised pastoral scenes and processions of priests and priestesses bearing strange ceremonial devices in adoration of a radiant god. The art is of the most phenomenal perfection, largely Hellenic in idea, yet strangely individual. It imparts an impression of terrible antiquity, as though it were the remotest rather than the immediate ancestor of Greek art. Nor can I doubt that every detail of this massive product was fashioned from the virgin hillside rock of our planet. It is palpably a part of the valley wall, though how the vast interior was ever excavated I cannot imagine. Perhaps a cavern or series of caverns furnished the nucleus. Neither age nor submersion has corroded the pristine grandeur of this awful fane—for fane indeed it must be—and today after thousands of years it rests untarnished and inviolate in the endless night and silence of an ocean chasm.

I cannot reckon the number of hours I spent in gazing at the sunken city with its buildings, arches, statues, and bridges, and the colossal temple with its beauty and mystery. Though I knew that death was near, my curiosity was consuming; and I threw the searchlight's beam about in eager quest. The shaft of light permitted me to learn many details, but refused to shew anything within the gaping door of the rock-hewn temple; and after a time I turned off the current, conscious of the need of conserving power. The rays were now perceptibly dimmer than they had been during the weeks of drifting.

And as if sharpened by the coming deprivation of light, my desire to explore the watery secrets grew. I, a German, should be the first to tread those aeon-forgotten ways!

I produced and examined a deep-sea diving suit of joined metal, and experimented with the portable light and air regenerator. Though I should have trouble in managing the double hatches alone, I believed I could overcome all obstacles with my scientific skill and actually walk about the dead city in person.

On August 16 I effected an exit from the U-29, and laboriously made my way through the ruined and mud-choked streets to the ancient river. I found no skeletons or other human remains, but gleaned a wealth of archaeological lore from sculptures and coins. Of this I cannot now speak save to utter my awe at a culture in the full noon of glory when cave-dwellers roamed Europe and the Nile flowed unwatched to the sea. Others, guided by this manuscript if it shall ever be found, must unfold the mysteries at which I can only hint. I returned to the boat as my electric batteries grew feeble, resolved to explore the rock temple on the following day.

On the 17th, as my impulse to search out the mystery of the temple waxed still more insistent, a great disappointment befell me; for I found that the materials needed to replenish the portable light had perished in the mutiny of those pigs in July. My rage was unbounded, yet my German sense forbade me to venture unprepared into an utterly black interior which might prove the lair of some indescribable marine monster or a labyrinth of passages from whose windings I could never extricate myself. All I could do was to turn on the waning searchlight of the U-29, and with its aid walk

up the temple steps and study the exterior carvings. The shaft of light entered the door at an upward angle, and I peered in to see if I could glimpse anything, but all in vain. Not even the roof was visible; and though I took a step or two inside after testing the floor with a staff, I dared not go farther. Moreover, for the first time in my life I experienced the emotion of dread. I began to realise how some of poor Klenze's moods had arisen, for as the temple drew me more and more, I feared its aqueous abysses with a blind and mounting terror. Returning to the submarine, I turned off the lights and sat thinking in the dark. Electricity must now be saved for emergencies.

Saturday the 18th I spent in total darkness, tormented by thoughts and memories that threatened to overcome my German will. Klenze had gone mad and perished before reaching this sinister remnant of a past unwholesomely remote, and had advised me to go with him. Was, indeed, Fate preserving my reason only to draw me irresistibly to an end more horrible and unthinkable than any man has dreamed of? Clearly, my nerves were sorely taxed, and I must cast off these impressions of weaker men.

I could not sleep Saturday night, and turned on the lights regardless of the future. It was annoying that the electricity should not last out the air and provisions. I revived my thoughts of euthanasia, and examined my automatic pistol. Toward morning I must have dropped asleep with the lights on, for I awoke in darkness yesterday afternoon to find the batteries dead. I struck several matches in succession, and desperately regretted the improvidence which had caused us long ago to use up the few candles we carried.

After the fading of the last match I dared to waste, I sat very quietly without a light. As I considered the inevitable end my mind ran over preceding events, and developed a hitherto dormant impression which would have caused a weaker and more superstitious man to shudder. The head of the radiant god in the sculptures on the rock temple is the same as that carven bit of ivory which the dead sailor brought from the sea and which poor Klenze carried back into the sea.

I was a little dazed by this coincidence, but did not become terrified. It is only the inferior thinker who hastens to explain the singular and the complex by the primitive short cut of supernaturalism. The coincidence was strange, but I was too sound a reasoner to connect circumstances which admit of no logical connexion, or to associate in any uncanny fashion the disastrous events which had led from the Victory affair to my present plight. Feeling the need of more rest, I took a sedative and secured some more sleep. My nervous condition was reflected in my dreams, for I seemed to hear the cries of drowning persons, and to see dead faces pressing against the portholes of the boat. And among the dead faces was the living, mocking face of the youth with the ivory image.

I must be careful how I record my awaking today, for I am unstrung, and much hallucination is necessarily mixed with fact. Psychologically my case is most interesting, and I regret that it cannot be observed scientifically by a competent German authority. Upon opening my eyes my first sensation was an overmastering desire to visit the rock temple; a desire which grew every instant, yet which I automatically sought to resist through some emotion of fear which operated in the reverse

direction. Next there came to me the impression of light amidst the darkness of dead batteries, and I seemed to see a sort of phosphorescent glow in the water through the porthole which opened toward the temple. This aroused my curiosity, for I knew of no deep-sea organism capable of emitting such luminosity. But before I could investigate there came a third impression which because of its irrationality caused me to doubt the objectivity of anything my senses might record. It was an aural delusion; a sensation of rhythmic, melodic sound as of some wild yet beautiful chant or choral hymn, coming from the outside through the absolutely sound-proof hull of the U-29. Convinced of my psychological and nervous abnormality, I lighted some matches and poured a stiff dose of sodium bromide solution, which seemed to calm me to the extent of dispelling the illusion of sound. But the phosphorescence remained, and I had difficulty in repressing a childish impulse to go to the porthole and seek its source. It was horribly realistic, and I could soon distinguish by its aid the familiar objects around me, as well as the empty sodium bromide glass of which I had had no former visual impression in its present location. The last circumstance made me ponder, and I crossed the room and touched the glass. It was indeed in the place where I had seemed to see it. Now I knew that the light was either real or part of an hallucination so fixed and consistent that I could not hope to dispel it, so abandoning all resistance I ascended to the conning tower to look for the luminous agency. Might it not actually be another U-boat, offering possibilities of rescue?

It is well that the reader accept nothing which follows as objective truth, for since the events transcend natural law, they are necessarily the subjective and unreal creations of my overtaxed mind. When I attained the conning tower I found the sea in general far less luminous than I had expected. There was no animal or vegetable phosphorescence about, and the city that sloped down to the river was invisible in blackness. What I did see was not spectacular, not grotesque or terrifying, yet it removed my last vestige of trust in my consciousness. For the door and windows of the undersea temple hewn from the rocky hill were vividly aglow with a flickering radiance, as from a mighty altar-flame far within.

Later incidents are chaotic. As I stared at the uncannily lighted door and windows, I became subject to the most extravagant visions—visions so extravagant that I cannot even relate them. I fancied that I discerned objects in the temple—objects both stationary and moving—and seemed to hear again the unreal chant that had floated to me when first I awaked. And over all rose thoughts and fears which centred in the youth from the sea and the ivory image whose carving was duplicated on the frieze and columns of the temple before me. I thought of poor Klenze, and wondered where his body rested with the image he had carried back into the sea. He had warned me of something, and I had not heeded—but he was a soft-headed Rhinelander who went mad at troubles a Prussian could bear with ease.

The rest is very simple. My impulse to visit and enter the temple has now become an inexplicable and imperious command which ultimately cannot be denied. My own German will no longer controls my acts, and volition is henceforward possible only in minor matters. Such madness it was which drove Klenze to his death, bareheaded and unprotected in the ocean; but I am a Prussian and a man of sense, and will use to the last what little will I have. When first I saw that I must go, I

prepared my diving suit, helmet, and air regenerator for instant donning; and immediately commenced to write this hurried chronicle in the hope that it may some day reach the world. I shall seal the manuscript in a bottle and entrust it to the sea as I leave the U-29 forever.

I have no fear, not even from the prophecies of the madman Klenze. What I have seen cannot be true, and I know that this madness of my own will at most lead only to suffocation when my air is gone. The light in the temple is a sheer delusion, and I shall die calmly, like a German, in the black and forgotten depths. This daemoniac laughter which I hear as I write comes only from my own weakening brain. So I will carefully don my diving suit and walk boldly up the steps into that primal shrine; that silent secret of unfathomed waters and uncounted years.

'...in the black and forgotten depths.'

H. P. Lovecraft

CASTING THE RUNES

BY M. R. JAMES

CASTING THE RUNES
April 15th, 190-

Dear Sir,

I am requested by the Council of the --- Association to return to you the draft of a paper on The Truth of Alchemy, which you have been good enough to offer to read at our forthcoming meeting, and to inform you that the Council do not see their way to including it in the programme.

I am,

Yours faithfully,

- Secretary.

* * * * *

April 18th

Dear Sir,

I am sorry to say that my engagements do not permit of my affording you an interview on the subject of your proposed paper. Nor do our laws allow of your discussing the matter with a Committee of our Council, as you suggest. Please allow me to assure you that the fullest consideration was given to the draft which you submitted, and that it was not declined without having been referred to the judgement of a most competent authority. No personal question (it can hardly be necessary for me to add) can have had the slightest influence on the decision of the Council.

Believe me (ut supra).

* * * * *

April 20th

The Secretary of the --- Association begs respectfully to inform Mr. Karswell that it is impossible for him to communicate the name of any person or persons to whom the draft of Mr. Karswell's paper may have been submitted; and further desires to intimate that he cannot undertake to reply to any further letters on this subject.

* * * * *

'And who is Mr. Karswell?' inquired the Secretary's wife. She had called at his office, and (perhaps unwarrantably) had picked up the last of these three letters, which the typist had just brought in.

'Why, my dear, just at present Mr. Karswell is a very angry man. But I don't know much about him otherwise, except that he is a person of wealth, his address is Lufford Abbey, Warwickshire, and he's an alchemist, apparently, and wants to tell us all about it; and that's about all---except that I don't want to meet him for the next week or two. Now, if you're ready to leave this place, I am.'

'What have you been doing to make him angry?' asked Mrs. Secretary.

'The usual thing, my dear, the usual thing: he sent in a draft of a paper he wanted to read at the next meeting, and we referred it to Edward Dunning---almost the only man in England who knows about these things---and he said it was perfectly hopeless, so we declined it. So Karswell has been pelting me with letters ever since. The last thing he wanted was the name of the man we referred his nonsense to; you saw my answer to that. But don't you say anything about it, for goodness' sake.'

'I should think not, indeed. Did I ever do such a thing? I do hope, though, he won't get to know that it was poor Mr. Dunning.'

'Poor Mr. Dunning? I don't know why you call him that; he's a very happy man, is Dunning. Lots of hobbies and a comfortable home, and all his time to himself.'

'I only meant I should be sorry for him if this man got hold of his name, and came and bothered him.'

'Oh, ah! yes. I dare say he would be poor Mr. Dunning then.'

The Secretary and his wife were lunching out, and the friends to whose house they were bound were Warwickshire people. So Mrs. Secretary had already settled it in her own mind that she would question them judiciously about Mr. Karswell. But she was saved the trouble of leading up to the subject, for the hostess said to the host,

before many minutes had passed, 'I saw the Abbot of Lufford this morning.' The host whistled. 'Did you? What in the world brings him up to town?' 'Goodness knows; he was coming out of the British Museum gate as I drove past.' It was not unnatural that Mrs. Secretary should inquire whether this was a real Abbot who was being spoken of. 'Oh no, my dear: only a neighbour of ours in the country who bought Lufford Abbey a few years ago. His real name is Karswell.' 'Is he a friend of yours?' asked Mr. Secretary, with a private wink to his wife. The question let loose a torrent of declamation. There was really nothing to be said for Mr. Karswell. Nobody knew what he did with himself: his servants were a horrible set of people; he had invented a new religion for himself, and practised no one could tell what appalling rites; he was very easily offended, and never forgave anybody; he had a dreadful face (so the lady insisted, her husband somewhat demurring); he never did a kind action, and whatever influence he did exert was mischievous. 'Do the poor man justice, dear,' the husband interrupted. 'You forget the treat he gave the school children.' 'Forget it, indeed! But I'm glad you mentioned it, because it gives an idea of the man. Now, Florence, listen to this. The first winter he was at Lufford this delightful neighbour of ours wrote to the clergyman of his parish (he's not ours, but we know him very well) and offered to show the school children some magic-lantern slides. He said he had some new kinds, which he thought would interest them. Well, the clergyman was rather surprised, because Mr. Karswell had shown himself inclined to be unpleasant to the children---complaining of their trespassing, or something of the sort; but of course he accepted, and the evening was fixed, and our friend went himself to see that everything went right. He said he never had been so thankful for anything as that his own children were all prevented from being there: they were at a children's party at our house, as a matter of fact. Because this Mr. Karswell had evidently set out with the intention of frightening these poor village children out of their wits, and I do believe, if he had been allowed to go on, he would actually have done so. He began with some comparatively mild things. Red Riding Hood was one, and even then, Mr. Farrer said, the wolf was so dreadful that several of the smaller children had to be taken out: and he said Mr. Karswell began the story by producing a noise like a wolf howling in the distance, which was the most gruesome thing he had ever heard. All the slides he showed, Mr. Farrer said, were most clever; they were absolutely realistic, and where he had got them or how he worked them he could not imagine. Well, the show went on, and the stories kept on becoming a little more terrifying each time, and the children were mesmerized into complete silence. At last he produced a series which represented a little boy passing through his own park---Lufford, I mean---in the evening. Every child in the room could recognize the place from the pictures. And this poor boy was followed, and at last pursued and over-taken, and either torn in pieces or somehow made away with, by a horrible hopping creature in white, which you saw first dodging about among the trees, and gradually it appeared more and more plainly. Mr. Farrer said it gave him one of the worst nightmares he ever remembered, and what it must have meant to the children doesn't bear thinking of. Of course this was too much, and he spoke very sharply indeed to Mr. Karswell, and said it couldn't go on. All he said was: "Oh, you think it's time to bring our little show to an end and send them home to their beds? Very well!" And then, if you please, he switched on another slide, which showed a great mass of snakes, cen-tipedes, and disgusting creatures with wings, and some-how or other he made it seem as if they were climbing

out of the picture and getting in amongst the audience; and this was accompanied by a sort of dry rustling noise which sent the children nearly mad, and of course they stampeded. A good many of them were rather hurt in getting out of the room, and I don't suppose one of them closed an eye that night. There was the most dreadful trouble in the village afterwards. Of course the mothers threw a good part of the blame on poor Mr. Farrer, and, if they could have got past the gates, I believe the fathers would have broken every window in the Abbey. Well, now, that's Mr. Karswell: that's the Abbot of Lufford, my dear, and you can imagine how we covet his society.'

'Yes, I think he has all the possibilities of a distinguished criminal, has Karswell,' said the host. 'I should be sorry for anyone who got into his bad books.'

'Is he the man, or am I mixing him up with someone else?' asked the Secretary (who for some minutes had been wearing the frown of the man who is trying to recollect something). 'Is he the man who brought out a History of Witchcraft some time back---ten years or more?'

'That's the man; do you remember the reviews of it?'

'Certainly I do; and what's equally to the point, I knew the author of the most incisive of the lot. So did you: you must remember John Harrington; he was at John's in our time.'

'Oh, very well indeed, though I don't think I saw or heard anything of him between the time I went down and the day I read the account of the inquest on him.'

'Inquest?' said one of the ladies. 'What has happened

to him?'

'Why, what happened was that he fell out of a tree and broke his neck. But the puzzle was, what could have induced him to get up there. It was a mysterious business, I must say. Here was this man---not an athletic fellow, was he? and with no eccentric twist about him that was ever noticed---walking home along a country road late in the evening---no tramps about---well known and liked in the place---and he suddenly begins to run like mad, loses his hat and stick, and finally shins up a tree---quite a difficult tree---growing in the hedgerow: a dead branch gives way, and he comes down with it and breaks his neck, and there he's found next morning with the most dreadful face of fear on him that could be imagined. It was pretty evident, of course, that he had been chased by something, and people talked of savage dogs, and beasts escaped out of menageries; but there was nothing to be made of that. That was in '89, and I believe his brother Henry (whom I remember as well at Cambridge, but you probably don't) has been trying to get on the track of an explanation ever since. He, of course, insists there was malice in it, but I don't know. It's difficult to see how it could have come in.'

After a time the talk reverted to the History of Witchcraft. 'Did you ever look into it?' asked the host.

'Yes, I did,' said the Secretary. 'I went so far as to read it.'

'Was it as bad as it was made out to be?'

'Oh, in point of style and form, quite hopeless. It deserved all the pulverizing it got. But, besides that, it was an evil book. The man believed every word of what he

was saying, and I'm very much mistaken if he hadn't tried the greater part of his receipts.'

'Well, I only remember Harrington's review of it, and I must say if I'd been the author it would have quenched my literary ambition for good. I should never have held up my head again.'

'It hasn't had that effect in the present case. But come, it's half-past three; I must be off.'

On the way home the Secretary's wife said, 'I do hope that horrible man won't find out that Mr. Dunning had anything to do with the rejection of his paper.' 'I don't think there's much chance of that,' said the Secretary. 'Dunning won't mention it himself, for these matters are confidential, and none of us will for the same reason. Karswell won't know his name, for Dunning hasn't published anything on the same subject yet. The only danger is that Karswell might find out, if he was to ask the British Museum people who was in the habit of consulting alchemical manuscripts: I can't very well tell them not to mention Dunning, can I? It would set them talking at once. Let's hope it won't occur to him.'

However, Mr. Karswell was an astute man.

* * * * *

This much is in the way of prologue. On an evening rather later in the same week, Mr. Edward Dunning was returning from the British Museum, where he had been engaged in Research, to the comfortable house in a suburb where he lived alone, tended by two excellent women who had been long with him. There is nothing to be add-

ed by way of description of him to what we have heard already. Let us follow him as he takes his sober course homewards.

* * * * *

A train took him to within a mile or two of his house, and an electric tram a stage farther. The line ended at a point some three hundred yards from his front door. He had had enough of reading when he got into the car, and indeed the light was not such as to allow him to do more than study the advertisements on the panes of glass that faced him as he sat. As was not unnatural, the advertisements in this particular line of cars were objects of his frequent contemplation, and, with the possible exception of the brilliant and convincing dialogue between Mr. Lamplough and an eminent K.C. on the subject of Pyretic Saline, none of them afforded much scope to his imagination. I am wrong: there was one at the corner of the car farthest from him which did not seem familiar. It was in blue letters on a yellow ground, and all that he could read of it was a name---John Harrington---and something like a date. It could be of no interest to him to know more; but for all that, as the car emptied, he was just curious enough to move along the seat until he could read it well. He felt to a slight extent repaid for his trouble; the advertisement was not of the usual type. It ran thus: 'In memory of John Harrington, F.S.A., of The Laurels, Ashbrooke. Died Sept. 18th, 1889. Three months were allowed.'

The car stopped. Mr. Dunning, still contemplating the blue letters on the yellow ground, had to be stimulated to rise by a word from the conductor. 'I beg your pardon,' he said, 'I was looking at that advertisement; it's a very

odd one, isn't it?' The conductor read it slowly. 'Well, my word,' he said, 'I never see that one before. Well, that is a cure, ain't it? Someone bin up to their jokes 'ere, I should think.' He got out a duster and applied it, not without saliva, to the pane and then to the outside. 'No,' he said, returning, 'that ain't no transfer; seems to me as if it was reg'lar in the glass, what I mean in the substance, as you may say. Don't you think so, sir?' Mr. Dunning examined it and rubbed it with his glove, and agreed. 'Who looks after these advertisements, and gives leave for them to be put up? I wish you would inquire. I will just take a note of the words.' At this moment there came a call from the driver: 'Look alive, George, time's up.' 'All right, all right; there's somethink else what's up at this end. You come and look at this 'ere glass.' 'What's gorn with the glass?' said the driver, approaching. 'Well, and oo's 'Arrington? What's it all about?' 'I was just asking who was responsible for putting the advertisements up in your cars, and saying it would be as well to make some inquiry about this one.' 'Well, sir, that's all done at the Company's orfice, that work is: it's our Mr. Timms, I believe, looks into that. When we put up tonight I'll leave word, and per'aps I'll be able to tell you tomorrer if you 'appen to be coming this way.'

This was all that passed that evening. Mr. Dunning did just go to the trouble of looking up Ashbrooke, and found that it was in Warwickshire.

Next day he went to town again. The car (it was the same car) was too full in the morning to allow of his getting a word with the conductor: he could only be sure that the curious advertisement had been made away with. The close of the day brought a further element of mystery into the transaction. He had missed the tram, or else preferred walking home, but at a rather late hour, while he was at work in his study, one of the maids came to say that two men from the tramways was very anxious to speak to him. This was a reminder of the advertisement, which he had, he says, nearly forgotten. He had the men in---they were the conductor and driver of the car---and when the matter of refreshment had been attended to, asked what Mr. Timms had had to say about the advertisement. 'Well, sir, that's what we took the liberty to step round about,' said the conductor. 'Mr. Timms 'e give William 'ere the rough side of his tongue about that: 'cordin' to 'im there warn't no advertisement of that description sent in, nor ordered, nor paid for, nor put up, nor nothink, let alone not bein' there, and we was playing the fool takin' up his time. "Well," I says, "if that's the case, all I ask of you, Mr. Timms," I says, "is to take and look at it for yourself," I says. "Of course if it ain't there," I says, "you may take and call me what you like." "Right," he says, "I will": and we went straight off. Now, I leave it to you, sir, if that ad., as we term 'em, with 'Arrington on it warn't as plain as ever you see anythink---blue letters on yeller glass, and as I says at the time, and you borne me out, reg'lar in the glass, because, if you remember, you recollect of me swabbing it with my duster.' 'To be sure I do, quite clearly---well?' 'You may say well, I don't think. Mr. Timms he gets in that car with a lightno, he told William to 'old the light outside. "Now," he says, "where's your precious ad. what we've 'eard so much about?" "'Ere it is," I says, "Mr. Timms," and I laid my 'and on it.' The conductor paused.

'Well,' said Mr. Dunning, 'it was gone, I suppose. Broken?'

'Broke!---not it. There warn't, if you'll believe me, no

more trace of them letters---blue letters they was---on that piece o' glass, than---well, it's no good me talkin'. I never see such a thing. I leave it to William here if---but there, as I says, where's the benefit in me going on about it?'

'And what did Mr. Timms say?'

'Why 'e did what I give 'im leave to---called us pretty much anythink he liked, and I don't know as I blame him so much neither. But what we thought, William and me did, was as we seen you take down a bit of a note about that---well, that letterin---"

'I certainly did that, and I have it now. Did you wish me to speak to Mr.
Timms myself, and show it to him? Was that what you came in about?'
'There, didn't I say as much?' said William. 'Deal with a gent if you can get on the track of one, that's my word. Now perhaps, George, you'll allow as I ain't took you very far wrong tonight.'

'Very well, William, very well; no need for you to go on as if you'd 'ad to frog's-march me 'ere. I come quiet, didn't I? All the same for that, we 'adn't ought to take up your time this way, sir; but if it so 'appened you could find time to step round to the Company's orfice in the morning and tell Mr. Timms what you seen for yourself, we should lay under a very 'igh obligation to you for the trouble. You see it ain't bein' called---well, one thing and another, as we mind, but if they got it into their 'ead at the orfice as we seen things as warn't there, why, one thing leads to another, and where we should be a twelvemunce 'ence---well, you can understand what I mean.'

Amid further elucidations of the proposition, George, conducted by

William, left the room.

The incredulity of Mr. Timms (who had a nodding acquaintance with Mr. Dunning) was greatly modified on the following day by what the latter could tell and show him; and any bad mark that might have been attached to the names of William and George was not suffered to remain on the Company's books; but explanation there was none.

Mr. Dunning's interest in the matter was kept alive by an incident of the following afternoon. He was walking from his club to the train, and he noticed some way ahead a man with a handful of leaflets such as are distributed to passers-by by agents of enterprising firms. This agent had not chosen a very crowded street for his operations: in fact, Mr. Dunning did not see him get rid of a single leaflet before he himself reached the spot. One was thrust into his hand as he passed: the hand that gave it touched his, and he experienced a sort of little shock as it did so. It seemed unnaturally rough and hot. He looked in passing at the giver, but the impression he got was so unclear that, however much he tried to reckon it up subsequently, nothing would come. He was walking quickly, and as he went on glanced at the paper. It was a blue one. The name of Harrington in large capitals caught his eye. He stopped, startled, and felt for his glasses. The next instant the leaflet was twitched out of his hand by a man who hurried past, and was irrecoverably gone. He ran back a few paces, but where was the passer-by? and where the distributor?

It was in a somewhat pensive frame of mind that Mr.

Dunning passed on the following day into the Select Manuscript Room of the British Museum, and filled up tickets for Harley 3586, and some other volumes. After a few minutes they were brought to him, and he was settling the one he wanted first upon the desk, when he thought he heard his own name whispered behind him. He turned round hastily, and in doing so, brushed his little portfolio of loose papers on to the floor. He saw no one he recognized except one of the staff in charge of the room, who nodded to him, and he proceeded to pick up his papers. He thought he had them all, and was turning to begin work, when a stout gentleman at the table behind him, who was just rising to leave, and had collected his own belongings, touched him on the shoulder, saying, 'May I give you this? I think it should be yours,' and handed him a missing quire. 'It is mine, thank you,' said Mr. Dunning. In another moment the man had left the room. Upon finishing his work for the afternoon, Mr. Dunning had some conversation with the assistant in charge, and took occasion to ask who the stout gentleman was. 'Oh, he's a man named Karswell,' said the assistant; 'he was asking me a week ago who were the great authorities on alchemy, and of course I told him you were the only one in the country. I'll see if I can't catch him: he'd like to meet you, I'm sure.'

'For heaven's sake don't dream of it!' said Mr. Dunning, 'I'm particularly anxious to avoid him.'

'Oh! very well,' said the assistant, 'he doesn't come here often: I dare say you won't meet him.'

More than once on the way home that day Mr. Dunning confessed to himself that he did not look forward with his usual cheerfulness to a solitary evening. It seemed to him

that something ill-defined and impalpable had stepped in between him and his fellow-men---had taken him in charge, as it were. He wanted to sit close up to his neighbours in the train and in the tram, but as luck would have it both train and car were markedly empty. The conductor George was thoughtful, and appeared to be absorbed in calculations as to the number of passengers. On arriving at his house he found Dr. Watson, his medical man, on his doorstep. 'I've had to upset your household arrangements, I'm sorry to say, Dunning. Both your servants hors de combat. In fact, I've had to send them to the Nursing Home.'

'Good heavens! what's the matter?'

'It's something like ptomaine poisoning, I should think: you've not suffered yourself, I can see, or you wouldn't be walking about. I think they'll pull through all right.'

'Dear, dear! Have you any idea what brought it on?'

'Well, they tell me they bought some shell-fish from a hawker at their dinner-time. It's odd. I've made inquiries, but I can't find that any hawker has been to other houses in the street. I couldn't send word to you; they won't be back for a bit yet. You come and dine with me tonight, anyhow, and we can make arrangements for going on. Eight o'clock. Don't be too anxious.'

The solitary evening was thus obviated; at the expense of some distress and inconvenience, it is true. Mr. Dunning spent the time pleasantly enough with the doctor (a rather recent settler), and returned to his lonely home at about 11.30. The night he passed is not one on which he looks back with any satisfaction. He was in bed and the

light was out. He was wondering if the charwoman would come early enough to get him hot water next morning, when he heard the unmistakable sound of his study door opening. No step followed it on the passage floor, but the sound must mean mischief, for he knew that he had shut the door that evening after putting his papers away in his desk. It was rather shame than courage that induced him to slip out into the passage and lean over the banister in his nightgown, listening. No light was visible; no further sound came: only a gust of warm, or even hot air played for an instant round his shins. He went back and decided to lock himself into his room. There was more unpleasantness, however. Either an economical suburban company had decided that their light would not be required in the small hours, and had stopped working, or else something was wrong with the meter; the effect was in any case that the electric light was off. The obvious course was to find a match, and also to consult his watch: he might as well know how many hours of discomfort awaited him. So he put his hand into the well-known nook under the pillow: only, it did not get so far. What he touched was, according to his account, a mouth, with teeth, and with hair about it, and, he declares, not the mouth of a human being. I do not think it is any use to guess what he said or did; but he was in a spare room with the door locked and his ear to it before he was clearly conscious again. And there he spent the rest of a most miserable night, looking every moment for some fumbling at the door: but nothing came.

The venturing back to his own room in the morning was attended with many listenings and quiverings. The door stood open, fortunately, and the blinds were up (the servants had been out of the house before the hour of drawing them down); there was, to be short, no trace of an inhabitant. The watch, too, was in its usual place; nothing was disturbed, only the wardrobe door had swung open, in accordance with its confirmed habit. A ring at the back door now announced the charwoman, who had been ordered the night before, and nerved Mr. Dunning, after letting her in, to continue his search in other parts of the house. It was equally fruitless.

The day thus begun went on dismally enough. He dared not go to the Museum: in spite of what the assistant had said, Karswell might turn up there, and Dunning felt he could not cope with a probably hostile stranger. His own house was odious; he hated sponging on the doctor. He spent some little time in a call at the Nursing Home, where he was slightly cheered by a good report of his housekeeper and maid. Towards lunch-time he betook himself to his club, again experiencing a gleam of satisfaction at seeing the Secretary of the Association. At luncheon Dunning told his friend the more material of his woes, but could not bring himself to speak of those that weighed most heavily on his spirits. 'My poor dear man,' said the Secretary, 'what an upset! Look here: we're alone at home, absolutely. You must put up with us. Yes! no excuse: send your things in this afternoon.' Dunning was unable to stand out: he was, in truth, becoming acutely anxious, as the hours went on, as to what that night might have waiting for him. He was almost happy as he hurried home to pack up.

His friends, when they had time to take stock of him, were rather shocked at his lorn appearance, and did their best to keep him up to the mark. Not altogether without success: but, when the two men were smoking alone later, Dunning became dull again. Suddenly he said, 'Gayton, I believe that alchemist man knows it was I who got his paper rejected.' Gayton whistled. 'What makes you think

that?' he said. Dunning told of his conversation with the Museum assistant, and Gayton could only agree that the guess seemed likely to be correct. 'Not that I care much,' Dunning went on, 'only it might be a nuisance if we were to meet. He's a bad-tempered party, I imagine.' Conversation dropped again; Gayton became more and more strongly impressed with the desolateness that came over Dunning's face and bearing, and finally---though with a considerable effort---he asked him point-blank whether something serious was not bothering him. Dunning gave an exclamation of relief. 'I was perishing to get it off my mind,' he said. 'Do you know anything about a man named John Harrington?' Gayton was thoroughly startled, and at the moment could only ask why. Then the complete story of Dunning's experiences came out--- what had happened in the tramcar, in his own house, and in the street, the troubling of spirit that had crept over him, and still held him; and he ended with the question he had begun with. Gayton was at a loss how to answer him. To tell the story of Harrington's end would perhaps be right; only, Dunning was in a nervous state, the story was a grim one, and he could not help asking himself whether there were not a connecting link between these two cases, in the person of Karswell. It was a difficult concession for a scientific man, but it could be eased by the phrase 'hypnotic suggestion'. In the end he decided that his answer tonight should be guarded; he would talk the situation over with his wife. So he said that he had known Harrington at Cambridge, and believed he had died suddenly in 1889, adding a few details about the man and his published work. He did talk over the matter with Mrs. Gayton, and, as he had anticipated, she leapt at once to the conclusion which had been hovering before him. It was she who reminded him of the surviving brother, Henry Harrington, and she also who suggested that he might be got hold of by means of their hosts of the day before. 'He might be a hopeless crank,' objected Gayton. 'That could be ascertained from the Bennetts, who knew him,' Mrs. Gayton retorted; and she undertook to see the Bennetts the very next day.

* * * * *

It is not necessary to tell in further detail the steps by which Henry Harrington and Dunning were brought together.

* * * * *

The next scene that does require to be narrated is a conversation that took place between the two. Dunning had told Harrington of the strange ways in which the dead man's name had been brought before him, and had said something, besides, of his own subsequent experiences. Then he had asked if Harrington was disposed, in return, to recall any of the circumstances connected with his brother's death. Harrington's surprise at what he heard can be imagined: but his reply was readily given.

'John,' he said, 'was in a very odd state, undeniably, from time to time, during some weeks before, though not immediately before, the catastrophe. There were several things; the principal notion he had was that he thought he was being followed. No doubt he was an impressionable man, but he never had had such fancies as this before. I cannot get it out of my mind that there was ill-will at work, and what you tell me about yourself reminds me very much of my brother. Can you think of any possible connecting link?'

'There is just one that has been taking shape vaguely

in my mind. I've been told that your brother reviewed a book very severely not long before he died, and just lately I have happened to cross the path of the man who wrote that book in a way he would resent.'

'Don't tell me the man was called Karswell.'

'Why not? that is exactly his name.'

Henry Harrington leant back. 'That is final to my mind. Now I must explain further. From something he said, I feel sure that my brother John was beginning to believe---very much against his will---that Karswell was at the bottom of his trouble. I want to tell you what seems to me to have a bearing on the situation. My brother was a great musician, and used to run up to concerts in town. He came back, three months before he died, from one of these, and gave me his programme to look at---an analytical programme: he always kept them. "I nearly missed this one," he said. "I suppose I must have dropped it: anyhow, I was looking for it under my seat and in my pockets and so on, and my neighbour offered me his; said 'might he give it me, he had no further use for it,' and he went away just afterwards. I don't know who he was---a stout, clean-shaven man. I should have been sorry to miss it; of course I could have bought another, but this cost me nothing." At another time he told me that he had been very uncomfortable both on the way to his hotel and during the night. I piece things together now in thinking it over. Then, not very long after, he was going over these programmes, putting them in order to have them bound up, and in this particular one (which by the way I had hardly glanced at), he found quite near the beginning a strip of paper with some very odd writing on it in red and black---most carefully done---it looked to me more like Runic letters than anything else. "Why," he said, "this must belong to my fat neighbour. It looks as if it might be worth returning to him; it may be a copy of something; evidently someone has taken trouble over it. How can I find his address?" We talked it over for a little and agreed that it wasn't worth advertising about, and that my brother had better look out for the man at the next concert, to which he was going very soon. The paper was lying on the book and we were both by the fire; it was a cold, windy summer evening. I suppose the door blew open, though I didn't notice it: at any rate a gust---a warm gust it was--- came quite suddenly between us, took the paper and blew it straight into the fire: it was light, thin paper, and flared and went up the chimney in a single ash. "Well," I said, "you can't give it back now." He said nothing for a min- ute: then rather crossly, "No, I can't; but why you should keep on saying so I don't know." I remarked that I didn't say it more than once. "Not more than four times, you mean," was all he said. I remember all that very clearly, without any good reason; and now to come to the point. I don't know if you looked at that book of Karswell's which my unfortunate brother reviewed. It's not likely that you should: but I did, both before his death and after it. The first time we made game of it together. It was written in no style at all---split infinitives, and every sort of thing that makes an Oxford gorge rise. Then there was nothing that the man didn't swallow: mixing up classical myths, and stories out of the Golden Legend with reports of sav- age customs of today---all very proper, no doubt, if you know how to use them, but he didn't: he seemed to put the Golden Legend and the Golden Bough exactly on a par, and to believe both: a pitiable exhibition, in short. Well, after the misfortune, I looked over the book again. It was no better than before, but the impression which it left this time on my mind was different. I suspected---as I

told you---that Karswell had borne ill-will to my brother, even that he was in some way responsible for what had happened; and now his book seemed to me to be a very sinister performance indeed. One chapter in particular struck me, in which he spoke of "casting the Runes" on people, either for the purpose of gaining their affection or of getting them out of the way---perhaps more especially the latter: he spoke of all this in a way that really seemed to me to imply actual knowledge. I've not time to go into details, but the upshot is that I am pretty sure from information received that the civil man at the concert was Karswell: I suspect---I more than suspect---that the paper was of importance: and I do believe that if my brother had been able to give it back, he might have been alive now. Therefore, it occurs to me to ask you whether you have anything to put beside what I have told you.'

By way of answer, Dunning had the episode in the Manuscript Room at the British Museum to relate. 'Then he did actually hand you some papers; have you examined them? No? because we must, if you'll allow it, look at them at once, and very carefully.'

They went to the still empty house---empty, for the two servants were not yet able to return to work. Dunning's portfolio of papers was gathering dust on the writing-table. In it were the quires of small-sized scribbling paper which he used for his transcripts: and from one of these, as he took it up, there slipped and fluttered out into the room with uncanny quickness, a strip of thin light paper. The window was open, but Harrington slammed it to, just in time to intercept the paper, which he caught. 'I thought so,' he said; 'it might be the identical thing that was given to my brother. You'll have to look out, Dunning; this may mean something quite serious for you.'

A long consultation took place. The paper was narrowly examined. As Harrington had said, the characters on it were more like Runes than anything else, but not decipherable by either man, and both hesitated to copy them, for fear, as they confessed, of perpetuating whatever evil purpose they might conceal. So it has remained impossible (if I may anticipate a little) to ascertain what was conveyed in this curious message or commission. Both Dunning and Harrington are firmly convinced that it had the effect of bringing its possessors into very undesirable company. That it must be returned to the source whence it came they were agreed, and further, that the only safe and certain way was that of personal service; and here contrivance would be necessary, for Dunning was known by sight to Karswell. He must, for one thing, alter his appearance by shaving his beard. But then might not the blow fall first? Harrington thought they could time it. He knew the date of the concert at which the 'black spot' had been put on his brother: it was June 18th. The death had followed on Sept. 18th. Dunning reminded him that three months had been mentioned on the inscription on the car-window. 'Perhaps,' he added, with a cheerless laugh, 'mine may be a bill at three months too. I believe I can fix it by my diary. Yes, April 23rd was the day at the Museum; that brings us to July 23rd. Now, you know, it becomes extremely important to me to know anything you will tell me about the progress of your brother's trouble, if it is possible for you to speak of it.' 'Of course. Well, the sense of being watched whenever he was alone was the most distressing thing to him. After a time I took to sleeping in his room, and he was the better for that: still, he talked a great deal in his sleep. What about? Is it wise to dwell on that, at least before things are straightened out? I think not, but I can tell you this: two things came

for him by post during those weeks, both with a London postmark, and addressed in a commercial hand. One was a woodcut of Bewick's, roughly torn out of the page: one which shows a moonlit road and a man walking along it, followed by an awful demon creature. Under it were written the lines out of the "Ancient Mariner" (which I suppose the cut illustrates) about one who, having once looked round---

> 'walks on,
> And turns no more his head,
> Because he knows a frightful fiend
> Doth close behind him tread.'

The other was a calendar, such as tradesmen often send. My brother paid no attention to this, but I looked at it after his death, and found that everything after Sept. 18 had been torn out. You may be surprised at his having gone out alone the evening he was killed, but the fact is that during the last ten days or so of his life he had been quite free from the sense of being followed or watched.'

The end of the consultation was this. Harrington, who knew a neighbour of Karswell's, thought he saw a way of keeping a watch on his movements. It would be Dunning's part to be in readiness to try to cross Karswell's path at any moment, to keep the paper safe and in a place of ready access.

They parted. The next weeks were no doubt a severe strain upon Dunning's nerves: the intangible barrier which had seemed to rise about him on the day when he received the paper, gradually developed into a brooding blackness that cut him off from the means of escape to which one might have thought he might resort. No one was at hand who was likely to suggest them to him, and he seemed robbed of all initiative. He waited with inexpressible anxiety as May, June, and early July passed on, for a mandate from Harrington. But all this time Karswell remained immovable at Lufford.

At last, in less than a week before the date he had come to look upon as the end of his earthly activities, came a telegram: 'Leaves Victoria by boat train Thursday night. Do not miss. I come to you to-night. Harrington.'

He arrived accordingly, and they concocted plans. The train left Victoria at nine and its last stop before Dover was Croydon West. Harrington would mark down Karswell at Victoria, and look out for Dunning at Croydon, calling to him if need were by a name agreed upon. Dunning, disguised as far as might be, was to have no label or initials on any hand luggage, and must at all costs have the paper with him.

Dunning's suspense as he waited on the Croydon platform I need not attempt to describe. His sense of danger during the last days had only been sharpened by the fact that the cloud about him had perceptibly been lighter; but relief was an ominous symptom, and, if Karswell eluded him now, hope was gone: and there were so many chances of that. The rumour of the journey might be itself a device. The twenty minutes in which he paced the platform and persecuted every porter with inquiries as to the boat train were as bitter as any he had spent. Still, the train came, and Harrington was at the window. It was important, of course, that there should be no recognition: so Dunning got in at the farther end of the corridor carriage, and only gradually made his way to the compartment where Harrington and Karswell were. He was

pleased, on the whole, to see that the train was far from full.

Karswell was on the alert, but gave no sign of recognition. Dunning took the seat not immediately facing him, and attempted, vainly at first, then with increasing command of his faculties, to reckon the possibilities of making the desired transfer. Opposite to Karswell, and next to Dunning, was a heap of Karswell's coats on the seat. It would be of no use to slip the paper into these---he would not be safe, or would not feel so, unless in some way it could be proffered by him and accepted by the other. There was a handbag, open, and with papers in it. Could he manage to conceal this (so that perhaps Karswell might leave the carriage without it), and then find and give it to him? This was the plan that suggested itself. If he could only have counselled with Harrington! but that could not be. The minutes went on. More than once Karswell rose and went out into the corridor. The second time Dunning was on the point of attempting to make the bag fall off the seat, but he caught Harrington's eye, and read in it a warning. Karswell, from the corridor, was watching: probably to see if the two men recognized each other. He returned, but was evidently restless: and, when he rose the third time, hope dawned, for something did slip off his seat and fall with hardly a sound to the floor. Karswell went out once more, and passed out of range of the corridor window. Dunning picked up what had fallen, and saw that the key was in his hands in the form of one of Cook's ticket-cases, with tickets in it. These cases have a pocket in the cover, and within very few seconds the paper of which we have heard was in the pocket of this one. To make the operation more secure, Harrington stood in the doorway of the compartment and fiddled with the blind. It was done, and done at the right time, for the train was now slowing down towards Dover.

In a moment more Karswell re-entered the compartment. As he did so, Dunning, managing, he knew not how, to suppress the tremble in his voice, handed him the ticket-case, saying, 'May I give you this, sir? I believe it is yours.' After a brief glance at the ticket inside, Karswell uttered the hoped-for response, 'Yes, it is; much obliged to you, sir,' and he placed it in his breast pocket.

Even in the few moments that remained---moments of tense anxiety, for they knew not to what a premature finding of the paper might lead---both men noticed that the carriage seemed to darken about them and to grow warmer; that Karswell was fidgety and oppressed; that he drew the heap of loose coats near to him and cast it back as if it repelled him; and that he then sat upright and glanced anxiously at both. They, with sickening anxiety, busied themselves in collecting their belongings; but they both thought that Karswell was on the point of speaking when the train stopped at Dover Town. It was natural that in the short space between town and pier they should both go into the corridor.

At the pier they got out, but so empty was the train that they were forced to linger on the platform until Karswell should have passed ahead of them with his porter on the way to the boat, and only then was it safe for them to exchange a pressure of the hand and a word of concentrated congratulation. The effect upon Dunning was to make him almost faint. Harrington made him lean up against the wall, while he himself went forward a few yards within sight of the gangway to the boat, at which Karswell had now arrived. The man at the head of it examined his ticket, and, laden with coats, he passed down into the boat.

Suddenly the official called after him, 'You, sir, beg pardon, did the other gentleman show his ticket?' 'What the devil do you mean by the other gentleman?' Karswell's snarling voice called back from the deck. The man bent over and looked at him. 'The devil? Well, I don't know, I'm sure,' Harrington heard him say to himself, and then aloud, 'My mistake, sir; must have been your rugs! ask your pardon.' And then, to a subordinate near him, "Ad he got a dog with him, or what? Funny thing: I could 'a' swore 'e wasn't alone. Well, whatever it was, they'll 'ave to see to it aboard. She's off now. Another week and we shall be gettin' the 'oliday customers.' In five minutes more there was nothing but the lessening lights of the boat, the long line of the Dover lamps, the night breeze, and the moon.

Long and long the two sat in their room at the 'Lord Warden'. In spite of the removal of their greatest anxiety, they were oppressed with a doubt, not of the lightest. Had they been justified in sending a man to his death, as they believed they had? Ought they not to warn him, at least? 'No,' said Harrington; 'if he is the murderer I think him, we have done no more than is just. Still, if you think it better---but how and where can you warn him?' 'He was booked to Abbeville only,' said Dunning. 'I saw that. If I wired to the hotels there in Joanne's Guide, "Examine your ticket-case, Dunning," I should feel happier. This is the 21st: he will have a day. But I am afraid he has gone into the dark.' So telegrams were left at the hotel office.

It is not clear whether these reached their destination, or whether, if they did, they were understood. All that is known is that, on the afternoon of the 23rd, an English traveller, examining the front of St Wulfram's Church at Abbeville, then under extensive repair, was struck on the head and instantly killed by a stone falling from the scaffold erected round the north-western tower, there being, as was clearly proved, no workman on the scaffold at that moment: and the traveller's papers identified him as Mr. Karswell.

Only one detail shall be added. At Karswell's sale a set of Bewick, sold with all faults, was acquired by Harrington. The page with the woodcut of the traveller and the demon was, as he had expected, mutilated. Also, after a judicious interval, Harrington repeated to Dunning something of what he had heard his brother say in his sleep: but it was not long before Dunning stopped him.

'Funny thing: I could 'a' swore 'e wasn't alone.'

CASTING THE RUNES

The Shadow over Innsmouth

by H. P. Lovecraft

I.

During the winter of 1927–28 officials of the Federal government made a strange and secret investigation of certain conditions in the ancient Massachusetts seaport of Innsmouth. The public first learned of it in February, when a vast series of raids and arrests occurred, followed by the deliberate burning and dynamiting—under suitable precautions—of an enormous number of crumbling, worm-eaten, and supposedly empty houses along the abandoned waterfront. Uninquiring souls let this occurrence pass as one of the major clashes in a spasmodic war on liquor.

Keener news-followers, however, wondered at the prodigious number of arrests, the abnormally large force of men used in making them, and the secrecy surrounding the disposal of the prisoners. No trials, or even definite charges, were reported; nor were any of the captives seen thereafter in the regular gaols of the nation. There were vague statements about disease and concentration camps, and later about dispersal in various naval and military prisons, but nothing positive ever developed. Innsmouth itself was left almost depopulated, and is even now only beginning to shew signs of a sluggishly revived existence.

Complaints from many liberal organisations were met with long confidential discussions, and representatives were taken on trips to certain camps and prisons. As a result, these societies became surprisingly passive and reticent. Newspaper men were harder to manage, but seemed largely to coöperate with the government in the end. Only one paper—a tabloid always discounted because of its wild policy—mentioned the deep-diving submarine that discharged torpedoes downward in the marine abyss just beyond Devil Reef. That item, gathered by chance in a haunt of sailors, seemed indeed rather far-fetched; since the low, black reef lies a full mile and a half out from Innsmouth Harbour.

People around the country and in the nearby towns muttered a great deal among themselves, but said very little to the outer world. They had talked about dying and half-deserted Innsmouth for nearly a century, and nothing new could be wilder or more hideous than what they had whispered and hinted years before. Many things had taught them secretiveness, and there was now no need to exert pressure on them. Besides, they really knew very little; for wide salt marshes, desolate and unpeopled, keep neighbours off from Innsmouth on the landward side.

But at last I am going to defy the ban on speech about this thing. Results, I am certain, are so thorough that no public harm save a shock of repulsion could ever accrue from a hinting of what was found by those horrified raiders at Innsmouth. Besides, what was found might possibly have more than one explanation. I do not know just how much of the whole tale has been told even to me, and I have many reasons for not wishing to probe deeper.

For my contact with this affair has been closer than that of any other layman, and I have carried away impressions which are yet to drive me to drastic measures.

It was I who fled frantically out of Innsmouth in the early morning hours of July 16, 1927, and whose frightened appeals for government inquiry and action brought on the whole reported episode. I was willing enough to stay mute while the affair was fresh and uncertain; but now that it is an old story, with public interest and curiosity gone, I have an odd craving to whisper about those few frightful hours in that ill-rumoured and evilly shadowed seaport of death and blasphemous abnormality. The mere telling helps me to restore confidence in my own faculties; to reassure myself that I was not simply the first to succumb to a contagious nightmare hallucination. It helps me, too, in making up my mind regarding a certain terrible step which lies ahead of me.

I never heard of Innsmouth till the day before I saw it for the first and—so far—last time. I was celebrating my coming of age by a tour of New England—sightseeing, antiquarian, and genealogical—and had planned to go directly from ancient Newburyport to Arkham, whence my mother's family was derived. I had no car, but was travelling by train, trolley, and motor-coach, always seeking the cheapest possible route. In Newburyport they told me that the steam train was the thing to take to Arkham; and it was only at the station ticket-office, when I demurred at the high fare, that I learned about Innsmouth. The stout, shrewd-faced agent, whose speech shewed him to be no local man, seemed sympathetic toward my efforts at economy, and made a suggestion that none of my other informants had offered.

"You could take that old bus, I suppose," he said with a certain hesitation, "but it ain't thought much of hereabouts. It goes through Innsmouth—you may have heard about that—and so the people don't like it. Run by an Innsmouth fellow—Joe Sargent—but never gets any custom from here, or Arkham either, I guess. Wonder it keeps running at all. I s'pose it's cheap enough, but I never see more'n two or three people in it—nobody but those Innsmouth folks. Leaves the Square—front of Hammond's Drug Store—at 10 a.m. and 7 p.m. unless they've changed lately. Looks like a terrible rattletrap—I've never ben on it."

That was the first I ever heard of shadowed Innsmouth. Any reference to a town not shewn on common maps or listed in recent guide-books would have interested me, and the agent's odd manner of allusion roused something like real curiosity. A town able to inspire such dislike in its neighbours, I thought, must be at least rather unusual, and worthy of a tourist's attention. If it came before Arkham I would stop off there—and so I asked the agent to tell me something about it. He was very deliberate, and spoke with an air of feeling slightly superior to what he said.

"Innsmouth? Well, it's a queer kind of a town down at the mouth of the Manuxet. Used to be almost a city—quite a port before the War of 1812—but all gone to pieces in the last hundred years or so. No railroad now—B. & M. never went through, and the branch line from Rowley was given up years ago.

"More empty houses than there are people, I guess, and no business to speak of except fishing and lobstering. Everybody trades mostly here or in Arkham or Ipswich.

Once they had quite a few mills, but nothing's left now except one gold refinery running on the leanest kind of part time.

"That refinery, though, used to be a big thing, and Old Man Marsh, who owns it, must be richer'n Croesus. Queer old duck, though, and sticks mighty close in his home. He's supposed to have developed some skin disease or deformity late in life that makes him keep out of sight. Grandson of Captain Obed Marsh, who founded the business. His mother seems to've ben some kind of foreigner—they say a South Sea islander—so everybody raised Cain when he married an Ipswich girl fifty years ago. They always do that about Innsmouth people, and folks here and hereabouts always try to cover up any Innsmouth blood they have in 'em. But Marsh's children and grandchildren look just like anyone else so far's I can see. I've had 'em pointed out to me here—though, come to think of it, the elder children don't seem to be around lately. Never saw the old man.

"And why is everybody so down on Innsmouth? Well, young fellow, you mustn't take too much stock in what people around here say. They're hard to get started, but once they do get started they never let up. They've ben telling things about Innsmouth—whispering 'em, mostly—for the last hundred years, I guess, and I gather they're more scared than anything else. Some of the stories would make you laugh—about old Captain Marsh driving bargains with the devil and bringing imps out of hell to live in Innsmouth, or about some kind of devil-worship and awful sacrifices in some place near the wharves that people stumbled on around 1845 or thereabouts—but I come from Panton, Vermont, and that kind of story don't go down with me.

"You ought to hear, though, what some of the old-timers tell about the black reef off the coast—Devil Reef, they call it. It's well above water a good part of the time, and never much below it, but at that you could hardly call it an island. The story is that there's a whole legion of devils seen sometimes on that reef—sprawled about, or darting in and out of some kind of caves near the top. It's a rugged, uneven thing, a good bit over a mile out, and toward the end of shipping days sailors used to make big detours just to avoid it.

"That is, sailors that didn't hail from Innsmouth. One of the things they had against old Captain Marsh was that he was supposed to land on it sometimes at night when the tide was right. Maybe he did, for I dare say the rock formation was interesting, and it's just barely possible he was looking for pirate loot and maybe finding it; but there was talk of his dealing with daemons there. Fact is, I guess on the whole it was really the Captain that gave the bad reputation to the reef.

"That was before the big epidemic of 1846, when over half the folks in Innsmouth was carried off. They never did quite figure out what the trouble was, but it was probably some foreign kind of disease brought from China or somewhere by the shipping. It surely was bad enough—there was riots over it, and all sorts of ghastly doings that I don't believe ever got outside of town—and it left the place in awful shape. Never came back—there can't be more'n 300 or 400 people living there now.

"But the real thing behind the way folks feel is simply race prejudice—and I don't say I'm blaming those that hold it. I hate those Innsmouth folks myself, and I

wouldn't care to go to their town. I s'pose you know—though I can see you're a Westerner by your talk—what a lot our New England ships used to have to do with queer ports in Africa, Asia, the South Seas, and everywhere else, and what queer kinds of people they sometimes brought back with 'em. You've probably heard about the Salem man that came home with a Chinese wife, and maybe you know there's still a bunch of Fiji Islanders somewhere around Cape Cod.

"Well, there must be something like that back of the Innsmouth people. The place always was badly cut off from the rest of the country by marshes and creeks, and we can't be sure about the ins and outs of the matter; but it's pretty clear that old Captain Marsh must have brought home some odd specimens when he had all three of his ships in commission back in the twenties and thirties. There certainly is a strange kind of streak in the Innsmouth folks today—I don't know how to explain it, but it sort of makes you crawl. You'll notice a little in Sargent if you take his bus. Some of 'em have queer narrow heads with flat noses and bulgy, stary eyes that never seem to shut, and their skin ain't quite right. Rough and scabby, and the sides of their necks are all shrivelled or creased up. Get bald, too, very young. The older fellows look the worst—fact is, I don't believe I've ever seen a very old chap of that kind. Guess they must die of looking in the glass! Animals hate 'em—they used to have lots of horse trouble before autos came in.

"Nobody around here or in Arkham or Ipswich will have anything to do with 'em, and they act kind of offish themselves when they come to town or when anyone tries to fish on their grounds. Queer how fish are always thick off Innsmouth Harbour when there ain't any anywhere

else around—but just try to fish there yourself and see how the folks chase you off! Those people used to come here on the railroad—walking and taking the train at Rowley after the branch was dropped—but now they use that bus.

"Yes, there's a hotel in Innsmouth—called the Gilman House—but I don't believe it can amount to much. I wouldn't advise you to try it. Better stay over here and take the ten o'clock bus tomorrow morning; then you can get an evening bus there for Arkham at eight o'clock. There was a factory inspector who stopped at the Gilman a couple of years ago, and he had a lot of unpleasant hints about the place. Seems they get a queer crowd there, for this fellow heard voices in other rooms—though most of 'em was empty—that gave him the shivers. It was foreign talk, he thought, but he said the bad thing about it was the kind of voice that sometimes spoke. It sounded so unnatural—slopping-like, he said—that he didn't dare undress and go to sleep. Just waited up and lit out the first thing in the morning. The talk went on most all night.

"This fellow—Casey, his name was—had a lot to say about how the Innsmouth folks watched him and seemed kind of on guard. He found the Marsh refinery a queer place—it's in an old mill on the lower falls of the Manuxet. What he said tallied up with what I'd heard. Books in bad shape, and no clear account of any kind of dealings. You know it's always ben a kind of mystery where the Marshes get the gold they refine. They've never seemed to do much buying in that line, but years ago they shipped out an enormous lot of ingots.

"Used to be talk of a queer foreign kind of jewellery that the sailors and refinery men sometimes sold on the

sly, or that was seen once or twice on some of the Marsh womenfolks. People allowed maybe old Captain Obed traded for it in some heathen port, especially since he was always ordering stacks of glass beads and trinkets such as seafaring men used to get for native trade. Others thought and still think he'd found an old pirate cache out on Devil Reef. But here's a funny thing. The old Captain's ben dead these sixty years, and there ain't ben a good-sized ship out of the place since the Civil War; but just the same the Marshes still keep on buying a few of those native trade things—mostly glass and rubber gewgaws, they tell me. Maybe the Innsmouth folks like 'em to look at themselves—Gawd knows they've gotten to be about as bad as South Sea cannibals and Guinea savages.

"That plague of '46 must have taken off the best blood in the place. Anyway, they're a doubtful lot now, and the Marshes and the other rich folks are as bad as any. As I told you, there probably ain't more'n 400 people in the whole town in spite of all the streets they say there are. I guess they're what they call 'white trash' down South—lawless and sly, and full of secret doings. They get a lot of fish and lobsters and do exporting by truck. Queer how the fish swarm right there and nowhere else.

"Nobody can ever keep track of these people, and state school officials and census men have a devil of a time. You can bet that prying strangers ain't welcome around Innsmouth. I've heard personally of more'n one business or government man that's disappeared there, and there's loose talk of one who went crazy and is out at Danvers now. They must have fixed up some awful scare for that fellow.

"That's why I wouldn't go at night if I was you. I've

never ben there and have no wish to go, but I guess a daytime trip couldn't hurt you—even though the people hereabouts will advise you not to make it. If you're just sightseeing, and looking for old-time stuff, Innsmouth ought to be quite a place for you."

And so I spent part of that evening at the Newburyport Public Library looking up data about Innsmouth. When I had tried to question the natives in the shops, the lunch room, the garages, and the fire station, I had found them even harder to get started than the ticket-agent had predicted; and realised that I could not spare the time to overcome their first instinctive reticences. They had a kind of obscure suspiciousness, as if there were something amiss with anyone too much interested in Innsmouth. At the Y.M.C.A., where I was stopping, the clerk merely discouraged my going to such a dismal, decadent place; and the people at the library shewed much the same attitude. Clearly, in the eyes of the educated, Innsmouth was merely an exaggerated case of civic degeneration.

The Essex County histories on the library shelves had very little to say, except that the town was founded in 1643, noted for shipbuilding before the Revolution, a seat of great marine prosperity in the early nineteenth century, and later a minor factory centre using the Manuxet as power. The epidemic and riots of 1846 were very sparsely treated, as if they formed a discredit to the county.

References to decline were few, though the significance of the later record was unmistakable. After the Civil War all industrial life was confined to the Marsh Refining Company, and the marketing of gold ingots formed the only remaining bit of major commerce aside from the eternal fishing. That fishing paid less and less as the

price of the commodity fell and large-scale corporations offered competition, but there was never a dearth of fish around Innsmouth Harbour. Foreigners seldom settled there, and there was some discreetly veiled evidence that a number of Poles and Portuguese who had tried it had been scattered in a peculiarly drastic fashion.

Most interesting of all was a glancing reference to the strange jewellery vaguely associated with Innsmouth. It had evidently impressed the whole countryside more than a little, for mention was made of specimens in the museum of Miskatonic University at Arkham, and in the display room of the Newburyport Historical Society. The fragmentary descriptions of these things were bald and prosaic, but they hinted to me an undercurrent of persistent strangeness. Something about them seemed so odd and provocative that I could not put them out of my mind, and despite the relative lateness of the hour I resolved to see the local sample—said to be a large, queerly proportioned thing evidently meant for a tiara—if it could possibly be arranged.

The librarian gave me a note of introduction to the curator of the Society, a Miss Anna Tilton, who lived nearby, and after a brief explanation that ancient gentlewoman was kind enough to pilot me into the closed building, since the hour was not outrageously late. The collection was a notable one indeed, but in my present mood I had eyes for nothing but the bizarre object which glistened in a corner cupboard under the electric lights.

It took no excessive sensitiveness to beauty to make me literally gasp at the strange, unearthly splendour of the alien, opulent phantasy that rested there on a purple velvet cushion. Even now I can hardly describe what I saw, though it was clearly enough a sort of tiara, as the description had said. It was tall in front, and with a very large and curiously irregular periphery, as if designed for a head of almost freakishly elliptical outline. The material seemed to be predominantly gold, though a weird lighter lustrousness hinted at some strange alloy with an equally beautiful and scarcely identifiable metal. Its condition was almost perfect, and one could have spent hours in studying the striking and puzzlingly untraditional designs—some simply geometrical, and some plainly marine—chased or moulded in high relief on its surface with a craftsmanship of incredible skill and grace.

The longer I looked, the more the thing fascinated me; and in this fascination there was a curiously disturbing element hardly to be classified or accounted for. At first I decided that it was the queer other-worldly quality of the art which made me uneasy. All other art objects I had ever seen either belonged to some known racial or national stream, or else were consciously modernistic defiances of every recognised stream. This tiara was neither. It clearly belonged to some settled technique of infinite maturity and perfection, yet that technique was utterly remote from any—Eastern or Western, ancient or modern—which I had ever heard of or seen exemplified. It was as if the workmanship were that of another planet.

However, I soon saw that my uneasiness had a second and perhaps equally potent source residing in the pictorial and mathematical suggestions of the strange designs. The patterns all hinted of remote secrets and unimaginable abysses in time and space, and the monotonously aquatic nature of the reliefs became almost sinister. Among these reliefs were fabulous monsters of abhorrent grotesqueness and malignity—half ichthyic

and half batrachian in suggestion—which one could not dissociate from a certain haunting and uncomfortable sense of pseudo-memory, as if they called up some image from deep cells and tissues whose retentive functions are wholly primal and awesomely ancestral. At times I fancied that every contour of these blasphemous fish-frogs was overflowing with the ultimate quintessence of unknown and inhuman evil.

In odd contrast to the tiara's aspect was its brief and prosy history as related by Miss Tilton. It had been pawned for a ridiculous sum at a shop in State Street in 1873, by a drunken Innsmouth man shortly afterward killed in a brawl. The Society had acquired it directly from the pawnbroker, at once giving it a display worthy of its quality. It was labelled as of probable East-Indian or Indo-Chinese provenance, though the attribution was frankly tentative.

Miss Tilton, comparing all possible hypotheses regarding its origin and its presence in New England, was inclined to believe that it formed part of some exotic pirate hoard discovered by old Captain Obed Marsh. This view was surely not weakened by the insistent offers of purchase at a high price which the Marshes began to make as soon as they knew of its presence, and which they repeated to this day despite the Society's unvarying determination not to sell.

As the good lady shewed me out of the building she made it clear that the pirate theory of the Marsh fortune was a popular one among the intelligent people of the region. Her own attitude toward shadowed Innsmouth—which she had never seen—was one of disgust at a community slipping far down the cultural scale, and she assured me that the rumours of devil-worship were partly justified by a peculiar secret cult which had gained force there and engulfed all the orthodox churches.

It was called, she said, "The Esoteric Order of Dagon", and was undoubtedly a debased, quasi-pagan thing imported from the East a century before, at a time when the Innsmouth fisheries seemed to be going barren. Its persistence among a simple people was quite natural in view of the sudden and permanent return of abundantly fine fishing, and it soon came to be the greatest influence on the town, replacing Freemasonry altogether and taking up headquarters in the old Masonic Hall on New Church Green.

All this, to the pious Miss Tilton, formed an excellent reason for shunning the ancient town of decay and desolation; but to me it was merely a fresh incentive. To my architectural and historical anticipations was now added an acute anthropological zeal, and I could scarcely sleep in my small room at the "Y" as the night wore away.

II.

Shortly before ten the next morning I stood with one small valise in front of Hammond's Drug Store in old Market Square waiting for the Innsmouth bus. As the hour for its arrival drew near I noticed a general drift of the loungers to other places up the street, or to the Ideal Lunch across the square. Evidently the ticket-agent had not exaggerated the dislike which local people bore toward Innsmouth and its denizens. In a few moments a small motor-coach of extreme decrepitude and dirty grey

colour rattled down State Street, made a turn, and drew up at the curb beside me. I felt immediately that it was the right one; a guess which the half-illegible sign on the windshield—"Arkham-Innsmouth-Newb'port"—soon verified.

There were only three passengers—dark, unkempt men of sullen visage and somewhat youthful cast—and when the vehicle stopped they clumsily shambled out and began walking up State Street in a silent, almost furtive fashion. The driver also alighted, and I watched him as he went into the drug store to make some purchase. This, I reflected, must be the Joe Sargent mentioned by the ticket-agent; and even before I noticed any details there spread over me a wave of spontaneous aversion which could be neither checked nor explained. It suddenly struck me as very natural that the local people should not wish to ride on a bus owned and driven by this man, or to visit any oftener than possible the habitat of such a man and his kinsfolk.

When the driver came out of the store I looked at him more carefully and tried to determine the source of my evil impression. He was a thin, stoop-shouldered man not much under six feet tall, dressed in shabby blue civilian clothes and wearing a frayed grey golf cap. His age was perhaps thirty-five, but the odd, deep creases in the sides of his neck made him seem older when one did not study his dull, expressionless face. He had a narrow head, bulging, watery blue eyes that seemed never to wink, a flat nose, a receding forehead and chin, and singularly undeveloped ears. His long, thick lip and coarse-pored, greyish cheeks seemed almost beardless except for some sparse yellow hairs that straggled and curled in irregular patches; and in places the surface seemed queerly irregular, as if peeling from some cutaneous disease. His hands were large and heavily veined, and had a very unusual greyish-blue tinge. The fingers were strikingly short in proportion to the rest of the structure, and seemed to have a tendency to curl closely into the huge palm. As he walked toward the bus I observed his peculiarly shambling gait and saw that his feet were inordinately immense. The more I studied them the more I wondered how he could buy any shoes to fit them.

A certain greasiness about the fellow increased my dislike. He was evidently given to working or lounging around the fish docks, and carried with him much of their characteristic smell. Just what foreign blood was in him I could not even guess. His oddities certainly did not look Asiatic, Polynesian, Levantine, or negroid, yet I could see why the people found him alien. I myself would have thought of biological degeneration rather than alienage.

I was sorry when I saw that there would be no other passengers on the bus. Somehow I did not like the idea of riding alone with this driver. But as leaving time obviously approached I conquered my qualms and followed the man aboard, extending him a dollar bill and murmuring the single word "Innsmouth". He looked curiously at me for a second as he returned forty cents change without speaking. I took a seat far behind him, but on the same side of the bus, since I wished to watch the shore during the journey.

At length the decrepit vehicle started with a jerk, and rattled noisily past the old brick buildings of State Street amidst a cloud of vapour from the exhaust. Glancing at the people on the sidewalks, I thought I detected in them

a curious wish to avoid looking at the bus—or at least a wish to avoid seeming to look at it. Then we turned to the left into High Street, where the going was smoother; flying by stately old mansions of the early republic and still older colonial farmhouses, passing the Lower Green and Parker River, and finally emerging into a long, monotonous stretch of open shore country.

The day was warm and sunny, but the landscape of sand, sedge-grass, and stunted shrubbery became more and more desolate as we proceeded. Out the window I could see the blue water and the sandy line of Plum Island, and we presently drew very near the beach as our narrow road veered off from the main highway to Rowley and Ipswich. There were no visible houses, and I could tell by the state of the road that traffic was very light hereabouts. The small, weather-worn telephone poles carried only two wires. Now and then we crossed crude wooden bridges over tidal creeks that wound far inland and promoted the general isolation of the region.

Once in a while I noticed dead stumps and crumbling foundation-walls above the drifting sand, and recalled the old tradition quoted in one of the histories I had read, that this was once a fertile and thickly settled countryside. The change, it was said, came simultaneously with the Innsmouth epidemic of 1846, and was thought by simple folk to have a dark connexion with hidden forces of evil. Actually, it was caused by the unwise cutting of woodlands near the shore, which robbed the soil of its best protection and opened the way for waves of wind-blown sand.

At last we lost sight of Plum Island and saw the vast expanse of the open Atlantic on our left. Our narrow course began to climb steeply, and I felt a singular sense of disquiet in looking at the lonely crest ahead where the rutted roadway met the sky. It was as if the bus were about to keep on in its ascent, leaving the sane earth altogether and merging with the unknown arcana of upper air and cryptical sky. The smell of the sea took on ominous implications, and the silent driver's bent, rigid back and narrow head became more and more hateful. As I looked at him I saw that the back of his head was almost as hairless as his face, having only a few straggling yellow strands upon a grey scabrous surface.

Then we reached the crest and beheld the outspread valley beyond, where the Manuxet joins the sea just north of the long line of cliffs that culminate in Kingsport Head and veer off toward Cape Ann. On the far, misty horizon I could just make out the dizzy profile of the Head, topped by the queer ancient house of which so many legends are told; but for the moment all my attention was captured by the nearer panorama just below me. I had, I realised, come face to face with rumour-shadowed Innsmouth.

It was a town of wide extent and dense construction, yet one with a portentous dearth of visible life. From the tangle of chimney-pots scarcely a wisp of smoke came, and the three tall steeples loomed stark and unpainted against the seaward horizon. One of them was crumbling down at the top, and in that and another there were only black gaping holes where clock-dials should have been. The vast huddle of sagging gambrel roofs and peaked gables conveyed with offensive clearness the idea of wormy decay, and as we approached along the now descending road I could see that many roofs had wholly caved in. There were some large square Georgian houses, too, with hipped roofs, cupolas, and railed "widow's walks". These

were mostly well back from the water, and one or two seemed to be in moderately sound condition. Stretching inland from among them I saw the rusted, grass-grown line of the abandoned railway, with leaning telegraph-poles now devoid of wires, and the half-obscured lines of the old carriage roads to Rowley and Ipswich.

The decay was worst close to the waterfront, though in its very midst I could spy the white belfry of a fairly well-preserved brick structure which looked like a small factory. The harbour, long clogged with sand, was enclosed by an ancient stone breakwater; on which I could begin to discern the minute forms of a few seated fishermen, and at whose end were what looked like the foundations of a bygone lighthouse. A sandy tongue had formed inside this barrier, and upon it I saw a few decrepit cabins, moored dories, and scattered lobster-pots. The only deep water seemed to be where the river poured out past the belfried structure and turned southward to join the ocean at the breakwater's end.

Here and there the ruins of wharves jutted out from the shore to end in indeterminate rottenness, those farthest south seeming the most decayed. And far out at sea, despite a high tide, I glimpsed a long, black line scarcely rising above the water yet carrying a suggestion of odd latent malignancy. This, I knew, must be Devil Reef. As I looked, a subtle, curious sense of beckoning seemed superadded to the grim repulsion; and oddly enough, I found this overtone more disturbing than the primary impression.

We met no one on the road, but presently began to pass deserted farms in varying stages of ruin. Then I noticed a few inhabited houses with rags stuffed in the broken windows and shells and dead fish lying about the littered yards. Once or twice I saw listless-looking people working in barren gardens or digging clams on the fishy-smelling beach below, and groups of dirty, simian-visaged children playing around weed-grown doorsteps. Somehow these people seemed more disquieting than the dismal buildings, for almost every one had certain peculiarities of face and motions which I instinctively disliked without being able to define or comprehend them. For a second I thought this typical physique suggested some picture I had seen, perhaps in a book, under circumstances of particular horror or melancholy; but this pseudo-recollection passed very quickly.

As the bus reached a lower level I began to catch the steady note of a waterfall through the unnatural stillness. The leaning, unpainted houses grew thicker, lined both sides of the road, and displayed more urban tendencies than did those we were leaving behind. The panorama ahead had contracted to a street scene, and in spots I could see where a cobblestone pavement and stretches of brick sidewalk had formerly existed. All the houses were apparently deserted, and there were occasional gaps where tumbledown chimneys and cellar walls told of buildings that had collapsed. Pervading everything was the most nauseous fishy odour imaginable.

Soon cross streets and junctions began to appear; those on the left leading to shoreward realms of unpaved squalor and decay, while those on the right shewed vistas of departed grandeur. So far I had seen no people in the town, but there now came signs of a sparse habitation—curtained windows here and there, and an occasional battered motor-car at the curb. Pavement and sidewalks were increasingly well defined, and though most of the

houses were quite old—wood and brick structures of the early nineteenth century—they were obviously kept fit for habitation. As an amateur antiquarian I almost lost my olfactory disgust and my feeling of menace and repulsion amidst this rich, unaltered survival from the past.

But I was not to reach my destination without one very strong impression of poignantly disagreeable quality. The bus had come to a sort of open concourse or radial point with churches on two sides and the bedraggled remains of a circular green in the centre, and I was looking at a large pillared hall on the right-hand junction ahead. The structure's once white paint was now grey and peeling, and the black and gold sign on the pediment was so faded that I could only with difficulty make out the words "Esoteric Order of Dagon". This, then, was the former Masonic Hall now given over to a degraded cult. As I strained to decipher this inscription my notice was distracted by the raucous tones of a cracked bell across the street, and I quickly turned to look out the window on my side of the coach.

The sound came from a squat-towered stone church of manifestly later date than most of the houses, built in a clumsy Gothic fashion and having a disproportionately high basement with shuttered windows. Though the hands of its clock were missing on the side I glimpsed, I knew that those hoarse strokes were telling the hour of eleven. Then suddenly all thoughts of time were blotted out by an onrushing image of sharp intensity and unaccountable horror which had seized me before I knew what it really was. The door of the church basement was open, revealing a rectangle of blackness inside. And as I looked, a certain object crossed or seemed to cross that dark rectangle; burning into my brain a momentary conception of nightmare which was all the more maddening because analysis could not shew a single nightmarish quality in it.

It was a living object—the first except the driver that I had seen since entering the compact part of the town—and had I been in a steadier mood I would have found nothing whatever of terror in it. Clearly, as I realised a moment later, it was the pastor; clad in some peculiar vestments doubtless introduced since the Order of Dagon had modified the ritual of the local churches. The thing which had probably caught my first subconscious glance and supplied the touch of bizarre horror was the tall tiara he wore; an almost exact duplicate of the one Miss Tilton had shewn me the previous evening. This, acting on my imagination, had supplied namelessly sinister qualities to the indeterminate face and robed, shambling form beneath it. There was not, I soon decided, any reason why I should have felt that shuddering touch of evil pseudo-memory. Was it not natural that a local mystery cult should adopt among its regimentals an unique type of head-dress made familiar to the community in some strange way—perhaps as treasure-trove?

A very thin sprinkling of repellent-looking youngish people now became visible on the sidewalks—lone individuals, and silent knots of two or three. The lower floors of the crumbling houses sometimes harboured small shops with dingy signs, and I noticed a parked truck or two as we rattled along. The sound of waterfalls became more and more distinct, and presently I saw a fairly deep river-gorge ahead, spanned by a wide, iron-railed highway bridge beyond which a large square opened out. As we clanked over the bridge I looked out on both sides and observed some factory buildings on the edge of the

grassy bluff or part way down. The water far below was very abundant, and I could see two vigorous sets of falls upstream on my right and at least one downstream on my left. From this point the noise was quite deafening. Then we rolled into the large semicircular square across the river and drew up on the right-hand side in front of a tall, cupola-crowned building with remnants of yellow paint and with a half-effaced sign proclaiming it to be the Gilman House.

I was glad to get out of that bus, and at once proceeded to check my valise in the shabby hotel lobby. There was only one person in sight—an elderly man without what I had come to call the "Innsmouth look"—and I decided not to ask him any of the questions which bothered me; remembering that odd things had been noticed in this hotel. Instead, I strolled out on the square, from which the bus had already gone, and studied the scene minutely and appraisingly.

One side of the cobblestoned open space was the straight line of the river; the other was a semicircle of slant-roofed brick buildings of about the 1800 period, from which several streets radiated away to the southeast, south, and southwest. Lamps were depressingly few and small—all low-powered incandescents—and I was glad that my plans called for departure before dark, even though I knew the moon would be bright. The buildings were all in fair condition, and included perhaps a dozen shops in current operation; of which one was a grocery of the First National chain, others a dismal restaurant, a drug store, and a wholesale fish-dealer's office, and still another, at the eastern extremity of the square near the river, an office of the town's only industry—the Marsh Refining Company. There were perhaps ten people visible, and four or five automobiles and motor trucks stood scattered about. I did not need to be told that this was the civic centre of Innsmouth. Eastward I could catch blue glimpses of the harbour, against which rose the decaying remains of three once beautiful Georgian steeples. And toward the shore on the opposite bank of the river I saw the white belfry surmounting what I took to be the Marsh refinery.

For some reason or other I chose to make my first inquiries at the chain grocery, whose personnel was not likely to be native to Innsmouth. I found a solitary boy of about seventeen in charge, and was pleased to note the brightness and affability which promised cheerful information. He seemed exceptionally eager to talk, and I soon gathered that he did not like the place, its fishy smell, or its furtive people. A word with any outsider was a relief to him. He hailed from Arkham, boarded with a family who came from Ipswich, and went back home whenever he got a moment off. His family did not like him to work in Innsmouth, but the chain had transferred him there and he did not wish to give up his job.

There was, he said, no public library or chamber of commerce in Innsmouth, but I could probably find my way about. The street I had come down was Federal. West of that were the fine old residence streets—Broad, Washington, Lafayette, and Adams—and east of it were the shoreward slums. It was in these slums—along Main Street—that I would find the old Georgian churches, but they were all long abandoned. It would be well not to make oneself too conspicuous in such neighbourhoods—especially north of the river—since the people were sullen and hostile. Some strangers had even disappeared.

Certain spots were almost forbidden territory, as he had learned at considerable cost. One must not, for example, linger much around the Marsh refinery, or around any of the still used churches, or around the pillared Order of Dagon Hall at New Church Green. Those churches were very odd—all violently disavowed by their respective denominations elsewhere, and apparently using the queerest kind of ceremonials and clerical vestments. Their creeds were heterodox and mysterious, involving hints of certain marvellous transformations leading to bodily immortality—of a sort—on this earth. The youth's own pastor—Dr. Wallace of Asbury M. E. Church in Arkham—had gravely urged him not to join any church in Innsmouth.

As for the Innsmouth people—the youth hardly knew what to make of them. They were as furtive and seldom seen as animals that live in burrows, and one could hardly imagine how they passed the time apart from their desultory fishing. Perhaps—judging from the quantities of bootleg liquor they consumed—they lay for most of the daylight hours in an alcoholic stupor. They seemed sullenly banded together in some sort of fellowship and understanding—despising the world as if they had access to other and preferable spheres of entity. Their appearance—especially those staring, unwinking eyes which one never saw shut—was certainly shocking enough; and their voices were disgusting. It was awful to hear them chanting in their churches at night, and especially during their main festivals or revivals, which fell twice a year on April 30th and October 31st.

They were very fond of the water, and swam a great deal in both river and harbour. Swimming races out to Devil Reef were very common, and everyone in sight seemed well able to share in this arduous sport. When one came to think of it, it was generally only rather young people who were seen about in public, and of these the oldest were apt to be the most tainted-looking. When exceptions did occur, they were mostly persons with no trace of aberrancy, like the old clerk at the hotel. One wondered what became of the bulk of the older folk, and whether the "Innsmouth look" were not a strange and insidious disease-phenomenon which increased its hold as years advanced.

Only a very rare affliction, of course, could bring about such vast and radical anatomical changes in a single individual after maturity—changes involving osseous factors as basic as the shape of the skull—but then, even this aspect was no more baffling and unheard-of than the visible features of the malady as a whole. It would be hard, the youth implied, to form any real conclusions regarding such a matter; since one never came to know the natives personally no matter how long one might live in Innsmouth.

The youth was certain that many specimens even worse than the worst visible ones were kept locked indoors in some places. People sometimes heard the queerest kind of sounds. The tottering waterfront hovels north of the river were reputedly connected by hidden tunnels, being thus a veritable warren of unseen abnormalities. What kind of foreign blood—if any—these beings had, it was impossible to tell. They sometimes kept certain especially repulsive characters out of sight when government agents and others from the outside world came to town.

It would be of no use, my informant said, to ask the natives anything about the place. The only one who

would talk was a very aged but normal-looking man who lived at the poorhouse on the north rim of the town and spent his time walking about or lounging around the fire station. This hoary character, Zadok Allen, was ninety-six years old and somewhat touched in the head, besides being the town drunkard. He was a strange, furtive creature who constantly looked over his shoulder as if afraid of something, and when sober could not be persuaded to talk at all with strangers. He was, however, unable to resist any offer of his favourite poison; and once drunk would furnish the most astonishing fragments of whispered reminiscence.

After all, though, little useful data could be gained from him; since his stories were all insane, incomplete hints of impossible marvels and horrors which could have no source save in his own disordered fancy. Nobody ever believed him, but the natives did not like him to drink and talk with strangers; and it was not always safe to be seen questioning him. It was probably from him that some of the wildest popular whispers and delusions were derived.

Several non-native residents had reported monstrous glimpses from time to time, but between old Zadok's tales and the malformed denizens it was no wonder such illusions were current. None of the non-natives ever stayed out late at night, there being a widespread impression that it was not wise to do so. Besides, the streets were loathsomely dark.

As for business—the abundance of fish was certainly almost uncanny, but the natives were taking less and less advantage of it. Moreover, prices were falling and competition was growing. Of course the town's real business was the refinery, whose commercial office was on the square only a few doors east of where we stood. Old Man Marsh was never seen, but sometimes went to the works in a closed, curtained car.

There were all sorts of rumours about how Marsh had come to look. He had once been a great dandy, and people said he still wore the frock-coated finery of the Edwardian age, curiously adapted to certain deformities. His sons had formerly conducted the office in the square, but latterly they had been keeping out of sight a good deal and leaving the brunt of affairs to the younger generation. The sons and their sisters had come to look very queer, especially the elder ones; and it was said that their health was failing.

One of the Marsh daughters was a repellent, reptilian-looking woman who wore an excess of weird jewellery clearly of the same exotic tradition as that to which the strange tiara belonged. My informant had noticed it many times, and had heard it spoken of as coming from some secret hoard, either of pirates or of daemons. The clergymen—or priests, or whatever they were called nowadays—also wore this kind of ornament as a head-dress; but one seldom caught glimpses of them. Other specimens the youth had not seen, though many were rumoured to exist around Innsmouth.

The Marshes, together with the other three gently bred families of the town—the Waites, the Gilmans, and the Eliots—were all very retiring. They lived in immense houses along Washington Street, and several were reputed to harbour in concealment certain living kinsfolk whose personal aspect forbade public view, and whose deaths had been reported and recorded.

Warning me that many of the street signs were down, the youth drew for my benefit a rough but ample and painstaking sketch map of the town's salient features. After a moment's study I felt sure that it would be of great help, and pocketed it with profuse thanks. Disliking the dinginess of the single restaurant I had seen, I bought a fair supply of cheese crackers and ginger wafers to serve as a lunch later on. My programme, I decided, would be to thread the principal streets, talk with any non-natives I might encounter, and catch the eight o'clock coach for Arkham. The town, I could see, formed a significant and exaggerated example of communal decay; but being no sociologist I would limit my serious observations to the field of architecture.

Thus I began my systematic though half-bewildered tour of Innsmouth's narrow, shadow-blighted ways. Crossing the bridge and turning toward the roar of the lower falls, I passed close to the Marsh refinery, which seemed oddly free from the noise of industry. This building stood on the steep river bluff near a bridge and an open confluence of streets which I took to be the earliest civic centre, displaced after the Revolution by the present Town Square.

Re-crossing the gorge on the Main Street bridge, I struck a region of utter desertion which somehow made me shudder. Collapsing huddles of gambrel roofs formed a jagged and fantastic skyline, above which rose the ghoulish, decapitated steeple of an ancient church. Some houses along Main Street were tenanted, but most were tightly boarded up. Down unpaved side streets I saw the black, gaping windows of deserted hovels, many of which leaned at perilous and incredible angles through the sinking of part of the foundations. Those windows stared so spectrally that it took courage to turn eastward toward the waterfront. Certainly, the terror of a deserted house swells in geometrical rather than arithmetical progression as houses multiply to form a city of stark desolation. The sight of such endless avenues of fishy-eyed vacancy and death, and the thought of such linked infinities of black, brooding compartments given over to cobwebs and memories and the conqueror worm, start up vestigial fears and aversions that not even the stoutest philosophy can disperse.

Fish Street was as deserted as Main, though it differed in having many brick and stone warehouses still in excellent shape. Water Street was almost its duplicate, save that there were great seaward gaps where wharves had been. Not a living thing did I see, except for the scattered fishermen on the distant breakwater, and not a sound did I hear save the lapping of the harbour tides and the roar of the falls in the Manuxet. The town was getting more and more on my nerves, and I looked behind me furtively as I picked my way back over the tottering Water Street bridge. The Fish Street bridge, according to the sketch, was in ruins.

North of the river there were traces of squalid life— active fish-packing houses in Water Street, smoking chimneys and patched roofs here and there, occasional sounds from indeterminate sources, and infrequent shambling forms in the dismal streets and unpaved lanes—but I seemed to find this even more oppressive than the southerly desertion. For one thing, the people were more hideous and abnormal than those near the centre of the town; so that I was several times evilly reminded of something utterly fantastic which I could

431

not quite place. Undoubtedly the alien strain in the Innsmouth folk was stronger here than farther inland—unless, indeed, the "Innsmouth look" were a disease rather than a blood strain, in which case this district might be held to harbour the more advanced cases.

One detail that annoyed me was the distribution of the few faint sounds I heard. They ought naturally to have come wholly from the visibly inhabited houses, yet in reality were often strongest inside the most rigidly boarded-up facades. There were creakings, scurryings, and hoarse doubtful noises; and I thought uncomfortably about the hidden tunnels suggested by the grocery boy. Suddenly I found myself wondering what the voices of those denizens would be like. I had heard no speech so far in this quarter, and was unaccountably anxious not to do so.

Pausing only long enough to look at two fine but ruinous old churches at Main and Church Streets, I hastened out of that vile waterfront slum. My next logical goal was New Church Green, but somehow or other I could not bear to repass the church in whose basement I had glimpsed the inexplicably frightening form of that strangely diademed priest or pastor. Besides, the grocery youth had told me that the churches, as well as the Order of Dagon Hall, were not advisable neighbourhoods for strangers.

Accordingly I kept north along Main to Martin, then turning inland, crossing Federal Street safely north of the Green, and entering the decayed patrician neighbourhood of northern Broad, Washington, Lafayette, and Adams Streets. Though these stately old avenues were ill-surfaced and unkempt, their elm-shaded dignity had not entirely departed. Mansion after mansion claimed my gaze, most of them decrepit and boarded up amidst neglected grounds, but one or two in each street shewing signs of occupancy. In Washington Street there was a row of four or five in excellent repair and with finely tended lawns and gardens. The most sumptuous of these—with wide terraced parterres extending back the whole way to Lafayette Street—I took to be the home of Old Man Marsh, the afflicted refinery owner.

In all these streets no living thing was visible, and I wondered at the complete absense of cats and dogs from Innsmouth. Another thing which puzzled and disturbed me, even in some of the best-preserved mansions, was the tightly shuttered condition of many third-story and attic windows. Furtiveness and secretiveness seemed universal in this hushed city of alienage and death, and I could not escape the sensation of being watched from ambush on every hand by sly, staring eyes that never shut.

I shivered as the cracked stroke of three sounded from a belfry on my left. Too well did I recall the squat church from which those notes came. Following Washington Street toward the river, I now faced a new zone of former industry and commerce; noting the ruins of a factory ahead, and seeing others, with the traces of an old railway station and covered railway bridge beyond, up the gorge on my right.

The uncertain bridge now before me was posted with a warning sign, but I took the risk and crossed again to the south bank where traces of life reappeared. Furtive, shambling creatures stared cryptically in my direction, and more normal faces eyed me coldly and curiously. Innsmouth was rapidly becoming intolerable, and I

turned down Paine Street toward the Square in the hope of getting some vehicle to take me to Arkham before the still-distant starting-time of that sinister bus.

It was then that I saw the tumbledown fire station on my left, and noticed the red-faced, bushy-bearded, watery-eyed old man in nondescript rags who sat on a bench in front of it talking with a pair of unkempt but not abnormal-looking firemen. This, of course, must be Zadok Allen, the half-crazed, liquorish nonagenarian whose tales of old Innsmouth and its shadow were so hideous and incredible.

III.

It must have been some imp of the perverse—or some sardonic pull from dark, hidden sources—which made me change my plans as I did. I had long before resolved to limit my observations to architecture alone, and I was even then hurrying toward the Square in an effort to get quick transportation out of this festering city of death and decay; but the sight of old Zadok Allen set up new currents in my mind and made me slacken my pace uncertainly.

I had been assured that the old man could do nothing but hint at wild, disjointed, and incredible legends, and I had been warned that the natives made it unsafe to be seen talking to him; yet the thought of this aged witness to the town's decay, with memories going back to the early days of ships and factories, was a lure that no amount of reason could make me resist. After all, the strangest and maddest of myths are often merely symbols or allegories based upon truth—and old Zadok must have seen everything which went on around Innsmouth for the last ninety years. Curiosity flared up beyond sense and caution, and in my youthful egotism I fancied I might be able to sift a nucleus of real history from the confused, extravagant outpouring I would probably extract with the aid of raw whiskey.

I knew that I could not accost him then and there, for the firemen would surely notice and object. Instead, I reflected, I would prepare by getting some bootleg liquor at a place where the grocery boy had told me it was plentiful. Then I would loaf near the fire station in apparent casualness, and fall in with old Zadok after he had started on one of his frequent rambles. The youth said that he was very restless, seldom sitting around the station for more than an hour or two at a time.

A quart bottle of whiskey was easily, though not cheaply, obtained in the rear of a dingy variety-store just off the Square in Eliot Street. The dirty-looking fellow who waited on me had a touch of the staring "Innsmouth look", but was quite civil in his way; being perhaps used to the custom of such convivial strangers—truckmen, gold-buyers, and the like—as were occasionally in town.

Reëntering the Square I saw that luck was with me; for—shuffling out of Paine Street around the corner of the Gilman House—I glimpsed nothing less than the tall, lean, tattered form of old Zadok Allen himself. In accordance with my plan, I attracted his attention by brandishing my newly purchased bottle; and soon realised that he had begun to shuffle wistfully after me as I turned into Waite Street on my way to the most deserted region I could think of.

I was steering my course by the map the grocery boy had prepared, and was aiming for the wholly abandoned stretch of southern waterfront which I had previously visited. The only people in sight there had been the fishermen on the distant breakwater; and by going a few squares south I could get beyond the range of these, finding a pair of seats on some abandoned wharf and being free to question old Zadok unobserved for an indefinite time. Before I reached Main Street I could hear a faint and wheezy "Hey, Mister!" behind me, and I presently allowed the old man to catch up and take copious pulls from the quart bottle.

I began putting out feelers as we walked along to Water Street and turned southward amidst the omnipresent desolation and crazily tilted ruins, but found that the aged tongue did not loosen as quickly as I had expected. At length I saw a grass-grown opening toward the sea between crumbling brick walls, with the weedy length of an earth-and-masonry wharf projecting beyond. Piles of moss-covered stones near the water promised tolerable seats, and the scene was sheltered from all possible view by a ruined warehouse on the north. Here, I thought, was the ideal place for a long secret colloquy; so I guided my companion down the lane and picked out spots to sit in among the mossy stones. The air of death and desertion was ghoulish, and the smell of fish almost insufferable; but I was resolved to let nothing deter me.

About four hours remained for conversation if I were to catch the eight o'clock coach for Arkham, and I began to dole out more liquor to the ancient tippler; meanwhile eating my own frugal lunch. In my donations I was careful not to overshoot the mark, for I did not wish Zadok's vinous garrulousness to pass into a stupor. After an hour his furtive taciturnity shewed signs of disappearing, but much to my disappointment he still sidetracked my questions about Innsmouth and its shadow-haunted past. He would babble of current topics, revealing a wide acquaintance with newspapers and a great tendency to philosophise in a sententious village fashion.

Toward the end of the second hour I feared my quart of whiskey would not be enough to produce results, and was wondering whether I had better leave old Zadok and go back for more. Just then, however, chance made the opening which my questions had been unable to make; and the wheezing ancient's rambling took a turn that caused me to lean forward and listen alertly. My back was toward the fishy-smelling sea, but he was facing it, and something or other had caused his wandering gaze to light on the low, distant line of Devil Reef, then shewing plainly and almost fascinatingly above the waves. The sight seemed to displease him, for he began a series of weak curses which ended in a confidential whisper and a knowing leer. He bent toward me, took hold of my coat lapel, and hissed out some hints that could not be mistaken.

"Thar's whar it all begun—that cursed place of all wickedness whar the deep water starts. Gate o' hell— sheer drop daown to a bottom no saoundin'-line kin tech. Ol' Cap'n Obed done it—him that faound aout more'n was good fer him in the Saouth Sea islands.

"Everybody was in a bad way them days. Trade fallin' off, mills losin' business—even the new ones—an' the best of our menfolks kilt a-privateerin' in the War of 1812 or lost with the Elizy brig an' the Ranger snow—both of 'em

Gilman venters. Obed Marsh he had three ships afloat—brigantine Columby, brig Hetty, an' barque Sumatry Queen. He was the only one as kep' on with the East-Injy an' Pacific trade, though Esdras Martin's barkentine Malay Pride made a venter as late as 'twenty-eight.

"Never was nobody like Cap'n Obed—old limb o' Satan! Heh, heh! I kin mind him a-tellin' abaout furren parts, an' callin' all the folks stupid fer goin' to Christian meetin' an' bearin' their burdens meek an' lowly. Says they'd orter git better gods like some o' the folks in the Injies—gods as ud bring 'em good fishin' in return for their sacrifices, an' ud reely answer folks's prayers.

"Matt Eliot, his fust mate, talked a lot, too, only he was agin' folks's doin' any heathen things. Told abaout an island east of Otaheité whar they was a lot o' stone ruins older'n anybody knew anything abaout, kind o' like them on Ponape, in the Carolines, but with carvin's of faces that looked like the big statues on Easter Island. They was a little volcanic island near thar, too, whar they was other ruins with diff'rent carvin's—ruins all wore away like they'd ben under the sea onct, an' with picters of awful monsters all over 'em.

"Wal, Sir, Matt he says the natives araound thar had all the fish they cud ketch, an' sported bracelets an' armlets an' head rigs made aout of a queer kind o' gold an' covered with picters o' monsters jest like the ones carved over the ruins on the little island—sorter fish-like frogs or frog-like fishes that was drawed in all kinds o' positions like they was human bein's. Nobody cud git aout o' them whar they got all the stuff, an' all the other natives wondered haow they managed to find fish in plenty even when the very next islands had lean pickin's.

Matt he got to wonderin' too, an' so did Cap'n Obed. Obed he notices, besides, that lots of the han'some young folks ud drop aout o' sight fer good from year to year, an' that they wa'n't many old folks araound. Also, he thinks some of the folks looks durned queer even fer Kanakys.

"It took Obed to git the truth aout o' them heathen. I dun't know haow he done it, but he begun by tradin' fer the gold-like things they wore. Ast 'em whar they come from, an' ef they cud git more, an' finally wormed the story aout o' the old chief—Walakea, they called him. Nobody but Obed ud ever a believed the old yeller devil, but the Cap'n cud read folks like they was books. Heh, heh! Nobody never believes me naow when I tell 'em, an' I dun't s'pose you will, young feller—though come to look at ye, ye hev kind o' got them sharp-readin' eyes like Obed had."

The old man's whisper grew fainter, and I found myself shuddering at the terrible and sincere portentousness of his intonation, even though I knew his tale could be nothing but drunken phantasy.

"Wal, Sir, Obed he larnt that they's things on this arth as most folks never heerd abaout—an' wouldn't believe ef they did hear. It seems these Kanakys was sacrificin' heaps o' their young men an' maidens to some kind o' god-things that lived under the sea, an' gittin' all kinds o' favour in return. They met the things on the little islet with the queer ruins, an' it seems them awful picters o' frog-fish monsters was supposed to be picters o' these things. Mebbe they was the kind o' critters as got all the mermaid stories an' sech started. They had all kinds o' cities on the sea-bottom, an' this island was heaved up from thar. Seems they was some of the things alive in

the stone buildin's when the island come up sudden to the surface. That's haow the Kanakys got wind they was daown thar. Made sign-talk as soon as they got over bein' skeert, an' pieced up a bargain afore long.

"Them things liked human sacrifices. Had had 'em ages afore, but lost track o' the upper world arter a time. What they done to the victims it ain't fer me to say, an' I guess Obed wa'n't none too sharp abaout askin'. But it was all right with the heathens, because they'd ben havin' a hard time an' was desp'rate abaout everything. They give a sarten number o' young folks to the sea-things twict every year—May-Eve an' Hallowe'en—reg'lar as cud be. Also give some o' the carved knick-knacks they made. What the things agreed to give in return was plenty o' fish—they druv 'em in from all over the sea—an' a few gold-like things naow an' then.

"Wal, as I says, the natives met the things on the little volcanic islet—goin' thar in canoes with the sacrifices et cet'ry, and bringin' back any of the gold-like jools as was comin' to 'em. At fust the things didn't never go onto the main island, but arter a time they come to want to. Seems they hankered arter mixin' with the folks, an' havin' j'int ceremonies on the big days—May-Eve an' Hallowe'en. Ye see, they was able to live both in an' aout o' water—what they call amphibians, I guess. The Kanakys told 'em as haow folks from the other islands might wanta wipe 'em aout ef they got wind o' their bein' thar, but they says they dun't keer much, because they cud wipe aout the hull brood o' humans ef they was willin' to bother—that is, any as didn't hev sarten signs sech as was used onct by the lost Old Ones, whoever they was. But not wantin' to bother, they'd lay low when anybody visited the island.

"When it come to matin' with them toad-lookin' fishes, the Kanakys kind o' balked, but finally they larnt something as put a new face on the matter. Seems that human folks has got a kind o' relation to sech water-beasts—that everything alive come aout o' the water onct, an' only needs a little change to go back agin. Them things told the Kanakys that cf they mixed bloods there'd be children as ud look human at fust, but later turn more'n more like the things, till finally they'd take to the water an' jine the main lot o' things daown thar. An' this is the important part, young feller—them as turned into fish things an' went into the water wouldn't never die. Them things never died excep' they was kilt violent.

"Wal, Sir, it seems by the time Obed knowed them islanders they was all full o' fish blood from them deep-water things. When they got old an' begun to shew it, they was kep' hid until they felt like takin' to the water an' quittin' the place. Some was more teched than others, an' some never did change quite enough to take to the water; but mostly they turned aout jest the way them things said. Them as was born more like the things changed arly, but them as was nearly human sometimes stayed on the island till they was past seventy, though they'd usually go daown under fer trial trips afore that. Folks as had took to the water gen'rally come back a good deal to visit, so's a man ud often be a-talkin' to his own five-times-great-grandfather, who'd left the dry land a couple o' hundred years or so afore.

"Everybody got aout o' the idee o' dyin'—excep' in canoe wars with the other islanders, or as sacrifices to the sea-gods daown below, or from snake-bite or plague or sharp gallopin' ailments or somethin' afore they cud take to the water—but simply looked forrad to a kind o' change that wa'n't a bit horrible arter a while. They thought what they'd got was well wuth all they'd had to give up—an' I guess Obed kind o' come to think the same hisself when he'd chewed over old Walakea's story a bit. Walakea, though, was one of the few as hadn't got none of the fish blood—bein' of a royal line that intermarried with royal lines on other islands.

"Walakea he shewed Obed a lot o' rites an' incantations as had to do with the sea-things, an' let him see some o' the folks in the village as had changed a lot from human shape. Somehaow or other, though, he never would let him see one of the reg'lar things from right aout o' the water. In the end he give him a funny kind o' thingumajig made aout o' lead or something, that he said ud bring up the fish things from any place in the water whar they might be a nest of 'em. The idee was to drop it daown with the right kind o' prayers an' sech. Walakea allaowed as the things was scattered all over the world, so's anybody that looked abaout cud find a nest an' bring 'em up ef they was wanted.

"Matt he didn't like this business at all, an' wanted Obed shud keep away from the island; but the Cap'n was sharp fer gain, an' faound he cud git them gold-like things so cheap it ud pay him to make a specialty of 'em. Things went on that way fer years, an' Obed got enough o' that gold-like stuff to make him start the refinery in Waite's old run-daown fullin' mill. He didn't dass sell the pieces like they was, fer folks ud be all the time askin' questions. All the same his crews ud git a piece an' dispose of it naow and then, even though they was swore to keep quiet; an' he let his women-folks wear some o' the pieces as was more human-like than most.

"Wal, come abaout 'thutty-eight—when I was seven year' old—Obed he faound the island people all wiped aout between v'yages. Seems the other islanders had got wind o' what was goin' on, an' had took matters into their own hands. S'pose they musta had, arter all, them old magic signs as the sea-things says was the only things they was afeard of. No tellin' what any o' them Kanakys will chance to git a holt of when the sea-bottom throws up some island with ruins older'n the deluge. Pious cusses, these was—they didn't leave nothin' standin' on either the main island or the little volcanic islet excep' what parts of the ruins was too big to knock daown. In some places they was little stones strewed abaout—like charms—with somethin' on 'em like what ye call a swastika naowadays. Prob'ly them was the Old Ones' signs. Folks all wiped aout, no trace o' no gold-like things, an' none o' the nearby Kanakys ud breathe a word abaout the matter. Wouldn't even admit they'd ever ben any people on that island.

"That naturally hit Obed pretty hard, seein' as his normal trade was doin' very poor. It hit the whole of Innsmouth, too, because in seafarin' days what profited the master of a ship gen'lly profited the crew proportionate. Most o' the folks araound the taown took the hard times kind o' sheep-like an' resigned, but they was in bad shape because the fishin' was peterin' aout an' the mills wa'n't doin' none too well.

"Then's the time Obed he begun a-cursin' at the folks fer bein' dull sheep an' prayin' to a Christian heaven as didn't help 'em none. He told 'em he'd knowed of folks as prayed to gods that give somethin' ye reely need, an' says ef a good bunch o' men ud stand by him, he cud mebbe git a holt o' sarten paowers as ud bring plenty o' fish an' quite a bit o' gold. O' course them as sarved

on the Sumatry Queen an' seed the island knowed what he meant, an' wa'n't none too anxious to git clost to sea-things like they'd heerd tell on, but them as didn't know what 'twas all abaout got kind o' swayed by what Obed had to say, an' begun to ast him what he cud do to set 'em on the way to the faith as ud bring 'em results."

Here the old man faltered, mumbled, and lapsed into a moody and apprehensive silence; glancing nervously over his shoulder and then turning back to stare fascinatedly at the distant black reef. When I spoke to him he did not answer, so I knew I would have to let him finish the bottle. The insane yarn I was hearing interested me profoundly, for I fancied there was contained within it a sort of crude allegory based upon the strangenesses of Innsmouth and elaborated by an imagination at once creative and full of scraps of exotic legend. Not for a moment did I believe that the tale had any really substantial foundation; but none the less the account held a hint of genuine terror, if only because it brought in references to strange jewels clearly akin to the malign tiara I had seen at Newburyport. Perhaps the ornaments had, after all, come from some strange island; and possibly the wild stories were lies of the bygone Obed himself rather than of this antique toper.

I handed Zadok the bottle, and he drained it to the last drop. It was curious how he could stand so much whiskey, for not even a trace of thickness had come into his high, wheezy voice. He licked the nose of the bottle and slipped it into his pocket, then beginning to nod and whisper softly to himself. I bent close to catch any articulate words he might utter, and thought I saw a sardonic smile behind the stained, bushy whiskers. Yes—he was really forming words, and I could grasp a fair proportion of them.

"Poor Matt—Matt he allus was agin' it—tried to line up the folks on his side, an' had long talks with the preachers—no use—they run the Congregational parson aout o' taown, an' the Methodist feller quit—never did see Resolved Babcock, the Baptist parson, agin—Wrath o' Jehovy—I was a mighty little critter, but I heerd what I heerd an' seen what I seen—Dagon an' Ashtoreth—Belial an' Beëlzebub—Golden Caff an' the idols o' Canaan an' the Philistines—Babylonish abominations—Mene, mene, tekel, upharsin—"

He stopped again, and from the look in his watery blue eyes I feared he was close to a stupor after all. But when I gently shook his shoulder he turned on me with astonishing alertness and snapped out some more obscure phrases.

"Dun't believe me, hey? Heh, heh, heh—then jest tell me, young feller, why Cap'n Obed an' twenty odd other folks used to row aout to Devil Reef in the dead o' night an' chant things so laoud ye cud hear 'em all over taown when the wind was right? Tell me that, hey? An' tell me why Obed was allus droppin' heavy things daown into the deep water t'other side o' the reef whar the bottom shoots daown like a cliff lower'n ye kin saound? Tell me what he done with that funny-shaped lead thingumajig as Walakea give him? Hey, boy? An' what did they all haowl on May-Eve, an' agin the next Hallowe'en? An' why'd the new church parsons—fellers as used to be sailors—wear them queer robes an' cover theirselves with them gold-like things Obed brung? Hey?"

The watery blue eyes were almost savage and maniacal

now, and the dirty white beard bristled electrically. Old Zadok probably saw me shrink back, for he had begun to cackle evilly.

"Heh, heh, heh, heh! Beginnin' to see, hey? Mebbe ye'd like to a ben me in them days, when I seed things at night aout to sea from the cupalo top o' my haouse. Oh, I kin tell ye, little pitchers hev big ears, an' I wa'n't missin' nothin' o' what was gossiped abaout Cap'n Obed an' the folks aout to the reef! Heh, heh, heh! Haow abaout the night I took my pa's ship's glass up to the cupalo an' seed the reef a-bristlin' thick with shapes that dove off quick soon's the moon riz? Obed an' the folks was in a dory, but them shapes dove off the far side into the deep water an' never come up. . . . Haow'd ye like to be a little shaver alone up in a cupalo a-watchin' shapes as wa'n't human shapes? . . . Hey? . . . Heh, heh, heh, heh. . . ."

The old man was getting hysterical, and I began to shiver with a nameless alarm. He laid a gnarled claw on my shoulder, and it seemed to me that its shaking was not altogether that of mirth.

"S'pose one night ye seed somethin' heavy heaved offen Obed's dory beyond the reef, an' then larned nex' day a young feller was missin' from home? Hey? Did anybody ever see hide or hair o' Hiram Gilman agin? Did they? An' Nick Pierce, an' Luelly Waite, an' Adoniram Saouthwick, an' Henry Garrison? Hey? Heh, heh, heh, heh. . . . Shapes talkin' sign language with their hands . . . them as had reel hands. . . .

"Wal, Sir, that was the time Obed begun to git on his feet agin. Folks see his three darters a-wearin' gold-like things as nobody'd never see on 'em afore, an' smoke started comin' aout o' the refin'ry chimbly. Other folks were prosp'rin', too—fish begun to swarm into the harbour fit to kill, an' heaven knows what sized cargoes we begun to ship aout to Newb'ryport, Arkham, an' Boston. 'Twas then Obed got the ol' branch railrud put through. Some Kingsport fishermen heerd abaout the ketch an' come up in sloops, but they was all lost. Nobody never see 'em agin. An' jest then our folks organised the Esoteric Order o' Dagon, an' bought Masonic Hall offen Calvary Commandery for it . . . heh, heh, heh! Matt Eliot was a Mason an' agin' the sellin', but he dropped aout o' sight jest then.

"Remember, I ain't sayin' Obed was set on hevin' things jest like they was on that Kanaky isle. I dun't think he aimed at fust to do no mixin', nor raise no younguns to take to the water an' turn into fishes with eternal life. He wanted them gold things, an' was willin' to pay heavy, an' I guess the others was satisfied fer a while. . . .

"Come in 'forty-six the taown done some lookin' an' thinkin' fer itself. Too many folks missin'—too much wild preachin' at meetin' of a Sunday—too much talk abaout that reef. I guess I done a bit by tellin' Selectman Mowry what I see from the cupalo. They was a party one night as follered Obed's craowd aout to the reef, an' I heerd shots betwixt the dories. Nex' day Obed an' thutty-two others was in gaol, with everbody a-wonderin' jest what was afoot an' jest what charge agin' 'em cud be got to holt. God, ef anybody'd look'd ahead . . . a couple o' weeks later, when nothin' had ben throwed into the sea fer that long.
. . ."

Zadok was shewing signs of fright and exhaustion, and I let him keep silence for a while, though glancing apprehensively at my watch. The tide had turned and was coming in now, and the sound of the waves seemed to arouse him. I was glad of that tide, for at high water the fishy smell might not be so bad. Again I strained to catch his whispers.

"That awful night . . . I seed 'em . . . I was up in the cupalo . . . hordes of 'em . . . swarms of 'em . . . all over the reef an' swimmin' up the harbour into the Manuxet. . . . God, what happened in the streets of Innsmouth that night . . . they rattled our door, but pa wouldn't open . . . then he clumb aout the kitchen winder with his musket to find Selectman Mowry an' see what he cud do. . . . Maounds o' the dead an' the dyin' . . . shots an' screams . . . shaoutin' in Ol' Squar an' Taown Squar an' New Church Green . . . gaol throwed open . . . proclamation . . . treason . . . called it the plague when folks come in an' faound haff our people missin' . . . nobody left but them as ud jine in with Obed an' them things or else keep quiet . . . never heerd o' my pa no more. . . ."

The old man was panting, and perspiring profusely. His grip on my shoulder tightened.

"Everything cleaned up in the mornin'—but they was traces. . . . Obed he kinder takes charge an' says things is goin' to be changed . . . others'll worship with us at meetin'-time, an' sarten haouses hez got to entertain guests . . . they wanted to mix like they done with the Kanakys, an' he fer one didn't feel baound to stop 'em. Far gone, was Obed . . . jest like a crazy man on the subjeck. He says they brung us fish an' treasure, an' shud hev what they hankered arter. . . .

"Nothin' was to be diff'runt on the aoutside, only

we was to keep shy o' strangers ef we knowed what was good fer us. We all hed to take the Oath o' Dagon, an' later on they was secon' an' third Oaths that some on us took. Them as ud help special, ud git special rewards— gold an' sech— No use balkin', fer they was millions of 'em daown thar. They'd ruther not start risin' an' wipin' aout humankind, but ef they was gave away an' forced to, they cud do a lot toward jest that. We didn't hev them old charms to cut 'em off like folks in the Saouth Sea did, an' them Kanakys wudn't never give away their secrets.

"Yield up enough sacrifices an' savage knick-knacks an' harbourage in the taown when they wanted it, an' they'd let well enough alone. Wudn't bother no strangers as might bear tales aoutside—that is, withaout they got pryin'. All in the band of the faithful—Order o' Dagon— an' the children shud never die, but go back to the Mother Hydra an' Father Dagon what we all come from onct—Iä! Iä! Cthulhu fhtagn! Ph'nglui mglw'nafh Cthulhu R'lyeh wgah-nagl fhtagn—"

Old Zadok was fast lapsing into stark raving, and I held my breath. Poor old soul—to what pitiful depths of hallucination had his liquor, plus his hatred of the decay, alienage, and disease around him, brought that fertile, imaginative brain! He began to moan now, and tears were coursing down his channelled cheeks into the depths of his beard.

"God, what I seen senct I was fifteen year' old— Mene, mene, tekel, upharsin!—the folks as was missin', an' them as kilt theirselves—them as told things in Arkham or Ipswich or sech places was all called crazy, like you're a-callin' me right naow—but God, what I seen— They'd a kilt me long ago fer what I know, only I'd took the fust

an' secon' Oaths o' Dagon offen Obed, so was pertected unlessen a jury of 'em proved I told things knowin' an' delib'rit . . . but I wudn't take the third Oath—I'd a died ruther'n take that—

"It got wuss araound Civil War time, when children born senct 'forty-six begun to grow up—some of 'em, that is. I was afeard—never did no pryin' arter that awful night, an' never see one of—them—clost to in all my life. That is, never no full-blooded one. I went to the war, an' ef I'd a had any guts or sense I'd a never come back, but settled away from here. But folks wrote me things wa'n't so bad. That, I s'pose, was because gov'munt draft men was in taown arter 'sixty-three. Arter the war it was jest as bad agin. People begun to fall off—mills an' shops shet daown—shippin' stopped an' the harbour choked up—railrud give up—but they . . . they never stopped swimmin' in an' aout o' the river from that cursed reef o' Satan—an' more an' more attic winders got a-boarded up, an' more an' more noises was heerd in haouses as wa'n't s'posed to hev nobody in 'em. . . .

"Folks aoutside hev their stories abaout us—s'pose you've heerd a plenty on 'em, seein' what questions ye ast—stories abaout things they've seed naow an' then, an' abaout that queer joolry as still comes in from somewhars an' ain't quite all melted up—but nothin' never gits def'nite. Nobody'll believe nothin'. They call them gold-like things pirate loot, an' allaow the Innsmouth folks hez furren blood or is distempered or somethin'. Besides, them that lives here shoo off as many strangers as they kin, an' encourage the rest not to git very cur'ous, specially raound night time. Beasts balk at the critters—hosses wuss'n mules—but when they got autos that was all right.

"In 'forty-six Cap'n Obed took a second wife that nobody in the taown never see—some says he didn't want to, but was made to by them as he'd called in—had three children by her—two as disappeared young, but one gal as looked like anybody else an' was eddicated in Europe. Obed finally got her married off by a trick to an Arkham feller as didn't suspect nothin'. But nobody aoutside'll hev nothin' to do with Innsmouth folks naow. Barnabas Marsh that runs the refin'ry naow is Obed's grandson by his fust wife—son of Onesiphorus, his eldest son, but his mother was another o' them as wa'n't never seed aoutdoors.

"Right naow Barnabas is abaout changed. Can't shet his eyes no more, an' is all aout o' shape. They say he still wears clothes, but he'll take to the water soon. Mebbe he's tried it already—they do sometimes go daown fer little spells afore they go fer good. Ain't ben seed abaout in public fer nigh on ten year'. Dun't know haow his poor wife kin feel—she come from Ipswich, an' they nigh lynched Barnabas when he courted her fifty odd year' ago. Obed he died in 'seventy-eight, an' all the next gen'ration is gone naow—the fust wife's children dead, an' the rest . . . God knows. . . ."

The sound of the incoming tide was now very insistent, and little by little it seemed to change the old man's mood from maudlin tearfulness to watchful fear. He would pause now and then to renew those nervous glances over his shoulder or out toward the reef, and despite the wild absurdity of his tale, I could not help beginning to share his vague apprehensiveness. Zadok now grew shriller, and seemed to be trying to whip up his courage with louder speech.

"Hey, yew, why dun't ye say somethin'? Haow'd ye like to be livin' in a taown like this, with everything a-rottin' an' a-dyin', an' boarded-up monsters crawlin' an' bleatin' an' barkin' an' hoppin' araoun' black cellars an' attics every way ye turn? Hey? Haow'd ye like to hear the haowlin' night arter night from the churches an' Order o' Dagon Hall, an' know what's doin' part o' the haowlin'? Haow'd ye like to hear what comes from that awful reef every May-Eve an' Hallowmass? Hey? Think the old man's crazy, eh? Wal, Sir, let me tell ye that ain't the wust!"

Zadok was really screaming now, and the mad frenzy of his voice disturbed me more than I care to own.

"Curse ye, dun't set thar a-starin' at me with them eyes—I tell Obed Marsh he's in hell, an' hez got to stay thar! Heh, heh . . . in hell, I says! Can't git me—I hain't done nothin' nor told nobody nothin'—

"Oh, you, young feller? Wal, even ef I hain't told nobody nothin' yet, I'm a-goin' to naow! You jest set still an' listen to me, boy—this is what I ain't never told nobody. . . . I says I didn't do no pryin' arter that night— but I faound things aout jest the same!

"Yew want to know what the reel horror is, hey? Wal, it's this—it ain't what them fish devils hez done, but what they're a-goin' to do! They're a-bringin' things up aout o' whar they come from into the taown—ben doin' it fer years, an' slackenin' up lately. Them haouses north o' the river betwixt Water an' Main Streets is full of 'em—them devils an' what they brung—an' when they git ready. . . . I say, when they git ready . . . ever hear tell of a shoggoth? . . .

"Hey, d'ye hear me? I tell ye I know what them things be—I seen 'em one night when . . . EH—AHHHH—AH! E'YAAHHHH. . . ."

The hideous suddenness and inhuman frightfulness of the old man's shriek almost made me faint. His eyes, looking past me toward the malodorous sea, were positively starting from his head; while his face was a mask of fear worthy of Greek tragedy. His bony claw dug monstrously into my shoulder, and he made no motion as I turned my head to look at whatever he had glimpsed.

There was nothing that I could see. Only the incoming tide, with perhaps one set of ripples more local than the long-flung line of breakers. But now Zadok was shaking me, and I turned back to watch the melting of that fear-frozen face into a chaos of twitching eyelids and mumbling gums. Presently his voice came back—albeit as a trembling whisper.

"Git aout o' here! Git aout o' here! They seen us— git aout fer your life! Dun't wait fer nothin'—they know naow— Run fer it—quick—aout o' this taown—"

Another heavy wave dashed against the loosening masonry of the bygone wharf, and changed the mad ancient's whisper to another inhuman and blood-curdling scream.

"E—YAAHHHH! . . . YHAAAAAAA! . . ."

Before I could recover my scattered wits he had relaxed his clutch on my shoulder and dashed wildly inland toward the street, reeling northward around the ruined warehouse wall.

I glanced back at the sea, but there was nothing there. And when I reached Water Street and looked along it toward the north there was no remaining trace of Zadok Allen.

IV.

I can hardly describe the mood in which I was left by this harrowing episode—an episode at once mad and pitiful, grotesque and terrifying. The grocery boy had prepared me for it, yet the reality left me none the less bewildered and disturbed. Puerile though the story was, old Zadok's insane earnestness and horror had communicated to me a mounting unrest which joined with my earlier sense of loathing for the town and its blight of intangible shadow.

Later I might sift the tale and extract some nucleus of historic allegory; just now I wished to put it out of my head. The hour had grown perilously late—my watch said 7:15, and the Arkham bus left Town Square at eight—so I tried to give my thoughts as neutral and practical a cast as possible, meanwhile walking rapidly through the deserted streets of gaping roofs and leaning houses toward the hotel where I had checked my valise and would find my bus.

Though the golden light of late afternoon gave the ancient roofs and decrepit chimneys an air of mystic loveliness and peace, I could not help glancing over my shoulder now and then. I would surely be very glad to get out of malodorous and fear-shadowed Innsmouth, and wished there were some other vehicle than the bus driven by that sinister-looking fellow Sargent. Yet I did not hurry too precipitately, for there were architectural details worth viewing at every silent corner; and I could easily, I calculated, cover the necessary distance in a half-hour.

Studying the grocery youth's map and seeking a route I had not traversed before, I chose Marsh Street instead of State for my approach to Town Square. Near the corner of Fall Street I began to see scattered groups of furtive whisperers, and when I finally reached the Square I saw that almost all the loiterers were congregated around the door of the Gilman House. It seemed as if many bulging, watery, unwinking eyes looked oddly at me as I claimed my valise in the lobby, and I hoped that none of these unpleasant creatures would be my fellow-passengers on the coach.

The bus, rather early, rattled in with three passengers somewhat before eight, and an evil-looking fellow on the sidewalk muttered a few indistinguishable words to the driver. Sargent threw out a mail-bag and a roll of newspapers, and entered the hotel; while the passengers—the same men whom I had seen arriving in Newburyport that morning—shambled to the sidewalk and exchanged some faint guttural words with a loafer in a language I could have sworn was not English. I boarded the empty coach and took the same seat I had taken before, but was hardly settled before Sargent reappeared and began mumbling in a throaty voice of peculiar repulsiveness.

I was, it appeared, in very bad luck. There had been something wrong with the engine, despite the excellent time made from Newburyport, and the bus could not complete the journey to Arkham. No, it could not

possibly be repaired that night, nor was there any other way of getting transportation out of Innsmouth, either to Arkham or elsewhere. Sargent was sorry, but I would have to stop over at the Gilman. Probably the clerk would make the price easy for me, but there was nothing else to do. Almost dazed by this sudden obstacle, and violently dreading the fall of night in this decaying and half-unlighted town, I left the bus and reëntered the hotel lobby; where the sullen, queer-looking night clerk told me I could have Room 428 on next the top floor—large, but without running water—for a dollar.

Despite what I had heard of this hotel in Newburyport, I signed the register, paid my dollar, let the clerk take my valise, and followed that sour, solitary attendant up three creaking flights of stairs past dusty corridors which seemed wholly devoid of life. My room, a dismal rear one with two windows and bare, cheap furnishings, overlooked a dingy courtyard otherwise hemmed in by low, deserted brick blocks, and commanded a view of decrepit westward-stretching roofs with a marshy countryside beyond. At the end of the corridor was a bathroom—a discouraging relique with ancient marble bowl, tin tub, faint electric light, and musty wooden panelling around all the plumbing fixtures.

It being still daylight, I descended to the Square and looked around for a dinner of some sort; noticing as I did so the strange glances I received from the unwholesome loafers. Since the grocery was closed, I was forced to patronise the restaurant I had shunned before; a stooped, narrow-headed man with staring, unwinking eyes, and a flat-nosed wench with unbelievably thick, clumsy hands being in attendance. The service was of the counter type, and it relieved me to find that much was evidently served from cans and packages. A bowl of vegetable soup with crackers was enough for me, and I soon headed back for my cheerless room at the Gilman; getting an evening paper and a flyspecked magazine from the evil-visaged clerk at the rickety stand beside his desk.

As twilight deepened I turned on the one feeble electric bulb over the cheap, iron-framed bed, and tried as best I could to continue the reading I had begun. I felt it advisable to keep my mind wholesomely occupied, for it would not do to brood over the abnormalities of this ancient, blight-shadowed town while I was still within its borders. The insane yarn I had heard from the aged drunkard did not promise very pleasant dreams, and I felt I must keep the image of his wild, watery eyes as far as possible from my imagination.

Also, I must not dwell on what that factory inspector had told the Newburyport ticket-agent about the Gilman House and the voices of its nocturnal tenants—not on that, nor on the face beneath the tiara in the black church doorway; the face for whose horror my conscious mind could not account. It would perhaps have been easier to keep my thoughts from disturbing topics had the room not been so gruesomely musty. As it was, the lethal mustiness blended hideously with the town's general fishy odour and persistently focussed one's fancy on death and decay.

Another thing that disturbed me was the absence of a bolt on the door of my room. One had been there, as marks clearly shewed, but there were signs of recent removal. No doubt it had become out of order, like so many other things in this decrepit edifice. In my nervousness I looked around and discovered a bolt on

the clothes-press which seemed to be of the same size, judging from the marks, as the one formerly on the door. To gain a partial relief from the general tension I busied myself by transferring this hardware to the vacant place with the aid of a handy three-in-one device including a screw-driver which I kept on my key-ring. The bolt fitted perfectly, and I was somewhat relieved when I knew that I could shoot it firmly upon retiring. Not that I had any real apprehension of its need, but that any symbol of security was welcome in an environment of this kind. There were adequate bolts on the two lateral doors to connecting rooms, and these I proceeded to fasten.

I did not undress, but decided to read till I was sleepy and then lie down with only my coat, collar, and shoes off. Taking a pocket flashlight from my valise, I placed it in my trousers, so that I could read my watch if I woke up later in the dark. Drowsiness, however, did not come; and when I stopped to analyse my thoughts I found to my disquiet that I was really unconsciously listening for something—listening for something which I dreaded but could not name. That inspector's story must have worked on my imagination more deeply than I had suspected. Again I tried to read, but found that I made no progress.

After a time I seemed to hear the stairs and corridors creak at intervals as if with footsteps, and wondered if the other rooms were beginning to fill up. There were no voices, however, and it struck me that there was something subtly furtive about the creaking. I did not like it, and debated whether I had better try to sleep at all. This town had some queer people, and there had undoubtedly been several disappearances. Was this one of those inns where travellers were slain for their money? Surely I had no look of excessive prosperity. Or were the townsfolk really so resentful about curious visitors? Had my obvious sightseeing, with its frequent map-consultations, aroused unfavourable notice? It occurred to me that I must be in a highly nervous state to let a few random creakings set me off speculating in this fashion—but I regretted none the less that I was unarmed.

At length, feeling a fatigue which had nothing of drowsiness in it, I bolted the newly outfitted hall door, turned off the light, and threw myself down on the hard, uneven bed—coat, collar, shoes, and all. In the darkness every faint noise of the night seemed magnified, and a flood of doubly unpleasant thoughts swept over me. I was sorry I had put out the light, yet was too tired to rise and turn it on again. Then, after a long, dreary interval, and prefaced by a fresh creaking of stairs and corridor, there came that soft, damnably unmistakable sound which seemed like a malign fulfilment of all my apprehensions. Without the least shadow of a doubt, the lock on my hall door was being tried—cautiously, furtively, tentatively— with a key.

My sensations upon recognising this sign of actual peril were perhaps less rather than more tumultuous because of my previous vague fears. I had been, albeit without definite reason, instinctively on my guard— and that was to my advantage in the new and real crisis, whatever it might turn out to be. Nevertheless the change in the menace from vague premonition to immediate reality was a profound shock, and fell upon me with the force of a genuine blow. It never once occurred to me that the fumbling might be a mere mistake. Malign purpose was all I could think of, and I kept deathly quiet, awaiting the would-be intruder's next move.

After a time the cautious rattling ceased, and I heard the room to the north entered with a pass-key. Then the lock of the connecting door to my room was softly tried. The bolt held, of course, and I heard the floor creak as the prowler left the room. After a moment there came another soft rattling, and I knew that the room to the south of me was being entered. Again a furtive trying of a bolted connecting door, and again a receding creaking. This time the creaking went along the hall and down the stairs, so I knew that the prowler had realised the bolted condition of my doors and was giving up his attempt for a greater or lesser time, as the future would shew.

The readiness with which I fell into a plan of action proves that I must have been subconsciously fearing some menace and considering possible avenues of escape for hours. From the first I felt that the unseen fumbler meant a danger not to be met or dealt with, but only to be fled from as precipitately as possible. The one thing to do was to get out of that hotel alive as quickly as I could, and through some channel other than the front stairs and lobby.

Rising softly and throwing my flashlight on the switch, I sought to light the bulb over my bed in order to choose and pocket some belongings for a swift, valiseless flight. Nothing, however, happened; and I saw that the power had been cut off. Clearly, some cryptic, evil movement was afoot on a large scale—just what, I could not say. As I stood pondering with my hand on the now useless switch I heard a muffled creaking on the floor below, and thought I could barely distinguish voices in conversation. A moment later I felt less sure that the deeper sounds were voices, since the apparent hoarse barkings and loose-syllabled croakings bore so little resemblance to recognised human speech. Then I thought with renewed force of what the factory inspector had heard in the night in this mouldering and pestilential building.

Having filled my pockets with the flashlight's aid, I put on my hat and tiptoed to the windows to consider chances of descent. Despite the state's safety regulations there was no fire escape on this side of the hotel, and I saw that my windows commanded only a sheer three-story drop to the cobbled courtyard. On the right and left, however, some ancient brick business blocks abutted on the hotel; their slant roofs coming up to a reasonable jumping distance from my fourth-story level. To reach either of these lines of buildings I would have to be in a room two doors from my own—in one case on the north and in the other case on the south—and my mind instantly set to work calculating what chances I had of making the transfer.

I could not, I decided, risk an emergence into the corridor; where my footsteps would surely be heard, and where the difficulties of entering the desired room would be insuperable. My progress, if it was to be made at all, would have to be through the less solidly built connecting doors of the rooms; the locks and bolts of which I would have to force violently, using my shoulder as a battering-ram whenever they were set against me. This, I thought, would be possible owing to the rickety nature of the house and its fixtures; but I realised I could not do it noiselessly. I would have to count on sheer speed, and the chance of getting to a window before any hostile forces became coördinated enough to open the right door toward me with a pass-key. My own outer door I reinforced by pushing the bureau against it—little by little, in order to make a minimum of sound.

I perceived that my chances were very slender, and was fully prepared for any calamity. Even getting to another roof would not solve the problem, for there would then remain the task of reaching the ground and escaping from the town. One thing in my favour was the deserted and ruinous state of the abutting buildings, and the number of skylights gaping blackly open in each row.

Gathering from the grocery boy's map that the best route out of town was southward, I glanced first at the connecting door on the south side of the room. It was designed to open in my direction, hence I saw—after drawing the bolt and finding other fastenings in place—it was not a favourable one for forcing. Accordingly abandoning it as a route, I cautiously moved the bedstead against it to hamper any attack which might be made on it later from the next room. The door on the north was hung to open away from me, and this—though a test proved it to be locked or bolted from the other side—I knew must be my route. If I could gain the roofs of the buildings in Paine Street and descend successfully to the ground level, I might perhaps dart through the courtyard and the adjacent or opposite buildings to Washington or Bates—or else emerge in Paine and edge around southward into Washington. In any case, I would aim to strike Washington somehow and get quickly out of the Town Square region. My preference would be to avoid Paine, since the fire station there might be open all night.

As I thought of these things I looked out over the squalid sea of decaying roofs below me, now brightened by the beams of a moon not much past full. On the right the black gash of the river-gorge clove the panorama; abandoned factories and railway station clinging barnacle-like to its sides. Beyond it the rusted railway and the Rowley road led off through a flat, marshy terrain dotted with islets of higher and dryer scrub-grown land. On the left the creek-threaded countryside was nearer, the narrow road to Ipswich gleaming white in the moonlight. I could not see from my side of the hotel the southward route toward Arkham which I had determined to take.

I was irresolutely speculating on when I had better attack the northward door, and on how I could least audibly manage it, when I noticed that the vague noises underfoot had given place to a fresh and heavier creaking of the stairs. A wavering flicker of light shewed through my transom, and the boards of the corridor began to groan with a ponderous load. Muffled sounds of possible vocal origin approached, and at length a firm knock came at my outer door.

For a moment I simply held my breath and waited. Eternities seemed to elapse, and the nauseous fishy odour of my environment seemed to mount suddenly and spectacularly. Then the knocking was repeated—continuously, and with growing insistence. I knew that the time for action had come, and forthwith drew the bolt of the northward connecting door, bracing myself for the task of battering it open. The knocking waxed louder, and I hoped that its volume would cover the sound of my efforts. At last beginning my attempt, I lunged again and again at the thin panelling with my left shoulder, heedless of shock or pain. The door resisted even more than I had expected, but I did not give in. And all the while the clamour at the outer door increased.

Finally the connecting door gave, but with such a crash that I knew those outside must have heard. Instantly

the outside knocking became a violent battering, while keys sounded ominously in the hall doors of the rooms on both sides of me. Rushing through the newly opened connexion, I succeeded in bolting the northerly hall door before the lock could be turned; but even as I did so I heard the hall door of the third room—the one from whose window I had hoped to reach the roof below— being tried with a pass-key.

For an instant I felt absolute despair, since my trapping in a chamber with no window egress seemed complete. A wave of almost abnormal horror swept over me, and invested with a terrible but unexplainable singularity the flashlight-glimpsed dust prints made by the intruder who had lately tried my door from this room. Then, with a dazed automatism which persisted despite hopelessness, I made for the next connecting door and performed the blind motion of pushing at it in an effort to get through and—granting that fastenings might be as providentially intact as in this second room—bolt the hall door beyond before the lock could be turned from outside.

Sheer fortunate chance gave me my reprieve—for the connecting door before me was not only unlocked but actually ajar. In a second I was through, and had my right knee and shoulder against a hall door which was visibly opening inward. My pressure took the opener off guard, for the thing shut as I pushed, so that I could slip the well-conditioned bolt as I had done with the other door. As I gained this respite I heard the battering at the two other doors abate, while a confused clatter came from the connecting door I had shielded with the bedstead. Evidently the bulk of my assailants had entered the southerly room and were massing in a lateral attack. But at the same moment a pass-key sounded in the next door

to the north, and I knew that a nearer peril was at hand.

The northward connecting door was wide open, but there was no time to think about checking the already turning lock in the hall. All I could do was to shut and bolt the open connecting door, as well as its mate on the opposite side—pushing a bedstead against the one and a bureau against the other, and moving a washstand in front of the hall door. I must, I saw, trust to such makeshift barriers to shield me till I could get out the window and on the roof of the Paine Street block. But even in this acute moment my chief horror was something apart from the immediate weakness of my defences. I was shuddering because not one of my pursuers, despite some hideous pantings, gruntings, and subdued barkings at odd intervals, was uttering an unmuffled or intelligible vocal sound.

As I moved the furniture and rushed toward the windows I heard a frightful scurrying along the corridor toward the room north of me, and perceived that the southward battering had ceased. Plainly, most of my opponents were about to concentrate against the feeble connecting door which they knew must open directly on me. Outside, the moon played on the ridgepole of the block below, and I saw that the jump would be desperately hazardous because of the steep surface on which I must land.

Surveying the conditions, I chose the more southerly of the two windows as my avenue of escape; planning to land on the inner slope of the roof and make for the nearest skylight. Once inside one of the decrepit brick structures I would have to reckon with pursuit; but I hoped to descend and dodge in and out of yawning

doorways along the shadowed courtyard, eventually getting to Washington Street and slipping out of town toward the south.

The clatter at the northerly connecting door was now terrific, and I saw that the weak panelling was beginning to splinter. Obviously, the besiegers had brought some ponderous object into play as a battering-ram. The bedstead, however, still held firm; so that I had at least a faint chance of making good my escape. As I opened the window I noticed that it was flanked by heavy velour draperies suspended from a pole by brass rings, and also that there was a large projecting catch for the shutters on the exterior. Seeing a possible means of avoiding the dangerous jump, I yanked at the hangings and brought them down, pole and all; then quickly hooking two of the rings in the shutter catch and flinging the drapery outside. The heavy folds reached fully to the abutting roof, and I saw that the rings and catch would be likely to bear my weight. So, climbing out of the window and down the improvised rope ladder, I left behind me forever the morbid and horror-infested fabric of the Gilman House.

I landed safely on the loose slates of the steep roof, and succeeded in gaining the gaping black skylight without a slip. Glancing up at the window I had left, I observed it was still dark, though far across the crumbling chimneys to the north I could see lights ominously blazing in the Order of Dagon Hall, the Baptist church, and the Congregational church which I recalled so shiveringly. There had seemed to be no one in the courtyard below, and I hoped there would be a chance to get away before the spreading of a general alarm. Flashing my pocket lamp into the skylight, I saw that there were no steps down. The distance was slight, however, so I clambered over the brink and dropped; striking a dusty floor littered with crumbling boxes and barrels.

The place was ghoulish-looking, but I was past minding such impressions and made at once for the staircase revealed by my flashlight—after a hasty glance at my watch, which shewed the hour to be 2 a.m. The steps creaked, but seemed tolerably sound; and I raced down past a barn-like second story to the ground floor. The desolation was complete, and only echoes answered my footfalls. At length I reached the lower hall, at one end of which I saw a faint luminous rectangle marking the ruined Paine Street doorway. Heading the other way, I found the back door also open; and darted out and down five stone steps to the grass-grown cobblestones of the courtyard.

The moonbeams did not reach down here, but I could just see my way about without using the flashlight. Some of the windows on the Gilman House side were faintly glowing, and I thought I heard confused sounds within. Walking softly over to the Washington Street side I perceived several open doorways, and chose the nearest as my route out. The hallway inside was black, and when I reached the opposite end I saw that the street door was wedged immovably shut. Resolved to try another building, I groped my way back toward the courtyard, but stopped short when close to the doorway.

For out of an opened door in the Gilman House a large crowd of doubtful shapes was pouring—lanterns bobbing in the darkness, and horrible croaking voices exchanging low cries in what was certainly not English. The figures moved uncertainly, and I realised to my relief that they did not know where I had gone; but for all that they sent

a shiver of horror through my frame. Their features were indistinguishable, but their crouching, shambling gait was abominably repellent. And worst of all, I perceived that one figure was strangely robed, and unmistakably surmounted by a tall tiara of a design altogether too familiar. As the figures spread throughout the courtyard, I felt my fears increase. Suppose I could find no egress from this building on the street side? The fishy odour was detestable, and I wondered I could stand it without fainting. Again groping toward the street, I opened a door off the hall and came upon an empty room with closely shuttered but sashless windows. Fumbling in the rays of my flashlight, I found I could open the shutters; and in another moment had climbed outside and was carefully closing the aperture in its original manner.

I was now in Washington Street, and for the moment saw no living thing nor any light save that of the moon. From several directions in the distance, however, I could hear the sound of hoarse voices, of footsteps, and of a curious kind of pattering which did not sound quite like footsteps. Plainly I had no time to lose. The points of the compass were clear to me, and I was glad that all the street-lights were turned off, as is often the custom on strongly moonlit nights in unprosperous rural regions. Some of the sounds came from the south, yet I retained my design of escaping in that direction. There would, I knew, be plenty of deserted doorways to shelter me in case I met any person or group who looked like pursuers.

I walked rapidly, softly, and close to the ruined houses. While hatless and dishevelled after my arduous climb, I did not look especially noticeable; and stood a good chance of passing unheeded if forced to encounter any casual wayfarer. At Bates Street I drew into a yawning vestibule while two shambling figures crossed in front of me, but was soon on my way again and approaching the open space where Eliot Street obliquely crosses Washington at the intersection of South. Though I had never seen this space, it had looked dangerous to me on the grocery youth's map; since the moonlight would have free play there. There was no use trying to evade it, for any alternative course would involve detours of possibly disastrous visibility and delaying effect. The only thing to do was to cross it boldly and openly; imitating the typical shamble of the Innsmouth folk as best I could, and trusting that no one—or at least no pursuer of mine— would be there.

Just how fully the pursuit was organised—and indeed, just what its purpose might be—I could form no idea. There seemed to be unusual activity in the town, but I judged that the news of my escape from the Gilman had not yet spread. I would, of course, soon have to shift from Washington to some other southward street; for that party from the hotel would doubtless be after me. I must have left dust prints in that last old building, revealing how I had gained the street.

The open space was, as I had expected, strongly moonlit; and I saw the remains of a park-like, iron-railed green in its centre. Fortunately no one was about, though a curious sort of buzz or roar seemed to be increasing in the direction of Town Square. South Street was very wide, leading directly down a slight declivity to the waterfront and commanding a long view out at sea; and I hoped that no one would be glancing up it from afar as I crossed in the bright moonlight.

My progress was unimpeded, and no fresh sound

arose to hint that I had been spied. Glancing about me, I involuntarily let my pace slacken for a second to take in the sight of the sea, gorgeous in the burning moonlight at the street's end. Far out beyond the breakwater was the dim, dark line of Devil Reef, and as I glimpsed it I could not help thinking of all the hideous legends I had heard in the last thirty-four hours—legends which portrayed this ragged rock as a veritable gateway to realms of unfathomed horror and inconceivable abnormality.

Then, without warning, I saw the intermittent flashes of light on the distant reef. They were definite and unmistakable, and awaked in my mind a blind horror beyond all rational proportion. My muscles tightened for panic flight, held in only by a certain unconscious caution and half-hypnotic fascination. And to make matters worse, there now flashed forth from the lofty cupola of the Gilman House, which loomed up to the northeast behind me, a series of analogous though differently spaced gleams which could be nothing less than an answering signal.

Controlling my muscles, and realising afresh how plainly visible I was, I resumed my brisker and feignedly shambling pace; though keeping my eyes on that hellish and ominous reef as long as the opening of South Street gave me a seaward view. What the whole proceeding meant, I could not imagine; unless it involved some strange rite connected with Devil Reef, or unless some party had landed from a ship on that sinister rock. I now bent to the left around the ruinous green; still gazing toward the ocean as it blazed in the spectral summer moonlight, and watching the cryptical flashing of those nameless, unexplainable beacons.

It was then that the most horrible impression of all was borne in upon me—the impression which destroyed my last vestige of self-control and set me running frantically southward past the yawning black doorways and fishily staring windows of that deserted nightmare street. For at a closer glance I saw that the moonlit waters between the reef and the shore were far from empty. They were alive with a teeming horde of shapes swimming inward toward the town; and even at my vast distance and in my single moment of perception I could tell that the bobbing heads and flailing arms were alien and aberrant in a way scarcely to be expressed or consciously formulated.

My frantic running ceased before I had covered a block, for at my left I began to hear something like the hue and cry of organised pursuit. There were footsteps and guttural sounds, and a rattling motor wheezed south along Federal Street. In a second all my plans were utterly changed—for if the southward highway were blocked ahead of me, I must clearly find another egress from Innsmouth. I paused and drew into a gaping doorway, reflecting how lucky I was to have left the moonlit open space before these pursuers came down the parallel street.

A second reflection was less comforting. Since the pursuit was down another street, it was plain that the party was not following me directly. It had not seen me, but was simply obeying a general plan of cutting off my escape. This, however, implied that all roads leading out of Innsmouth were similarly patrolled; for the denizens could not have known what route I intended to take. If this were so, I would have to make my retreat across country away from any road; but how could I do that in view of the marshy and creek-riddled nature of all the surrounding region? For a moment my brain reeled—

both from sheer hopelessness and from a rapid increase in the omnipresent fishy odour.

Then I thought of the abandoned railway to Rowley, whose solid line of ballasted, weed-grown earth still stretched off to the northwest from the crumbling station on the edge of the river-gorge. There was just a chance that the townsfolk would not think of that; since its brier-choked desertion made it half-impassable, and the unlikeliest of all avenues for a fugitive to choose. I had seen it clearly from my hotel window, and knew about how it lay. Most of its earlier length was uncomfortably visible from the Rowley road, and from high places in the town itself; but one could perhaps crawl inconspicuously through the undergrowth. At any rate, it would form my only chance of deliverance, and there was nothing to do but try it.

Drawing inside the hall of my deserted shelter, I once more consulted the grocery boy's map with the aid of the flashlight. The immediate problem was how to reach the ancient railway; and I now saw that the safest course was ahead to Babson Street, then west to Lafayette—there edging around but not crossing an open space homologous to the one I had traversed—and subsequently back northward and westward in a zigzagging line through Lafayette, Bates, Adams, and Bank Streets—the latter skirting the river-gorge—to the abandoned and dilapidated station I had seen from my window. My reason for going ahead to Babson was that I wished neither to re-cross the earlier open space nor to begin my westward course along a cross street as broad as South.

Starting once more, I crossed the street to the

right-hand side in order to edge around into Babson as inconspicuously as possible. Noises still continued in Federal Street, and as I glanced behind me I thought I saw a gleam of light near the building through which I had escaped. Anxious to leave Washington Street, I broke into a quiet dog-trot, trusting to luck not to encounter any observing eye. Next the corner of Babson Street I saw to my alarm that one of the houses was still inhabited, as attested by curtains at the window; but there were no lights within, and I passed it without disaster.

In Babson Street, which crossed Federal and might thus reveal me to the searchers, I clung as closely as possible to the sagging, uneven buildings; twice pausing in a doorway as the noises behind me momentarily increased. The open space ahead shone wide and desolate under the moon, but my route would not force me to cross it. During my second pause I began to detect a fresh distribution of the vague sounds; and upon looking cautiously out from cover beheld a motor-car darting across the open space, bound outward along Eliot Street, which there intersects both Babson and Lafayette.

As I watched—choked by a sudden rise in the fishy odour after a short abatement—I saw a band of uncouth, crouching shapes loping and shambling in the same direction; and knew that this must be the party guarding the Ipswich road, since that highway forms an extension of Eliot Street. Two of the figures I glimpsed were in voluminous robes, and one wore a peaked diadem which glistened whitely in the moonlight. The gait of this figure was so odd that it sent a chill through me—for it seemed to me the creature was almost hopping.

When the last of the band was out of sight I resumed

my progress; darting around the corner into Lafayette Street, and crossing Eliot very hurriedly lest stragglers of the party be still advancing along that thoroughfare. I did hear some croaking and clattering sounds far off toward Town Square, but accomplished the passage without disaster. My greatest dread was in re-crossing broad and moonlit South Street—with its seaward view—and I had to nerve myself for the ordeal. Someone might easily be looking, and possible Eliot Street stragglers could not fail to glimpse me from either of two points. At the last moment I decided I had better slacken my trot and make the crossing as before in the shambling gait of an average Innsmouth native.

When the view of the water again opened out— this time on my right—I was half-determined not to look at it at all. I could not, however, resist; but cast a sidelong glance as I carefully and imitatively shambled toward the protecting shadows ahead. There was no ship visible, as I had half expected there would be. Instead, the first thing which caught my eye was a small rowboat pulling in toward the abandoned wharves and laden with some bulky, tarpaulin-covered object. Its rowers, though distantly and indistinctly seen, were of an especially repellent aspect. Several swimmers were still discernible; while on the far black reef I could see a faint, steady glow unlike the winking beacon visible before, and of a curious colour which I could not precisely identify. Above the slant roofs ahead and to the right there loomed the tall cupola of the Gilman House, but it was completely dark. The fishy odour, dispelled for a moment by some merciful breeze, now closed in again with maddening intensity.

I had not quite crossed the street when I heard a muttering band advancing along Washington from the north. As they reached the broad open space where I had had my first disquieting glimpse of the moonlit water I could see them plainly only a block away—and was horrified by the bestial abnormality of their faces and the dog-like sub-humanness of their crouching gait. One man moved in a positively simian way, with long arms frequently touching the ground; while another figure—robed and tiaraed—seemed to progress in an almost hopping fashion. I judged this party to be the one I had seen in the Gilman's courtyard—the one, therefore, most closely on my trail. As some of the figures turned to look in my direction I was transfixed with fright, yet managed to preserve the casual, shambling gait I had assumed. To this day I do not know whether they saw me or not. If they did, my stratagem must have deceived them, for they passed on across the moonlit space without varying their course—meanwhile croaking and jabbering in some hateful guttural patois I could not identify.

Once more in shadow, I resumed my former dog-trot past the leaning and decrepit houses that stared blankly into the night. Having crossed to the western sidewalk I rounded the nearest corner into Bates Street, where I kept close to the buildings on the southern side. I passed two houses shewing signs of habitation, one of which had faint lights in upper rooms, yet met with no obstacle. As I turned into Adams Street I felt measurably safer, but received a shock when a man reeled out of a black doorway directly in front of me. He proved, however, too hopelessly drunk to be a menace; so that I reached the dismal ruins of the Bank Street warehouses in safety.

No one was stirring in that dead street beside the river-gorge, and the roar of the waterfalls quite drowned my footsteps. It was a long dog-trot to the ruined station,

and the great brick warehouse walls around me seemed somehow more terrifying than the fronts of private houses. At last I saw the ancient arcaded station—or what was left of it—and made directly for the tracks that started from its farther end.

The rails were rusty but mainly intact, and not more than half the ties had rotted away. Walking or running on such a surface was very difficult; but I did my best, and on the whole made very fair time. For some distance the line kept on along the gorge's brink, but at length I reached the long covered bridge where it crossed the chasm at a dizzy height. The condition of this bridge would determine my next step. If humanly possible, I would use it; if not, I would have to risk more street wandering and take the nearest intact highway bridge.

The vast, barn-like length of the old bridge gleamed spectrally in the moonlight, and I saw that the ties were safe for at least a few feet within. Entering, I began to use my flashlight, and was almost knocked down by the cloud of bats that flapped past me. About half way across there was a perilous gap in the ties which I feared for a moment would halt me; but in the end I risked a desperate jump which fortunately succeeded.

I was glad to see the moonlight again when I emerged from that macabre tunnel. The old tracks crossed River Street at grade, and at once veered off into a region increasingly rural and with less and less of Innsmouth's abhorrent fishy odour. Here the dense growth of weeds and briers hindered me and cruelly tore my clothes, but I was none the less glad that they were there to give me concealment in case of peril. I knew that much of my route must be visible from the Rowley road.

The marshy region began very shortly, with the single track on a low, grassy embankment where the weedy growth was somewhat thinner. Then came a sort of island of higher ground, where the line passed through a shallow open cut choked with bushes and brambles. I was very glad of this partial shelter, since at this point the Rowley road was uncomfortably near according to my window view. At the end of the cut it would cross the track and swerve off to a safer distance; but meanwhile I must be exceedingly careful. I was by this time thankfully certain that the railway itself was not patrolled.

Just before entering the cut I glanced behind me, but saw no pursuer. The ancient spires and roofs of decaying Innsmouth gleamed lovely and ethereal in the magic yellow moonlight, and I thought of how they must have looked in the old days before the shadow fell. Then, as my gaze circled inland from the town, something less tranquil arrested my notice and held me immobile for a second.

What I saw—or fancied I saw—was a disturbing suggestion of undulant motion far to the south; a suggestion which made me conclude that a very large horde must be pouring out of the city along the level Ipswich road. The distance was great, and I could distinguish nothing in detail; but I did not at all like the look of that moving column. It undulated too much, and glistened too brightly in the rays of the now westering moon. There was a suggestion of sound, too, though the wind was blowing the other way—a suggestion of bestial scraping and bellowing even worse than the muttering of the parties I had lately overheard.

All sorts of unpleasant conjectures crossed my mind. I thought of those very extreme Innsmouth types said to be hidden in crumbling, centuried warrens near the waterfront. I thought, too, of those nameless swimmers I had seen. Counting the parties so far glimpsed, as well as those presumably covering other roads, the number of my pursuers must be strangely large for a town as depopulated as Innsmouth.

Whence could come the dense personnel of such a column as I now beheld? Did those ancient, unplumbed warrens teem with a twisted, uncatalogued, and unsuspected life? Or had some unseen ship indeed landed a legion of unknown outsiders on that hellish reef? Who were they? Why were they there? And if such a column of them was scouring the Ipswich road, would the patrols on the other roads be likewise augmented?

I had entered the brush-grown cut and was struggling along at a very slow pace when that damnable fishy odour again waxed dominant. Had the wind suddenly changed eastward, so that it blew in from the sea and over the town? It must have, I concluded, since I now began to hear shocking guttural murmurs from that hitherto silent direction. There was another sound, too—a kind of wholesale, colossal flopping or pattering which somehow called up images of the most detestable sort. It made me think illogically of that unpleasantly undulating column on the far-off Ipswich road.

And then both stench and sounds grew stronger, so that I paused shivering and grateful for the cut's protection. It was here, I recalled, that the Rowley road drew so close to the old railway before crossing westward and diverging. Something was coming along that road, and I must lie low till its passage and vanishment in the distance. Thank heaven these creatures employed no dogs for tracking—though perhaps that would have been impossible amidst the omnipresent regional odour. Crouched in the bushes of that sandy cleft I felt reasonably safe, even though I knew the searchers would have to cross the track in front of me not much more than a hundred yards away. I would be able to see them, but they could not, except by a malign miracle, see me.

All at once I began dreading to look at them as they passed. I saw the close moonlit space where they would surge by, and had curious thoughts about the irredeemable pollution of that space. They would perhaps be the worst of all Innsmouth types—something one would not care to remember.

The stench waxed overpowering, and the noises swelled to a bestial babel of croaking, baying, and barking without the least suggestion of human speech. Were these indeed the voices of my pursuers? Did they have dogs after all? So far I had seen none of the lower animals in Innsmouth. That flopping or pattering was monstrous—I could not look upon the degenerate creatures responsible for it. I would keep my eyes shut till the sounds receded toward the west. The horde was very close now—the air foul with their hoarse snarlings, and the ground almost shaking with their alien-rhythmed footfalls. My breath nearly ceased to come, and I put every ounce of will power into the task of holding my eyelids down.

I am not even yet willing to say whether what followed was a hideous actuality or only a nightmare hallucination. The later action of the government, after my frantic appeals, would tend to confirm it as a monstrous truth;

but could not an hallucination have been repeated under the quasi-hypnotic spell of that ancient, haunted, and shadowed town? Such places have strange properties, and the legacy of insane legend might well have acted on more than one human imagination amidst those dead, stench-cursed streets and huddles of rotting roofs and crumbling steeples. Is it not possible that the germ of an actual contagious madness lurks in the depths of that shadow over Innsmouth? Who can be sure of reality after hearing things like the tale of old Zadok Allen? The government men never found poor Zadok, and have no conjectures to make as to what became of him. Where does madness leave off and reality begin? Is it possible that even my latest fear is sheer delusion?

But I must try to tell what I thought I saw that night under the mocking yellow moon—saw surging and hopping down the Rowley road in plain sight in front of me as I crouched among the wild brambles of that desolate railway cut. Of course my resolution to keep my eyes shut had failed. It was foredoomed to failure—for who could crouch blindly while a legion of croaking, baying entities of unknown source flopped noisomely past, scarcely more than a hundred yards away?

I thought I was prepared for the worst, and I really ought to have been prepared considering what I had seen before. My other pursuers had been accursedly abnormal—so should I not have been ready to face a strengthening of the abnormal element; to look upon forms in which there was no mixture of the normal at all? I did not open my eyes until the raucous clamour came loudly from a point obviously straight ahead. Then I knew that a long section of them must be plainly in sight where the sides of the cut flattened out and the road crossed the track—and I could no longer keep myself from sampling whatever horror that leering yellow moon might have to shew.

It was the end, for whatever remains to me of life on the surface of this earth, of every vestige of mental peace and confidence in the integrity of Nature and of the human mind. Nothing that I could have imagined— nothing, even, that I could have gathered had I credited old Zadok's crazy tale in the most literal way—would be in any way comparable to the daemoniac, blasphemous reality that I saw—or believe I saw. I have tried to hint what it was in order to postpone the horror of writing it down baldly. Can it be possible that this planet has actually spawned such things; that human eyes have truly seen, as objective flesh, what man has hitherto known only in febrile phantasy and tenuous legend?

And yet I saw them in a limitless stream—flopping, hopping, croaking, bleating—surging inhumanly through the spectral moonlight in a grotesque, malignant saraband of fantastic nightmare. And some of them had tall tiaras of that nameless whitish-gold metal . . . and some were strangely robed . . . and one, who led the way, was clad in a ghoulishly humped black coat and striped trousers, and had a man's felt hat perched on the shapeless thing that answered for a head. . . .

I think their predominant colour was a greyish-green, though they had white bellies. They were mostly shiny and slippery, but the ridges of their backs were scaly. Their forms vaguely suggested the anthropoid, while their heads were the heads of fish, with prodigious bulging eyes that never closed. At the sides of their necks were palpitating gills, and their long paws were webbed.

They hopped irregularly, sometimes on two legs and sometimes on four. I was somehow glad that they had no more than four limbs. Their croaking, baying voices, clearly used for articulate speech, held all the dark shades of expression which their staring faces lacked.

But for all of their monstrousness they were not unfamiliar to me. I knew too well what they must be—for was not the memory of that evil tiara at Newburyport still fresh? They were the blasphemous fish-frogs of the nameless design—living and horrible—and as I saw them I knew also of what that humped, tiaraed priest in the black church basement had so fearsomely reminded me. Their number was past guessing. It seemed to me that there were limitless swarms of them—and certainly my momentary glimpse could have shewn only the least fraction. In another instant everything was blotted out by a merciful fit of fainting; the first I had ever had.

V.

It was a gentle daylight rain that awaked me from my stupor in the brush-grown railway cut, and when I staggered out to the roadway ahead I saw no trace of any prints in the fresh mud. The fishy odour, too, was gone. Innsmouth's ruined roofs and toppling steeples loomed up greyly toward the southeast, but not a living creature did I spy in all the desolate salt marshes around. My watch was still going, and told me that the hour was past noon.

The reality of what I had been through was highly uncertain in my mind, but I felt that something hideous lay in the background. I must get away from evil-shadowed Innsmouth—and accordingly I began to test my cramped, wearied powers of locomotion. Despite weakness, hunger, horror, and bewilderment I found myself after a long time able to walk; so started slowly along the muddy road to Rowley. Before evening I was in the village, getting a meal and providing myself with presentable clothes. I caught the night train to Arkham, and the next day talked long and earnestly with government officials there; a process I later repeated in Boston. With the main result of these colloquies the public is now familiar—and I wish, for normality's sake, there were nothing more to tell. Perhaps it is madness that is overtaking me—yet perhaps a greater horror—or a greater marvel—is reaching out.

As may well be imagined, I gave up most of the foreplanned features of the rest of my tour—the scenic, architectural, and antiquarian diversions on which I had counted so heavily. Nor did I dare look for that piece of strange jewellery said to be in the Miskatonic University Museum. I did, however, improve my stay in Arkham by collecting some genealogical notes I had long wished to possess; very rough and hasty data, it is true, but capable of good use later on when I might have time to collate and codify them. The curator of the historical society there— Mr. E. Lapham Peabody—was very courteous about assisting me, and expressed unusual interest when I told him I was a grandson of Eliza Orne of Arkham, who was born in 1867 and had married James Williamson of Ohio at the age of seventeen.

It seemed that a maternal uncle of mine had been there many years before on a quest much like my own; and that my grandmother's family was a topic of some local curiosity. There had, Mr. Peabody said, been considerable discussion about the marriage of her father, Benjamin Orne, just after the Civil War; since the ancestry of the bride was peculiarly puzzling. That bride was understood to have been an orphaned Marsh of New Hampshire—a cousin of the Essex County Marshes—but her education had been in France and she knew very little of her family. A guardian had deposited funds in a Boston bank to maintain her and her French governess; but that guardian's name was unfamiliar to Arkham people, and in time he dropped out of sight, so that the governess assumed his role by court appointment. The Frenchwoman—now long dead—was very taciturn, and there were those who said she could have told more than she did.

But the most baffling thing was the inability of anyone to place the recorded parents of the young woman—Enoch and Lydia (Meserve) Marsh—among the known families of New Hampshire. Possibly, many suggested, she was the natural daughter of some Marsh of prominence—she certainly had the true Marsh eyes. Most of the puzzling was done after her early death, which took place at the birth of my grandmother—her only child. Having formed some disagreeable impressions connected with the name of Marsh, I did not welcome the news that it belonged on my own ancestral tree; nor was I pleased by Mr. Peabody's suggestion that I had the true Marsh eyes myself. However, I was grateful for data which I knew would prove valuable; and took copious notes and lists of book references regarding the well-documented Orne family.

I went directly home to Toledo from Boston, and later spent a month at Maumee recuperating from my ordeal. In September I entered Oberlin for my final year, and from then till the next June was busy with studies and other wholesome activities—reminded of the bygone terror only by occasional official visits from government men in connexion with the campaign which my pleas and evidence had started. Around the middle of July—just a year after the Innsmouth experience—I spent a week with my late mother's family in Cleveland; checking some of my new genealogical data with the various notes, traditions, and bits of heirloom material in existence there, and seeing what kind of connected chart I could construct.

I did not exactly relish the task, for the atmosphere of the Williamson home had always depressed me. There was a strain of morbidity there, and my mother had never encouraged my visiting her parents as a child, although she always welcomed her father when he came to Toledo. My Arkham-born grandmother had seemed strange and almost terrifying to me, and I do not think I grieved when she disappeared. I was eight years old then, and it was said that she had wandered off in grief after the suicide of my uncle Douglas, her eldest son. He had shot himself after a trip to New England—the same trip, no doubt, which had caused him to be recalled at the Arkham Historical Society.

This uncle had resembled her, and I had never liked him either. Something about the staring, unwinking expression of both of them had given me a vague, unaccountable uneasiness. My mother and uncle Walter had not looked like that. They were like their father, though poor little cousin Lawrence—Walter's son—had been an almost perfect duplicate of his grandmother before his condition took him to the permanent seclusion of a sanitarium at Canton. I had not seen him in four years,

but my uncle once implied that his state, both mental and physical, was very bad. This worry had probably been a major cause of his mother's death two years before.

My grandfather and his widowed son Walter now comprised the Cleveland household, but the memory of older times hung thickly over it. I still disliked the place, and tried to get my researches done as quickly as possible. Williamson records and traditions were supplied in abundance by my grandfather; though for Orne material I had to depend on my uncle Walter, who put at my disposal the contents of all his files, including notes, letters, cuttings, heirlooms, photographs, and miniatures.

It was in going over the letters and pictures on the Orne side that I began to acquire a kind of terror of my own ancestry. As I have said, my grandmother and uncle Douglas had always disturbed me. Now, years after their passing, I gazed at their pictured faces with a measurably heightened feeling of repulsion and alienation. I could not at first understand the change, but gradually a horrible sort of comparison began to obtrude itself on my unconscious mind despite the steady refusal of my consciousness to admit even the least suspicion of it. It was clear that the typical expression of these faces now suggested something it had not suggested before—something which would bring stark panic if too openly thought of.

But the worst shock came when my uncle shewed me the Orne jewellery in a downtown safe-deposit vault. Some of the items were delicate and inspiring enough, but there was one box of strange old pieces descended from my mysterious great-grandmother which my uncle was almost reluctant to produce. They were, he said, of very grotesque and almost repulsive design, and had never to his knowledge been publicly worn; though my grandmother used to enjoy looking at them. Vague legends of bad luck clustered around them, and my great-grandmother's French governess had said they ought not to be worn in New England, though it would be quite safe to wear them in Europe.

As my uncle began slowly and grudgingly to unwrap the things he urged me not to be shocked by the strangeness and frequent hideousness of the designs. Artists and archaeologists who had seen them pronounced the workmanship superlatively and exotically exquisite, though no one seemed able to define their exact material or assign them to any specific art tradition. There were two armlets, a tiara, and a kind of pectoral; the latter having in high relief certain figures of almost unbearable extravagance.

During this description I had kept a tight rein on my emotions, but my face must have betrayed my mounting fears. My uncle looked concerned, and paused in his unwrapping to study my countenance. I motioned to him to continue, which he did with renewed signs of reluctance. He seemed to expect some demonstration when the first piece—the tiara—became visible, but I doubt if he expected quite what actually happened. I did not expect it, either, for I thought I was thoroughly forewarned regarding what the jewellery would turn out to be. What I did was to faint silently away, just as I had done in that brier-choked railway cut a year before.

From that day on my life has been a nightmare of brooding and apprehension, nor do I know how much

is hideous truth and how much madness. My great-grandmother had been a Marsh of unknown source whose husband lived in Arkham—and did not old Zadok say that the daughter of Obed Marsh by a monstrous mother was married to an Arkham man through a trick? What was it the ancient toper had muttered about the likeness of my eyes to Captain Obed's? In Arkham, too, the curator had told me I had the true Marsh eyes. Was Obed Marsh my own great-great-grandfather? Who—or what—then, was my great-great-grandmother? But perhaps this was all madness. Those whitish-gold ornaments might easily have been bought from some Innsmouth sailor by the father of my great-grandmother, whoever he was. And that look in the staring-eyed faces of my grandmother and self-slain uncle might be sheer fancy on my part—sheer fancy, bolstered up by the Innsmouth shadow which had so darkly coloured my imagination. But why had my uncle killed himself after an ancestral quest in New England?

For more than two years I fought off these reflections with partial success. My father secured me a place in an insurance office, and I buried myself in routine as deeply as possible. In the winter of 1930–31, however, the dreams began. They were very sparse and insidious at first, but increased in frequency and vividness as the weeks went by. Great watery spaces opened out before me, and I seemed to wander through titanic sunken porticos and labyrinths of weedy Cyclopean walls with grotesque fishes as my companions. Then the other shapes began to appear, filling me with nameless horror the moment I awoke. But during the dreams they did not horrify me at all—I was one with them; wearing their unhuman trappings, treading their aqueous ways, and praying monstrously at their evil sea-bottom temples.

There was much more than I could remember, but even what I did remember each morning would be enough to stamp me as a madman or a genius if ever I dared write it down. Some frightful influence, I felt, was seeking gradually to drag me out of the sane world of wholesome life into unnamable abysses of blackness and alienage; and the process told heavily on me. My health and appearance grew steadily worse, till finally I was forced to give up my position and adopt the static, secluded life of an invalid. Some odd nervous affliction had me in its grip, and I found myself at times almost unable to shut my eyes.

It was then that I began to study the mirror with mounting alarm. The slow ravages of disease are not pleasant to watch, but in my case there was something subtler and more puzzling in the background. My father seemed to notice it, too, for he began looking at me curiously and almost affrightedly. What was taking place in me? Could it be that I was coming to resemble my grandmother and uncle Douglas?

One night I had a frightful dream in which I met my grandmother under the sea. She lived in a phosphorescent palace of many terraces, with gardens of strange leprous corals and grotesque brachiate efflorescences, and welcomed me with a warmth that may have been sardonic. She had changed—as those who take to the water change—and told me she had never died. Instead, she had gone to a spot her dead son had learned about, and had leaped to a realm whose wonders—destined for him as well—he had spurned with a smoking pistol. This was to be my realm, too—I could not escape it. I would never die, but would live with those who had lived since

before man ever walked the earth.

I met also that which had been her grandmother. For eighty thousand years Pth'thya-l'yi had lived in Y'ha-nthlei, and thither she had gone back after Obed Marsh was dead. Y'ha-nthlei was not destroyed when the upper-earth men shot death into the sea. It was hurt, but not destroyed. The Deep Ones could never be destroyed, even though the palaeogean magic of the forgotten Old Ones might sometimes check them. For the present they would rest; but some day, if they remembered, they would rise again for the tribute Great Cthulhu craved. It would be a city greater than Innsmouth next time. They had planned to spread, and had brought up that which would help them, but now they must wait once more. For bringing the upper-earth men's death I must do a penance, but that would not be heavy. This was the dream in which I saw a shoggoth for the first time, and the sight set me awake in a frenzy of screaming. That morning the mirror definitely told me I had acquired the Innsmouth look.

So far I have not shot myself as my uncle Douglas did. I bought an automatic and almost took the step, but certain dreams deterred me. The tense extremes of horror are lessening, and I feel queerly drawn toward the unknown sea-deeps instead of fearing them. I hear and do strange things in sleep, and awake with a kind of exaltation instead of terror. I do not believe I need to wait for the full change as most have waited. If I did, my father would probably shut me up in a sanitarium as my poor little cousin is shut up. Stupendous and unheard-of splendours await me below, and I shall seek them soon. Iä-R'lyeh! Cthulhu fhtagn! Iä! Iä! No, I shall not shoot myself—I cannot be made to shoot myself!

I shall plan my cousin's escape from that Canton madhouse, and together we shall go to marvel-shadowed Innsmouth. We shall swim out to that brooding reef in the sea and dive down through black abysses to Cyclopean and many-columned Y'ha-nthlei, and in that lair of the Deep Ones we shall dwell amidst wonder and glory for ever.

'The older fellows look the worst...'

Oh, Whistle, and I'll Come to You, My Lad

by M. R. James

'I suppose you will be getting away pretty soon, now Full term is over, Professor,' said a person not in the story to the Professor of Ontography, soon after they had sat down next to each other at a feast in the hospitable hall of St. James's College.

The Professor was young, neat, and precise in speech.

'Yes,' he said; 'my friends have been making me take up golf this term, and I mean to go to the East Coast—in point of fact to Burnstow—(I dare say you know it) for a week or ten days, to improve my game. I hope to get off to-morrow.'

'Oh, Parkins,' said his neighbour on the other side, 'if you are going to Burnstow, I wish you would look at the site of the Templars' preceptory, and let me know if you think it would be any good to have a dig there in the summer.'

It was, as you might suppose, a person of antiquarian pursuits who said this, but, since he merely appears in this prologue, there is no need to give his entitlements.

'Certainly,' said Parkins, the Professor: 'if you will describe to me whereabouts the site is, I will do my best to give you an idea of the lie of the land when I get back; or I could write to you about it, if you would tell me where you are likely to be.'

'Don't trouble to do that, thanks. It's only that I'm thinking of taking my family in that direction in the Long, and it occurred to me that, as very few of the English preceptories have ever been properly planned, I might have an opportunity of doing something useful on off-days.'

The Professor rather sniffed at the idea that planning out a preceptory could be described as useful. His neighbour continued:

'The site—I doubt if there is anything showing above ground—must be down quite close to the beach now. The sea has encroached tremendously, as you know, all along that bit of coast. I should think, from the map, that it must be about three-quarters of a mile from the Globe Inn, at the north end of the town. Where are you going to stay?'

'Well, at the Globe Inn, as a matter of fact,' said Parkins; 'I have engaged a room there. I couldn't get in anywhere else; most of the lodging-houses are shut up in winter, it seems; and, as it is, they tell me that the only room of any size I can have is really a double-bedded one, and that they haven't a corner in which to store the other bed, and so on. But I must have a fairly large room, for I am taking some books down, and mean to do a bit of work; and though I don't quite fancy having an empty bed—not to speak of two—in what I may call for the time being my study, I suppose I can manage to rough it for the short time I shall be there.'

'Do you call having an extra bed in your room roughing it, Parkins?' said a bluff person opposite. 'Look here, I shall come down and occupy it for a bit; it'll be company for you.'

The Professor quivered, but managed to laugh in a courteous manner.

'By all means, Rogers; there's nothing I should like better. But I'm afraid you would find it rather dull; you don't play golf, do you?'

'No, thank Heaven!' said rude Mr. Rogers.

'Well, you see, when I'm not writing I shall most likely be out on the links, and that, as I say, would be rather dull for you, I'm afraid.'

'Oh, I don't know! There's certain to be somebody I know in the place; but, of course, if you don't want me, speak the word, Parkins; I shan't be offended. Truth, as you always tell us, is never offensive.'

Parkins was, indeed, scrupulously polite and strictly truthful. It is to be feared that Mr. Rogers sometimes practised upon his knowledge of these characteristics. In Parkins's breast there was a conflict now raging, which for a moment or two did not allow him to answer. That interval being over, he said:

'Well, if you want the exact truth, Rogers, I was considering whether the room I speak of would really be large enough to accommodate us both comfortably; and also whether (mind, I shouldn't have said this if you hadn't pressed me) you would not constitute something in the nature of a hindrance to my work.'

Rogers laughed loudly.

'Well done, Parkins!' he said. 'It's all right. I promise not to interrupt your work; don't you disturb yourself about that. No, I won't come if you don't want me; but I thought I should do so nicely to keep the ghosts off.' Here he might have been seen to wink and to nudge his next neighbour. Parkins might also have been seen to become pink. 'I beg pardon, Parkins,' Rogers continued; 'I oughtn't to have said that. I forgot you didn't like levity on these topics.'

'Well,' Parkins said, 'as you have mentioned the matter, I freely own that I do not like careless talk about what you call ghosts. A man in my position,' he went on, raising his voice a little, 'cannot, I find, be too careful about appearing to sanction the current beliefs on such subjects. As you know, Rogers, or as you ought to know; for I think I have never concealed my views——'

'No, you certainly have not, old man,' put in Rogers sotto voce.

'——I hold that any semblance, any appearance of concession to the view that such things might exist is to me a renunciation of all that I hold most sacred. But I'm afraid I have not succeeded in securing your attention.'

'Your undivided attention, was what Dr. Blimber

actually said,'[1] Rogers interrupted, with every appearance of an earnest desire for accuracy. 'But I beg your pardon, Parkins: I'm stopping you.'

'No, not at all,' said Parkins. 'I don't remember Blimber; perhaps he was before my time. But I needn't go on. I'm sure you know what I mean.'

'Yes, yes,' said Rogers, rather hastily—'just so. We'll go into it fully at Burnstow, or somewhere.'

In repeating the above dialogue I have tried to give the impression which it made on me, that Parkins was something of an old woman—rather henlike, perhaps, in his little ways; totally destitute, alas! of the sense of humour, but at the same time dauntless and sincere in his convictions, and a man deserving of the greatest respect. Whether or not the reader has gathered so much, that was the character which Parkins had.

On the following day Parkins did, as he had hoped, succeed in getting away from his college, and in arriving at Burnstow. He was made welcome at the Globe Inn, was safely installed in the large double-bedded room of which we have heard, and was able before retiring to rest to arrange his materials for work in apple-pie order upon a commodious table which occupied the outer end of the room, and was surrounded on three sides by windows looking out seaward; that is to say, the central window looked straight out to sea, and those on the left and right commanded prospects along the shore to the north and south respectively. On the south you saw the village of Burnstow. On the north no houses were to be seen, but only the beach and the low cliff backing it. Immediately in front was a strip—not considerable—of rough grass, dotted with old anchors, capstans, and so forth; then a broad path; then the beach. Whatever may have been the original distance between the Globe Inn and the sea, not more than sixty yards now separated them.

The rest of the population of the inn was, of course, a golfing one, and included few elements that call for a special description. The most conspicuous figure was, perhaps, that of an ancien militaire, secretary of a London club, and possessed of a voice of incredible strength, and of views of a pronouncedly Protestant type. These were apt to find utterance after his attendance upon the ministrations of the Vicar, an estimable man with inclinations towards a picturesque ritual, which he gallantly kept down as far as he could out of deference to East Anglian tradition.

Professor Parkins, one of whose principal characteristics was pluck, spent the greater part of the day following his arrival at Burnstow in what he had called improving his game, in company with this Colonel Wilson: and during the afternoon—whether the process of improvement were to blame or not, I am not sure— the Colonel's demeanour assumed a colouring so lurid that even Parkins jibbed at the thought of walking home with him from the links. He determined, after a short and furtive look at that bristling moustache and those incarnadined features, that it would be wiser to allow the influences of tea and tobacco to do what they could with the Colonel before the dinner-hour should render a meeting inevitable.

'I might walk home to-night along the beach,' he reflected—'yes, and take a look—there will be light enough for that—at the ruins of which Disney was talking. I don't exactly know where they are, by the way; but I expect I can hardly help stumbling on them.'

This he accomplished, I may say, in the most literal sense, for in picking his way from the links to the shingle beach his foot caught, partly in a gorse-root and partly in a biggish stone, and over he went. When he got up and surveyed his surroundings, he found himself in a patch of somewhat broken ground covered with small depressions and mounds. These latter, when he came to examine them, proved to be simply masses of flints embedded in mortar and grown over with turf. He must, he quite rightly concluded, be on the site of the preceptory he had promised to look at. It seemed not unlikely to reward the spade of the explorer; enough of the foundations was probably left at no great depth to throw a good deal of light on the general plan. He remembered vaguely that the Templars, to whom this site had belonged, were in the habit of building round churches, and he thought a particular series of the humps or mounds near him did appear to be arranged in something of a circular form. Few people can resist the temptation to try a little amateur research in a department quite outside their own, if only for the satisfaction of showing how successful they would have been had they only taken it up seriously. Our Professor, however, if he felt something of this mean desire, was also truly anxious to oblige Mr. Disney. So he paced with care the circular area he had noticed, and wrote down its rough dimensions in his pocket-book. Then he

Oh, Whistle, and I'll Come to You, My Lad proceeded to examine an oblong eminence which lay east of the centre of the circle, and seemed to his thinking likely to be the base of a platform or altar. At one end of it, the northern, a patch of the turf was gone—removed by some boy or other creature ferae naturae. It might, he thought, be as well to probe the soil here for evidences of masonry, and he took out his knife and began scraping away the earth. And now followed another little discovery: a portion of soil fell inward as he scraped, and disclosed a small cavity. He lighted one match after another to help him to see of what nature the hole was, but the wind was too strong for them all. By tapping and scratching the sides with his knife, however, he was able to make out that it must be an artificial hole in masonry. It was rectangular, and the sides, top, and bottom, if not actually plastered, were smooth and regular. Of course it was empty. No! As he withdrew the knife he heard a metallic clink, and when he introduced his hand it met with a cylindrical object lying on the floor of the hole. Naturally enough, he picked it up, and when he brought it into the light, now fast fading, he could see that it, too, was of man's making—a metal tube about four inches long, and evidently of some considerable age.

By the time Parkins had made sure that there was nothing else in this odd receptacle, it was too late and too dark for him to think of undertaking any further search. What he had done had proved so unexpectedly interesting that he determined to sacrifice a little more of the daylight on the morrow to archæology. The object which he now had safe in his pocket was bound to be of some slight value at least, he felt sure.

Bleak and solemn was the view on which he took a

last look before starting homeward. A faint yellow light in the west showed the links, on which a few figures moving towards the club-house were still visible, the squat martello tower, the lights of Aldsey village, the pale ribbon of sands intersected at intervals by black wooden groynings, the dim and murmuring sea. The wind was bitter from the north, but was at his back when he set out for the Globe. He quickly rattled and clashed through the shingle and gained the sand, upon which, but for the groynings which had to be got over every few yards, the going was both good and quiet. One last look behind, to measure the distance he had made since leaving the ruined Templars' church, showed him a prospect of company on his walk, in the shape of a rather indistinct personage in the distance, who seemed to be making great efforts to catch up with him, but made little, if any, progress. I mean that there was an appearance of running about his movements, but that the distance between him and Parkins did not seem materially to lessen. So, at least, Parkins thought, and decided that he almost certainly did not know him, and that it would be absurd to wait until he came up. For all that, company, he began to think, would really be very welcome on that lonely shore, if only you could choose your companion. In his unenlightened days he had read of meetings in such places which even now would hardly bear thinking of. He went on thinking of them, however, until he reached home, and particularly of one which catches most people's fancy at some time of their childhood. 'Now I saw in my dream that Christian had gone but a very little way when he saw a foul fiend coming over the field to meet him.' 'What should I do now,' he thought, 'if I looked back and caught sight of a black figure sharply defined against the yellow sky, and saw that it had horns and wings? I wonder whether I should stand or run for it. Luckily, the gentleman behind is not of that kind, and he seems to be about as far off now as when I saw him first. Well, at this rate he won't get his dinner as soon as I shall; and, dear me! it's within a quarter of an hour of the time now. I must run!'

Parkins had, in fact, very little time for dressing. When he met the Colonel at dinner, Peace—or as much of her as that gentleman could manage—reigned once more in the military bosom; nor was she put to flight in the hours of bridge that followed dinner, for Parkins was a more than respectable player. When, therefore, he retired towards twelve o'clock, he felt that he had spent his evening in quite a satisfactory way, and that, even for so long as a fortnight or three weeks, life at the Globe would be supportable under similar conditions—'especially,' thought he, 'if I go on improving my game.'

As he went along the passages he met the boots of the Globe, who stopped and said:

'Beg your pardon, sir, but as I was a-brushing your coat just now there was somethink fell out of the pocket. I put it on your chest of drawers, sir, in your room, sir—a piece of a pipe or somethink of that, sir. Thank you, sir. You'll find it on your chest of drawers, sir—yes, sir. Good-night, sir.'

The speech served to remind Parkins of his little discovery of that afternoon. It was with some considerable curiosity that he turned it over by the light of his candles. It was of bronze, he now saw, and was shaped very much after the manner of the modern dog-whistle; in fact it was—yes, certainly it was—actually no more nor less than a whistle. He put it to his lips, but it was quite full of a fine, caked-up sand or earth, which would not yield to knocking, but must be loosened with a knife. Tidy as ever in his habits, Parkins cleared out the earth on to a piece of paper, and took the latter to the window to empty it out. The night was clear and bright, as he saw when he had opened the casement, and he stopped for an instant to look at the sea and note a belated wanderer stationed on the shore in front of the inn. Then he shut the window, a little surprised at the late hours people kept at Burnstow, and took his whistle to the light again. Why, surely there were marks on it, and not merely marks, but letters! A very little rubbing rendered the deeply-cut inscription quite legible, but the Professor had to confess, after some earnest thought, that the meaning of it was as obscure to him as the writing on the wall to Belshazzar. There were legends both on the front and on the back of the whistle. The one read thus:

FUR FLA
FLE BIS

The other:

✝QUIS · EST · ISTE · QUI · UENIT✝

'I ought to be able to make it out,' he thought; 'but I suppose I am a little rusty in my Latin. When I come to think of it, I don't believe I even know the word for a whistle. The long one does seem simple enough. It ought to mean, "Who is this who is coming?" Well, the best way to find out is evidently to whistle for him.'

He blew tentatively and stopped suddenly, startled and yet pleased at the note he had elicited. It had a quality of infinite distance in it, and, soft as it was, he somehow felt it must be audible for miles round. It was a sound, too, that seemed to have the power (which many scents possess) of forming pictures in the brain. He saw quite clearly for a moment a vision of a wide, dark expanse at night, with a fresh wind blowing, and in the midst a lonely figure—how employed, he could not tell. Perhaps he would have seen more had not the picture been broken by the sudden surge of a gust of wind against his casement, so sudden that it made him look up, just in time to see the white glint of a sea-bird's wing somewhere outside the dark panes.

The sound of the whistle had so fascinated him that he could not help trying it once more, this time more boldly. The note was little, if at all, louder than before, and repetition broke the illusion—no picture followed, as he had half hoped it might. 'But what is this? Goodness! what force the wind can get up in a few minutes! What a tremendous gust! There! I knew that window-fastening was no use! Ah! I thought so—both candles out. It is enough to tear the room to pieces.'

The first thing was to get the window shut. While you might count twenty Parkins was struggling with the small casement, and felt almost as if he were pushing back a sturdy burglar, so strong was the pressure. It slackened all at once, and the window banged to and latched itself. Now to relight the candles and see what damage, if any, had been done. No, nothing seemed amiss; no glass even was broken in the casement. But the noise had evidently roused at least one member of the household: the Colonel was to be heard stumping in his stockinged feet on the floor above, and growling.

Quickly as it had risen, the wind did not fall at once. On it went, moaning and rushing past the house, at times rising to a cry so desolate that, as Parkins disinterestedly said, it might have made fanciful people feel quite uncomfortable; even the unimaginative, he thought after a quarter of an hour, might be happier without it.

Whether it was the wind, or the excitement of golf, or of the researches in the preceptory that kept Parkins awake, he was not sure. Awake he remained, in any case, long enough to fancy (as I am afraid I often do myself under such conditions) that he was the victim of all manner of fatal disorders: he would lie counting the beats of his heart, convinced that it was going to stop work every moment, and would entertain grave suspicions of his lungs, brain, liver, etc.—suspicions which he was sure would be dispelled by the return of daylight, but which until then refused to be put aside. He found a little vicarious comfort in the idea that someone else was in the same boat. A near neighbour (in the darkness it was not easy to tell his direction) was tossing and rustling in his bed, too.

The next stage was that Parkins shut his eyes and determined to give sleep every chance. Here again over-excitement asserted itself in another form—that of making pictures. Experto crede, pictures do come to the closed eyes of one trying to sleep, and often his pictures are so little to his taste that he must open his eyes and disperse the images.

Parkins's experience on this occasion was a very distressing one. He found that the picture which presented itself to him was continuous. When he opened his eyes, of course, it went; but when he shut them once more it framed itself afresh, and acted itself out again, neither quicker nor slower than before. What he saw was this:

A long stretch of shore—shingle edged by sand, and intersected at short intervals with black groynes running down to the water—a scene, in fact, so like that of his afternoon's walk that, in the absence of any landmark, it could not be distinguished therefrom. The light was obscure, conveying an impression of gathering storm, late winter evening, and slight cold rain. On this bleak stage at first no actor was visible. Then, in the distance, a bobbing black object appeared; a moment more, and it was a man running, jumping, clambering over the groynes, and every few seconds looking eagerly back. The nearer he came the more obvious it was that he was not only anxious, but even terribly frightened, though his face was not to be distinguished. He was, moreover, almost at the end of his strength. On he came; each successive obstacle seemed to cause him more difficulty than the last. 'Will he get over this next one?' thought Parkins; 'it seems a little higher than the others.' Yes; half climbing, half throwing himself, he did get over, and fell all in a heap on the other side (the side nearest to the spectator). There, as if really unable to get up again, he remained crouching under the groyne, looking up in an attitude of painful anxiety.

So far no cause whatever for the fear of the runner had been shown; but now there began to be seen, far up the shore, a little flicker of something light-coloured moving to and fro with great swiftness and irregularity. Rapidly growing larger, it, too, declared itself as a figure in pale, fluttering draperies, ill-defined. There was something about its motion which made Parkins very unwilling to see it at close quarters. It would stop, raise arms, bow itself toward the sand, then run stooping across the beach to the water-edge and back again; and then, rising upright, once more continue its course forward at a speed that was startling and terrifying. The moment came when the pursuer was hovering about from left to right only a few yards beyond the groyne where the runner lay in hiding. After two or three ineffectual castings hither and thither it came to a stop, stood upright, with arms raised high, and then darted straight forward towards the groyne.

It was at this point that Parkins always failed in his resolution to keep his eyes shut. With many misgivings as to incipient failure of eyesight, overworked brain, excessive smoking, and so on, he finally resigned himself to light his candle, get out a book, and pass the night waking, rather than be tormented by this persistent panorama, which he saw clearly enough could only be a morbid reflection of his walk and his thoughts on that very day.

The scraping of match on box and the glare of light must have startled some creatures of the night—rats or what not—which he heard scurry across the floor from the side of his bed with much rustling. Dear, dear! the match is out! Fool that it is! But the second one burnt better, and a candle and book were duly procured, over which Parkins pored till sleep of a wholesome kind came upon him, and that in no long space. For about the first time in his orderly and prudent life he forgot to blow out the candle, and when he was called next morning at eight there was still a flicker in the socket and a sad mess of guttered grease on the top of the little table.

After breakfast he was in his room, putting the finishing touches to his golfing costume—fortune had again allotted the Colonel to him for a partner—when one of the maids came in.

'Oh, if you please,' she said, 'would you like any extra blankets on your bed, sir?'

'Ah! thank you,' said Parkins. 'Yes, I think I should like one. It seems likely to turn rather colder.'

In a very short time the maid was back with the blanket.

'Which bed should I put it on, sir?' she asked.

'What? Why, that one—the one I slept in last night,' he said, pointing to it.

'Oh yes! I beg your pardon, sir, but you seemed to have tried both of 'em; leastways, we had to make 'em both up this morning.'

'Really? How very absurd!' said Parkins. 'I certainly never touched the other, except to lay some things on it. Did it actually seem to have been slept in?'

'Oh yes, sir!' said the maid. 'Why, all the things was crumpled and throwed about all ways, if you'll excuse me, sir—quite as if anyone 'adn't passed but a very poor night, sir.'

'Dear me,' said Parkins. 'Well, I may have disordered it more than I thought when I unpacked my things. I'm very sorry to have given you the extra trouble, I'm sure. I expect a friend of mine soon, by the way—a gentleman from Cambridge—to come and occupy it for a night or two. That will be all right, I suppose, won't it?'

'Oh yes, to be sure, sir. Thank you, sir. It's no trouble, I'm sure,' said the maid, and departed to giggle with her colleagues.

Parkins set forth, with a stern determination to improve his game.

I am glad to be able to report that he succeeded so far in this enterprise that the Colonel, who had been rather repining at the prospect of a second day's play in his company, became quite chatty as the morning advanced; and his voice boomed out over the flats, as certain also of our own minor poets have said, 'like some great bourdon in a minster tower.'

'Extraordinary wind, that, we had last night,' he said. 'In my old home we should have said someone had been whistling for it.'

'Should you, indeed!' said Parkins. 'Is there a superstition of that kind still current in your part of the country?'

'I don't know about superstition,' said the Colonel. 'They believe in it all over Denmark and Norway, as well as on the Yorkshire coast; and my experience is, mind you, that there's generally something at the bottom of what these country-folk hold to, and have held to for generations. But it's your drive' (or whatever it might have been: the golfing reader will have to imagine appropriate digressions at the proper intervals).

When conversation was resumed, Parkins said, with a slight hesitancy:

'Apropos of what you were saying just now, Colonel, I think I ought to tell you that my own views on such subjects are very strong. I am, in fact, a convinced disbeliever in what is called the "supernatural."'

'What!' said the Colonel, 'do you mean to tell me you don't believe in second-sight, or ghosts, or anything of that kind?'

'In nothing whatever of that kind,' returned Parkins firmly.

'Well,' said the Colonel, 'but it appears to me at that rate, sir, that you must be little better than a Sadducee.'

Parkins was on the point of answering that, in his opinion, the Sadducees were the most sensible persons he had ever read of in the Old Testament; but, feeling some doubt as to whether much mention of them was to be found in that work, he preferred to laugh the accusation off.

'Perhaps I am,' he said; 'but—— Here, give me my cleek, boy!—Excuse me one moment, Colonel.' A short interval. 'Now, as to whistling for the wind, let me give you my theory about it. The laws which govern winds are really not at all perfectly known—to fisher-folk and such, of course, not known at all. A man or woman of eccentric habits, perhaps, or a stranger, is seen repeatedly on the beach at some unusual hour, and is heard whistling. Soon afterwards a violent wind rises; a man who could read the sky perfectly or who possessed a barometer could have foretold that it would. The simple people of a fishing-village have no barometers, and only a few rough rules for prophesying weather. What more natural than that the eccentric personage I postulated should be regarded as having raised the wind, or that he or she should clutch eagerly at the reputation of being able to do so? Now, take last night's wind: as it happens, I myself was whistling. I blew a whistle twice, and the wind seemed to come absolutely in answer to my call. If anyone had seen me——'

The audience had been a little restive under this harangue, and Parkins had, I fear, fallen somewhat into the tone of a lecturer; but at the last sentence the Colonel stopped.

'Whistling, were you?' he said. 'And what sort of whistle did you use? Play this stroke first.' Interval.

'About that whistle you were asking, Colonel. It's rather a curious one. I have it in my—— No; I see I've left it in my room. As a matter of fact, I found it yesterday.'

And then Parkins narrated the manner of his discovery of the whistle, upon hearing which the Colonel grunted, and opined that, in Parkins's place, he should himself be careful about using a thing that had belonged to a set of Papists, of whom, speaking generally, it might be affirmed that you never knew what they might not have been up to. From this topic he diverged to the enormities of the Vicar, who had given notice on the previous Sunday that Friday would be the Feast of St. Thomas the Apostle, and that there would be service at eleven o'clock in the church. This and other similar proceedings constituted in the Colonel's view a strong presumption that the Vicar was a concealed Papist, if not a Jesuit; and Parkins, who could not very readily follow the Colonel in this region, did not disagree with him. In fact, they got on so well together in the morning that there was no talk on either side of their separating after lunch.

Both continued to play well during the afternoon, or, at least, well enough to make them forget everything else until the light began to fail them. Not until then did Parkins remember that he had meant to do some more investigating at the preceptory; but it was of no great importance, he reflected. One day was as good as another; he might as well go home with the Colonel.

As they turned the corner of the house, the Colonel was almost knocked down by a boy who rushed into him at the very top of his speed, and then, instead of running away, remained hanging on to him and panting. The first words of the warrior were naturally those of reproof and objurgation, but he very quickly discerned that the boy was almost speechless with fright. Inquiries were useless at first. When the boy got his breath he began to howl, and still clung to the Colonel's legs. He was at last detached, but continued to howl.

'What in the world is the matter with you? What have you been up to? What have you seen?' said the two men.

'Ow, I seen it wive at me out of the winder,' wailed the boy, 'and I don't like it.'

'What window?' said the irritated Colonel. 'Come, pull yourself together, my boy.'

'The front winder it was, at the 'otel,' said the boy.

At this point Parkins was in favour of sending the boy home, but the Colonel refused; he wanted to get to the bottom of it, he said; it was most dangerous to give a boy such a fright as this one had had, and if it turned out that people had been playing jokes, they should suffer for it in some way. And by a series of questions he made out this story: The boy had been playing about on the grass in front of the Globe with some others; then they had gone home to their teas, and he was just going, when he happened to look up at the front winder and see it a-wiving at him. It seemed to be a figure of some sort, in white as far as he knew—couldn't see its face; but it wived at him, and it warn't a right thing—not to say not a right person. Was there a light in the room? No, he didn't think to look if there was a light. Which was the window? Was it the top one or the second one? The seckind one it was—the big winder what got two little uns at the sides.

'Very well, my boy,' said the Colonel, after a few more questions. 'You run away home now. I expect it was some person trying to give you a start. Another time, like a brave English boy, you just throw a stone—well, no, not that exactly, but you go and speak to the waiter, or to Mr. Simpson, the landlord, and—yes—and say that I advised you to do so.'

The boy's face expressed some of the doubt he felt as to the likelihood of Mr. Simpson's lending a favourable ear to his complaint, but the Colonel did not appear to perceive this, and went on:

'And here's a sixpence—no, I see it's a shilling—and you be off home, and don't think any more about it.'

The youth hurried off with agitated thanks, and the Colonel and Parkins went round to the front of the Globe and reconnoitred. There was only one window answering to the description they had been hearing.

'Well, that's curious,' said Parkins; 'it's evidently my window the lad was talking about. Will you come up for a moment, Colonel Wilson? We ought to be able to see if anyone has been taking liberties in my room.'

They were soon in the passage, and Parkins made as if to open the door. Then he stopped and felt in his pockets.

'This is more serious than I thought,' was his next remark. 'I remember now that before I started this morning I locked the door. It is locked now, and, what is more, here is the key.' And he held it up. 'Now,' he went on, 'if the servants are in the habit of going into one's room during the day when one is away, I can only say that—well, that I don't approve of it at all.' Conscious of a somewhat weak climax, he busied himself in opening the door (which was indeed locked) and in lighting candles. 'No,' he said, 'nothing seems disturbed.'

'Except your bed,' put in the Colonel.

'Excuse me, that isn't my bed,' said Parkins. 'I don't use that one. But it does look as if someone had been playing tricks with it.'

It certainly did: the clothes were bundled up and twisted together in a most tortuous confusion. Parkins pondered.

'That must be it,' he said at last: 'I disordered the clothes last night in unpacking, and they haven't made it since. Perhaps they came in to make it, and that boy saw them through the window; and then they were called away and locked the door after them. Yes, I think that must be it.'

'Well, ring and ask,' said the Colonel, and this appealed to Parkins as practical.

The maid appeared, and, to make a long story short, deposed that she had made the bed in the morning when the gentleman was in the room, and hadn't been there since. No, she hadn't no other key. Mr. Simpson he kep' the keys; he'd be able to tell the gentleman if anyone had been up.

This was a puzzle. Investigation showed that nothing of value had been taken, and Parkins remembered the disposition of the small objects on tables and so forth well enough to be pretty sure that no pranks had been played with them. Mr. and Mrs. Simpson furthermore agreed that neither of them had given the duplicate key of the room to any person whatever during the day. Nor could Parkins, fair-minded man as he was, detect anything in the demeanour of master, mistress, or maid that indicated guilt. He was much more inclined to think that the boy had been imposing on the Colonel.

The latter was unwontedly silent and pensive at dinner and throughout the evening. When he bade good-night to Parkins, he murmured in a gruff undertone:

'You know where I am if you want me during the night.'

'Why, yes, thank you, Colonel Wilson, I think I do; but there isn't much prospect of my disturbing you, I hope. By the way,' he added, 'did I show you that old whistle I spoke of? I think not. Well, here it is.'

The Colonel turned it over gingerly in the light of the candle.

'Can you make anything of the inscription?' asked Parkins, as he took it back.

'No, not in this light. What do you mean to do with it?'

'Oh, well, when I get back to Cambridge I shall submit it to some of the archæologists there, and see what they think of it; and very likely, if they consider it worth having, I may present it to one of the museums.'

''M!' said the Colonel. 'Well, you may be right. All I know is that, if it were mine, I should chuck it straight into the sea. It's no use talking, I'm well aware, but I expect that with you it's a case of live and learn. I hope so, I'm sure, and I wish you a good-night.'

He turned away, leaving Parkins in act to speak at the bottom of the stair, and soon each was in his own bedroom.

By some unfortunate accident, there were neither blinds nor curtains to the windows of the Professor's room. The previous night he had thought little of this, but to-night there seemed every prospect of a bright moon rising to shine directly on his bed, and probably wake him later on. When he noticed this he was a good deal annoyed, but, with an ingenuity which I can only envy, he succeeded in rigging up, with the help of a railway-rug, some safety-pins, and a stick and umbrella, a screen which, if it only held together, would completely keep the moonlight off his bed. And shortly afterwards he was comfortably in that bed. When he had read a somewhat solid work long enough to produce a decided wish for sleep, he cast a drowsy glance round the room, blew out the candle, and fell back upon the pillow.

He must have slept soundly for an hour or more, when a sudden clatter shook him up in a most unwelcome manner. In a moment he realized what had happened: his carefully-constructed screen had given way, and a very bright frosty moon was shining directly on his face. This was highly annoying. Could he possibly get up and reconstruct the screen? or could he manage to sleep if he did not?

For some minutes he lay and pondered over the possibilities; then he turned over sharply, and with all his eyes open lay breathlessly listening. There had been a movement, he was sure, in the empty bed on the opposite side of the room. To-morrow he would have it moved, for there must be rats or something playing about in it. It was quiet now. No! the commotion began again. There was a rustling and shaking: surely more than any rat could cause

I can figure to myself something of the Professor's bewilderment and horror, for I have in a dream thirty years back seen the same thing happen; but the reader will hardly, perhaps, imagine how dreadful it was to him to see a figure suddenly sit up in what he had known was an empty bed. He was out of his own bed in one bound, and made a dash towards the window, where lay his only weapon, the stick with which he had propped his screen. This was, as it turned out, the worst thing he could have done, because the personage in the empty bed, with a sudden smooth motion, slipped from the bed and took up a position, with outspread arms, between the two beds, and in front of the door. Parkins watched it in a horrid perplexity. Somehow, the idea of getting past it and escaping through the door was intolerable to him; he could not have borne—he didn't know why—to touch it; and as for its touching him, he would sooner dash himself through the window than have that happen. It stood for the moment in a band of dark shadow, and he had not seen what its face was like. Now it began to move, in a stooping posture, and all at once the spectator realized, with some horror and some relief, that it must be blind, for it seemed to feel about it with its muffled arms in a groping and random fashion. Turning half away from him, it became suddenly conscious of the bed he had just left, and darted towards it, and bent and felt over the pillows in a way which made Parkins shudder as he had never in his life thought it possible. In a very few moments it seemed to know that the bed was empty, and then, moving forward into the area of light and facing the window, it showed for the first time what manner of thing it was.

Parkins, who very much dislikes being questioned about it, did once describe something of it in my hearing, and I gathered that what he chiefly remembers about it is a horrible, an intensely horrible, face of crumpled linen. What expression he read upon it he could not or would not tell, but that the fear of it went nigh to maddening him is certain.

But he was not at leisure to watch it for long. With formidable quickness it moved into the middle of the room, and, as it groped and waved, one corner of its draperies swept across Parkins's face. He could not, though he knew how perilous a sound was—he could not keep back a cry of disgust, and this gave the searcher an instant clue. It leapt towards him upon the instant, and the next moment he was halfway through the window backwards, uttering cry upon cry at the utmost pitch of his voice, and the linen face was thrust close into his own. At this, almost the last possible second, deliverance came, as you will have guessed: the Colonel burst the door open, and was just in time to see the dreadful group at the window. When he reached the figures only one was left. Parkins sank forward into the room in a faint, and before him on the floor lay a tumbled heap of bed-clothes.

Colonel Wilson asked no questions, but busied himself

keeping everyone else out of the room and in getting Parkins back to his bed; and himself, wrapped in a rug, occupied the other bed, for the rest of the night. Early on the next day Rogers arrived, more welcome than he would have been a day before, and the three of them held a very long consultation in the Professor's room. At the end of it the Colonel left the hotel door carrying a small object between his finger and thumb, which he cast as far into the sea as a very brawny arm could send it. Later on the smoke of a burning ascended from the back premises of the Globe.

Exactly what explanation was patched up for the staff and visitors at the hotel I must confess I do not recollect. The Professor was somehow cleared of the ready suspicion of delirium tremens, and the hotel of the reputation of a troubled house.

There is not much question as to what would have happened to Parkins if the Colonel had not intervened when he did. He would either have fallen out of the window or else lost his wits. But it is not so evident what more the creature that came in answer to the whistle could have done than frighten. There seemed to be absolutely nothing material about it save the bed-clothes of which it had made itself a body. The Colonel, who remembered a not very dissimilar occurrence in India, was of opinion that if Parkins had closed with it it could really have done very little, and that its one power was that of frightening. The whole thing, he said, served to confirm his opinion of the Church of Rome.

There is really nothing more to tell, but, as you may imagine, the Professor's views on certain points are less clear cut than they used to be. His nerves, too, have suffered: he cannot even now see a surplice hanging on a door quite unmoved, and the spectacle of a scarecrow in a field late on a winter afternoon has cost him more than one sleepless night.

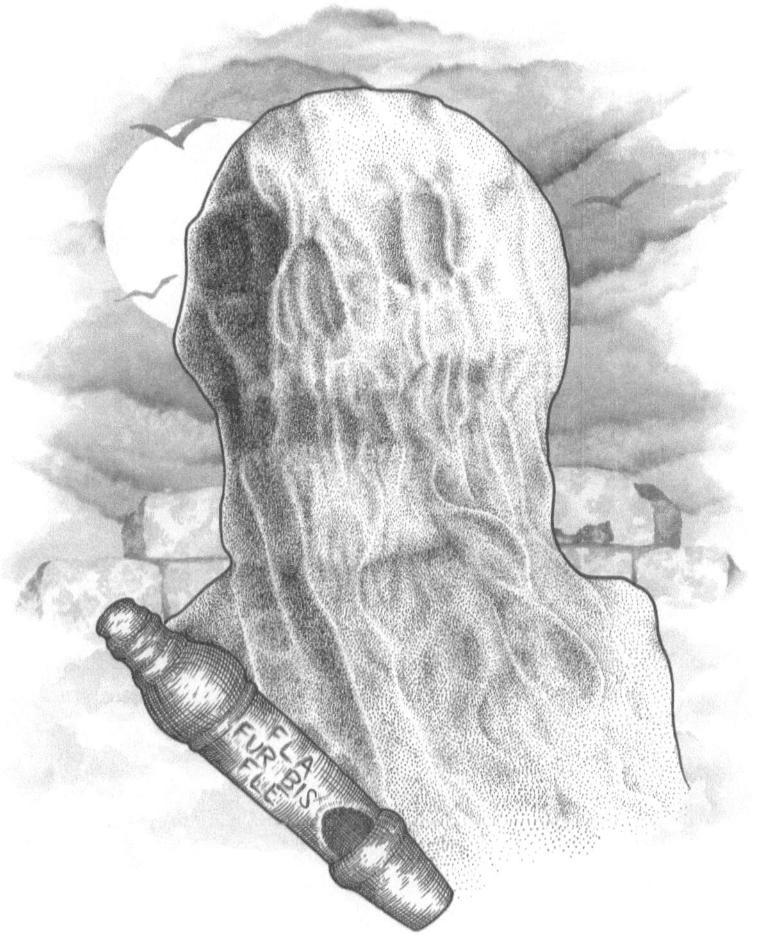

"Who is this who is coming?"

524

THE CALL OF CTHULHU

BY H. P. LOVECRAFT

(Found Among the Papers of the Late
Francis Wayland Thurston, of Boston)

"Of such great powers or beings there may be conceivably a survival . . . a survival of a hugely remote period when . . . consciousness was manifested, perhaps, in shapes and forms long since withdrawn before the tide of advancing humanity . . . forms of which poetry and legend alone have caught a flying memory and called them gods, monsters, mythical beings of all sorts and kinds. . . ."

—Algernon Blackwood.

I.

The Horror in Clay.

The most merciful thing in the world, I think, is the inability of the human mind to correlate all its contents. We live on a placid island of ignorance in the midst of black seas of infinity, and it was not meant that we should voyage far. The sciences, each straining in its own direction, have hitherto harmed us little; but some day the piecing together of dissociated knowledge will open up such terrifying vistas of reality, and of our frightful position therein, that we shall either go mad from the revelation or flee from the deadly light into the peace and safety of a new dark age.

Theosophists have guessed at the awesome grandeur of the cosmic cycle wherein our world and human race form transient incidents. They have hinted at strange survivals in terms which would freeze the blood if not masked by a bland optimism. But it is not from them that there came the single glimpse of forbidden aeons which chills me when I think of it and maddens me when I dream of it. That glimpse, like all dread glimpses of truth, flashed out from an accidental piecing together of separated things—in this case an old newspaper item and the notes of a dead professor. I hope that no one else will accomplish this piecing out; certainly, if I live, I shall never knowingly supply a link in so hideous a chain. I think that the professor, too, intended to keep silent regarding the part he knew, and that he would have destroyed his notes had not sudden death seized him.

My knowledge of the thing began in the winter of 1926–27 with the death of my grand-uncle George Gammell Angell, Professor Emeritus of Semitic Languages in Brown University, Providence, Rhode Island. Professor Angell was widely known as an authority on ancient inscriptions, and had frequently been resorted to by the heads of prominent museums; so that his passing at the age of ninety-two may be recalled by many. Locally, interest was intensified by the obscurity of the cause of death. The professor had been stricken whilst returning from the Newport boat; falling suddenly, as witnesses said, after having been jostled by a nautical-looking negro who had come from one of the queer dark courts on the precipitous hillside which formed a short cut from the waterfront to the deceased's home in Williams Street. Physicians were unable to find any visible disorder, but concluded after perplexed debate that some obscure lesion of the heart, induced by the brisk ascent of so steep a hill by so elderly a man, was responsible for the end. At the time I saw no reason to dissent from this dictum, but latterly I am inclined to wonder—and more than wonder.

As my grand-uncle's heir and executor, for he died a childless widower, I was expected to go over his papers with some thoroughness; and for that purpose moved his entire set of files and boxes to my quarters in Boston. Much of the material which I correlated will be later published by the American Archaeological Society, but there was one box which I found exceedingly puzzling, and which I felt much averse from shewing to other eyes. It had been locked, and I did not find the key till it occurred to me to examine the personal ring which the professor carried always in his pocket. Then indeed I succeeded in opening it, but when I did so seemed only to be confronted by a greater and more closely locked barrier. For what could be the meaning of the queer clay bas-relief and the disjointed jottings, ramblings, and cuttings which I found? Had my uncle, in his latter years, become credulous of the most superficial impostures? I resolved to search out the eccentric sculptor responsible for this apparent disturbance of an old man's peace of mind.

The bas-relief was a rough rectangle less than an inch thick and about five by six inches in area; obviously of modern origin. Its designs, chowever, were far from modern in atmosphere and suggestion; for although the vagaries of cubism and futurism are many and wild, they do not often reproduce that cryptic regularity which lurks in prehistoric writing. And writing of some kind the bulk of these designs seemed certainly to be; though my memory, despite much familiarity with the papers

and collections of my uncle, failed in any way to identify this particular species, or even to hint at its remotest affiliations.

Above these apparent hieroglyphics was a figure of evidently pictorial intent, though its impressionistic execution forbade a very clear idea of its nature. It seemed to be a sort of monster, or symbol representing a monster, of a form which only a diseased fancy could conceive. If I say that my somewhat extravagant imagination yielded simultaneous pictures of an octopus, a dragon, and a human caricature, I shall not be unfaithful to the spirit of the thing. A pulpy, tentacled head surmounted a grotesque and scaly body with rudimentary wings; but it was the general outline of the whole which made it most shockingly frightful. Behind the figure was a vague suggestion of a Cyclopean architectural background.

The writing accompanying this oddity was, aside from a stack of press cuttings, in Professor Angell's most recent hand; and made no pretence to literary style. What seemed to be the main document was headed "CTHULHU CULT" in characters painstakingly printed to avoid the erroneous reading of a word so unheard-of. The manuscript was divided into two sections, the first of which was headed "1925—Dream and Dream Work of H. A. Wilcox, 7 Thomas St., Providence, R.I.", and the second, "Narrative of Inspector John R. Legrasse, 121 Bienville St., New Orleans, La., at 1908 A. A. S. Mtg.—Notes on Same, & Prof. Webb's Acct." The other manuscript papers were all brief notes, some of them accounts of the queer dreams of different persons, some of them citations from theosophical books and magazines (notably W. Scott-Elliot's Atlantis and the Lost Lemuria), and the rest comments on long-surviving secret societies and hidden cults, with references to passages in such mythological and anthropological source-books as Frazer's Golden Bough and Miss Murray's Witch-Cult in Western Europe. The cuttings largely alluded to outré mental illnesses and outbreaks of group folly or mania in the spring of 1925.

The first half of the principal manuscript told a very peculiar tale. It appears that on March 1st, 1925, a thin, dark young man of neurotic and excited aspect had called upon Professor Angell bearing the singular clay bas-relief, which was then exceedingly damp and fresh. His card bore the name of Henry Anthony Wilcox, and my uncle had recognised him as the youngest son of an excellent family slightly known to him, who had latterly been studying sculpture at the Rhode Island School of Design and living alone at the Fleur-de-Lys Building near that institution. Wilcox was a precocious youth of known genius but great eccentricity, and had from childhood excited attention through the strange stories and odd dreams he was in the habit of relating. He called himself "psychically hypersensitive", but the staid folk of the ancient commercial city dismissed him as merely "queer". Never mingling much with his kind, he had dropped gradually from social visibility, and was now known only to a small group of aesthetes from other towns. Even the Providence Art Club, anxious to preserve its conservatism, had found him quite hopeless.

On the occasion of the visit, ran the professor's manuscript, the sculptor abruptly asked for the benefit of his host's archaeological knowledge in identifying the hieroglyphics on the bas-relief. He spoke in a dreamy, stilted manner which suggested pose and alienated sympathy; and my uncle shewed some sharpness in replying, for the conspicuous freshness of the tablet

implied kinship with anything but archaeology. Young Wilcox's rejoinder, which impressed my uncle enough to make him recall and record it verbatim, was of a fantastically poetic cast which must have typified his whole conversation, and which I have since found highly characteristic of him. He said, "It is new, indeed, for I made it last night in a dream of strange cities; and dreams are older than brooding Tyre, or the contemplative Sphinx, or garden-girdled Babylon."

It was then that he began that rambling tale which suddenly played upon a sleeping memory and won the fevered interest of my uncle. There had been a slight earthquake tremor the night before, the most considerable felt in New England for some years; and Wilcox's imagination had been keenly affected. Upon retiring, he had had an unprecedented dream of great Cyclopean cities of titan blocks and sky-flung monoliths, all dripping with green ooze and sinister with latent horror. Hieroglyphics had covered the walls and pillars, and from some undetermined point below had come a voice that was not a voice; a chaotic sensation which only fancy could transmute into sound, but which he attempted to render by the almost unpronounceable jumble of letters, "Cthulhu fhtagn".

This verbal jumble was the key to the recollection which excited and disturbed Professor Angell. He questioned the sculptor with scientific minuteness; and studied with almost frantic intensity the bas-relief on which the youth had found himself working, chilled and clad only in his night-clothes, when waking had stolen bewilderingly over him. My uncle blamed his old age, Wilcox afterward said, for his slowness in recognising both hieroglyphics and pictorial design. Many of his questions seemed highly out-of-place to his visitor, especially those which tried to connect the latter with strange cults or societies; and Wilcox could not understand the repeated promises of silence which he was offered in exchange for an admission of membership in some widespread mystical or paganly religious body. When Professor Angell became convinced that the sculptor was indeed ignorant of any cult or system of cryptic lore, he besieged his visitor with demands for future reports of dreams. This bore regular fruit, for after the first interview the manuscript records daily calls of the young man, during which he related startling fragments of nocturnal imagery whose burden was always some terrible Cyclopean vista of dark and dripping stone, with a subterrene voice or intelligence shouting monotonously in enigmatical sense-impacts uninscribable save as gibberish. The two sounds most frequently repeated are those rendered by the letters "Cthulhu" and "R'lyeh".

On March 23d, the manuscript continued, Wilcox failed to appear; and inquiries at his quarters revealed that he had been stricken with an obscure sort of fever and taken to the home of his family in Waterman Street. He had cried out in the night, arousing several other artists in the building, and had manifested since then only alternations of unconsciousness and delirium. My uncle at once telephoned the family, and from that time forward kept close watch of the case; calling often at the Thayer Street office of Dr. Tobey, whom he learned to be in charge. The youth's febrile mind, apparently, was dwelling on strange things; and the doctor shuddered now and then as he spoke of them. They included not only a repetition of what he had formerly dreamed, but touched wildly on a gigantic thing "miles high" which walked or lumbered about. He at no time fully described this object, but occasional frantic words, as repeated by Dr. Tobey, convinced the professor that it must be identical with the nameless monstrosity he had sought to depict in his dream-sculpture. Reference to this object, the doctor added, was invariably a prelude to the young man's subsidence into lethargy. His temperature, oddly enough, was not greatly above normal; but his whole condition was otherwise such as to suggest true fever rather than mental disorder.

On April 2nd at about 3 p.m. every trace of Wilcox's malady suddenly ceased. He sat upright in bed, astonished to find himself at home and completely ignorant of what had happened in dream or reality since the night of March 22nd. Pronounced well by his physician, he returned to his quarters in three days; but to Professor Angell he was of no further assistance. All traces of strange dreaming had vanished with his recovery, and my uncle kept no record of his night-thoughts after a week of pointless and irrelevant accounts of thoroughly usual visions.

Here the first part of the manuscript ended, but references to certain of the scattered notes gave me much material for thought—so much, in fact, that only the ingrained scepticism then forming my philosophy can account for my continued distrust of the artist. The notes in question were those descriptive of the dreams of various persons covering the same period as that in which young Wilcox had had his strange visitations. My uncle, it seems, had quickly instituted a prodigiously far-flung body of inquiries amongst nearly all the friends whom he could question without impertinence, asking for nightly reports of their dreams, and the dates of any notable visions for some time past. The reception of his request seems to have been varied; but he must, at the very least, have received more responses than any ordinary man could have handled without a secretary. This original correspondence was not preserved, but his notes formed a thorough and really significant digest. Average people in society and business—New England's traditional "salt of the earth"—gave an almost completely negative result, though scattered cases of uneasy but formless nocturnal impressions appear here and there, always between March 23d and April 2nd—the period of young Wilcox's delirium. Scientific men were little more affected, though four cases of vague description suggest fugitive glimpses of strange landscapes, and in one case there is mentioned a dread of something abnormal.

It was from the artists and poets that the pertinent answers came, and I know that panic would have broken loose had they been able to compare notes. As it was, lacking their original letters, I half suspected the compiler of having asked leading questions, or of having edited the correspondence in corroboration of what he had latently resolved to see. That is why I continued to feel that Wilcox, somehow cognisant of the old data which my uncle had possessed, had been imposing on the veteran scientist. These responses from aesthetes told a disturbing tale. From February 28th to April 2nd a large proportion of them had dreamed very bizarre things, the intensity of the dreams being immeasurably the stronger during the period of the sculptor's delirium. Over a fourth of those who reported anything, reported scenes and half-sounds not unlike those which Wilcox had described; and some of the dreamers confessed acute fear of the gigantic nameless thing visible toward the last. One case, which the note describes with emphasis, was very sad. The subject, a widely known architect with leanings toward theosophy and occultism, went violently

insane on the date of young Wilcox's seizure, and expired several months later after incessant screamings to be saved from some escaped denizen of hell. Had my uncle referred to these cases by name instead of merely by number, I should have attempted some corroboration and personal investigation; but as it was, I succeeded in tracing down only a few. All of these, however, bore out the notes in full. I have often wondered if all the objects of the professor's questioning felt as puzzled as did this fraction. It is well that no explanation shall ever reach them.

The press cuttings, as I have intimated, touched on cases of panic, mania, and eccentricity during the given period. Professor Angell must have employed a cutting bureau, for the number of extracts was tremendous and the sources scattered throughout the globe. Here was a nocturnal suicide in London, where a lone sleeper had leaped from a window after a shocking cry. Here likewise a rambling letter to the editor of a paper in South America, where a fanatic deduces a dire future from visions he has seen. A despatch from California describes a theosophist colony as donning white robes en masse for some "glorious fulfilment" which never arrives, whilst items from India speak guardedly of serious native unrest toward the end of March. Voodoo orgies multiply in Hayti, and African outposts report ominous mutterings. American officers in the Philippines find certain tribes bothersome about this time, and New York policemen are mobbed by hysterical Levantines on the night of March 22–23. The west of Ireland, too, is full of wild rumour and legendry, and a fantastic painter named Ardois-Bonnot hangs a blasphemous "Dream Landscape" in the Paris spring salon of 1926. And so numerous are the recorded troubles in insane asylums, that only a miracle can have stopped the medical fraternity from noting strange parallelisms and drawing mystified conclusions. A weird bunch of cuttings, all told; and I can at this date scarcely envisage the callous rationalism with which I set them aside. But I was then convinced that young Wilcox had known of the older matters mentioned by the professor.

II.
The Tale of Inspector Legrasse.

The older matters which had made the sculptor's dream and bas-relief so significant to my uncle formed the subject of the second half of his long manuscript. Once before, it appears, Professor Angell had seen the hellish outlines of the nameless monstrosity, puzzled over the unknown hieroglyphics, and heard the ominous syllables which can be rendered only as "Cthulhu"; and all this in so stirring and horrible a connexion that it is small wonder he pursued young Wilcox with queries and demands for data.

The earlier experience had come in 1908, seventeen years before, when the American Archaeological Society held its annual meeting in St. Louis. Professor Angell, as befitted one of his authority and attainments, had had a prominent part in all the deliberations; and was one of the first to be approached by the several outsiders who took advantage of the convocation to offer questions for correct answering and problems for expert solution.

The chief of these outsiders, and in a short time the focus of interest for the entire meeting, was a commonplace-looking middle-aged man who had travelled all the way from New Orleans for certain

special information unobtainable from any local source. His name was John Raymond Legrasse, and he was by profession an Inspector of Police. With him he bore the subject of his visit, a grotesque, repulsive, and apparently very ancient stone statuette whose origin he was at a loss to determine. It must not be fancied that Inspector Legrasse had the least interest in archaeology. On the contrary, his wish for enlightenment was prompted by purely professional considerations. The statuette, idol, fetish, or whatever it was, had been captured some months before in the wooded swamps south of New Orleans during a raid on a supposed voodoo meeting; and so singular and hideous were the rites connected with it, that the police could not but realise that they had stumbled on a dark cult totally unknown to them, and infinitely more diabolic than even the blackest of the African voodoo circles. Of its origin, apart from the erratic and unbelievable tales extorted from the captured members, absolutely nothing was to be discovered; hence the anxiety of the police for any antiquarian lore which might help them to place the frightful symbol, and through it track down the cult to its fountain-head.

Inspector Legrasse was scarcely prepared for the sensation which his offering created. One sight of the thing had been enough to throw the assembled men of science into a state of tense excitement, and they lost no time in crowding around him to gaze at the diminutive figure whose utter strangeness and air of genuinely abysmal antiquity hinted so potently at unopened and archaic vistas. No recognised school of sculpture had animated this terrible object, yet centuries and even thousands of years seemed recorded in its dim and greenish surface of unplaceable stone.

The figure, which was finally passed slowly from man to man for close and careful study, was between seven and eight inches in height, and of exquisitely artistic workmanship. It represented a monster of vaguely anthropoid outline, but with an octopus-like head whose face was a mass of feelers, a scaly, rubbery-looking body, prodigious claws on hind and fore feet, and long, narrow wings behind. This thing, which seemed instinct with a fearsome and unnatural malignancy, was of a somewhat bloated corpulence, and squatted evilly on a rectangular block or pedestal covered with undecipherable characters. The tips of the wings touched the back edge of the block, the seat occupied the centre, whilst the long, curved claws of the doubled-up, crouching hind legs gripped the front edge and extended a quarter of the way down toward the bottom of the pedestal. The cephalopod head was bent forward, so that the ends of the facial feelers brushed the backs of huge fore paws which clasped the croucher's elevated knees. The aspect of the whole was abnormally life-like, and the more subtly fearful because its source was so totally unknown. Its vast, awesome, and incalculable age was unmistakable; yet not one link did it shew with any known type of art belonging to civilisation's youth—or indeed to any other time. Totally separate and apart, its very material was a mystery; for the soapy, greenish-black stone with its golden or iridescent flecks and striations resembled nothing familiar to geology or mineralogy. The characters along the base were equally baffling; and no member present, despite a representation of half the world's expert learning in this field, could form the least notion of even their remotest linguistic kinship. They, like the subject and material, belonged to something horribly remote and distinct from mankind as we know it; something frightfully suggestive of old and unhallowed cycles of life in which our world and our

conceptions have no part.

And yet, as the members severally shook their heads and confessed defeat at the Inspector's problem, there was one man in that gathering who suspected a touch of bizarre familiarity in the monstrous shape and writing, and who presently told with some diffidence of the odd trifle he knew. This person was the late William Channing Webb, Professor of Anthropology in Princeton University, and an explorer of no slight note. Professor Webb had been engaged, forty-eight years before, in a tour of Greenland and Iceland in search of some Runic inscriptions which he failed to unearth; and whilst high up on the West Greenland coast had encountered a singular tribe or cult of degenerate Esquimaux whose religion, a curious form of devil-worship, chilled him with its deliberate bloodthirstiness and repulsiveness. It was a faith of which other Esquimaux knew little, and which they mentioned only with shudders, saying that it had come down from horribly ancient aeons before ever the world was made. Besides nameless rites and human sacrifices there were certain queer hereditary rituals addressed to a supreme elder devil or tornasuk; and of this Professor Webb had taken a careful phonetic copy from an aged angekok or wizard-priest, expressing the sounds in Roman letters as best he knew how. But just now of prime significance was the fetish which this cult had cherished, and around which they danced when the aurora leaped high over the ice cliffs. It was, the professor stated, a very crude bas-relief of stone, comprising a hideous picture and some cryptic writing. And so far as he could tell, it was a rough parallel in all essential features of the bestial thing now lying before the meeting.

This data, received with suspense and astonishment

by the assembled members, proved doubly exciting to Inspector Legrasse; and he began at once to ply his informant with questions. Having noted and copied an oral ritual among the swamp cult-worshippers his men had arrested, he besought the professor to remember as best he might the syllables taken down amongst the diabolist Esquimaux. There then followed an exhaustive comparison of details, and a moment of really awed silence when both detective and scientist agreed on the virtual identity of the phrase common to two hellish rituals so many worlds of distance apart. What, in substance, both the Esquimau wizards and the Louisiana swamp-priests had chanted to their kindred idols was something very like this—the word-divisions being guessed at from traditional breaks in the phrase as chanted aloud:

"Ph'nglui mglw'nafh Cthulhu R'lyeh wgah'nagl fhtagn."

Legrasse had one point in advance of Professor Webb, for several among his mongrel prisoners had repeated to him what older celebrants had told them the words meant. This text, as given, ran something like this:

"In his house at R'lyeh dead Cthulhu waits dreaming."

And now, in response to a general and urgent demand, Inspector Legrasse related as fully as possible his experience with the swamp worshippers; telling a story to which I could see my uncle attached profound significance. It savoured of the wildest dreams of myth-maker and theosophist, and disclosed an astonishing degree of cosmic imagination among such half-castes and pariahs as might be least expected to possess it.

On November 1st, 1907, there had come to the New Orleans police a frantic summons from the swamp and lagoon country to the south. The squatters there, mostly primitive but good-natured descendants of Lafitte's men, were in the grip of stark terror from an unknown thing which had stolen upon them in the night. It was voodoo, apparently, but voodoo of a more terrible sort than they had ever known; and some of their women and children had disappeared since the malevolent tom-tom had begun its incessant beating far within the black haunted woods where no dweller ventured. There were insane shouts and harrowing screams, soul-chilling chants and dancing devil-flames; and, the frightened messenger added, the people could stand it no more.

So a body of twenty police, filling two carriages and an automobile, had set out in the late afternoon with the shivering squatter as a guide. At the end of the passable road they alighted, and for miles splashed on in silence through the terrible cypress woods where day never came. Ugly roots and malignant hanging nooses of Spanish moss beset them, and now and then a pile of dank stones or fragment of a rotting wall intensified by its hint of morbid habitation a depression which every malformed tree and every fungous islet combined to create. At length the squatter settlement, a miserable huddle of huts, hove in sight; and hysterical dwellers ran out to cluster around the group of bobbing lanterns. The muffled beat of tom-toms was now faintly audible far, far ahead; and a curdling shriek came at infrequent intervals when the wind shifted. A reddish glare, too, seemed to filter through the pale undergrowth beyond endless avenues of forest night. Reluctant even to be left alone again, each one of the cowed squatters refused point-blank to advance another inch toward the scene of unholy worship, so Inspector Legrasse and his nineteen colleagues plunged on unguided into black arcades of horror that none of them had ever trod before.

The region now entered by the police was one of traditionally evil repute, substantially unknown and untraversed by white men. There were legends of a hidden lake unglimpsed by mortal sight, in which dwelt a huge, formless white polypous thing with luminous eyes; and squatters whispered that bat-winged devils flew up out of caverns in inner earth to worship it at midnight. They said it had been there before D'Iberville, before La Salle, before the Indians, and before even the wholesome beasts and birds of the woods. It was nightmare itself, and to see it was to die. But it made men dream, and so they knew enough to keep away. The present voodoo orgy was, indeed, on the merest fringe of this abhorred area, but that location was bad enough; hence perhaps the very place of the worship had terrified the squatters more than the shocking sounds and incidents.

Only poetry or madness could do justice to the noises heard by Legrasse's men as they ploughed on through the black morass toward the red glare and the muffled tom-toms. There are vocal qualities peculiar to men, and vocal qualities peculiar to beasts; and it is terrible to hear the one when the source should yield the other. Animal fury and orgiastic licence here whipped themselves to daemoniac heights by howls and squawking ecstasies that tore and reverberated through those nighted woods like pestilential tempests from the gulfs of hell. Now and then the less organised ululation would cease, and from what seemed a well-drilled chorus of hoarse voices would rise in sing-song chant that hideous phrase or ritual:

"Ph'nglui mglw'nafh Cthulhu R'lyeh wgah'nagl fhtagn."

Then the men, having reached a spot where the trees were thinner, came suddenly in sight of the spectacle itself. Four of them reeled, one fainted, and two were shaken into a frantic cry which the mad cacophony of the orgy fortunately deadened. Legrasse dashed swamp water on the face of the fainting man, and all stood trembling and nearly hypnotised with horror.

In a natural glade of the swamp stood a grassy island of perhaps an acre's extent, clear of trees and tolerably dry. On this now leaped and twisted a more indescribable horde of human abnormality than any but a Sime or an Angarola could paint. Void of clothing, this hybrid spawn were braying, bellowing, and writhing about a monstrous ring-shaped bonfire; in the centre of which, revealed by occasional rifts in the curtain of flame, stood a great granite monolith some eight feet in height; on top of which, incongruous with its diminutiveness, rested the noxious carven statuette. From a wide circle of ten scaffolds set up at regular intervals with the flame-girt monolith as a centre hung, head downward, the oddly marred bodies of the helpless squatters who had disappeared. It was inside this circle that the ring of worshippers jumped and roared, the general direction of the mass motion being from left to right in endless Bacchanal between the ring of bodies and the ring of fire.

It may have been only imagination and it may have been only echoes which induced one of the men, an excitable Spaniard, to fancy he heard antiphonal responses to the ritual from some far and unillumined spot deeper within the wood of ancient legendry and horror. This man, Joseph D. Galvez, I later met and questioned; and he proved distractingly imaginative. He indeed went so far as to hint of the faint beating of great wings, and of a glimpse of shining eyes and a mountainous white bulk beyond the remotest trees—but I suppose he had been hearing too much native superstition.

Actually, the horrified pause of the men was of comparatively brief duration. Duty came first; and although there must have been nearly a hundred mongrel celebrants in the throng, the police relied on their firearms and plunged determinedly into the nauseous rout. For five minutes the resultant din and chaos were beyond description. Wild blows were struck, shots were fired, and escapes were made; but in the end Legrasse was able to count some forty-seven sullen prisoners, whom he forced to dress in haste and fall into line between two rows of policemen. Five of the worshippers lay dead, and two severely wounded ones were carried away on improvised stretchers by their fellow-prisoners. The image on the monolith, of course, was carefully removed and carried back by Legrasse.

Examined at headquarters after a trip of intense strain and weariness, the prisoners all proved to be men of a very low, mixed-blooded, and mentally aberrant type. Most were seamen, and a sprinkling of negroes and mulattoes, largely West Indians or Brava Portuguese from the Cape Verde Islands, gave a colouring of voodooism to the heterogeneous cult. But before many questions were asked, it became manifest that something far deeper and older than negro fetichism was involved. Degraded and ignorant as they were, the creatures held with surprising consistency to the central idea of their loathsome faith.

They worshipped, so they said, the Great Old Ones who lived ages before there were any men, and who came to the young world out of the sky. Those Old Ones were gone now, inside the earth and under the sea; but their dead bodies had told their secrets in dreams to the first men, who formed a cult which had never died. This was that cult, and the prisoners said it had always existed and always would exist, hidden in distant wastes and dark places all over the world until the time when the great priest Cthulhu, from his dark house in the mighty city of R'lyeh under the waters, should rise and bring the earth again beneath his sway. Some day he would call, when the stars were ready, and the secret cult would always be waiting to liberate him.

Meanwhile no more must be told. There was a secret which even torture could not extract. Mankind was not absolutely alone among the conscious things of earth, for shapes came out of the dark to visit the faithful few. But these were not the Great Old Ones. No man had ever seen the Old Ones. The carven idol was great Cthulhu, but none might say whether or not the others were precisely like him. No one could read the old writing now, but things were told by word of mouth. The chanted ritual was not the secret—that was never spoken aloud, only whispered. The chant meant only this: "In his house at R'lyeh dead Cthulhu waits dreaming."

Only two of the prisoners were found sane enough to be hanged, and the rest were committed to various institutions. All denied a part in the ritual murders, and averred that the killing had been done by Black Winged Ones which had come to them from their immemorial meeting-place in the haunted wood. But of those mysterious allies no coherent account could ever be gained. What the police did extract, came mainly from an immensely aged mestizo named Castro, who claimed to have sailed to strange ports and talked with undying leaders of the cult in the mountains of China.

Old Castro remembered bits of hideous legend that paled the speculations of theosophists and made man and the world seem recent and transient indeed. There had been aeons when other Things ruled on the earth, and They had had great cities. Remains of Them, he said the deathless Chinamen had told him, were still to be found as Cyclopean stones on islands in the Pacific. They all died vast epochs of time before men came, but there were arts which could revive Them when the stars had come round again to the right positions in the cycle of eternity. They had, indeed, come themselves from the stars, and brought Their images with Them.

These Great Old Ones, Castro continued, were not composed altogether of flesh and blood. They had shape—for did not this star-fashioned image prove it?—but that shape was not made of matter. When the stars were right, They could plunge from world to world through the sky; but when the stars were wrong, They could not live. But although They no longer lived, They would never really die. They all lay in stone houses in Their great city of R'lyeh, preserved by the spells of mighty Cthulhu for a glorious resurrection when the stars and the earth might once more be ready for Them. But at that time some force from outside must serve to liberate Their bodies. The spells that preserved Them intact likewise prevented Them from making an initial move, and They could only lie awake in the dark and think whilst uncounted millions of years rolled by. They knew all that was occurring in the universe, but Their mode of speech was transmitted

thought. Even now They talked in Their tombs. When, after infinities of chaos, the first men came, the Great Old Ones spoke to the sensitive among them by moulding their dreams; for only thus could Their language reach the fleshly minds of mammals.

Then, whispered Castro, those first men formed the cult around small idols which the Great Ones shewed them; idols brought in dim aeras from dark stars. That cult would never die till the stars came right again, and the secret priests would take great Cthulhu from His tomb to revive His subjects and resume His rule of earth. The time would be easy to know, for then mankind would have become as the Great Old Ones; free and wild and beyond good and evil, with laws and morals thrown aside and all men shouting and killing and revelling in joy. Then the liberated Old Ones would teach them new ways to shout and kill and revel and enjoy themselves, and all the earth would flame with a holocaust of ecstasy and freedom. Meanwhile the cult, by appropriate rites, must keep alive the memory of those ancient ways and shadow forth the prophecy of their return.

In the elder time chosen men had talked with the entombed Old Ones in dreams, but then something had happened. The great stone city R'lyeh, with its monoliths and sepulchres, had sunk beneath the waves; and the deep waters, full of the one primal mystery through which not even thought can pass, had cut off the spectral intercourse. But memory never died, and high-priests said that the city would rise again when the stars were right. Then came out of the earth the black spirits of earth, mouldy and shadowy, and full of dim rumours picked up in caverns beneath forgotten sea-bottoms. But of them old Castro dared not speak much. He cut himself off hurriedly, and no amount of persuasion or subtlety could elicit more in this direction. The size of the Old Ones, too, he curiously declined to mention. Of the cult, he said that he thought the centre lay amid the pathless deserts of Arabia, where Irem, the City of Pillars, dreams hidden and untouched. It was not allied to the European witch-cult, and was virtually unknown beyond its members. No book had ever really hinted of it, though the deathless Chinamen said that there were double meanings in the Necronomicon of the mad Arab Abdul Alhazred which the initiated might read as they chose, especially the much-discussed couplet:

"That is not dead which can eternal lie,
And with strange aeons even death may die."

Legrasse, deeply impressed and not a little bewildered, had inquired in vain concerning the historic affiliations of the cult. Castro, apparently, had told the truth when he said that it was wholly secret. The authorities at Tulane University could shed no light upon either cult or image, and now the detective had come to the highest authorities in the country and met with no more than the Greenland tale of Professor Webb.

The feverish interest aroused at the meeting by Legrasse's tale, corroborated as it was by the statuette, is echoed in the subsequent correspondence of those who attended; although scant mention occurs in the formal publications of the society. Caution is the first care of those accustomed to face occasional charlatanry and imposture. Legrasse for some time lent the image to Professor Webb, but at the latter's death it was returned to him and remains in his possession, where I viewed it not long ago. It is truly a terrible thing, and unmistakably

akin to the dream-sculpture of young Wilcox.

That my uncle was excited by the tale of the sculptor I did not wonder, for what thoughts must arise upon hearing, after a knowledge of what Legrasse had learned of the cult, of a sensitive young man who had dreamed not only the figure and exact hieroglyphics of the swamp-found image and the Greenland devil tablet, but had come in his dreams upon at least three of the precise words of the formula uttered alike by Esquimau diabolists and mongrel Louisianans? Professor Angell's instant start on an investigation of the utmost thoroughness was eminently natural; though privately I suspected young Wilcox of having heard of the cult in some indirect way, and of having invented a series of dreams to heighten and continue the mystery at my uncle's expense. The dream-narratives and cuttings collected by the professor were, of course, strong corroboration; but the rationalism of my mind and the extravagance of the whole subject led me to adopt what I thought the most sensible conclusions. So, after thoroughly studying the manuscript again and correlating the theosophical and anthropological notes with the cult narrative of Legrasse, I made a trip to Providence to see the sculptor and give him the rebuke I thought proper for so boldly imposing upon a learned and aged man.

Wilcox still lived alone in the Fleur-de-Lys Building in Thomas Street, a hideous Victorian imitation of seventeenth-century Breton architecture which flaunts its stuccoed front amidst the lovely colonial houses on the ancient hill, and under the very shadow of the finest Georgian steeple in America. I found him at work in his rooms, and at once conceded from the specimens scattered about that his genius is indeed profound and authentic. He will, I believe, some time be heard from as one of the great decadents; for he has crystallised in clay and will one day mirror in marble those nightmares and phantasies which Arthur Machen evokes in prose, and Clark Ashton Smith makes visible in verse and in painting.

Dark, frail, and somewhat unkempt in aspect, he turned languidly at my knock and asked me my business without rising. When I told him who I was, he displayed some interest; for my uncle had excited his curiosity in probing his strange dreams, yet had never explained the reason for the study. I did not enlarge his knowledge in this regard, but sought with some subtlety to draw him out. In a short time I became convinced of his absolute sincerity, for he spoke of the dreams in a manner none could mistake. They and their subconscious residuum had influenced his art profoundly, and he shewed me a morbid statue whose contours almost made me shake with the potency of its black suggestion. He could not recall having seen the original of this thing except in his own dream bas-relief, but the outlines had formed themselves insensibly under his hands. It was, no doubt, the giant shape he had raved of in delirium. That he really knew nothing of the hidden cult, save from what my uncle's relentless catechism had let fall, he soon made clear; and again I strove to think of some way in which he could possibly have received the weird impressions.

He talked of his dreams in a strangely poetic fashion; making me see with terrible vividness the damp Cyclopean city of slimy green stone—whose geometry, he oddly said, was all wrong—and hear with frightened expectancy the ceaseless, half-mental calling from underground: "Cthulhu fhtagn", "Cthulhu fhtagn". These

words had formed part of that dread ritual which told of dead Cthulhu's dream-vigil in his stone vault at R'lyeh, and I felt deeply moved despite my rational beliefs. Wilcox, I was sure, had heard of the cult in some casual way, and had soon forgotten it amidst the mass of his equally weird reading and imagining. Later, by virtue of its sheer impressiveness, it had found subconscious expression in dreams, in the bas-relief, and in the terrible statue I now beheld; so that his imposture upon my uncle had been a very innocent one. The youth was of a type, at once slightly affected and slightly ill-mannered, which I could never like; but I was willing enough now to admit both his genius and his honesty. I took leave of him amicably, and wish him all the success his talent promises.

The matter of the cult still remained to fascinate me, and at times I had visions of personal fame from researches into its origin and connexions. I visited New Orleans, talked with Legrasse and others of that old-time raiding-party, saw the frightful image, and even questioned such of the mongrel prisoners as still survived. Old Castro, unfortunately, had been dead for some years. What I now heard so graphically at first-hand, though it was really no more than a detailed confirmation of what my uncle had written, excited me afresh; for I felt sure that I was on the track of a very real, very secret, and very ancient religion whose discovery would make me an anthropologist of note. My attitude was still one of absolute materialism, as I wish it still were, and I discounted with almost inexplicable perversity the coincidence of the dream notes and odd cuttings collected by Professor Angell.

One thing I began to suspect, and which I now fear I know, is that my uncle's death was far from natural. He fell on a narrow hill street leading up from an ancient waterfront swarming with foreign mongrels, after a careless push from a negro sailor. I did not forget the mixed blood and marine pursuits of the cult-members in Louisiana, and would not be surprised to learn of secret methods and poison needles as ruthless and as anciently known as the cryptic rites and beliefs. Legrasse and his men, it is true, have been let alone; but in Norway a certain seaman who saw things is dead. Might not the deeper inquiries of my uncle after encountering the sculptor's data have come to sinister ears? I think Professor Angell died because he knew too much, or because he was likely to learn too much. Whether I shall go as he did remains to be seen, for I have learned much now.

III.

The Madness from the Sea.

If heaven ever wishes to grant me a boon, it will be a total effacing of the results of a mere chance which fixed my eye on a certain stray piece of shelf-paper. It was nothing on which I would naturally have stumbled in the course of my daily round, for it was an old number of an Australian journal, the Sydney Bulletin for April 18, 1925. It had escaped even the cutting bureau which had at the time of its issuance been avidly collecting material for my uncle's research.

I had largely given over my inquiries into what Professor Angell called the "Cthulhu Cult", and was visiting a learned friend in Paterson, New Jersey; the curator of a local museum and a mineralogist of note. Examining one day the reserve specimens roughly set on the storage shelves in a rear room of the museum, my eye was caught by an odd picture in one of the old papers

spread beneath the stones. It was the Sydney Bulletin I have mentioned, for my friend has wide affiliations in all conceivable foreign parts; and the picture was a half-tone cut of a hideous stone image almost identical with that which Legrasse had found in the swamp.

Eagerly clearing the sheet of its precious contents, I scanned the item in detail; and was disappointed to find it of only moderate length. What it suggested, however, was of portentous significance to my flagging quest; and I carefully tore it out for immediate action. It read as follows:

MYSTERY DERELICT FOUND AT SEA
Vigilant Arrives With Helpless Armed New Zealand Yacht in Tow.
One Survivor and Dead Man Found Aboard. Tale of Desperate Battle and Deaths at Sea.
Rescued Seaman Refuses
Particulars of Strange Experience.
Odd Idol Found in His Possession. Inquiry to Follow.

The Morrison Co.'s freighter Vigilant, bound from Valparaiso, arrived this morning at its wharf in Darling Harbour, having in tow the battled and disabled but heavily armed steam yacht Alert of Dunedin, N. Z., which was sighted April 12th in S. Latitude 34° 21', W. Longitude 152° 17' with one living and one dead man aboard.

The Vigilant left Valparaiso March 25th, and on April 2nd was driven considerably south of her course by exceptionally heavy storms and monster waves. On April 12th the derelict was sighted; and though apparently deserted, was found upon boarding to contain one survivor in a half-delirious condition and one man who had evidently been dead for more than a week. The living man was clutching a horrible stone idol of unknown origin, about a foot in height, regarding whose nature authorities at Sydney University, the Royal Society, and the Museum in College Street all profess complete bafflement, and which the survivor says he found in the cabin of the yacht, in a small carved shrine of common pattern.

This man, after recovering his senses, told an exceedingly strange story of piracy and slaughter. He is Gustaf Johansen, a Norwegian of some intelligence, and had been second mate of the two-masted schooner Emma of Auckland, which sailed for Callao February 20th with a complement of eleven men. The Emma, he says, was delayed and thrown widely south of her course by the great storm of March 1st, and on March 22nd, in S. Latitude 49° 51', W. Longitude 128° 34', encountered the Alert, manned by a queer and evil-looking crew of Kanakas and half-castes. Being ordered peremptorily to turn back, Capt. Collins refused; whereupon the strange crew began to fire savagely and without warning upon the schooner with a peculiarly heavy battery of brass cannon forming part of the yacht's equipment. The Emma's men shewed fight, says the survivor, and though the schooner began to sink from shots beneath the waterline they managed to heave alongside their enemy and board her, grappling with the savage crew on the yacht's deck, and being forced to kill them all, the number being slightly superior, because of their particularly abhorrent and desperate though rather clumsy mode of fighting.

Three of the Emma's men, including Capt. Collins and

First Mate Green, were killed; and the remaining eight under Second Mate Johansen proceeded to navigate the captured yacht, going ahead in their original direction to see if any reason for their ordering back had existed. The next day, it appears, they raised and landed on a small island, although none is known to exist in that part of the ocean; and six of the men somehow died ashore, though Johansen is queerly reticent about this part of his story, and speaks only of their falling into a rock chasm. Later, it seems, he and one companion boarded the yacht and tried to manage her, but were beaten about by the storm of April 2nd. From that time till his rescue on the 12th the man remembers little, and he does not even recall when William Briden, his companion, died. Briden's death reveals no apparent cause, and was probably due to excitement or exposure. Cable advices from Dunedin report that the Alert was well known there as an island trader, and bore an evil reputation along the waterfront. It was owned by a curious group of half-castes whose frequent meetings and night trips to the woods attracted no little curiosity; and it had set sail in great haste just after the storm and earth tremors of March 1st. Our Auckland correspondent gives the Emma and her crew an excellent reputation, and Johansen is described as a sober and worthy man. The admiralty will institute an inquiry on the whole matter beginning tomorrow, at which every effort will be made to induce Johansen to speak more freely than he has done hitherto.

This was all, together with the picture of the hellish image; but what a train of ideas it started in my mind! Here were new treasuries of data on the Cthulhu Cult, and evidence that it had strange interests at sea as well as on land. What motive prompted the hybrid crew to order back the Emma as they sailed about with their hideous idol? What was the unknown island on which six of the Emma's crew had died, and about which the mate Johansen was so secretive? What had the vice-admiralty's investigation brought out, and what was known of the noxious cult in Dunedin? And most marvellous of all, what deep and more than natural linkage of dates was this which gave a malign and now undeniable significance to the various turns of events so carefully noted by my uncle?

March 1st—our February 28th according to the International Date Line—the earthquake and storm had come. From Dunedin the Alert and her noisome crew had darted eagerly forth as if imperiously summoned, and on the other side of the earth poets and artists had begun to dream of a strange, dank Cyclopean city whilst a young sculptor had moulded in his sleep the form of the dreaded Cthulhu. March 23d the crew of the Emma landed on an unknown island and left six men dead; and on that date the dreams of sensitive men assumed a heightened vividness and darkened with dread of a giant monster's malign pursuit, whilst an architect had gone mad and a sculptor had lapsed suddenly into delirium! And what of this storm of April 2nd—the date on which all dreams of the dank city ceased, and Wilcox emerged unharmed from the bondage of strange fever? What of all this—and of those hints of old Castro about the sunken, star-born Old Ones and their coming reign; their faithful cult and their mastery of dreams? Was I tottering on the brink of cosmic horrors beyond man's power to bear? If so, they must be horrors of the mind alone, for in some way the second of April had put a stop to whatever monstrous menace had begun its siege of mankind's soul.

That evening, after a day of hurried cabling and

arranging, I bade my host adieu and took a train for San Francisco. In less than a month I was in Dunedin; where, however, I found that little was known of the strange cult-members who had lingered in the old sea-taverns. Waterfront scum was far too common for special mention; though there was vague talk about one inland trip these mongrels had made, during which faint drumming and red flame were noted on the distant hills. In Auckland I learned that Johansen had returned with yellow hair turned white after a perfunctory and inconclusive questioning at Sydney, and had thereafter sold his cottage in West Street and sailed with his wife to his old home in Oslo. Of his stirring experience he would tell his friends no more than he had told the admiralty officials, and all they could do was to give me his Oslo address.

After that I went to Sydney and talked profitlessly with seamen and members of the vice-admiralty court. I saw the Alert, now sold and in commercial use, at Circular Quay in Sydney Cove, but gained nothing from its non-committal bulk. The crouching image with its cuttlefish head, dragon body, scaly wings, and hieroglyphed pedestal, was preserved in the Museum at Hyde Park; and I studied it long and well, finding it a thing of balefully exquisite workmanship, and with the same utter mystery, terrible antiquity, and unearthly strangeness of material which I had noted in Legrasse's smaller specimen. Geologists, the curator told me, had found it a monstrous puzzle; for they vowed that the world held no rock like it. Then I thought with a shudder of what old Castro had told Legrasse about the primal Great Ones: "They had come from the stars, and had brought Their images with Them."

Shaken with such a mental revolution as I had never before known, I now resolved to visit Mate Johansen in Oslo. Sailing for London, I reëmbarked at once for the Norwegian capital; and one autumn day landed at the trim wharves in the shadow of the Egeberg. Johansen's address, I discovered, lay in the Old Town of King Harold Haardrada, which kept alive the name of Oslo during all the centuries that the greater city masqueraded as "Christiana". I made the brief trip by taxicab, and knocked with palpitant heart at the door of a neat and ancient building with plastered front. A sad-faced woman in black answered my summons, and I was stung with disappointment when she told me in halting English that Gustaf Johansen was no more.

He had not survived his return, said his wife, for the doings at sea in 1925 had broken him. He had told her no more than he had told the public, but had left a long manuscript—of "technical matters" as he said—written in English, evidently in order to safeguard her from the peril of casual perusal. During a walk through a narrow lane near the Gothenburg dock, a bundle of papers falling from an attic window had knocked him down. Two Lascar sailors at once helped him to his feet, but before the ambulance could reach him he was dead. Physicians found no adequate cause for the end, and laid it to heart trouble and a weakened constitution.

I now felt gnawing at my vitals that dark terror which will never leave me till I, too, am at rest; "accidentally" or otherwise. Persuading the widow that my connexion with her husband's "technical matters" was sufficient to entitle me to his manuscript, I bore the document away and began to read it on the London boat. It was a simple, rambling thing—a naive sailor's effort at a post-facto

diary—and strove to recall day by day that last awful voyage. I cannot attempt to transcribe it verbatim in all its cloudiness and redundance, but I will tell its gist enough to shew why the sound of the water against the vessel's sides became so unendurable to me that I stopped my ears with cotton.

Johansen, thank God, did not know quite all, even though he saw the city and the Thing, but I shall never sleep calmly again when I think of the horrors that lurk ceaselessly behind life in time and in space, and of those unhallowed blasphemies from elder stars which dream beneath the sea, known and favoured by a nightmare cult ready and eager to loose them on the world whenever another earthquake shall heave their monstrous stone city again to the sun and air.

Johansen's voyage had begun just as he told it to the vice-admiralty. The Emma, in ballast, had cleared Auckland on February 20th, and had felt the full force of that earthquake-born tempest which must have heaved up from the sea-bottom the horrors that filled men's dreams. Once more under control, the ship was making good progress when held up by the Alert on March 22nd, and I could feel the mate's regret as he wrote of her bombardment and sinking. Of the swarthy cult-fiends on the Alert he speaks with significant horror. There was some peculiarly abominable quality about them which made their destruction seem almost a duty, and Johansen shews ingenuous wonder at the charge of ruthlessness brought against his party during the proceedings of the court of inquiry. Then, driven ahead by curiosity in their captured yacht under Johansen's command, the men sight a great stone pillar sticking out of the sea, and in S. Latitude 47° 9', W. Longitude 126° 43' come upon a coast-line of mingled mud, ooze, and weedy Cyclopean masonry which can be nothing less than the tangible substance of earth's supreme terror—the nightmare corpse-city of R'lyeh, that was built in measureless aeons behind history by the vast, loathsome shapes that seeped down from the dark stars. There lay great Cthulhu and his hordes, hidden in green slimy vaults and sending out at last, after cycles incalculable, the thoughts that spread fear to the dreams of the sensitive and called imperiously to the faithful to come on a pilgrimage of liberation and restoration. All this Johansen did not suspect, but God knows he soon saw enough!

I suppose that only a single mountain-top, the hideous monolith-crowned citadel whereon great Cthulhu was buried, actually emerged from the waters. When I think of the extent of all that may be brooding down there I almost wish to kill myself forthwith. Johansen and his men were awed by the cosmic majesty of this dripping Babylon of elder daemons, and must have guessed without guidance that it was nothing of this or of any sane planet. Awe at the unbelievable size of the greenish stone blocks, at the dizzying height of the great carven monolith, and at the stupefying identity of the colossal statues and bas-reliefs with the queer image found in the shrine on the Alert, is poignantly visible in every line of the mate's frightened description.

Without knowing what futurism is like, Johansen achieved something very close to it when he spoke of the city; for instead of describing any definite structure or building, he dwells only on broad impressions of vast angles and stone surfaces—surfaces too great to belong to any thing right or proper for this earth, and impious with horrible images and hieroglyphs. I mention his talk about

angles because it suggests something Wilcox had told me of his awful dreams. He had said that the geometry of the dream-place he saw was abnormal, non-Euclidean, and loathsomely redolent of spheres and dimensions apart from ours. Now an unlettered seaman felt the same thing whilst gazing at the terrible reality.

Johansen and his men landed at a sloping mud-bank on this monstrous Acropolis, and clambered slipperily up over titan oozy blocks which could have been no mortal staircase. The very sun of heaven seemed distorted when viewed through the polarising miasma welling out from this sea-soaked perversion, and twisted menace and suspense lurked leeringly in those crazily elusive angles of carven rock where a second glance shewed concavity after the first shewed convexity.

Something very like fright had come over all the explorers before anything more definite than rock and ooze and weed was seen. Each would have fled had he not feared the scorn of the others, and it was only half-heartedly that they searched—vainly, as it proved—for some portable souvenir to bear away.

It was Rodriguez the Portuguese who climbed up the foot of the monolith and shouted of what he had found. The rest followed him, and looked curiously at the immense carved door with the now familiar squid-dragon bas-relief. It was, Johansen said, like a great barn-door; and they all felt that it was a door because of the ornate lintel, threshold, and jambs around it, though they could not decide whether it lay flat like a trap-door or slantwise like an outside cellar-door. As Wilcox would have said, the geometry of the place was all wrong. One could not be sure that the sea and the ground were horizontal, hence the relative position of everything else seemed phantasmally variable.

Briden pushed at the stone in several places without result. Then Donovan felt over it delicately around the edge, pressing each point separately as he went. He climbed interminably along the grotesque stone moulding—that is, one would call it climbing if the thing was not after all horizontal—and the men wondered how any door in the universe could be so vast. Then, very softly and slowly, the acre-great panel began to give inward at the top; and they saw that it was balanced. Donovan slid or somehow propelled himself down or along the jamb and rejoined his fellows, and everyone watched the queer recession of the monstrously carven portal. In this phantasy of prismatic distortion it moved anomalously in a diagonal way, so that all the rules of matter and perspective seemed upset.

The aperture was black with a darkness almost material. That tenebrousness was indeed a positive quality; for it obscured such parts of the inner walls as ought to have been revealed, and actually burst forth like smoke from its aeon-long imprisonment, visibly darkening the sun as it slunk away into the shrunken and gibbous sky on flapping membraneous wings. The odour arising from the newly opened depths was intolerable, and at length the quick-eared Hawkins thought he heard a nasty, slopping sound down there. Everyone listened, and everyone was listening still when It lumbered slobberingly into sight and gropingly squeezed Its gelatinous green immensity through the black doorway into the tainted outside air of that poison city of madness.

Poor Johansen's handwriting almost gave out when he

wrote of this. Of the six men who never reached the ship, he thinks two perished of pure fright in that accursed instant. The Thing cannot be described—there is no language for such abysms of shrieking and immemorial lunacy, such eldritch contradictions of all matter, force, and cosmic order. A mountain walked or stumbled. God! What wonder that across the earth a great architect went mad, and poor Wilcox raved with fever in that telepathic instant? The Thing of the idols, the green, sticky spawn of the stars, had awaked to claim his own. The stars were right again, and what an age-old cult had failed to do by design, a band of innocent sailors had done by accident. After vigintillions of years great Cthulhu was loose again, and ravening for delight.

Three men were swept up by the flabby claws before anybody turned. God rest them, if there be any rest in the universe. They were Donovan, Guerrera, and Ångstrom. Parker slipped as the other three were plunging frenziedly over endless vistas of green-crusted rock to the boat, and Johansen swears he was swallowed up by an angle of masonry which shouldn't have been there; an angle which was acute, but behaved as if it were obtuse. So only Briden and Johansen reached the boat, and pulled desperately for the Alert as the mountainous monstrosity flopped down the slimy stones and hesitated floundering at the edge of the water.

Steam had not been suffered to go down entirely, despite the departure of all hands for the shore; and it was the work of only a few moments of feverish rushing up and down between wheel and engines to get the Alert under way. Slowly, amidst the distorted horrors of that indescribable scene, she began to churn the lethal waters; whilst on the masonry of that charnel shore that was not of earth the titan Thing from the stars slavered and gibbered like Polypheme cursing the fleeing ship of Odysseus. Then, bolder than the storied Cyclops, great Cthulhu slid greasily into the water and began to pursue with vast wave-raising strokes of cosmic potency. Briden looked back and went mad, laughing shrilly as he kept on laughing at intervals till death found him one night in the cabin whilst Johansen was wandering deliriously.

But Johansen had not given out yet. Knowing that the Thing could surely overtake the Alert until steam was fully up, he resolved on a desperate chance; and, setting the engine for full speed, ran lightning-like on deck and reversed the wheel. There was a mighty eddying and foaming in the noisome brine, and as the steam mounted higher and higher the brave Norwegian drove his vessel head on against the pursuing jelly which rose above the unclean froth like the stern of a daemon galleon. The awful squid-head with writhing feelers came nearly up to the bowsprit of the sturdy yacht, but Johansen drove on relentlessly. There was a bursting as of an exploding bladder, a slushy nastiness as of a cloven sunfish, a stench as of a thousand opened graves, and a sound that the chronicler would not put on paper. For an instant the ship was befouled by an acrid and blinding green cloud, and then there was only a venomous seething astern; where—God in heaven!—the scattered plasticity of that nameless sky-spawn was nebulously recombining in its hateful original form, whilst its distance widened every second as the Alert gained impetus from its mounting steam.

That was all. After that Johansen only brooded over the idol in the cabin and attended to a few matters of food for himself and the laughing maniac by his side. He

did not try to navigate after the first bold flight, for the reaction had taken something out of his soul. Then came the storm of April 2nd, and a gathering of the clouds about his consciousness. There is a sense of spectral whirling through liquid gulfs of infinity, of dizzying rides through reeling universes on a comet's tail, and of hysterical plunges from the pit to the moon and from the moon back again to the pit, all livened by a cachinnating chorus of the distorted, hilarious elder gods and the green, bat-winged mocking imps of Tartarus.

Out of that dream came rescue—the Vigilant, the vice-admiralty court, the streets of Dunedin, and the long voyage back home to the old house by the Egeberg. He could not tell—they would think him mad. He would write of what he knew before death came, but his wife must not guess. Death would be a boon if only it could blot out the memories.

That was the document I read, and now I have placed it in the tin box beside the bas-relief and the papers of Professor Angell. With it shall go this record of mine— this test of my own sanity, wherein is pieced together that which I hope may never be pieced together again. I have looked upon all that the universe has to hold of horror, and even the skies of spring and the flowers of summer must ever afterward be poison to me. But I do not think my life will be long. As my uncle went, as poor Johansen went, so I shall go. I know too much, and the cult still lives.

Cthulhu still lives, too, I suppose, again in that chasm of stone which has shielded him since the sun was young. His accursed city is sunken once more, for the Vigilant sailed over the spot after the April storm; but his ministers on earth still bellow and prance and slay around idol-capped monoliths in lonely places. He must have been trapped by the sinking whilst within his black abyss, or else the world would by now be screaming with fright and frenzy. Who knows the end? What has risen may sink, and what has sunk may rise. Loathsomeness waits and dreams in the deep, and decay spreads over the tottering cities of men. A time will come—but I must not and cannot think! Let me pray that, if I do not survive this manuscript, my executors may put caution before audacity and see that it meets no other eye.

'That is not dead which can eternal lie...'

THE CALL OF CTHULHU

H. P. Lovecraft